ZRAC

GEORGIA
COAST
ROMANCE

A SPARKLE *of* SILVER

LIZ JOHNSON

Revell

a division of Baker Publishing Group
Grand Rapids, Michigan

Published by Revell
a division of Baker Publishing Group
PO Box 6287, Grand Rapids, MI 49516-6287
www.revellbooks.com

Printed in the United States of America

Library of Congress Cataloging-in-Publication Data
Names: Johnson, Liz, 1981– author.
Title: A sparkle of silver / Liz Johnson.
Description: Grand Rapids, MI : Revell, a division of Baker Publishing Group, [2018] | Series: Georgia Coast romance ; 1
Identifiers: LCCN 2018014357 | ISBN 9780800729622 (softcover : acid-free paper)
Subjects: | GSAFD: Romantic suspense fiction. | Christian fiction.
Classification: LCC PS3610.O3633 S68 2018 | DDC 813/.6—dc23
LC record available at https://lccn.loc.gov/2018014357

Published in association with Books & Such Literary Management, 52 Mission Circle, Suite 122, PMB 170, Santa Rosa, CA 95409-5370, www.booksandsuch.com

18 19 20 21 22 23 24   7 6 5 4 3 2 1

For Aunt Chris,
who invited me to fall in love with books when I was a child
and to visit her on St. Simons Island when I was an adult.
You are a brilliant cheerleader and an incredible woman.
I'm so thankful you're my aunt.

The greedy stir up conflict
but those who trust in the LORD will prosper.
Proverbs 28:25

ONE

There were some things Millie Sullivan would rather forget. The long gravel lane up to this home. The drab interior walls that melted into sticky carpet and stained tile floors. The fact that she could afford nothing better for the woman she loved most.

But every time she stepped into her Grandma Joy's room, Millie tried to be thankful her grandmother could remember anything at all.

"Who are you?" Grandma Joy squinted from across the small studio apartment, her hooded eyes suspicious and the wrinkles at the corners of her mouth growing deeper. "I don't know you. What are you doing here? What do you want?"

Her breath caught in the back of her throat, and Millie tried to recall what she'd done last time. What had the doctor said? *Speak in low tones, calming words.*

"It's all right." She held out her hands, palms up, an invitation. Taking two slow steps, she dipped her chin and lowered her voice another half an octave. "You're safe. You're in your home."

"I know that. What do you take me for?" Grandma Joy

looked like she had half a mind to hop out of her overstuffed rocker at such an offense. "I want to know who you are and what you're doing here."

Fair question.

Try to use familiar words and phrases.

"I'm Mil—Camilla."

Grandma Joy's eyes narrowed further, nearly disappearing beneath loose skin. "Camilla?" Her tone held a hint of recognition.

Millie's chin hitched, a smile already spreading into place. "Yes, Camilla. I'm Robert's daughter."

"Robert?" Any sign of clarity vanished, and her too-pink lips smacked together. "Never heard of him."

Wrapping her arms across her stomach, Millie nodded. "Okay." But it wasn't, not even a little bit. Nearly everything she knew about her dad, she'd learned from his mother. And today Grandma Joy couldn't even remember him.

Her stomach heaved like a boat on stormy waves. What if last time was the last time Grandma Joy remembered her? What if last time was the last time she heard Grandma Joy's laugh? What if last time was the last time Grandma Joy kissed her forehead and promised that all was well?

The back of her eyes burned, and Millie pressed her hands over her face. Holding every muscle as tight as she could, she forced a smile in place and held it there for three seconds before meeting her grandma's gaze again.

Yes, a smile. That's what she needed. Even if she didn't feel it, Grandma Joy would see it. And even if she didn't recognize Millie's smile specifically, well . . . everyone appreciated a smile. Right?

The smile in question trembled behind the cover of her

hands, and Millie sucked in a quick breath between pinched lips.

Remember. She just had to remember. This woman—the one in the faded purple rocking chair—wasn't the one who had raised Millie. She wasn't the one who had taken in her only grandchild and provided for her every need. At best she was a facsimile.

But the only thing Millie could do about it was paste a smile on her face and try to help her remember. And pray that Grandma Joy would come back to her.

Please, God. Let me have her a little longer.

"Miss Sullivan?"

Millie jumped, a shiver racing down her spine. She knew that voice, and it never brought good news. But she was paid up. She was. Her last check hadn't bounced, and Golden Isles had cashed it immediately.

Turning toward the woman at the open door, Millie bestowed the smile she'd been saving for her grandma on Virginia Baker.

The woman's sleek bob wobbled in greeting, but she didn't bother returning the grin. "May I have a word?"

A word, sure. It was imagining the second, third, fourth, and fifth that sent her stomach into a nosedive. Still, Millie turned her back on Grandma Joy and walked toward the door.

Virginia held out her hand in a silent invitation for Millie to step into the hallway. Millie tried to take a steadying breath. The rumble in her stomach was far too much like that time she'd been called into the principal's office for falling asleep in class during high school. She hung her head the same way she had all those years ago as she stepped past

Virginia from the warm tones of Grandma Joy's room into the garish lights of the hallway.

"Miss Sullivan, there's just no easy way to say this."

Suddenly it was hard to breathe. She pressed a hand to her throat and tried to gasp a thread of air, but it didn't help. Neither did Virginia's unforgiving monologue.

"She's getting worse." When Millie opened her mouth to offer an argument, Virginia shook her head. "I'm not telling you anything that you don't already know."

Millie risked a glance toward Grandma Joy, who had closed her eyes and let her mouth drop open. The even creaking of her chair had ceased, and she looked at peace. No longer disturbed by the arrival of a woman she couldn't recognize.

With a sigh Millie nodded. She knew. And no matter how much she wanted to deny it, there had been no evidence to indicate otherwise.

Grandma Joy wasn't going to get better. Her memories weren't going to come back—at least not for longer than a few minutes. But they were in there, and every so often one surfaced, only to nosedive back into oblivion before Millie could use it to pull her grandma closer.

"Your grandmother needs better care. More personalized. She needs someone to look after her one-on-one. All day. And night."

"I know, but—"

Virginia held up her hand. "I know money is a concern."

That was the understatement of the century. Money wasn't just *a* concern. It was the only one. It was all that was holding Millie back from giving Grandma Joy the finest room in the best memory-care facility.

But she couldn't make money where there was none. As

far as she knew, it was still illegal to print her own. Besides, she'd need a printer for that, and she highly doubted the library would let her use theirs. Not that she would do such a thing even if she could, of course.

"There is government help available."

"I know. I've applied for all of it. But they've turned her down. Her diagnosis isn't severe enough or something."

Virginia rubbed her chin, a frown tugging at the corners of her lips. "Then you have to appeal. Get a lawyer and take it to court."

Millie held back a snort, but only just. That required money too—a lot of it. And time, which was hard to come by when she was working two jobs just to make ends meet. And even then she'd been late with her own rent again last month.

Maybe Virginia read her face, because she moved on to another option with a hopeful lilt in her tone. "Well then, what about her Social Security?"

"What about it? It doesn't even cover half of your fine establishment's fee every month." As if on cue, the fluorescent light above them flickered, and Virginia's shoulders drooped.

"I'm sorry," Millie said, forcing her sarcasm to stay in check. It wasn't Virginia's fault. None of it. And she couldn't afford to alienate the home's administrator. "I've tried everything I can think of, but we're out of options. Golden Isles is our only choice."

Chewing on her lower lip, Virginia shook her head. "We have a list of people who belong here waiting to get in. I'll give you ninety days. And then you're going to need to find her other arrangements."

"Three months? You can't be serious." Millie's voice rose

with each word, her heart skipping every other beat until the chair in her grandma's apartment resumed squeaking. She couldn't look across the room and could barely breathe. "What am I supposed to do?"

Well, that was a silly question. And Virginia seemed to have only a silly answer.

"Some people find in-home care to be a better choice."

Millie's chin fell against her chest, and she wrapped her arms around her middle as a chill swept down her spine. She'd tried caring for Grandma Joy at home, but the first time she'd been called home from her job at the diner to find her grandma wandering down the road in little more than a threadbare robe, she'd known that they needed help.

That's where Golden Isles Assisted Living had come in. They were desperately understaffed and in a building older than any of their residents, but bless their hearts, they tried. That was all Millie asked for. A safe place with people who genuinely cared for Grandma Joy.

But now they were kicking her out. And leaving Millie in a pickle too big to swallow.

"Please." She hated the way the word came out—desperate, strangled. Taking a deep breath, she tried again. "There has to be another option. I could . . . I could pay you more. I could pay for an extra night nurse."

Yeah, right. She didn't have that kind of money, and she didn't have a clue how to get it. Maybe she could get an extra shift at the diner. That would get her approximately one percent of the way there. The truth was, there weren't enough shifts at the Hermit Crab Café to cover that kind of offer. Not that Virginia Baker was inclined to accept it anyway.

"This isn't a negotiation, Miss Sullivan. She has to move."

Virginia dropped her voice on the last sentence, a small consolation to the complete rejection in her words. "I'll begin preparing her paperwork. Let me know if you need some recommendations. I have some literature in my office." She didn't wait for Millie to respond before patting her shoulder and walking away, head high.

Millie slumped against the wall and stared hard at the gray laces of her tennis shoes. She was pretty sure they'd only had one previous owner, the best pair she'd ever found at the thrift store. She pressed her toe into the carpet, wishing there was some sort of pedal she could push that would reveal a solution, but it wasn't that easy.

It never was.

"You're just like your dad."

Her chin snapped up, and she peeked into the room. Grandma Joy's eyes were still closed, but there was a tension in her features that suggested she was awake and—dare Millie even hope?—lucid.

"He never knew what to say to bad news either."

"My dad?"

"My Robert." Grandma Joy readjusted her folded hands over her middle and sighed. "He was so smart, but sometimes he couldn't find the words. He said he always wanted to go to college. Then he up and met your mama, and he couldn't tear his eyes away from her."

Millie took a tentative step into the room, careful to avoid the groans in the old floor, careful not to spook her grandma out of this bout of memory.

"He made mistakes, but he loved me. Just like I know you do."

Millie pressed her lips together and tried to form a picture in her mind of the man she'd last seen when she was four. But the memories were too faded. Maybe that was what it felt like for Grandma Joy, looking for the past that remained elusive.

"Yep. You're so much like your father."

She wanted to ask if that was a compliment. Even though the memories were thin, her perception of her father was anything but. Everything she knew about him was tainted with a thick layer of cynicism based on his selfishness.

But before she could ask, Grandma Joy kept going. "You are your father's daughter. But I'm not."

Millie's eyebrows rose, and she met Grandma Joy's gaze. "You're not what? Not your father's daughter?" That couldn't be. Grandma Joy's dad, Henry, was a good man. There had been pictures of him all over the farmhouse where Millie had grown up.

Grandma Joy's lips twitched, a sparkle in her eyes promising a good secret.

"You're joking, right?" Millie couldn't hold it back.

"My mother, Ruth, was a guest at the Chateau. Before she married Henry."

"Chateau Dawkins?"

Grandma Joy chuckled. "Is there another one?"

A picture of the grand estate on the coast, built by Howard Dawkins, flashed across her mind. Three stories of gleaming white glory reached by curving white staircases and rich archways, surrounded by lush lawns and waving palms. They said at night the lights could be seen half a mile across the ocean, glowing like a beacon, brighter than the island's famous lighthouse. The Chateau adorned postcards in every St. Simons Island gift shop, and the library carried a whole shelf of books about the mansion and its short-lived golden era.

"I just. . ." Millie shook her head, trying to find her words. "You never said."

"Oh, Mama mentioned it a time or two. I think she fell in love there."

Her stomach lurched as Grandma Joy's ramblings suddenly began to make sense. Ruth—Great-Grandma Ruth—had stayed at the wealthiest estate in Georgia during the late 1920s and fell in love there. And Grandma Joy wasn't her father's daughter, which meant . . .

Millie gasped and dropped to her grandma's bed, perching on the edge.

Grandma Joy was the illegitimate child of one of the wealthy guests. Oil and newspapers, real estate and coal—Dawkins had been connected to millionaires of every ilk.

And even an illegitimate heir deserved something from the estate of her father. Right?

"Who was it?" Millie clapped a hand over her mouth. "I'm sorry," she whispered between her fingers. "That was crass. I just meant . . . do you know who your father is?"

That twinkle in Grandma Joy's eyes returned, mischief personified. "She would never say. She didn't put his name on my birth certificate. After all, she was married to Henry before I was born. She said it was between her and her diary. And she hid that away at the estate. After all, she didn't want the treasure map in it to get into the wrong hands."

Ben Thornton scribbled another name on the list. Judith Tulley. That made twenty-three. Twenty-three people identified. Twenty-three lines in his notebook. Each one a ruined life.

"You hear me, Ben?"

He glared at the phone on his desk, faceup and glowing. The thick Southern drawl on the other end echoed in his empty classroom but still managed to make his skin shiver.

"Judith Tulley from Augusta. Ninety-one."

"I heard you, Owen. Why wasn't she in the case?"

Owen shuffled some papers on the other end. "I don't know. Maybe they couldn't find her. Maybe she didn't . . . Well, you know. She's old. Maybe she just didn't want to bother."

"With justice?"

Owen sighed, and Ben could picture the young lawyer running a hand through his too-long hair. "With the hassle," Owen said. "It's not easy. It takes time. A lot of it. Y'all know that."

Yes, Ben knew that litigation had a tendency to drag on. And maybe Judith didn't want to spend what was left of her time on earth trying to see a woman pay for her crimes.

But Ben was young. And he would see that her crimes were paid for and her victims compensated.

"Ben, there's something else." Owen's voice took a decidedly deep turn.

Ben leaned an elbow against the desktop, pushed an essay he'd been grading out of his way, and rested his forehead against his open palm. "What is it?"

"She's filed for bankruptcy."

His groan was entirely involuntary, and he doubled all the way over, face against his desk. "She's going to get away with it." There was no question involved, just a dull certainty that throbbed at the base of his skull.

"If she has no assets, she can't repay the claimants."

That sounded about right. Maybe it had been her plan all along. If she lived lavishly off other people's money, she'd never have to repay all that she'd stolen. And without another mark, she had no source of income.

"I guess that's all we can do." Owen sounded defeated. Even after he'd won the trial and put a swindler behind bars.

But jail time wasn't restitution. It wouldn't give those people back their savings. It wouldn't make their lives any easier. And if she was claiming bankruptcy, then there was no one to pay them back, no one to make things right.

No one but him.

"Have a good day," Owen said before hanging up the phone.

Standing, Ben took a deep breath of the stale classroom air. He strolled through the rows of empty desks, stooping to pick up a crumpled piece of paper.

He wasn't exactly responsible for cleaning up the classroom. It was only his for three classes a week, after all. Still, the sparse furniture made it easy to tell if the room had been picked up or not. He wasn't about to leave a mess for the tenured professor who would teach the next course here.

Bending over, he snagged a pen that a student had dropped before tossing it into the cup on his desk for anyone who showed up to class without a writing utensil. If only it were as easy to clean up after the mess his mom had made.

And he would have to. It wasn't even a question.

As he slid back into his desk chair and straightened the pile of essays that had been turned in, he gave another hard look at the list in his notebook. There were a lot of names there and few dollars in his checking account. He needed another job. Maybe two.

TWO

A scuffle down the hallway made her gasp, and Millie flung herself against the bookcase behind the door. Holding her breath, she pressed her eye to the crack above a hinge, searching the corridor beyond for the source of the commotion and praying that the pounding of her heart was only audible to her own ears.

If she was caught, her grand plan—her only plan—would be ruined. It had taken her three weeks to cook up the scheme, land a job at the Chateau, and begin searching for her great-grandmother's diary. And as long as she was here, there was hope. At least an inkling that she could find a treasure that would save Grandma Joy.

Whether the treasure was marked on the map in the journal with a big red X or Ruth's words revealed the identity of Grandma Joy's father, the Chateau was her only hope. She couldn't afford to be found out of place on her third night at work, or she'd certainly be fired.

Peeking into the hallway, she could only see the pale yellow lines of the wallpaper through the opening.

Until a small child pressed his chubby face into the crack. "What are you doing in there?"

Her pulse galloped as she blinked at the little intruder. She tried to find her breath and her words. "Shh." Adjusting her dress to lower herself to his level, she pressed her finger to her lips. "I'm playing a game. We have to be silent."

"Can I play?" He clearly didn't understand the definition of silent, his voice bouncing down the generous corridor and probably down the spiral stone staircase at the end of it.

"Your mom and dad will miss you. You should go find them."

He wiped the back of his hand across his mouth, and in the flickering light from the antique sconces, she could make out a trickle of green from the corner of his lips to his chin. Apparently he'd indulged in some mint ice cream at the gift shop by the front gate. And now his sticky fingers were pressed against a wooden door older than his great-great-grandparents.

"No. I don't want to. This house is boring."

Boring? For a five-year-old, maybe. For all of the other tourists who paid the entrance fee, Chateau Dawkins was an entry to the past. A window into what had once been. And it held more than enough secrets to keep her interested. But arguing the point wasn't going to get her little visitor to leave her alone. And letting him stay would only alert others to her location.

She patted her hips as though the sleek silk gown would magically grow pockets and a stash of candy in them. But she had nothing to distract him. Nothing she could even use to bribe him.

And all the motion did was remind her how strange the

dress felt, even on her third shift. Her simple cotton wardrobe didn't include anything half as luxurious as the knee-length evening gown with its feather embellishments at the shoulder. It was a few decades out of style, but exactly what her Great-Grandma Ruth might have worn when she visited this estate.

But if she wasn't careful, Millie might never find out anything more about Ruth.

Her gaze darted around the room on this side of the door. Cloth-covered books in faded blues and greens and burgundies lined every inch of the deep cherry shelves. Like china in a cabinet, many of them were hemmed in by locked doors, the windows replaced with chicken wire so trapped humidity wouldn't ruin the precious tomes. A turn-of-the-century sofa took up the majority of the center of the room. The matching gray wingback chair in front of the empty fireplace looked perfect for curling up with one of the thousands of stories on these shelves. On any other night, in any other situation, she might have done just that. But none of this would distract her young visitor.

The red velvet rope across the doorway hadn't stopped her from entering. And it wasn't likely to keep out someone who could so easily go under the barrier.

The little guy made a move to duck under it, his eyes bright with mischief, and she lunged around the door, blocking his entry before slinking into the shadows on the opposite side.

"You have to go back to your family. Please."

Perfect. Now she was begging a five-year-old. She might not have had a lot of experience with kids, but even she knew that showing her desperation was bound to end poorly.

"But I don't want to. I want to play the game."

The game? Right. The one where they were silent.

Except it would be anything but when the kid's parents noticed he was missing. Every flickering light in the house would be turned on, every employee—from security all the way to reenactors like her—would be sent out to find him.

Maybe she could convince him to go back with a different tactic. "Where did you last see your parents?"

He waved a finger past the room that had once served as Howard Dawkins's study and toward the stairwell at the end of the hall. "Over there."

"What did the room look like?"

His eyebrows, so fair that they nearly disappeared into his pale skin, rose halfway up his forehead. "There was a big table."

"The dining room?" Oh dear. That was on the far side of the house. How had he wandered so far?

He shook his head. "It was for playing a game."

She let out a quick breath and offered a soft smile. "The billiard room?"

He shrugged. "Maybe."

Well, as far as confirmations went, "maybe" was pretty weak. But it would have to suffice. The game room was at the foot of the stairs, and she couldn't think of another room in the house with a big table.

Glancing behind her once more at the rows of unsearched books, she sighed. They would have to wait for another night.

She unlatched the velvet rope from its gold post, slipped past him, and held out her hand. "Let's go for a walk."

"Is this part of the game?"

"Um, yes."

With a nod and a skip, he led the way down the corridor,

the sound of his little feet echoing off the arched ceilings. At the top of the stairs, he turned back to her. "What do we do next?"

Sure, he'd ask her about the rules of a game she'd only made up to distract him.

"Well . . ."

"Jamie! Jamie, where are you? Come here now."

Saved by the call of a frantic mom. Millie heaved a sigh of relief, and Jamie must have recognized a tone that meant business. Grabbing onto the relatively recently installed handrail, he disappeared down the spiral staircase. Within moments his mother's audible relief reached the upper hallway.

"I was so worried about you. Where did you go?"

"I was playing a game with the lady."

"What lady?"

There was a long pause, and Millie's heart jumped to her throat. This was it. The moment they rushed up the stairs and she was discovered at the very last place she should be— in the room she most needed to search.

"That lady with all the books."

"Don't be silly. There's no one up there. Now, come along."

"But there is, Mama. There's a woman in red."

Jamie's mother must have dragged him back to join the rest of the tour group, his voice disappearing but remaining adamant.

Millie smoothed down the front of her red evening gown, and even through her white gloves the silk was cool beneath her suddenly trembling fingers. Too close. This was all too close.

And it might all be for nothing.

There was no telling how much of Grandma Joy's story

had been true. Probably less than was false. Still, she had seemed so certain. There had been something about the fragile old woman's eyes that gleamed with excitement and hope. *"It's in the room with the books. Find it. It's in there."*

"Find it," Millie muttered to herself as she slipped across the hallway and let herself back into the library. "No problem. Find a book in a library." It was like finding a particular piece of hay in a haystack. Every single binding could be the journal she hunted for.

But after two tries, she wasn't sure any of them really were.

Running a finger down the blue spine of a classic by Jules Verne, she sighed. The three cases to her left had all been history and architecture. Then there were several rows of poetry. Where the dust was too thick to read the gilded titles, she brushed it away, whispering every name to herself, lest she skip the only book she really wanted to find.

"Leaves of Grass. Poems by Emily Dickinson. The Road Not Taken and Other Poems."

No. No. No. Not what she needed.

The clock on the mantel above the fireplace chimed a tinny, hollow sound, its bells long since coated with the same film that covered every other surface of the room. But it couldn't be ignored. Nine o'clock. The last tour would be wrapping up in fifteen minutes. If she wasn't in her place in the theater room in ten, she'd be missed. And then she'd be fired.

But she was so close. There was only one more bookcase. She hurried over to it, her finger almost but not quite touching every cover as she moved from poetry to prose.

"Poe. Hawthorne. Melville. Alcott."

Whoever had organized this library was a fan of neither Mr. Dewey nor the English alphabet. But she couldn't very well argue with them, as they'd likely been gone for as long as her Great-Grandma Ruth. Longer than Millie had been alive.

A shiver raced down her spine at the very thought. Ruth had been in this room, maybe perused these same tomes searching for a summer read to indulge in on the beach or on the deck of the estate's swimming pool.

Ruth had been here. At least according to Grandma Joy. Though nearly ninety years apart, great-grandmother and great-granddaughter had found their way to the same place.

If only Millie could find Ruth's journal and the map Grandma Joy had promised would be in it.

The ever-present ticking of the clock reminded her that she had to hurry. If she wanted another chance at searching this room, she'd have to stay on the payroll.

She sighed, her shoulders slumping as she rested her hand on the final volume in the third row from the bottom. Tucked between the wooden column built into the wall and Edith Wharton's *The Age of Innocence* was a slender volume. Its dark brown cover wasn't the same quality leather as its compatriots, but that wasn't the most interesting thing about it. It didn't have either a title or an author printed on it.

Holding her breath, she gave it a gentle tug. The book and a tumble of cobwebs pulled loose. Heart thudding harder than it had when Jamie's mother had come after him, she gingerly opened the front cover.

In perfect script someone had written *Ruthie Holiday—1929.*

"Oh." It was more breath than actual word, but the moment seemed to require something to recognize its importance.

Then, because she did the same with every book she'd

ever read, she turned it over and opened to the last page to read the last line.

Let it be there. Please, let it be right there.

"Come on, come on," she whispered.

"Come on out of there."

The deep voice made her drop the journal.

Ben stared hard at the woman in the shadows on the far side of the room. Partly because she'd pulled him from a warm cup of coffee in the security office. And partly because he couldn't believe that little Jamie Grammer had been right.

There really was a woman in red in the room with all the books. But she didn't look anything like the other visitors finishing up the final tour of the night.

He let his gaze sweep over her costume. The shimmering red fabric of her dress skimmed her thin frame and swished as she turned toward him. With wide eyes she stared back, the angle of her chin both certain and stubborn.

He couldn't make out her coloring under the too-yellow lights of the library, but her fair hair was held in place by a red headband that sparkled with every hitch of her breath. All of the actresses on the property had costumes covered with too many ornaments, and sometimes it seemed the outfits from the twenties wore the women.

Not the case with this one. Her firm shoulders and staunch posture could have easily placed her in the Chateau's heyday. But she wasn't an apparition. She was an actress. And she had broken at least half the rules in the relatively short employee handbook.

"Come on out," he said again.

She froze, her gloved hands fixed behind her.

"What's your name?"

She still didn't respond, but neither did she drop her gaze.

The clock on the wall to his right chimed the quarter hour, and they both turned toward it. Her shoulders slumped. No doubt she'd missed her last post of the night. She would have lost her job even if he hadn't found her beyond the red velvet rope. "Where are you supposed to be?"

"The theater."

He nodded. "Are you ready to go?"

As she stepped into the beam of light from the hallway, she shook her head. The feather tucked into the band around her head dipped and brushed her cheek, only emphasizing her impossibly smooth skin.

He had no business noticing that. He had a job to do, and two weeks into his new job at the Chateau, he didn't intend to lose it for a pretty face. After all, there were twenty-three other faces counting on him. Sure, he hadn't seen them. That didn't mean he didn't owe them.

Squaring his shoulders, he cleared his throat and pulled himself up to his full height. "Let's go, theater girl."

"It's Millie—Camilla, actually. Please. Plea—"

"You know the rules." His tone carried a hint of bitterness, and he tried to dial it back. "We'll both be here late enough filling out paperwork."

"But I . . ." Her voice trailed off as her eyebrows bunched above her nose. "You don't have to turn me in."

If he'd expected her to beg for a reprieve, he was disappointed. While distress was scripted across her features, her voice never wavered.

"I was looking for something. It belonged to my family."

"Ha!" He couldn't help but bark out the laugh. "Are you a Dawkins?"

Her pale features turned even more wan in the dim light, and she opened her mouth, only to close it again without a peep.

"I'll take that as a no."

Still she made no motion to step out of history and into the present. Into the hallway with him. So he unclipped the rope from its gold stand.

"Let's go, Camilla."

"It's Millie." The knot in her jaw suddenly relaxed, and she pressed her shoulders back. When she spoke again, her voice was stronger. Certain. "My name is Millie Sullivan, and my great-grandmother was a guest here. She left behind a journal. It's—it has some family history. I need it."

As she spoke, he couldn't tear his gaze away from the red line of her lips—the same shocking shade as her dress. There was a firmness to their set, a quiet line at each side that seemed to swear to the truth of her words.

Oh, if they were true. How incredible it would be to find family history in this great castle looming along the Georgia shore.

And how very unlikely.

He had an early class in the morning and no time for fairy tales. "Come on." He grabbed her arm right above her elbow at the top of her white evening glove. "Let's get going."

"Wait! Wait!" She tugged on her elbow, trying to free it from his grip, but he refused to let go. Whatever other wild stories she might concoct, he wasn't interested. At more than fifteen bucks an hour, this was the best part-time job he'd been able to find on short notice. That it happened to be at the island's most famous historical locale was just a perk.

Fear and hope flashed in her blue eyes, promising that whatever she was about to claim would almost certainly land him minus one job. And he didn't have any to spare.

"I don't think so. Let's go."

Beneath his fingers, her muscles flexed. "There's a lost treasure."

His eyebrows pulled together, his forehead wrinkling.

"In my great-grandmother's journal." She took a ragged breath and struggled again, but he shook his head hard. Best to put a stop to this and get her to the office, where her manager could take care of the situation.

But she was still going, as though more words would somehow convince him. "It's on the property. Here. At the estate. Don't you see?"

"I understand what you're saying." He let his gaze narrow in on her front teeth, which bit into her full lower lip, picking up a tint of the red there. "Doesn't mean I think it's true."

The way her eyes widened, it was clear she did. Whoever had sold her a tall tale about some riches hidden at the Chateau had fully convinced her. That didn't mean he needed to be as gullible. He'd read nearly every book about this old property, and then he'd taught a class about it. History 103: "Georgia's Past to the Present."

Sure, every now and then a rumor emerged about lost treasure in the area. There were even a few rumors of buried treasures dating back as far as the heyday of pirates, but every single one of them had been debunked. There was no treasure here except fifteen bucks an hour. And he wasn't about to give that up.

"Look, lady."

Her eyebrows darted together, a storm cloud rising.

He quickly modified his comment. "Millie, I'm sorry. There's nothing I can do. You're clearly not where you're supposed to be, and that's grounds for termination. You know that."

Gaze darting toward the floor, she nodded. The landmark's supervisors were pretty clear about actors only going where they were assigned—the parlor and pool deck mostly. It was about preserving the historical integrity of the old house as long as possible. Even without extra foot traffic, the carpets had begun to wear in strange patterns. And peeling patches of fabric wallpaper would soon require repairs, another piece of history gone.

"I know. But can't you make an exception?"

"No."

He sounded like a jerk. Maybe he was a jerk. But what if he let her go and someone found out? He couldn't risk that.

Trying to keep his grip firm but gentle, he gave her a small tug. "Come on. We'll get this sorted out at the office."

"Please." There was a tremor in her voice, as though more than a fictional gold chest was at stake, but her spine remained straight, her chin at a stubborn angle.

"Let's go."

Her feet slid along the rug, its maroon and gold thread already thin in patches, and he almost stopped so she wouldn't damage the original carpet. Almost. With a quick glance over her shoulder, she let out a faint sob and pointed toward a book on the floor. "It's all in there. In the diary."

A boulder dropped in his stomach.

"And I'll split it with you."

Well, that was interesting.

THREE

*S*o what happened? Did you get sick or something? You missed your whole last act!"

Ben risked a slow look out of the side of his eye at Millie as she took her manager's scolding, the older woman clearly doubtful about her subordinate's claim. Millie's long arms were wrapped around her middle, her eyes glistening with something that certainly looked like tears. They had the strangely unfocused look of someone truly ill, although she'd never even hinted that she wasn't feeling well. And her shoulders twitched with the uneven rhythm of shivers. Or maybe she was just nervous under the firm eye of her boss. If he hadn't known better, he'd have guessed she really had the flu rather than a case of the nerves.

Juliet Covington, the manager of all the talent at the Chateau, sucked on her front tooth, her dark gaze moving from Millie to him and back again. "And *you* just so happened to find her." Skepticism dripped from her words.

"Yes. I was looking for the woman the little boy saw. It must have been Millie." His voice nearly cracked on the last word, and he could have shot his own foot. He was botching this performance. Juliet didn't believe them. Or rather, she didn't believe him. Millie could have convinced the world she was Princess Anastasia—a century late and blonde to boot.

What had he been thinking? He never should have agreed to any of this. It was a ridiculous plan. And the chances of there actually being any treasure on this property—besides the gold-plated tiles in the swimming pool and other adornments—were beyond slim.

Stupid. Foolhardy. Reckless.

He was banking everything—his job, his reputation, and maybe even his position at the college—on a silly story from Millie's grandmother and the evidence in an old journal. And all for what?

A chance to repay the people he owed.

The truth struck him like a punch to the gut. It didn't matter how many times he reminded himself of what he owed them. It always hurt. It always stole his breath.

Paying back those people was worth it. It had to be. And at least if he was along for the ride, he could keep an eye on Millie and make sure she didn't walk away with anything that didn't belong to her.

He sucked in a quick breath as Juliet's gaze traveled from him to Millie and back again. He should just give the journal to Juliet. His hands itched to reach for the book carefully tucked into the back of his waistband, covered by his black security jacket, but he fisted them at his sides instead.

"Uh-huh." Juliet huffed and leaned back in the chair behind her desk, which was twice as large as it should have been for an office so small. "You two just *happened* to be in the same place. And you lost track of time."

The way her gaze volleyed back and forth left little room to wonder what Juliet was thinking. She assumed that when single co-workers disappeared, they were taking advantage of one of the hundreds of dim corners or shadowed alcoves. She assumed they'd been up to something.

And they definitely had been—just not what she assumed.

"Well, I knew what time it was," Millie said. "But I was answering Mr. Thornton's questions."

He shot her a hard stare. She made him sound like he was eighty. Well, he wasn't. Just because he liked to follow the rules—*normally*—well, that didn't mean he was an old fuddy-duddy.

He caught another glimpse of her profile, all smooth lines and porcelain skin. But she wasn't as young as she looked. There was an understanding in her eyes that reminded him of the pleading in her voice when they'd met in the library. She needed that treasure for some reason. She needed it badly enough that she was willing to share what she found. And she needed help to find it—his help.

Millie lifted her chin under Juliet's scrutiny, firmly setting her jaw. Most girls would have blabbered on, but Millie handled the weighty gaze with quiet solemnity.

Maybe it was because she knew that the journal was safely tucked away. But if she was fired, she wouldn't be free to search the grounds. Then it would be up to him to . . . what? Find a treasure that never existed?

He cringed at the thought. This was all a mess, and he'd gone and gotten himself wrapped up in it like a fool. If he ended up on the wrong side of the law, he wouldn't be in a position to repay all those names on his list.

Juliet squinted at him. "What are you two up to?"

Millie bit her lips until they disappeared, and Ben crossed his arms over his chest. Then dropped them to his side. Then crossed them again. Juliet's eyes followed every movement.

With a tap of the wooden desktop, Juliet said, "I should have you both fired."

Millie let out a little peep of anguish, and he had a sudden urge to put his hand on her shoulder. Of course, that was crazy. He didn't console women he didn't know. And he didn't have time to know many women. Besides, Juliet was threatening his job too.

"But . . ."

He let out a little sigh.

"I've barely gotten you trained, and I don't like to waste my time." Juliet stood to her full height, nearly as tall as Ben, and waved one finger at them both. "This is your only warning. Do you understand me? Next time you're not where you're supposed to be, I'll personally kick you off the property—both of you."

A knot in his chest that he hadn't even realized was there suddenly unraveled, and he gulped a deep breath.

"Yes, ma'am." Millie's voice dipped into a thicker, deeper accent in those words that every Southern child knew. Ben could only nod.

Juliet dismissed them both. Her mouth said, "I'll see you for your next shift." Her tone said, "I'll be watching you."

No doubt that would be true, which would not make searching for a treasure on the grounds easy. That is, if there even was one.

He backed out of the office and followed Millie toward the women's locker room. "I need to change and get my purse," she said. Her sapphire gaze was sharper than he'd ever seen it in the exactly thirty-two minutes he'd known her, and it was rather unnerving.

Actually, everything from this night was a little bit out of his norm and a whole lot out of his comfort zone.

"Do you know Coastal Coffee by the pier?"

He nodded.

"Let's meet there in about twenty minutes."

His forehead wrinkled so hard he could feel it, but her gaze never wavered from his.

She glanced toward his side, and after a brief moment, she gave a decisive nod. "You can keep the journal until then if that makes you feel better."

It didn't. Taking an antique book—even a handwritten one—off the property made his stomach feel like it had taken too many loops on a roller coaster.

The slow traffic across St. Simons Island didn't help the matter. By the time he pulled his car into the almost empty parking lot of the island's coffeehouse, loved by locals and generally missed by tourists, he'd decided this had all been a terrible mistake.

Millie had nearly gotten him fired, and he didn't hold out much hope that he'd be able to hang on to the job as long as he was running around with her. He couldn't work with her. But if he didn't, she was going to hunt on her own. What kind of trouble would she get into then?

Besides, if the diary did belong to her great-grandmother, then she was entitled to it. Right? He didn't exactly know the rules for these things—forgotten treasure and all that.

This was a bad idea. Terrible. The very worst. Maybe it wasn't too late to back out now.

Yet his hand had no problem resting on the journal riding

shotgun in his coupe. There was no telling the mysteries this book might reveal. It was a window into the Chateau at its most luxurious. It was an important piece of history.

And he wanted it for a stupid treasure map.

He pressed his forehead to the cracked steering wheel and took a deep breath. The cool summer air carried the scents of the sea, water, and fish. And home. But it did little to calm the speeding train threatening to run off his mind's track.

God, I think I'm in over my head here. I have no idea what to do now.

Two sharp raps on his window jerked him upright, and he stared into that blue gaze.

Whether Millie was an answer to prayer or just had uncanny timing, he'd never know.

Millie picked up her small black coffee and slipped into the corner booth. The blue vinyl cushion stuck to the back of her legs, and she suddenly missed the sleekness of silk. Her costumes all made her feel like she could slide through the eye of a needle. Should she ever need to.

But she'd left her silks at the Chateau, and apparently she'd deserted her good sense long before that. Whatever had convinced her to offer to split the reward they found had left behind only regret in its wake. What had she been thinking?

Oh, that's right. She hadn't been. She'd let her mouth run away with her because she'd been backed into a corner and couldn't see any other way out. But that didn't excuse her behavior. And now she was stuck. Stuck with a partner she didn't know. Stuck with a journal she had barely touched. Stuck with a clock that wouldn't stop counting down.

Sixty-three days. That's all she had left to find a miracle.

As Ben slid into the seat across from her, he laid the brown journal onto the table between them. It took everything inside her not to snatch it up and begin reading her great-grandmother's story and searching for the map Grandma Joy had said it contained. But the heavy weight of Ben's gaze kept her hands wrapped around her paper cup.

"So . . ." he began.

Back in the library she'd promised him the truth, but now that the moment was here, she wasn't quite sure it wouldn't sound a bit ridiculous. Actually, she was absolutely sure she would sound ridiculous. There just wasn't any other way around it.

"You see, it all started with my grandma."

His eyes shot toward the journal. "I thought you said she was your great-grandma."

"No. Yes." Millie rubbed her forehead, trying to figure out how to explain only the parts he needed to know—and there were certainly plenty of those—in a way that would make any sort of sense.

But there was also information he didn't need. Like the conversation she'd had with Grandma Joy. The news that Henry wasn't Grandma Joy's biological father. The realization that they might be heirs of a wealthy guest at the Chateau.

Ben, with his gaze that seemed to see straight through her, did not need to know about all of that. And he definitely didn't need to know that the most famous guest of the Chateau the summer of 1929 had been Claude Devereaux.

As Ben stared at her with unmoving eyes, every line of his face turned tight and expectant.

He'd said he was in. But somehow she knew if she didn't impress him right now, she was going to lose everything he could offer her search—the protection of a security guard on the grounds and the help of another set of eyes. Maybe it wouldn't be the worst thing to lose his help. But if she didn't know he was on her side, she couldn't be sure he wouldn't spill her secrets.

Under Juliet's watchful gaze, Millie would have to be extra careful not to be found out. And that's where Ben could help. A lot. Even if working with him meant sharing the money, there was more at stake here.

Her gut twisted as she thought about the secrecy it would take to search the estate. Grandma Joy would be appalled. Millie was nearly there herself. Sneaking around places she knew she wasn't supposed to be in wasn't how she would have chosen to find the treasure. But she hadn't been given a choice.

Grandma Joy needed a safe home—a permanent one. And she'd do whatever she needed to make that happen.

"My Grandma Joy was telling me stories about her mom—my Great-Grandma Ruth—a few weeks ago."

He nodded, scratching at his chin with his thumb.

"She—I mean Ruth—was a guest at the Chateau the summer of 1929."

His lips pursed, and he let out a low whistle just as his coffee reached his mouth. He tilted the cup up but never looked away, and her skin broke out in goose bumps under his scrutiny. But he said nothing else.

He clearly didn't need to be reminded that that was the last summer before the stock market crashed and the Great Depression settled over the country. He didn't need to be reminded that the guests had enjoyed every luxury money could buy. And he definitely didn't need to be reminded that the Chateau had never been the same after that summer.

"Grandma Joy said that her mom had mentioned a lost treasure at Howard Dawkins's home. Jewelry and diamonds and such."

His jaw locked, and he shook his head. "I've been studying the history of the barrier islands for more than a decade, and those are only rumors, old stories that have been tossed about for years. No one's ever proved there was anything on the property. What makes you think your grandma is telling the truth?"

Millie chewed on her lip and spun her coffee in a slow circle. What did make her think Grandma Joy was telling the truth? Especially given her diagnosis.

Sure, it was easier to believe that this was just another story concocted after a sleepless night or one too many prescriptions. But that didn't explain the most important element.

"She knew about the diary. It stands to reason she could be telling the truth about its contents too."

His blue eyes darted toward the book as his dark eyebrows pinched together. Three little furrows appeared above his nose, but he didn't speak for several long seconds. Finally he said, "You really think there's a map in there?"

"Only one way to find out." Inordinately proud of how confident she sounded, she reached for the diary.

He pressed his hand over hers to stop the movement. "Be careful."

"I know." Her voice had picked up a little tremor in the previous minute, and she clamped her lips closed to keep anything else from coming out. To keep anything else from giving away how very unsure she was about everything that had happened in the last two hours.

She'd discovered the journal, and now she had an accomplice on her mission. But she still hadn't read even one line of the book. Only God knew what she'd find in it.

With a steadying breath, she slipped her hand from under the heavy weight of his and eased the diary across the table. The supple brown leather glided over the wooden tabletop, and she slowly flipped the cover open. Page after page revealed only the narrow script of Ruth Holiday's penmanship. There were no drawings, no "X marks the spot" indicators.

With each turn of the page, her heart sank a little lower. It was in her shoes by the time she reached the last page.

Nothing. It wasn't a treasure map after all.

Grandma Joy had been wrong, and this had all been for nothing.

Her dejection must have shown across her face, because Ben reached toward her hand again, stopped short, and then drummed his fingertips next to his cup. "Maybe it's in there." He tried—and failed—to keep his tone light, and his words hit almost as hard as the truth had.

She shook her head, her chin bowing and her hair falling over her shoulders and across her face. Something deep in her chest longed to deny the truth. But it was like she'd woken from a dream right in the middle of it. Now she could only imagine how it might have ended. But she'd never know for sure.

Always a dream. Always past the tips of her fingers.

This diary had meant hope. And now . . . Now she was

exactly where she'd been when the doctor had said there was no cure.

"Maybe she wrote out the directions to the treasure." Ben shrugged. "She could have been a terrible artist."

Her head snapped up, the weight on her shoulders instantly lifting. "In the words. Of course!"

He grinned, his smile a little lopsided but filled with satisfaction.

"Why didn't I think of that?" Because she had a lot more on the line than he did, and the absence of a drawn map didn't define him.

"Hey, I've got a stake in this now too." He winked, and she laughed. "You can't be the only one coming up with ideas."

"Fair enough." She glanced back down at the diary. If—and that was still a big *if*—there was a treasure map in these pages, it was hidden in the words, somewhere in Ruth's memories. And someone was going to have to ferret it out.

Before she suggested that she take the diary home, Ben scooted across his bench seat and glanced at his watch with a shake of his head. "It's late. I have to be up for work in five hours."

"You work the day shift too?" The question popped out even before she fully formed the reason behind it. If he was at the Chateau during the day, maybe he could uncover information that she didn't have access to during her night shifts.

But he didn't give an affirmative reply. "No. I teach a couple classes at the Georgia Coast College in Brunswick on Tuesdays and Thursdays while I'm working on my PhD."

"Oh. That sounds nice." She sounded lame. And it sounded like he had to work two jobs and go to school. No wonder he was interested in the money.

With a shrug and a hand covering his yawn, he said, "It's not bad. Except the eight a.m. class is filled with a bunch of sleepers." The corner of his mouth ticked up a notch. "But that might not be a bad thing tomorrow. They won't mind if I cut class a little short."

"So what are we going to do?"

"I'm going to go home and get some sleep. And then we're going to find that treasure."

"You really think it's there?" Again her tongue got ahead of her, and she hated the uncertainty she'd just displayed. She wanted—maybe even *needed*—his help.

He lifted a shoulder. "I think your grandma knows something, like you said. That diary was just where she said it would be. So you better start reading."

"You're going to let me take it home?"

"Well, we can't read it at the same time, so one of us is going to have to go first. I figured since it's your family history, you should do it."

June 15, 1929

Dear Diary,

The Chateau is beyond anything I could have dreamed. I had heard of the opulence and luxury, of course. The stories reached clear to Madison and certainly into the heart of Atlanta. They likely go much farther. How could they not?

Mr. Dawkins's gilded roof must be visible from a mile out to sea. Three stories tall and more than enough lighted windows to guide a ship to safety. Now that I am here, I can hardly believe my good fortune.

Our party is quite diverse. Jane and I are first-time visitors, of course, but Mr. Dawkins has made us feel especially welcome as guests of his particular friend, Miss Lucille Globe. We met her at the bank and were too eager to hear her stories about being on the radio. Can you imagine? Her life is ever so glamorous. She spends her days on the studio stage and her evenings on the arm of one of the richest men in America. We could hardly believe that she would invite us to spend the summer with her on St. Simons Island. How could we decline?

The rest of our party is nearly as glamorous as Lucille. Angelique, a singer who nightly entertains us in the parlor, has been here often, accompanying her brother, Mr. Claude Devereaux. He is the most dashing radio producer, and I was seated next to him at dinner last evening. He spoke endlessly of his travels through Europe, visiting family in France and London.

I confess that I could not follow all of Mr. Devereaux's conversation for his most distracting mustache. It is sleek and trimmed and ever so handsome. I could not look away.

His eyes are rich like warm chocolate before bed, and they seemed to look right into me.

He invited me to go swimming this morning, and I accepted, perhaps faster than Mama would think proper. But what is the purpose of being at such a place without having some fun this summer?

I must prepare. We're to meet shortly.

June 16, 1929

Oh my! I can hardly breathe for recalling yesterday's ordeal.

I had planned to meet Mr. Devereaux at the agreed-upon time, and Jane had promised to accompany me. However, she awoke late and was still at breakfast when I went down to the pool.

There wasn't a soul around, but Mr. Devereaux had assured me he would meet me. So when I found the deck empty, I peeked around the Grecian columns to be sure he wasn't hiding. But they are too narrow to conceal a man of Mr. Devereaux's stature. His shoulders are so broad, and when he and his sister played lawn tennis, he rolled up his shirt sleeves enough to reveal rather sculpted forearms. He puts the statues in Mr. Dawkins's gallery to shame. He must do more than sit behind a desk at the radio network, or he could not possibly look as he does. And Mama would approve of a man who works hard, like the farmhands back home.

After several minutes, I decided to slip into the water. The sun was so warm, and I looked up as I stepped in. My foot landed on something slick on the top step. Perhaps it was one of the gold tiles Mr. Dawkins had installed along the bottom of the pool. I flung my arms about and screamed as I splashed into the water, but I hit my head on the edge of the deck, and then all went black.

I remember nothing until I woke up coughing and choking. It felt like my throat was on fire as my stomach writhed to release all I had swallowed. And then a face appeared right above me, the unforgiving deck to my back. The face was familiar, but I could not quite place it.

"Miss Holiday? Miss Holiday, are you well?" His voice was gentle and kind, his eyes even more so. They were so soft, like pasture grass warmed beneath the summer sun, but worry and concern filled them too. His skin held the deep tan of a man who worked outdoors.

Only after assessing all of that did I realize that his dark brown hair was dripping down his face. His pale blue shirt clung to his chest and around his arms as though he'd gone swimming in it.

"Miss Holiday, I'm going to go for help. Will you be all right here?"

His words did not immediately make any sense to me. Perhaps he read my confusion on my face, for he brushed a wet strand of hair off my forehead. His fingers were infinitely gentle, but my head suddenly felt like a melon crushed by a hammer. Mama would have been so embarrassed, but I could not help it. I began to cry.

He did not seem to mind, merely scooping me into his arms and carrying me like a child. He moved quickly but never jarred my still throbbing head, and quickly we arrived in the dining room.

Jane gasped and Lucille scrambled toward us, demanding to know what on earth had happened. Her high-

pitched squeal only made the pounding at my temple increase, but her hands quickly guided the man to the sofa. As he laid me down, he told them what had happened, then stepped away. I could only see him from the corner of my eye, his hands in front of him as though holding a hat.

Lucille asked if he had gone in after me, her gaze darting between us as though pursuing another story. As though there could possibly be any explanation other than the one he gave.

He looked up, and our gazes met. His was so warm that I nearly forgot to shiver in the cool house, my skin still damp and my hair soaked through. He gave her a "yes, ma'am" that was as sweet as peach preserves.

And then suddenly Jane was there, wrapping a blanket around me and holding me close. She apologized profusely for letting me go alone and begged to know if I was terribly hurt.

I tried to give her a small smile. But then Mr. Devereaux descended on the room, his apologies overflowing and rattling around my head.

Finally it was Mr. Dawkins who arrived, stilling the room with his quiet words. Shaking hands with the man who rescued me, he called him George and thanked him for his service before sending him to go clean up.

George looked at me again and gave a small nod, and I tried to thank him with my eyes. I would have surely drowned if not for his quick action. And I don't even know his last name.

Mr. Devereaux stayed nearby me for the rest of the day,

ever watchful until he saw me to my room. I decided to eat upstairs, as I could not manage to dress myself for dinner.

When we first arrived, Jane and I were assigned one of the cottages near the pool. However, after the ordeal, Lucille insisted we be in a room in the house, near her and Angelique and the two actresses from Mr. Devereaux's latest soap opera. It was quite kind of her, and I slept very well.

I am ashamed to admit it even here, but I dreamed about a blue cotton shirt stretched across a broad chest last night.

FOUR

*M*illie looked over her shoulder down the empty corridor, expecting someone to tell her to go back where she belonged. But the hall was empty, the only noise trickling from behind closed classroom doors. Well, that and the squeaking of the rubber soles of her shoes on the tile floor. No one peeked around the sterile corner at the end of the hall and told her to leave, so she took several more steps, swallowing the strange sensation that made the back of her throat itch.

Checking the scrap of paper in her hand, she confirmed the room number: 122. Ben had scratched it onto the back of her receipt from the coffee shop, along with directions to the history building at the college, before leaving the night before. She'd thanked him, mostly grateful that she didn't have to pay for another cup of coffee when they met up again. Such frivolities weren't in her budget.

The second-to-last door in the hallway was marked with a tan plaque identifying it. But this one was closed too.

That bothersome itch returned to her throat, and she scratched at her neck. Maybe this was an indicator that she shouldn't be here. She'd never even been on a college campus before.

But it wasn't her fault that she'd landed herself a partner. Or that he happened to be something of a smarty-pants.

She pressed her ear to the door just as a chorus of laughter broke out.

Was it possible he was funny too? There was only one way to find out. She turned the latch as silently as possible and opened the door a crack.

"Not quite, Mr. Thurber. The American Revolution wasn't started by a bunch of farmers with muskets looking for free tea." It was definitely Ben's voice, but there was a lightness to it, a bit of humor woven into every phrase, and she stepped toward it. "These men—Revere, Adams, Jefferson, Washington—they were facing the greatest military of the time, so they'd better believe in more than their right to drink tea."

Suddenly Ben looked directly at Millie, and his voice trailed off. She froze. Oh dear. She'd stepped all the way inside the room behind a dozen rows of desks. A push at the door behind her proved that it had shut all the way, and she tried for an apologetic smile. It felt more like a grimace.

But Ben didn't seem to mind. The corner of his mouth quirked up, and he raised his eyebrows as he nodded to an empty seat three rows down.

Sit. Right. That would be less conspicuous.

She slid into the chair, and the girl in the next seat glanced at her questioningly. But before Millie could respond, the other girl grinned. "I'd sneak into this class to see him too."

Millie almost swallowed her tongue.

At least she didn't have to respond. The girl turned back

toward the front of the room, propping her chin in her hand, a dreamy look settling across her features.

Millie tried to follow the exact path of her stare, which seemed to land on Ben as he paced before a large whiteboard. The student was clearly enamored. But Millie couldn't tell exactly why.

Tracing his movements, she stared hard. He wasn't particularly striking—certainly not the hero type in the books she loved to read. He couldn't serve as a stand-in for Sir Robert, the medieval knight in her current read. Tall and a little lanky, Ben wore a corduroy jacket that was a bit too big across his shoulders. The leather patches on the elbows made him look like a man lost in time, one who belonged two or three generations before.

A student in the second row raised her hand, and Ben pointed at her. "So what is it they believed in?" she asked.

Ben ran his fingers through his hair, ruffling his dark waves, and a broad smile broke free. "That's what I want to know." He turned his back to the room and picked up a black marker. "Three pages answering the question, Which of the Founding Fathers' beliefs would have prompted *you* to join them in the war with England?"

"All of them?"

He glanced over his shoulder at the boy who had interrupted. "Well, who'd you have in mind?" There was a long pause before Ben gave him a knowing smile. "Sam Adams, I suppose."

A wave of red crept up the boy's neck until his cheeks flamed.

"Yes, he brewed his own beer. No, you may not write an essay on his belief in good alcohol."

The whole class giggled as Ben finished outlining the

assignment on the whiteboard. "Might I suggest choosing one or two key topics and unpacking why those who supported them did so and why you agree? Don't try to cram all of them into one paper. I'm looking for a thoughtful consideration rather than a regurgitation of the Declaration of Independence. That's why I'm giving you a week." His eyebrows went up again. "Questions?"

When there were none, he dismissed the class.

Millie was glued to her seat. Her first college class. She'd just survived her first—and only. Okay, so it was more like the last seven minutes of the class. But still. It had been fun.

She frowned. Classes had never included laughter and teasing during her school years. They'd been focused and demanding and utterly boring. Somehow her teachers had even managed to make literature a yawn.

Could a good teacher make that much of a difference? Given the smiles and chatter of the students filing down the aisle and out of the classroom, apparently so.

She was so wrapped up in watching the interaction of the young students that she didn't notice she had an audience until his shadow fell across her desk. Glancing way up, she met Ben's deep blue gaze as he crossed his arms.

"I'm sorry. I didn't know you were going to be in the middle of class. I'd have waited outside."

The corner of his mouth tipped up. "No problem." There was an unspoken question in the squint of his eyes, but she couldn't quite make it out.

"I . . ." Searching for a response, she dropped her gaze to the line at the corner of his mouth.

Lips pinched together, he seemed to lean forward, waiting. On her.

"Um . . . I've never seen such a fun class." His grin returned, so she spit out another compliment. "I really enjoyed it."

Ben nodded, dropped his arms to his sides, and tilted his head toward the desk at the front of the room. "I'm glad. I had fun teaching it."

There was nothing to do but follow him, so she ambled a few paces behind him. "Is this . . . what class is it?"

"History 120—A Survey of American History."

"Summer school?"

He glanced up from where he straightened a stack of papers, his lips pursed to the side.

Stupid. Stupid. Stupid. Of course it was summer school. It was the middle of June. But the only thing she knew about school at this time of year was related to making up a geometry class that she'd bombed during the regular semester. Worst summer of her life.

"I mean, are they making up a class that they failed?" He probably thought she was an idiot.

His gaze darted to the closed door as a snort escaped the back of his throat. "Um, no."

"Oh." Perfect. Now he *knew* she was an idiot.

"Most of them are trying to get ahead so they can graduate early. Some of them are nontraditional students." He must have read the confusion on her face, and he quickly defined the unfamiliar term. "They have full-time jobs or families and can't take a full course load, so they take whatever classes they can squeeze into their schedules."

She pressed her hands together and frowned. That was an option—fitting in the classes you could manage? It hadn't been when she'd been in high school, which was why she'd ended up in summer school in the first place.

But there wasn't anything to do about it now. That summer was gone. And this one promised so much more. An extra job. A treasure hunt. Riches beyond anything even in her favorite novels.

And maybe even a new family name. Claude Devereaux might be her great-grandfather. Or he might not be. But it was clear even in the first few pages of Ruth's diary that she was smitten. And if the summer of 1929 played out as Millie hoped, she could be part of a family that had never had to pinch pennies. She closed her eyes and sighed, lost in the possibilities of that what-if until Ben cleared his throat, a question seeming to punctuate the sound.

Shaking off her daydream, Millie snapped her gaze to meet his. "Sorry. I must have . . ." Spaced out. Like the idiot he already knew she was. "You're pretty good at this." She waved at the whiteboard still covered in his neat block letters. "Why not do it full-time?"

Something close to a scowl flickered across his features. It was there only a moment and then vanished, but his eyes remained narrowed for a long second, and she was beyond thankful that the weight of his gaze fell on the loose pages in his hands.

"You know. Between working on my PhD and life. I guess there are extenuating circumstances."

"Like what?"

His eyes flashed in her direction, and she immediately looked around for a place to hide. No such luck, unless she crawled under one of the desks. "Never mind."

He stabbed his fingers through his hair, sending his hair into even more disarray. "It's been . . . these last few years have been tough."

Like Ramen noodles seven days a week, tough? Like splurging on a bike only because it meant not having to pay for gas? Like running the air-conditioning once a week as a special treat? He didn't confirm as much, but she knew a thing or two about those. Maybe that's why he didn't have to spell it all the way out. Sometimes she could just tell with people who shared the same struggles. It wasn't quite a secret handshake, but it might as well be. Theirs was a club no one wanted to join.

But if he was really a member, how had he reached this point? Not only a graduate of college but *teaching* at one.

She couldn't ask another impertinent question. And that was all she had.

Thankfully he saved her from testing the size of her mouth with her foot. "So, did you discover a map in the diary last night?" His scowl disappeared, replaced by the hint of a smile.

"No." She swung her bag onto a desk in the front row and cringed when it settled with a loud thunk. She shot a side glance at Ben, who paused as he put his stack of papers into his beaten-up messenger bag.

His look seemed to suggest that perhaps she ought to have a little more respect for a treasured artifact that, at the least, carried her family's history. At the most, it was the key to wealth that would change both of their lives. Forever.

"Sorry." She mouthed the word as she pulled out the brown paper bag–wrapped package, the diary just as she'd found it the night before—minus some dust that she'd blown off. Flipping open the first page, she paused, then glanced up from beneath her lashes.

His bag now packed, Ben had repositioned himself. Sitting on the edge of his desk, his long, khaki-covered legs stretched out before him, he crossed his arms. "So what did you find?"

"Um . . ." She tried not to look guilty, but the glint in his eyes was either humor or accusation. While she hoped it was the first, the rope around her chest suggested that it very well might be the second.

"I read the last line. First."

His eyebrows went up, but other than that he remained still.

"It's just a thing I do."

Those deep brown arches rose nearly to the matching wave sweeping across his forehead, and her neck immediately burned under his scrutiny.

Pressing a hand to her throat, she dropped her gaze to the diary. "I always read the last line of a book first." He opened his mouth to ask the same question that everyone else did, but she beat him with the response. "Of course, not mysteries. I'm not trying to ruin the book, but if I know where I'm going, I know if the journey is going to be worth it."

She glanced down at her feet, pressing one hand to the desk at her side and clutching the journal in the other. They were maybe three feet apart, but in his current pose, they could have been eye to eye if she'd looked up. Which she didn't.

She could only bring her gaze as far as his feet. The look of censure she was sure would be on his face kept her from lifting her eyes. She wasn't educated like he was. She didn't do things the way she was supposed to like he did. And she'd found herself in a position he could never understand.

He uncrossed his ankles, then crossed them again. "Isn't this a mystery?"

Her stomach seeped toward her toes. "I-I suppose." And it wasn't just any mystery. It was *the* mystery. Her past and present swept into one big question.

"So what does the last line say?"

She cringed. "There's another journal."

"What?" He grabbed for the book, his hands gentle but nothing less than intent. Flipping to the end, he scanned the last lines. Ones she'd memorized in a single read.

This summer is so different than I anticipated. There is more to share. It is a good thing Mama thought to pack a second journal, for I shall have no difficulty filling it.

"This is only the first volume?" The disbelief evident in his voice was just like hers had been the night before, and he smoothly flipped the pages before him, his eyes scanning them, clearly searching for a clue that had been missed.

But the only missing piece was from Grandma Joy, who had said the map would be here. She'd known about the diary, so how had she missed that there was a second one? Had she not known about it at all? Or, more likely, had she forgotten?

"What else did you find out?"

"Ruth was invited to the Chateau by Lucille Globe, who was"—she held up her fingers in air quotes—"'the particular friend of Howard Dawkins.'"

Ben's chuckle wasn't really humorous but spoke to the absurdity of the phrase.

"I know. It's amazing how they flaunted their inappropriate relationships."

He nodded. "But labeled them with the most unassuming titles."

"And everyone knew." She pointed at the journal. "Ruth wrote about it so matter-of-factly. It wasn't even questioned.

Lucille was the mistress of the Chateau—at least for the summer."

That scowl he'd worn before made its way back into place, the tip of his nose twitching. "Even though Dawkins had a wife and a son back in Chicago."

Her stomach did a full flip. "He did?"

"Sure." Ben shifted his weight against the desk beneath him, but he didn't attempt to make eye contact. "His son passed away about ten years ago. It was big news because it was on the eightieth anniversary of the stock market crash, and of course his dad had been hit hard by it."

Her insides shivered, and she wrapped her arms around her middle, not sure how to make sense of this bit of information or if it mattered at all. "I guess I assumed . . . Wasn't the Chateau passed down to his nephew or something?"

Ben nodded. "Maybe his son didn't want it. Maybe his wife didn't. There must have been a lot of bad memories wrapped up in the old place."

Millie had just assumed he'd been single. She wasn't naive enough to believe that married men were always faithful, but . . . In her first entries, Ruth had made it seem as though everyone liked Dawkins, that he was a man worthy of their respect.

But if Dawkins wasn't the man Millie had assumed him to be, then was Ruth a reliable narrator? Or was Millie missing the truth on the pages?

She hated those novels—the ones where she couldn't tell if the main character was lying to her. And now she had to wonder if her great-grandmother was doing the same. Was this all a wild goose chase or an elaborate hoax? Or was it possible that there was *some* truth—hidden though it might be—in what Ruth had written?

"Did the diary mention anyone else? Besides Dawkins and his girlfriend?"

Ben's question made her jump, and she jerked herself away from her own troubling inquiries. "Yes. A few. There was a gardener and her friend Jane. And Claude Devereaux." She stumbled on the name, but he didn't seem to notice, his jaw dropping and his eyes narrowing in on the leather volume dwarfed by his long fingers.

"Claude Devereaux? As in . . ." He found her gaze and held it for a long moment. "*The* Devereaux family? As in Henri Devereaux? As in the Louisiana Vanderbilts?"

Millie swallowed the lump that had suddenly formed in her throat, but it refused to fully dislodge, and she had to resort to a simple nod of response. Which felt rather pathetic given the incredulity of his tone.

She hadn't been surprised to see the name of one of the wealthiest families in the country written in her great-grandmother's handwriting. As soon as she'd learned that Ruth had spent time there, she'd begun to research that summer on the shore, and the Devereaux name had been mentioned. Perhaps not effusively, but it wasn't hidden either.

But Ben didn't need to know what that meant. After all, that information had zero effect on him. It wasn't tied to the treasure. Not really.

No. Not at all. They were definitely two very different searches.

"Henri was the oldest brother and inherited the majority of their father's estate," Ben said, "but Claude was no slouch. Wasn't he interested in radio?"

Millie nodded quickly, and Ben opened his mouth like he was going to explain, but she jumped in. She didn't have to read it in a textbook. She'd read about the prevalence of personal radios in a Depression-era novel. "Because television wasn't really around yet. Radio was the way most people kept in touch with the rest of the country. It was also a key source of entertainment."

Ben smiled. "Exactly."

"And of course Dawkins invested heavily in radio."

"Ha!" Ben's laugh was like a chocolate-covered caramel, all things pleasant and soothing. "How'd you know that?"

Pressing her hands to her hips, she cocked her head and shot him her best fake scowl. "You think I don't listen when the tour guides come through the Chateau?"

He crossed his arms and leaned back, but his lips twitched like they were fighting back a smile. "I would never presume such a thing."

"Good."

"But this isn't going to help us figure out where the treasure is hidden or the location of the second diary."

Fair point. But not really helpful. "So . . . I guess we go back to the start? It stands to reason that the second journal would be near the first."

Ben scrubbed his cheek with a flat hand and stared at a spot over her shoulder, but it was clear he wasn't really focused on it. Finally he gave a curt nod of his head. "Back to the library, then?"

"Unless you have a better idea."

June 19, 1929

I am glad to be fully recovered from the ordeal at the pool. The ache in my temple has finally subsided. However, Mr. Devereaux took it upon himself to inspect the injury. No man has ever asked if he could touch me so, but his fingers were terribly gentle, and it was all very decent in the company of his sister and Jane.

What was happening in my nerves was rather lacking in decency. He is a very handsome man, and I could not help but lean in toward him ever so slightly.

Willa and Betsy arrived in the midst of his examination, and they scowled at me as though I'd stolen their spots in his next production. Of course, I have not. He has said nothing about his work except in passing. Perhaps he does not realize that I long to pursue a career in radio. I have no desire to work as a bank teller forever, even if banking has made Mr. Dawkins sinfully rich.

Although I see Mr. Devereaux watching me, I am afraid I have missed several chances to spend time with him. Yesterday the whole of the house party took advantage of the stables, and I stayed in my room.

By the afternoon, the light through the window was too bright for me to keep my eyes closed. I wandered the house for a while and ended up thoroughly lost. I walked the hallways for an hour, trying to locate a familiar room or stairwell, but they all seemed to blend together. Just when I had decided to sit a spell on the floor, I discovered a small spiral staircase. I followed it down and found myself by the kitchen. It smelled of wonderful roasted duck and sautéed onions.

Everyone here has been so kind to me, but I could not

bring myself to ask for assistance. Instead I found a back door and snuck through it, successful in avoiding detection by any of the household staff.

That is, until I rounded the corner of the outside of the house. The sun nearly blinded me as it peeked around the column of one of the towers and through the Spanish moss hanging from the enormous oak trees. I promptly ran into what I thought was a brick wall. Then it grunted. Or rather, he grunted. When he spun around, he put his hand to my elbow, as I was dangerously close to toppling over after our collision. And that is when I realized who he was. It was George, the man who rescued me from the pool.

He dropped his hand, leaving behind a coolness in its absence, but his eyes were as warm as any I have ever seen.

He tugged on the corner of his brown cap before wiping his forehead with the back of his hand and called me Miss Holiday. The farmhands often made a similar movement when the sun burned so brightly. But here, so close to the coast, the breeze off the water keeps us cool beneath the ever-present summer sunshine.

He made no other movement, only holding a rake steady at his side. I held out my hand, and he stared at it for a long moment, making no motion to shake it. I told him that I owed him my gratitude, but when I went to call him by name, I trailed off, my face flushing. We hadn't been introduced, and I did not know his last name. The man had pulled me to safety and carried me through the house, and I knew absolutely nothing about him. Except that his eyes were the color of grass and his embrace was as gentle as a newborn kitten.

As his gaze rose to meet mine, he transferred his rake

from his right hand to his left. After a swipe of his fingers against his brown trousers, he shook my hand and supplied his name. Whitman. George Whitman. But he said everyone here just calls him George.

I tried to smile, but it wasn't easy given the strange tumult inside me that seemed to be tied to his grin. It was slightly lopsided. His front teeth are the slightest bit crooked, but it is endearing rather than off-putting.

"Ruth Holiday," I said. And then I nearly bit off my tongue. What on earth was wrong with me? He knew my name. He had called me by it many times by the side of the pool. I sputtered on, trying not to be even more inane, but there is no way to be certain if I succeeded. I bumbled on with my thank-yous, even specifying where he'd rescued me, though he certainly remembered the ordeal.

His chin dipped, but his gaze stayed locked on me. He said nothing else, so I was forced to continue.

I said that I hoped his clothes were not ruined. He responded only that they had already dried. Then I tried to ask him if he'd had someone wash them for him, but oh dear, I botched it terribly. Because suddenly it was the most important thing to know if there was a woman in his life who would take care of such things.

I felt a strange sensation in my stomach as he paused. Oh my. I've never experienced anything like that in all of my nineteen years. It was the oddest feeling.

Before I could fully analyze it, the corners of his eyes crinkled. There was no accompanying smile, but the planes of his face transformed with a humor that had not been there before.

He said he had managed, and he sounded fully capable.

However, it was not an answer to my question. And I think he knew it.

Before I could push further, he asked me what I was doing outside alone. And I was forced to tell the truth. George laughed so hard at my silly story of getting lost and wandering for an hour, pressing a hand to his side and leaning heavily on his rake.

When his humor finally abated, he agreed to show me the way. Mama would have said I was too forward asking for his help. But he had already saved my life once. How could a short stroll around the Chateau be wrong? No one was around to see us anyway.

It was a lovely walk.

June 20, 1929

The strangest thing has happened at the Chateau. Last night after dinner, we retired to the parlor and the men poured themselves drinks. Mr. Dawkins says that no matter what the government says, certain men will always have access to the best liquor. He is one of those men.

Some men indulge in their drink among friends. Some in private. But aren't all breaking the law?

I must say that Mr. Devereaux abstained from a drink last evening. When the butler offered him the highball glass filled with amber liquid, he caught my eye, waved the drink off, and winked at me from his place on the far sofa.

It was rather forward of him, but I smiled nonetheless. He is a handsome man and has been terribly attentive since my ordeal. I believe he blames himself for not being at the pool when he had said he would meet me there.

He stood then and walked toward me. But before he could even make it halfway around the circle of women playing cards at the center table, Angelique spoke loudly, declaring that Willa must be mistaken.

Every eye in the room, including mine and Jane's beside me, turned toward the four women.

Willa, the actress with deep chestnut hair, said she could see no other way around it. Her silver sapphire necklace and earrings were missing, and only the maid had been in her room. Lucille looked aghast and pleaded with Mr. Dawkins to tell Willa that she was mistaken.

Mr. Dawkins only reclined further in his chair and mumbled something about how it must have been misplaced. Willa seemed disinclined to agree, but she said that she would look again in the morning in fresh light.

But I thought it very strange, as Jane had lost a brooch just that morning.

FIVE

here's something strange going on."

Ben snapped his head toward Millie, still hunched over a low shelf, then in the direction of the library door, looking for any sign that they'd been caught beyond the burgundy velvet rope by his supervisor or hers. But the only thing there was the faint smell of summer rain wafting through the screened windows on the other side of the third-story corridor.

"What?" He kept his voice low, but an inch of frustration seeped into it. He didn't have any desire to identify the source of that irritation, but he took a deep breath anyway. Forcing his hands to unclench, he tried again. Gentler. Softer. "What do you mean?"

She didn't even bother to look up from where her finger scrolled below every leather-bound title on the shelf before her. Just as it had for the last forty-five minutes.

And they'd found nothing.

Frustration, meet your maker.

Rubbing his hands on the front of his navy-blue uniform pants, he tried not to focus on their wasted time, their blatant rule breaking, and the little voice in the back of his head that kept chiding him. *This is all for nothing. You're never going to find that money. Your life isn't going to change unless you change it.*

Yes, if he wanted a different future than the one he'd been handed, he was going to have to make it happen. There were debts to pay and he was going to have to pay them. And this sneaking around—even if it went against everything he believed—might be his only chance to pay them back before there was no one left to pay back.

There was another voice too, this one sweet and promising. And it tempted him with a future where he'd only have to work one job—one he loved. A future where the bills could be settled as soon as they arrived. A future where he didn't drive a coupe that only started when it felt like it. A future that wasn't cloaked in his mother's sins.

And he wanted that future. He'd worked for that future. He'd prayed for that future. Maybe this—meeting Millie and agreeing to help her search for her treasure—was some sort of answer to that request.

Or maybe he was ignoring the still small voice of God telling him to run.

"I said there was something going on at the Chateau."

"What? When?"

Stupid questions. He knew when. When it came to the two of them, there was only one *when*.

But she didn't harp on it. "In the diary. Ruth said that one of the guests lost a sapphire and silver necklace."

Looking up from where he'd knelt before the bottom shelf, he shot her a look that he hoped conveyed just how much he didn't care about a rich woman misplacing a necklace that could more than cover the down payment on the townhouse he'd been dreaming of for the last nine months. "So what?"

Her eyebrows rose, and he immediately regretted the sharp words. "I'm sorry." Scrubbing his hand down his face, he shook his head. "I'm just tired. I didn't mean to snap at you."

She glanced back down toward the shelf she'd been checking, her shoulders slumping beneath the gauzy weight of the navy-blue straps that crisscrossed below her neck. She had to be as exhausted as he was after a long shift at the Chateau, and it wasn't her fault that there was a second diary or that she hadn't known about it.

Taking a shallow breath, he tried for a softer tone. "What do you think was going on?"

Her gaze remained trained on the leather casings at her knee, and her volume stayed just as low. But there was a certainty in her tone when she finally spoke. "Someone stole them."

"Them?"

"Ruth's friend lost a brooch too. The same day."

"You think there was a thief?" He couldn't help the way his voice rose in astonishment, and he clapped a hand over his mouth at her startled glance. At least, he thought she was startled. The yellow and pink shadows from the low lamps played across her face, hiding some of her features. The big window in the wall adjacent to the empty fireplace didn't even let in the moonlight, a blanket of clouds covering the sky.

But there was no anger or palpable tension flowing from her, so he made his move. Tiptoeing to the door and ducking his head around to stare down the hallway, he held his breath, only releasing it when he'd confirmed that it was empty. "Coast is still clear."

"Lucky you. Unless you're *trying* to get us caught and banned from the premises."

He wrinkled his nose, and she giggled behind the fingers of an elbow-length white glove.

It wasn't surprising that she was teasing him. What was surprising was his laugh joining hers. It snuck up on him and popped out before he even realized it was coming. Or how much he liked the sound of their mingled laughter. He couldn't remember the last time he'd let himself enjoy a moment of humor with someone else.

Probably not since before his mother's arraignment.

A memory flashed against the back of his eyelids. The courtroom. The stern scowl on the judge's face. His mom's cold gaze. Her crisp black suit—most likely purchased with someone else's hard-earned money.

The images reached into his chest like spindly fingers and then clenched into a fist that had him doubling over before he knew it.

"You okay?"

He nodded quickly, rubbing at the spot over his heart and praying that the memories would subside.

Someday.

Someday he'd forget. When the debts were repaid.

And the treasure could take care of that. It could make at least half of his problems disappear. Redoubling his efforts to find that elusive second diary, he returned to his spot on the shelf and ignored the way her gaze stayed heavy on his back. He needed something to distract her.

"So how'd you say you knew about the first diary?" His

question popped out without much thought, and as soon as it did, he remembered that she'd already told him the answer.

"Um . . . my grandmother." The lilt at the end of her response made it sound more like a question, but he kept his back to her and his finger nearly tracing the outline of the books at hand.

"Any chance she could help us find the second? I mean, how did you know where to find it exactly?"

Millie cleared her throat, and it seemed more like an excuse to delay her response than a necessity. "Well . . . I'm pretty sure she told me everything she knows."

Looking over his shoulder, he squinted at her. "What exactly did she tell you?"

Tilting her head back and closing her eyes, she seemed to stretch for the words. "She said that her mom had often wished she had her journal from that summer."

"Single?"

"Yes. Just the one." Millie cracked an eye open at him as she smoothed her hand down the front of her dress. In the dim glow its fabric swished and shimmered like the sky in a midnight thunderstorm, but he kept his gaze on her face.

"She never said anything about there being two," she continued.

"So how'd you know where to find it?"

The look in her eyes shifted from seeing into the past to a very curious direct stare into the present. "She said, 'It's in the room with the books.' Why?"

He met her gaze with the same fortitude. "Maybe she could help us find the second. I think we should ask her."

Millie's lips—still outrageously red from her role that evening—nearly disappeared as she bit them together. Tugging up her gloves, she dropped her gaze to her fingers. "Sure. I'll ask her."

Ben frowned. That wasn't what he'd been proposing. And he had a gut feeling she knew it. She was keeping him away from something. Maybe it was a bit of key information. Or maybe it was . . . more.

He didn't have a clue what he was missing, but the longer she hemmed and hawed about it, the more he was going to press. And he'd get there. He'd figure it out. Digging up the past was his job. All three of his jobs, actually. He'd uncover the truth, whether she wanted to tell him or not.

"I meant *we* should talk to her. Together. What are you doing tomorrow?"

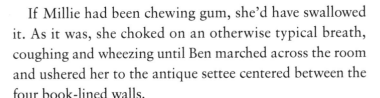

If Millie had been chewing gum, she'd have swallowed it. As it was, she choked on an otherwise typical breath, coughing and wheezing until Ben marched across the room and ushered her to the antique settee centered between the four book-lined walls.

"I'm fine." She held up a hand even as he nearly pushed her to the sofa. Its burgundy upholstery let out a little puff of dust, which only made her cough harder.

"Sure you are." He lowered himself to her side but refrained from the standard thump on the back, for which she was incredibly grateful. It was hard enough to catch her breath without being pounded into the lumpy cushion.

Ben pressed his hands to his thighs but didn't say a word for several long seconds as she tried to quell the tickle in the back of her throat that had turned into a forest fire.

"I'm okay. Good. Fine." And apparently a liar too.

An errant cough was the least of her worries. She closed her eyes, hoping that the truth hadn't spilled down her face as easily as the tears streaming there. After tugging off a glove, she swiped at them with her fingernail and managed to keep from adding a saltwater spot to her silk gown. Finally she sucked in a breath, the tension in her chest easing ever so slightly.

When she snuck a glance at Ben, he raised his eyebrows in an unspoken question.

"Yes. I'm okay." She gulped and swallowed the air with an extra measure of caution. "Sorry about that."

He nodded an acknowledgment, but there was something in his eyes that said her unplanned distraction hadn't distracted him at all. It promised that he wasn't going to let go of his idea.

That wouldn't—*couldn't*—happen. She couldn't take him to meet Grandma Joy for at least one very important reason, so she scrambled for another focus. "I can't believe you let me sit on this couch."

He looked down, and his face twisted like he'd suddenly realized he was sitting on a shark. Jumping up, he stared back at the furniture, shaking his head.

"And that's probably not great for the carpet," she said.

His gaze darted in the direction of his black work boots, his eyes bright and round. But it was his tiptoeing to the wooden floor that made her burst out laughing. Immediately she clamped her hand over her mouth. The tears that had been loosened before weren't so easily stemmed. Two big ones raced down her cheeks under his watchful glare.

"It really isn't good for the antiques, you know. And what if the sofa was damaged? They'd know we were in here."

"They'd know *someone* was in here." Her correction was cautious, thoughtful. They couldn't risk alerting the other private security personnel that there was anyone slinking through the shadows. If the historical preservation society thought that someone was sneaking around the property, they'd amp up security faster than Millie could fill a cup of coffee—which was quicker than any other waitress at the Hermit Crab Café.

That meant they had to leave everything precisely as they found it.

Slowly she rose from the hundred-year-old sofa, brushing at the dust she'd undoubtedly picked up and praying that it hadn't stuck to unmentionable areas. Twisting to check her backside, she nearly missed the set in his jaw, which should have tipped her off to what was to come.

"Do you really think the second journal is in here?"

No. But she wasn't about to give in that easily. "Why wouldn't it be?"

"Because we've searched every shelf—three times—and there's no sign of it."

"Okay . . ." As far as concessions went, it wasn't one. But she didn't have another comeback, so she stared at him. Hard. Maybe he'd back down.

He blinked, a slow smirk rolling across his lips.

All right. Back down unlikely.

"It's not in this room, Millie." He waved a hand toward the window. "Maybe it's somewhere else on the property. Maybe it's not at the Chateau at all. But one thing I know for sure. We need more information."

Ack. He was right back to where she didn't want him.

"We just need to read the diary." That sounded like a valid

point. It *was* a valid point. They had no idea the secrets that slim volume might hold, and the only way they'd find them is if they read the book.

If only she didn't have to get some sleep between her jobs.

She'd dozed off after just two short entries the night before. She'd wanted to keep reading, but her eyes refused to cooperate, drooping and closing without permission. One minute she'd been about to flip the page, and the next her alarm clock insisted she roll out of bed and race to the diner, or she'd be late. And late meant fired. She couldn't afford that until she—they—found whatever had been hidden on this estate.

"Sure, the book is important, but what if there's something in there that we don't know because we're missing the details?" He crossed his arms again, the shoulders of his jacket pulling almost as tight as the lines around his mouth. The faint wrinkles at the corners of his eyes deepened.

He'd make a good lawyer. She felt like she was on trial and he was about to act as judge and jury too.

"Of course. I'll ask her."

He began to shake his head slowly and then stopped in mid-motion. "I'll go with you."

"No—" It popped out like a firecracker, unexpected and loud, and she slapped a hand over her mouth, remembering too late that her lipstick would likely leave a mark against the white fabric. But that was the least of her worries if Ben's squinted glare was any indication.

"Is there a reason you don't want me to meet your grandmother?"

"Of course not."

Liar, liar. You know better.

Her conscience chided her, reminding her of the sermon her pastor had preached a few weeks before. *"Do not lie to each other."* It was somewhere in Colossians, but she couldn't remember exactly where. It didn't matter. She didn't need to know the reference to know lying was wrong. Even if her reasons were . . . mostly honorable.

He opened his mouth to respond, but she shook her head quickly, cutting him off. She could do better. She *would* do better.

"Grandma Joy is a wealth of knowledge, but . . . um . . . sometimes she requires a delicate touch. New people can overwhelm her." She closed her eyes and prayed for the words she needed, ones that made sense. "And her mom—Ruth— died when she was fairly young. The stories, the memories, are pretty old."

Ben stood a little taller and relaxed his arms a fraction. "She doesn't always remember?"

Well, that was a benign way of putting it.

Millie grimaced but leaned into the truth, hunting for words that were accurate but gentle. Because, while she'd wished at least once that she'd never even met him, she needed his help. And the truth—all of it—was more likely to make him run than stick around for the hard stuff.

"You could put it that way. Her memories aren't always particularly . . . crisp."

Oh, man. That was a stretch. Sometimes Grandma Joy's memory was sharper than a new knife. But sometimes— more often than either of them wanted to admit—her mind wouldn't cut through the mashed potatoes they served at the home.

When she looked up at Ben, his thick brows had dipped

until they met in the middle. The rest of his features pulled tight. "I'm sorry." He sounded like he actually meant it, and it surprised her how much those two little words warmed that spot in her chest that had to grow a little bit cold every time she saw Grandma Joy.

"Thank you." She sounded stupid, but really, what else was there to say?

Except, of course, a rapid reassurance that this wasn't all a waste of their time.

"She has good days. And she knew about the first journal. She knew—she knows. She's just—"

This time Ben stopped her, raising his hand with a sad grin. "I get it. My grandpa was forgetful too."

Forgetful? Sure. They could go with that. For a while.

Maybe Grandma Joy could even pull it off. For a while. But then what? What would she do if Ben witnessed one of Grandma Joy's more painful moments? What if he freaked out and took off and left Millie to do this all on her own?

That was where she had started anyway. But now it felt different.

She frowned and pressed a hand to her forehead. It wasn't different. It was just new. She'd been on her own most of her adult life. After her grandpa died, it had been just her and Grandma Joy. Those had been a good two years. Fun even. Until Grandma Joy started forgetting. Until the house had been sold.

Her lungs ached for a breath, but it was too painful to remember how everything had changed so suddenly. One moment Grandma Joy had been taking care of her. The next, Millie had to take care of Grandma Joy.

"I still think she's our best resource."

Millie tiptoed off the rug and then paced the narrow confines of the available hardwood floor, trying to rid herself of both the memories and Ben's suggestion. She couldn't take him to meet her grandmother. She just couldn't.

Except he was right. Grandma Joy knew more about Ruth's story than anyone else alive.

A question wiggled its way into the back of her brain, refusing to leave. What if Ben could do more than keep her out of hot water with Chateau security?

He'd already proven to be helpful. And he was an unabashed history nerd—from the leather patches on his tweed jacket to the way he riled up a classroom full of college students over the American Revolution. While he'd never said as much, she had a feeling that he hadn't picked up a part-time job at the Chateau because he loved being a security guard or because it paid particularly well. He loved the area and its history as much as anyone else. He knew things she'd never had the opportunity to learn.

Not that she would have chosen to learn what he had. But it would have been nice to have the option.

She swung a glance in his direction as she spun to make another trek over the open boards. He'd crossed his arms again, and his gaze had turned intense. But he didn't seem in a rush for her response.

Maybe he understood that introducing him to her grandmother was so much bigger than a lost treasure. It meant taking this from the page to real life. And her life didn't look like silk gowns, white gloves, and diamond necklaces.

There was more at stake than what once was lost on this estate.

"I'll see if she's up for a visitor."

June 25, 1929

Claude took me on a walk today, only the two of us. He insists that I call him Claude instead of Mr. Devereaux, and I have agreed. We have two more months together, and we must be friendly, so I have given him leave to call me Ruth. When he does, my entire spine tingles.

We strolled along the beach, and I didn't even mind that the breeze off the water whipped my hair about my face. Who needs to be able to see when such a strong, handsome man is walking at your side, the crook of his elbow a sure guide?

Oh, but he is a fascinating man. He's seen so much of the world and has such incredible stories to tell. He's even been to Africa and seen elephants and lions and something called a gazelle, which sounds like a deer. I could have listened to him talk all day about his adventures and his life. It's so foreign to me. The ships he sails on are nearly as luxurious as the Chateau, although that is hard to comprehend.

His life is so unlike anything I knew on the farm. There are no children running about his legs. I suppose that could be because all of his siblings are older. But even those he does not speak of, except Angelique, of course. They rarely have more than a casual greeting in the evenings before dinner, a simple kiss on the cheek or a mild embrace.

I cannot help but remember when I returned to the farm after my first month away. Jimmy, Sarah, Abraham, and Shirley raced to me, tangling in my skirts until I nearly fell to the yard, the air filled with their screams of delight. The farm is never quiet, but it is also never lonely.

Perhaps he has never known such a life.

We had walked nearly half a mile along the water before he stopped. There was no one else on the sand as far as I could see in either direction, so I let him take my hands in his. They were gentle and soft, not at all like George's hands with their rough calluses. Not that I have been thinking about him. I certainly have not.

Claude told me I am beautiful. When he looked into my eyes and said those words, my insides melted like butter over hot bread. I could only stare at him, and I do not think I even blinked.

Oh my, but he is handsome. His narrow mustache is so refined and elegant, and his smile makes me want to fall into his arms. Mama has always warned me away from men. "There ain't near enough good ones," she says. But surely Claude is one of the good ones. Certainly he's always been kind to me. And whatever his shortcomings may be, life with him would never be boring. There would be so many adventures, enough money to buy a house on the beach beside the Chateau. Perhaps near the creek to the south. I love the sound of it as it bubbles and gurgles its way to the ocean. The water is so clear that you can see right to the bottom of it.

On the beach, Claude lifted my hand and pressed his lips to my palm. If I had been wearing gloves, it would have been nothing but innocent.

I was not. But I could not make myself chastise him for any impropriety. Not even when he kissed the inside of my arm. All the way up to my elbow. Below the sleeve of my dress, his mustache tickling my arm, his breath warm against my skin, he stopped.

I did not want him to.

Am I so very wicked?

He sighed when he stopped, and I think he wanted to keep going as well. But he said only that I was truly beautiful and that I could be in the moving pictures, except then he would not get to work with me. I think that made him sad.

I managed a strangled giggle and tried to tell him how much I long to work with him. I could only focus on the shiver that ran across my arms and had absolutely nothing to do with the breeze off the water. Somehow the rolling waves and endless blue expanse had disappeared. There was only he and I. Together.

And when he raised his head, I let him kiss me.

June 26, 1929

My maid is gone. Jenny was not mine exactly, but she was one of the housemaids on loan to the guests each morning. She always brought fresh towels piled to the ceiling. They were so soft and fluffy and smelled of sunshine and gardenias. And she often laid out our clothes for the day, taking care of any wrinkles.

This morning she did not appear. My dress still hung in the armoire, simple cotton and decorated with all the wrinkles my trunk could give it. Jane's as well.

We did our best, taking special care with our hair. But when Jane stabbed herself for the third time while pinning up her great chestnut waves, she gave up and declared that she would much rather have one of those new short hairstyles. I almost think she is serious.

When we did finally make it to breakfast, Angelique and Willa and Betsy were whispering unabashedly just inside the dining room. I could not make out their words, but the tension was absolutely palpable. It drew us to them. We were merely moths and they the lamp. As we approached, their voices rose, and I could not help but wonder if this was a performance, and Jane and I the audience.

Willa squealed that we would never believe what had happened. Mr. Dawkins had fired her.

Jane and I looked at each other, both terribly confused. Angelique was quick to tell us that Jenny had been caught stealing from Betsy's room the night before. Betsy nodded right along, holding up the gold bracelet that had nearly been taken from her.

It is stunning. Truly. The golden band glistened in the light, the intricate design work as delicate as Betsy's wrist. Rubies and emeralds make it look like a Christmas decoration—one that costs more than Papa will earn in his entire life.

But I cannot begin to imagine why Jenny would want to take it. She would never be able to wear such a thing. It is so easy to recognize, especially on such a small island. And if she tried to sell it, she would have the same trouble.

Why on earth would Jenny try to take something so noticeable? If I were to steal something—not that I would ever ponder such an unlawful act—I would choose Angelique's string of pearls. So beautiful and as fresh as the oysters they came from. But they are common. Well, they are not common on a Georgia farm, but Mr. Dawkins gave Lucille a long string of them only a few nights ago. She tittered like they had come off of Mr. Ford's motorcar assembly line. They are stunning against the flawless skin at her neck.

None of this explains why Jenny is gone. Angelique said

Mr. Dawkins had to release her. There was no other way. He cannot have a thief in his employ, under his roof. I suppose she is right.

The whole situation bothered me so much that I snuck away from the rest of the party as they ventured out for another excursion. When Jane asked why I wasn't going to see the lighthouse, I begged another ache in my head. She wanted to know if it was from my accident. Of course not. But I was instantly reminded of George, and I wondered if I could find him somewhere beneath the shade of a tree. That would have been terribly inappropriate. Especially after my walk with Claude yesterday.

Instead I snuck up to the library to continue the novel I began last week. This is one by Jane Austen about a man and a woman who despise each other upon first meeting. I am thankful that Claude and I had quite a different introduction.

I fully enjoyed the book, but my mind kept wandering to Jenny. If she had indeed tried to steal the bracelet, had she also taken Jane's missing brooch? And what about the misplaced necklace? Where would she have hidden them in her little room?

SIX

"eet me in the maids' quarters."

Ben jumped as the hair on the back of his neck stood on end. The whisper in his ear traveled across his shoulders and down his arms, causing an uncontrollable shiver.

The voice was familiar, but the urgency was new since they'd searched the library three days before. There was no time to stop Millie as she brushed past him on her way into the parlor. She didn't even acknowledge him beyond that barely-there command, her gloved hand hooked into the elbow of a man in a black tux. She followed the man through the giant doorway and beneath the arch of carved wood showing ducks and dolphins and a turtle making its way down what was clearly a beach. Even after nearly ninety years, the animals were unmistakable.

Less clear was why she'd whispered so urgently in his ear. And the reason it still echoed inside him.

A herd of tourists thundered down the hallway, their stomps on the original wood floors dragging him from his wonderings. He looked up just in time to step out of the way of the guide, who strolled backward without a glance over her shoulder.

"Howard Dawkins loved to throw parties, but they weren't your typical evening soirees. He filled his home with guests all summer long, and his Chicago colleagues sometimes visited around the holidays to take advantage of the Georgia winters." The docent—he thought her name was Felicity, but he couldn't remember for sure—flicked her wrist in a wave toward the parlor behind her and offered each of the children a mischievous grin. "After dinner, Mr. Dawkins and his guests retired to the drawing room to play games and enjoy a drink. Let's see what they're doing this evening."

Like every one of the paid ticket holders, Ben leaned toward the entrance, Felicity's tone an undeniable invitation to peer into the past.

Taller than most, as he had been at nearly every stage of life, he had no problem looking over the heads of the group. They shuffled to the edge of the red carpet, breath held and eyes wide.

And that's when Millie made his heart stop.

Looking up from her hand of cards, her lashes long and black, she winked at her audience. "I suppose I'd better *let* him win tonight."

A burst of giggles followed, every eye in the group looking across the gaming table to the sleekly mustached man Millie had clung to on her way into the room. Everyone except Ben. He couldn't seem to look away from her cheeky smile and knowing eyes. Despite her scarlet evening gown and redder lipstick, this was the same Millie who had worn shorts to get coffee and nearly caused a scene in his class. This vision with a halo of golden curls pinned at the nape of her long, slender neck. They were one and the same, two parts of the whole.

Just like his mother, who had two sides.

His stomach took a leap, but Millie's laughter shook him free of his sudden plunge. So deep, so joyful. The sound trickled over him like the lightest summer rain, soothing and welcome. And the absolute opposite of Patty Thornton.

Millie wasn't like his mom. At least, he didn't want to believe she was.

But reasoning out the truth in his mind and knowing it in his heart when he looked at his partner were very different things. Millie played a role. And she'd been doing it since the night he met her. She put on a dress and performed her part for an audience. Then she changed into her cutoff jean shorts and played an entirely new part for him.

Patty had done the same. She'd doted on him, seeming the concerned parent. His lunches were packed for school every day. His clothes were clean and folded and on the foot of his bed every afternoon. His car had gas in it, and his wallet wasn't empty. From his perspective, she'd looked like the perfect mom. Most of the time.

The problem was the side he hadn't seen, the side that had been busy convincing near-retirees to let her invest their money. That was the side that had pocketed every dime. That was the side that had sat in a courtroom, so cold, so detached. That was the side that hadn't even apologized when the judge gave her the opportunity to do so.

That was the side she had hidden.

Or the side you refused to see.

He cringed at the memory. He'd been barely twenty at the time, but he'd been certain he knew his own mother. It had been just the two of them for so long that he'd convinced himself she was just what she appeared.

But he knew the truth. He'd been afraid to ask the hard questions, even the obvious ones.

Patty had never held down a job, so where did the money come from to pay the rent, keep the lights on, and buy him a car? He'd wanted to believe it could have come from his dad, but that lout hadn't even bothered with a wave as he walked out the door and never looked back.

His mom had straight-up swindled him right along with every one of her victims.

But Millie wasn't the same type of woman. Millie had been up-front from the beginning, hadn't she? She'd told him what she was looking for. He hadn't asked a lot of questions in that first conversation, and she'd told him just enough. There was a treasure, and at least some of it had belonged to Ruth. Millie was looking for what was rightfully hers. Right?

A tiny prick at the back of his skull jabbed him a few times.

Right?

Ugh.

The dull nudge turned into a sharp ache as most-likely-Felicity led her group away, leaving Ben and the thunder at his temples to focus on Millie, who had never once confirmed that Ruth held any claim on the treasure. Of course, she couldn't have confirmed his assumption because he'd never asked.

Brilliant.

Millie giggled at something her costar said, and she was back. No longer the sultry eyes and throaty laugh, she was the Millie he was coming to know, the Millie who read the last page of a book first. Who teased him for walking on carpet he'd never have considered treading on before. Who whispered to meet her in the maids' quarters.

But that was after his shift, which wasn't over yet, despite his wandering mind. Scrambling after the tour group, he gave her a little wave and caught the nod of her head just as he turned a red-carpeted corner.

"This isn't the maids' quarters."

"Of course it is." Millie fumbled for a folded sheet of paper that she'd procured at the front entrance, pulling it from the pocket of her shorts. "It says so right on the map." She pointed to the room on the second-floor blueprint.

Ben shrugged, a slow smile worming its way across his lips. A dimple appeared in each cheek, but she refused to let her scowl fade.

"Besides," she said, "you're the one who's late."

"I'm not late." He held up his hands, his smile growing more generous with each passing tick of the grandfather clock at the end of the hallway. It echoed in their pause. "I was right on time. *At the maids' quarters.*"

He leaned heavily on those words, and it made her stomach drop. "This *is* the maids' quarters, as previously established." She flapped her paper map again, but the impotent flop of her wrist did little to convince even her. Clearing her throat, she tried again. "See the beds and the dressers? And there's no running water."

Ben followed her command, ducking his head into the simple square of a room. Matching twin beds covered in unremarkable brown blankets abutted the far wall, and a simple wooden dresser along the adjacent wall clearly held two sets of toiletries.

He simply shook his head.

"But . . . the guide said so?" She hated the way she sounded so deflated, hated how he might be right. "How do you know? They always point this room out, and . . ." Again she flapped the map in his direction.

"And you believe everything they say on the tours?"

"No-o." She knew that some of the furniture passed off as antique was really a re-creation of pieces that had been destroyed during a fire in the fifties. She knew that the wallpaper in the dining room had been ripped and repatched with a mere fabrication. But those were important parts of the home's history. Surely they wouldn't have fabricated a maids' room.

"How do you know?" she asked again.

He shrugged, but his eyes never wavered from hers. "I just do."

"Have you been searching the house? Are you looking for the treasure yourself?" She clamped her mouth shut as his eyes grew to the size of the estate's gold-rimmed dinner plates, and he jerked back as if she'd smacked his shoulder. But when he opened his mouth, nothing came out.

"I'm sorry." Whispering through her fingers, she tried to find better words. But they weren't there. There was nothing to say after she'd accused him of double-crossing her—in so many words. She hadn't meant to. She hadn't even considered the possibility until that very moment. "I'm sorry. I don't think you're trying to . . ."

"Steal your treasure?" The words came out like they were being dragged over a gravel driveway.

She nodded. And then shook her head. "Are you?" This time it was her eyes that went wide, and she scrambled for an explanation. "I'm so sorry. I didn't realize I was . . ." Worried? Anxious? Uncertain of him?

Ben crossed his arms, his lean shoulders still broad enough to stretch the fabric of his knit T-shirt. Not that she'd noticed. But the heroine in the novel she was reading—Genevieve—had spent three pages thinking about her Sir Robert's shoulders.

Not that Ben was like the hero in her story. She didn't need a hero. She needed a fortune. She did not need broad shoulders and expressive blue eyes and a generous smile.

Nope. She didn't need or have time for any of that.

"Listen, I know we don't know each other very well. I totally get that. And you're trusting me with a lot."

That was it. He stopped right where he should have gone on. He offered no promise that she could trust him. He didn't assure her that he was a good guy or that he'd never take off with her money. He simply offered an unwavering gaze.

That was better than most promises. It was real.

When he did continue, he said only, "We both have something to bring to this partnership."

She didn't want to seem too eager, but her question came out before he even finished speaking. "Like what?"

"You have the journal and access to the only person who heard those stories firsthand."

She nodded slowly, and his arms relaxed to his sides before he went on. "I know the real history of this property and the location of the actual maids' rooms."

"Looks like I'm bringing more to this partnership than you are."

Lifting his eyebrows, he seemed to consider her argument for a long moment. Finally he said, "And I promised not to get you fired for sneaking around the estate at night."

Her giggle wouldn't be subdued even as she pressed the back of her hand to her mouth. "Fair enough. Partners?"

He looked down at her outstretched hand. "I thought we already were."

"Let's make it official. I'll trust you and you'll trust me. And neither of us will run off with the other's share."

A dark shadow slithered across his face. It was there and gone in an instant, but it left her cold, and she almost pulled her hand back. But he grabbed it before she could.

"Partners," he said.

"Partners who—"

He cut her off with a quick wave of his hand. "Sneak around the house and find the treasure."

Something deep in her stomach still rumbled with an uncertainty she couldn't name. He had said the right words, looked her directly in the eye. She could trust him. She had to, or she had to cut ties now. And that wasn't really an option. So she pushed down the uncertainty and moved forward.

"To the maids' room, then." Turning around, she began marching. He cleared his throat and she stopped midstep.

Peeking over her shoulder, she squinted in his direction. Ben said nothing. He just pointed over his shoulder with his thumb.

Spinning around again, she muttered under her breath, "Well, how was I supposed to know that?"

His grin set her insides to rolling as she tiptoed along. She couldn't afford to let an errant step on a squeaking floorboard announce their location to anyone in the area.

The thought made her slam on her brakes, and Ben ran smack into the middle of her back. They both wobbled for a precarious moment. Grasping her shoulders, he kept them standing by sheer force of will and firm footing.

"What is it?"

His breath at her ear sent shivers down her arms, and she couldn't help but wrap them around her middle. "We've been too cavalier, haven't we?"

"What do you mean? Do you think security is onto us?"

"They might be. Or Juliet." She lifted a shoulder, brushing against his arm. Which was warm and solid. That was just what the heroine in her book would think. And this was not like that. Not even a little bit. "We just haven't been very careful."

With a slow nod, he caught her hair against the whiskers on his cheek, tugging it gently. "Sure. But who do we have to hide from right now? The cameras are turned off after the last tour."

"Are you sure?"

"I did it myself tonight."

With a slow sigh, she let herself breathe again. She'd somehow forgotten to do just that for the last minute, and the air, warm and thick with humidity, was still somehow refreshing. "And the night guards?"

"Night guards?"

"You know, the ones who patrol the grounds at night?"

When he shook his head, she leaned away from him. Coolness washed down her back in his absence, and she subdued the shiver so eager to betray her. Glancing over her shoulder, she tried to read his face, but his smile was easy, indecipherable. "No night guards?"

"I think that you're giving far too much credit to the Chateau's security system, which generally consists of trying to keep riffraff off the lawns." He nodded toward the open window and the paved driveway beyond. "In its day, that gate was state-of-the-art. But that day was thirty years ago. Now . . . well, not so much."

She looked in the direction he'd indicated and could see only darkness.

"The historical preservation society doesn't have money to waste on overnight security—cameras or otherwise—when the estate is supposed to be closed. They figure once it's locked up for the night, it's safe."

"And let me guess, you're the locker-upper."

"You know that's right." He hooked his thumbs behind imaginary suspenders. "And here you thought I wouldn't come in handy."

"I never said . . ." Okay, she'd had her doubts, but that was neither here nor there.

They were alone inside the Chateau, alone on five acres of prime shoreline and surrounded by a ten-foot stone wall. She couldn't make out the stones or the gate she entered through in the barest hint of their neighbor's lights, which stretched through the Spanish moss hanging in the old sycamores. Draped in their finest, the trees masked the wall that surrounded the property from the shore to the entrance. Its imposing façade had been Howard Dawkins's idea—if the tour guides could be believed at least in that area.

Dawkins had been vigilant about protecting his guests and their privacy. And if he'd spent thousands of dollars—in the twenties, no less—to keep interlopers off his property, how much more vigilant was he about the ones he let in? Wouldn't he have interviewed Jenny the maid? There would have been letters of reference from her previous employers, right?

He wouldn't have been careless. He never would have hired Jenny if he didn't trust her. But he hadn't hesitated to fire her.

"We have to get to Jenny's room." She grabbed at his wrist and tugged.

He tripped on the sudden step but followed closely behind her. "Who's Jenny?"

"Ruth's maid. Well, not really Ruth's. She was a house-maid here, and she helped Ruth get dressed. She probably turned down their beds."

At a T in the hall, he pointed her to the left through an open archway that led to an exterior hall. She ran her fingers along the stucco wall, its open windows inviting in the night winds off the water. "She was sacked."

When they reached the top of a set of stone steps, Ben stopped. The humor in his features had disappeared, replaced by a mix of concern and curiosity. "For stealing?"

Millie paused too, able only to offer a slow nod. Then because it was clear he was waiting for even more clarifica-tion, she added, "From the guests."

"That's great."

Mouth dropping open, she paused, but he didn't expound on his thought. Stepping around her, he took the first three stairs in quick succession before turning around and offering his hand. There was no handrail inside the tightly spiraled stairwell, so she slipped her fingers into his grasp. And in-stantly regretted it.

It wasn't like that boy in junior high school who'd had sweaty palms. She'd pulled away from his damp grip im-mediately. And it wasn't like her high school boyfriend, who had used their linked hands to steer her wherever he pleased.

Ben's large fingers surrounded hers. Cool. Firm. Secure. Competent. He held on to her like he knew what he was doing. Like he was as concerned for her well-being as he was his own. Like the heroes in her books.

Nope. Not that again. You are not going down that path.

Her life wasn't a romance novel. But his touch did make her wonder what she'd been missing out on all these years, confining love between the covers of her favorite paperbacks.

She pulled her hand from his, and he looked back at her, a question flitting across his face. At least that's what she assumed. It was hard to tell for sure. The moon's light couldn't reach within the narrow confines of the stone walls, and a faint glow from the bottom kept him mostly in shadow.

Suddenly the silence felt heavier than the dark, and she stretched for anything to fill it. "I guess how great it is depends on who you are. Jenny probably didn't think it was very great."

He grunted something that sounded like agreement. "Did they search her room back then?"

"I'm not sure. Ruth didn't say anything about it, but I assume they would have checked. Wouldn't they?"

Pausing on the bottom step, he poked his head into the crossing hallway, looking each way. "Almost there," he said, leading her into what she'd assumed was a hallway. But the vast room was filled with an antique icebox, a cast-iron stove, and the largest island she'd ever seen. It was laid with wax fruits and faux meat that sat in a pool of moonlight shining through a row of windows to her left. To the right an open door showed a clear path to the butler's pantry. The opening was roped off with the telltale crimson velvet.

She stepped in that direction, but he tugged on her arm and ticked his head toward a barely-there panel hidden between the icebox and a sugar chest.

Millie tripped over her own feet and caught herself on the corner of the island. Her hand immediately burned, but not from the impact. Yanking it back, she clutched both hands to her chest, giving the exit a quick glance over her shoulder.

"There's a whole other hallway back here," Ben said.

"But . . . the house was built after the war. Didn't live-in help go out of style in the twenties?" She was blabbering, her thoughts suddenly jumbled and unclear, but a cleansing breath did absolutely nothing to help. Her skin tingled where she'd slapped the oak countertop.

She wanted to get to Jenny's old room. She wanted to know what was back there. The money, the jewelry, the evidence of who she really was. It could all be behind that thin door, painted green to blend into the surrounding wall.

Her heart gave a hard thump, then another, until she could feel it pounding at the base of her throat. "We aren't supposed to be here."

"What do you mean? This is where Jenny's room would have been."

Yes. She understood that. But there was something like a hook around her middle pulling her from the room. Something like fear that kept her from wanting to find what might actually be hidden nearby.

She wasn't doing this just for the sake of breaking the rules. There was more at stake than protecting the past, like freeing the truth. After all, the Bible said that if she found the truth it would set her free.

But what if she didn't like the truth she found?

"Are you all right?" He closed the distance between them, his grip on her elbow firm but understanding.

"I-I think so."

"Millie, what's your—" He let go of her and stabbed his fingers through his hair, his gaze trained on the floor.

His hesitation made her stomach do a couple flips, and she tried to step back from his warmth. The kitchen stayed relatively cool since the air-conditioning unit had been installed in the eighties, but within an arm's length of Ben, she suddenly wondered if she was suffering from the hot flashes that Grandma Joy complained about.

Letting out a slow breath angled toward her forehead, she tried to keep her face from turning red or her upper lip from breaking out in a stiff sweat.

He couldn't possibly know about Devereaux. He just couldn't. He hadn't read more than a handful of words in Ruth's diary, and Millie had been so careful. Of course, he knew that Devereaux had been a guest at the house that summer. They'd talked about that. But he didn't know about Ruth and the millionaire. He didn't know about walks along the beach or liberties taken beneath the afternoon sun or Ruth's dreams of being a radio actress. He knew nothing.

So why did she feel like she was about to be sick?

Would it be so bad if he knew?

Fair question. Just not one she knew the answer to. He might not care. Or he might insist she cough up half of whatever a Devereaux family connection might afford her. After all, she'd promised to share the treasure. Only she had no idea how much that might be. If it wasn't enough, she'd be right back where she started—without a fortune or a hope or any way of helping Grandma Joy.

She should tell him anyway.

"Ben . . . the thing is . . ."

When he finally looked up, his eyes were filled with determination. "Millie, what's your claim on this treasure?"

SEVEN

"Finders keepers?"

Ben let out a full-bellied laugh, bending at his waist and leaning a hand on his knee just to stay mostly upright. She put her hands on her hips and stuck out her bottom lip like she couldn't believe he was actually laughing at her.

He wasn't sure what he'd been anticipating, but "finders keepers" wasn't it, and the absurdity of it kept bubbling out of him on each guffaw.

"Hey now, mister." She straightened, and the look of disbelief turned into one of mock indignation. "There's no need to laugh. I mean, if someone just left it behind, we can keep it."

That was enough to swipe away all humor. It was too close to his mother's justification. *"If someone is stupid enough to give me their money, then I'll keep it."* And she'd done just that. She'd found more than a hundred marks willing to hand over their hard-earned savings. And while he only knew the names of the twenty-three on his list, the truth still applied. He wasn't going to begin stealing because it was a family trait. He wouldn't take money from the rightful owner of the Chateau's treasure. Whoever that might be.

"I'm not taking someone else's money."

Millie wiped the teasing look from her face. "What do you mean?"

"Just what I said. You said you'd share it with me, but who says it's yours to share?"

She looked at her empty hands as though expecting the journal to be there. "I mean, my great-grandmother knew about it. She had to tell my Grandma Joy. And she wrote about it."

"We think." He didn't know why he interrupted her. He didn't doubt that Ruth had been there and told Joy something that had sent her granddaughter on a chase. But if he and Millie never found a map, they'd never know for sure.

"She did." Millie looked on the verge of stomping her foot, her hand flapping behind her in the general direction of the icebox. "She wrote about the pieces of jewelry that were stolen."

"But none of them were hers, right?"

Her shoulders slumped like a deflated balloon. She took a deep breath, reinflating her stance. "Probably not." She paused for a moment, and then the truth just spilled out. "It was a feat for Georgia farmers to send their daughters to the city at all. There's no way Ruth's father could have bought her diamond bracelets or"—she twirled her finger at her throat as though looping it around the necklace she'd worn earlier—"pearls."

He scrubbed his hand down his face, something not far from disappointment swirling in his middle. "So what makes you so sure that what was taken belonged to her—belongs to you?"

Millie looked at the floor for far too long. "I'm not."

Her quiet honesty disarmed him, sending him stumbling back a few steps. He'd expected bravado and anger and insistence that she could do and take whatever she wanted. Instead, she looked up through lashes too long to be her own, her lips pulled tight and hands folded before her.

"It belongs to the owners of the estate at this point. At least that's the legal precedence here in Georgia. Dawkins's great-nephew still owns the property. He just contracted with the local historical preservation society to run it as a museum."

"You bothered to look that up, but you didn't bother to tell me as much?"

She nodded slowly, her face collapsing.

He couldn't hold back a scowl, hating the rising anger that churned in his stomach and took off along a fiery trail up his esophagus. "So you promised me half of something that isn't yours. That's very generous of you."

She blinked quickly, remaining otherwise still for a long second. But then she hurried forward two steps. "Yes, I was going to turn over what I found to the authorities so they could return it to the rightful owners. But what about a finder's fee? It's not unheard of for people to show their appreciation."

Good. They were on the same page at least. They weren't keeping someone else's money. But that didn't leave much. "What is it you think Dawkins's heirs are going to offer?"

"Maybe ten percent of whatever we find." The last word ended on an uptick, a question more than a statement. Uncertain. Hopeful. And probably utterly ridiculous.

He grunted and crossed his arms over his chest, the urge to

reassure her battling with the one to storm away. He wanted a treasure. Or half of one. It wouldn't come close to covering what he needed it to, but he'd pay off at least a few of those debts.

Half of a finder's fee wasn't what he'd signed up for.

"And how much do you think we'll find?"

She shrugged a shoulder, maybe a little too nonchalant about the whole situation. Sure, she'd had time to consider the rightful owners, and she'd known about this a lot longer than he had. But the difference between ten percent and a hundred barely seemed to register on her face.

"I don't have any idea. But I know it's worth something."

"Worth risking your job?"

He already knew the answer to that because she'd put her job on the line every day since he'd met her, and at least a few times before that.

Her chin tipped up as her eyes narrowed. "It's worth everything."

A shiver raced down his spine at the urgency in her voice, and the drop of her jaw revealed that she'd said more than she'd planned on. There was something more than money on the line for her. But he wasn't sure he wanted to be mixed up in it for a twenty-dollar payout.

You can't leave her on her own.

He wanted to punch whatever whispered that into his ear. But he couldn't argue the point. He'd promised to help her. Before he ever truly believed that there was even something to find, he'd promised.

"Aren't you at all curious about what's been hidden for so many years?" She closed one eye and raised the other eyebrow. "Imagine the history we could uncover. Imagine what it will tell us about the people who stayed here, the man who built it, the surrounding area."

That was clearly bait. The good kind too. But he hoped his glare told her he was onto her schemes.

Millie stepped closer before tipping her head toward the invisible hall behind her. "Have you been inside? Haven't you ever wondered what it looks like?"

He added a scowl to his glare, but her puppy-dog eyes never backed down. Innocent and compelling, she nudged him toward the nearly invisible door. "When you teach about the history of St. Simons Island, don't you wish you could see what the people back then saw? Don't you wish you could tell your students firsthand?"

He almost nodded, almost gave in. A flicker of a smile across her pert pink lips made him pause.

"When I teach about the history of the island, I spend about a minute on the Chateau." That was an understatement. He spent at least a couple sessions of his local history class talking about the Roaring Twenties. Men like Rockefeller, Ford, and Dawkins had made a name for themselves. Some of those men had reached the shores of St. Simons and changed it forever.

He'd give just about anything to see what the world had looked like through their eyes.

With that thought, he knew he was hooked. He was a bass and she a fisherman, and she had reeled him in with an expert hand. But he could put up one last fight.

"If you had a treasure at Christ Church of Frederica, we could talk."

She crossed her arms and turned her head in the direction of the small white church building. It wasn't visible from anywhere on the Chateau's first floor, but she looked like she could almost see its charcoal-gray pitched roof and jutting steeple beneath a shower of thick moss and surrounded by sentinels twice as tall.

Shaking her head, she took a step backward, then another. Skirting the corner of the kitchen island, she made steady progress across the room. "I can't help you there. But tonight I'm going into Jenny's room, and I'm going to dig until I find what I'm looking for."

Her determination made him grin, and he hurried in her direction. "What do you think you're going to find in there? Don't you think they searched it?"

He hadn't been trying to deflate her, but it sure looked like he had. Her shoulders slumped, and her face puckered with concern. "Of course. Yes." There was an unspoken "duh" in there somewhere, and she paused for a long second. "But maybe they missed something. If they had found the stolen jewelry—well, then there wouldn't be a lost treasure, right? Maybe there's a clue or something." She picked up speed as she crossed the room to the door, and he followed right behind her.

The flash of her teeth in the darkened room was nearly blinding, but he couldn't look away. The hidden door opened with a creak, letting loose an avalanche of dust, and Millie jumped back, straight into his arms.

He'd been aware of her before. Her hair smelled of citrus, and her laughter was contagious. He'd felt her presence somewhere deep inside him. Now he fully enjoyed it.

She was filled with life and verve that made his heart slam against his ribs. And she hadn't lied to him. She hadn't tried to convince him that the money belonged to her. She'd owned up to it. Even if something deep inside him whispered that she wasn't telling the whole truth. For now it would be enough.

Brushing his hands from her shoulders to her elbows, he leaned into her ear. "Okay?"

She wrinkled her nose. "I have to pay for my own dry cleaning if I make a mess of my costume." They both looked down at her black tank top and blue jean shorts. Then she shot him a guilty grin. "Force of habit, I guess."

As soon as the dust settled, she wiggled free, and he tried not to think about how empty his arms felt in that moment. There were more important things to consider. Like a hallway with four doors off of it. Millie shrugged and reached for the nearest brass knob. It turned and must have released faster than she'd expected as she sailed into the room.

Ben was right behind her, suddenly inside an empty space, the white paint on the four walls peeling in each corner and around the small window. The planks of the floor had obviously not been treated to the same restoration efforts as the rest of the house, and the room had never been anything more than what it was now. A strange juxtaposition to the rest of the house and its over-the-top grandeur.

Millie made a slow turn, her arms outstretched as though she'd like to see if she could reach from wall to wall. Almost.

"So if you lived in this room, where would you stash something?" She spun again, her gaze darting from corner to corner.

"Not just something—the most valuable things you'd ever seen."

She nodded, lips pursed and eyes narrowed.

"I guess I'd start with the last place anyone would look."

"Or the place they didn't know to."

Immediately they took off in different directions. He dropped to the floor, running his hands along the seams of the hardwood. Millie rushed toward an iron grate in the corner.

His fingers searched out any inconsistencies, any mismatched joints, for a hidden compartment beneath the floorboards. He rapped his middle knuckle against a soft spot, but the floor echoed like it should. It was solid and steady. He moved onto the next board, shuffling on his knees, but was quickly interrupted.

"Do you have a screwdriver?"

He shot her a lifted eyebrow and half frown. She was bent over the metal grate in the floor, her fingertips prying at the corner of it. "I must have forgotten it in my other tool belt."

She rolled her eyes and turned back to her pursuit. "There are a couple of screws on here, and if I could just. Get. Them. Out." She was nearly grunting by the end, her fingers twisting.

She was going to break a nail. Or worse.

Suddenly she sucked in a sharp breath and popped her finger into her mouth. But she didn't look over at him or wail her complaint. She simply went at the stubborn screw with her thumb instead.

Taking his turn with the eye roll, he dug into his pocket and pulled out the Swiss Army knife his mom's then-boyfriend had given him in the seventh grade. *"A man should always carry one of these. You never know when you're going to need a screwdriver or toothpick."* Tim had put it in his hand, patted his shoulder, and set the table for dinner.

Patty had packed up their car and moved them three states away the next week. Ben had never seen Tim again. But Tim's face was as clear as a picture in the deepest recesses of his mind. And he had been right. You never knew when you'd need a Swiss Army knife.

"Heads up." He waited for Millie to look at him before lobbing the knife in her direction.

She reached up with both hands and snagged it out of the air. "Thanks," she mumbled into her hands, then began pulling out and putting away the various tools until she found the blunt-tipped one that would work best.

He was so busy watching her work with hunched shoulders and purposeful movements that he almost forgot his own job. Even as he crawled along the floor, his hands running the length of the joints, his gaze kept wandering back to Millie, who had managed to get three screws out. But she was stuck on the last. She grunted once, pinched her eyes closed, and torqued it for all she was worth. The muscles in her arms shook, hands clasped together in front of her, and for a brief moment he worried about the safety of his knife.

"Let me." He was across the room before he even realized it.

"I've got it," she said between clenched teeth. "I'm almost—"

Suddenly her hand slipped, and she flew back on her rear end, slamming into the wall with a crash that almost brought the roof down.

"Ow." She moaned and rubbed the back of her head.

He squatted by her side, eye to eye. "You okay?"

She looked at him like she might enjoy seeing the roof come down on him. "Fine." But when she moved again, she cringed.

He reached for the back of her head, although he didn't

know precisely what he planned to do. He never got the chance to find out because she swung her arm up to stop him. "I'm fine. Really." The way she squeezed her eyes closed suggested that her head felt anything but.

Picking up the knife from where it had fallen, he took his turn at the remaining screw. Gritting his teeth, he gave it the full force of his strength. It wouldn't budge.

"Thought you could help, huh."

He glanced up just fast enough to catch her smirk before the knife twisted in his hand and the whole grate came free. "You were saying?"

She humphed and mumbled something under her breath about loosening it for him, but there was laughter in her voice, and he chuckled too.

"I'm sure you did."

But when they looked into the black hole of the vent, it didn't matter. Illuminated by the light on her phone, it wasn't any better.

The vent was clearly empty. No stash. No chest. No glittering diamonds.

The room was empty. So were the other three in the same hall. No secret holes or any evidence that there had ever been a treasure. No trace of even a secret hiding hole.

It was well after midnight by the time they slid the last grate back into place and examined the last section of flooring. Millie leaned a shoulder against the doorjamb, her head low and her other hand protecting the back of her head. "I was sure there would be something here."

Ben racked his brain for a piece of encouragement, but the only words that came to mind felt more like a slap than a boost. "Maybe there used to be."

Her long lashes blinked rapidly, but her gaze never strayed from the spot between her knockoff Converse sneakers. "You think someone beat us to it?"

He hadn't said that, but . . . "Could be. Maybe. I don't know."

"It would explain the missing second diary."

That felt like a punch to the gut. It was too true to ignore. "Ye-es . . ." He used every second of the dragged-out word to formulate his thoughts and then took an extra breath. "If someone else knew about the journal and took it, they might have already searched these rooms."

"But the dust and the cobwebs." She waved a hand toward the footprints they'd left behind.

"It could have been years—decades—ago."

Finally looking up at him, she gave him a pinched smile. "So we're looking for a treasure that was found years ago."

There was that jab to the gut again. Why? Because he wanted half of whatever that finder's fee might be. And because no matter how sarcastic she got, he hated to see her disappointed. At all.

Well, that was inconvenient.

"Did anyone else know about the diary? About the treasure?"

"I don't know. I don't think so."

"Your parents maybe?"

She whipped her head back and forth so fast that it jerked him to another realization. He didn't know a thing about her family situation. It was a blank beyond Ruth and Grandma Joy. And the fire in her eyes promised that pushing wasn't going to get her to give up any of that information. Not now and maybe not ever.

He knew a thing or two about that. He'd never told a soul about his mom.

"Then we better ask Grandma Joy."

She countered his argument in a voice suggesting she hoped he didn't notice that was exactly what she was doing. "There has to be a way to find out if a treasure was ever found at the Chateau."

"Of course there is." And he was such an idiot for not looking into it from the first.

"Whatcha lookin' at?"

Ben shrank away from the question and the man who asked it, shifting his shoulders in a vain attempt to cover the computer screen on the desk before him. "Nothing."

"Uh-huh." Carl Ingram crossed his arms over his chest and pursed his thin lips. If it was possible, his squinty eyes narrowed even more, trapping Ben into his small corner.

Ben could shrug the questioning gaze off, but he knew that was a bad idea for two reasons. One, Carl wasn't likely to let it go. He hadn't become the lead historical archivist at the Glynn County Library because he gave up on tracking down the details. Carl would pester him until he got to the truth. And two, Carl was his boss.

At least Carl was his boss at the library—his third job. Ben picked up a handful of hours every week helping Carl document and track the county's historical archives to bring in a few extra dollars—dollars that went out just as fast. And it was the kind of thing he enjoyed.

Leaning back in his chair and crossing his arms, Ben took a deep breath and revealed the screen he'd been hovering over for half an hour. The site specialized in detailing rumors and discoveries of treasure in the South, but at the moment, its flashing ads and blinking screen just made Carl recoil.

"How do you kids stare at that junk? It's enough to make a donkey run."

Ben chuckled. He wasn't familiar with the phrase, but that wasn't too surprising. Carl had a habit of making up words when he didn't know what to say.

"I was wondering about something. You ever hear about a lost treasure on St. Simons?"

Carl's bushy eyebrows did a little bop of surprise. "Sounds about the opposite of nothin'." His Southern drawl dragged the words out to twice their length.

Ben nodded. "Could be. But maybe not."

Carl peered at the screen before shaking his head and pulling his glasses out of the front pocket of his short-sleeve button-up, which was tucked into pants way too close to his armpits and much too far from the floor. Shoving the enormous frames farther up his face with one finger, he wrinkled his nose.

"Pirate treasure?" He waved at the webpage that still displayed the only St. Simons treasure Ben had been able to find.

"No."

Carl grunted and squinted again, this time directly at Ben. "What kind of treasure you looking for?"

Ben looked around Carl, giving the long room a careful survey. The far wall was lined with cabinets that housed many of Glynn County's and the island's historic documents, preserved and protected. A table in the center of the room held the project that Carl had been working on for two weeks, a series of letters donated to the county by one of St. Simons's wealthiest families.

Carl's desk in the opposite corner was pristine as always. Also per usual, he hadn't bothered to turn on his computer.

The room was empty, nothing out of place, so Ben took a deep breath. He wasn't quite sure why he had to steel himself for this conversation. Sure, he'd promised Millie that he wouldn't tell anyone else about Ruth's journal and the treasure. But picking the brain of the most knowledgeable historian in the area wasn't the same as announcing their search for treasure on the website he'd just been exploring.

"What about at the Chateau?"

Carl sniffed. "You mean other than the gold on the bottom of that ridiculous pool?"

With a low laugh Ben shook his head. "No. Not that gold. Something else. Something better, maybe."

Carl hitched up the leg of his polyester pants as he gazed toward the ceiling. When he looked back down, he seemed to be able to see through walls, his focus somewhere in the far distance. "You see something over there?"

Well, that wasn't an answer. And it certainly wasn't the response that he'd expected.

Maybe—*maybe*—Carl would have mentioned the rumors that sometimes surfaced around the great house. But Ben had really anticipated a flat-out denial.

He sat up straighter so he didn't have to tilt his head back quite so far to get a good view of Carl's expression. "No." The word came out about three times too long and couldn't even convince him.

"What'd you find?" Carl leaned forward, shoving his glasses up from the tip of his nose as he drew eye to eye with Ben.

"Nothing." Except Ruth's journal. And no one really knew what it held. Millie had been working her way through it, filling him in as she went, but she wasn't nearly finished yet. It was quite a bit longer than the thin tome had suggested, and the sometimes fading handwriting could take a while to decipher. She'd apologized for not reading faster, but he couldn't blame her. It wasn't easy juggling multiple jobs and needing to catch at least few hours of shut-eye at night.

The one thing they knew for sure was that there was a whole journal more to the story. But telling Carl about that meant breaking his promise to Millie, which he wasn't interested in doing.

A burst of fire shot up from his stomach, and he pressed a fist against his chest. Not that it was going to stop the heartburn. He had an antacid in his desk drawer, an arm's length away. But reaching for that would surely clue Carl in that he hadn't disclosed all he knew.

With a snort, Carl shook his head. "You know something, don't you? Might be better than the crumbs I've heard. Take your chalk, young man." He reached for another chair on wheels, rolling it over before falling into it. "Then we'll compare notes."

Apparently Carl could read his mind. Not helpful. Unless, of course, it meant Ben didn't have to say a word about Millie and Ruth and a treasure that had been lost for nearly a century.

He snatched the bottle from his drawer, popped three of the chalky disks into his mouth, and chewed them quickly. They tasted like fake oranges and regret. And they did absolutely nothing to stem the acid churning in his stomach.

"Tell me everything you've heard."

Ben rubbed his chest and swallowed thickly. "Why don't you start?"

"Because I fought in Korea, I raised four children, and I'm your boss."

He rolled his eyes but nodded. He wasn't sure why the first two mattered in this argument, but the third was enough. "I heard about . . ." He took another deep breath as he tried to sort his thoughts into something that would make sense. "I heard that someone was stealing from some of the guests that last summer before the crash."

Carl nodded appreciatively. "Jenny Russell. She was barely twenty when they ran her out of the house and off the island."

Jenny. The maid whose room showed exactly no evidence that she'd ever hidden anything there—or in any of the maids' rooms. "How do you know about that?"

"Oh, her firing made all the local papers. She was forced to move to Augusta just to find work, and her family was none too happy about it. That reputation followed her for the rest of her life."

Whether from the acid in his stomach or the certainty that Jenny hadn't committed the crimes she'd been accused of, his insides twisted. He didn't know who had stolen from the Chateau's guests, only that the wrong woman had been accused.

"'Course, none of those accusations amounted to a hill of beans," Carl said.

"You don't think she did it?"

"Oh, I doubt anyone—least of all Howard Dawkins—really thought she did it."

"Then why'd they . . . ?" Ben wasn't quite sure what he

was asking. Or maybe he already knew the answer and didn't want to confirm it.

Carl answered anyway. "People with power, my boy. People with power will do anything to protect that privilege."

"So what happened to the things that were stolen? Were they ever found?"

Leaning his forearms on his knees, Carl licked his lips, his gaze again focusing on something too distant to see or too long ago. "Far as I know, no one ever went looking for them."

"But how does an entire island just forget about something like that? Especially the ones who were stolen from."

"I'm not sure anyone knows just what was taken. There's no record of it."

Except Ruth's diary.

"There was a fire in the police records office around 1932. After that, no one cared enough to keep looking," Carl said. "Truth was, by that point, no one had cared for almost three years. Whatever was taken couldn't make up for all that was lost."

"You mean Dawkins?"

Carl tugged on his earlobe. "I suppose it's hard for a man to face something like that. To lose all of your money in an instant and to realize that everything you've worked for is suddenly worthless. The crash hit a lot of people hard."

"But the Vanderbilt and Rockefeller and Devereaux families all survived the Depression, wealth and name intact."

With a sigh and a sad shake of his head, Carl continued his train of thought as though Ben had never spoken. "Dawkins poured everything he had—and a whole lot of what he didn't—into building the Chateau. It was his masterpiece, his *Mona Lisa*. He never had the money of those other families, but he knew that the Chateau would give him the credibility to run in those crowds. And that's really all he ever wanted. So when the market crashed and his fancy furnishings were worth pennies on the dollar, he did what he thought was honorable."

Ben knew that part of the story and the rest. Dawkins, sure he would never recover his losses, had ended his own life. The house had been willed to his nephew instead of his wife, who probably didn't want a thing to do with it and the reminders of his life without her that it contained. But by the seventies it had fallen into disrepair, so Phillip Dawkins had partnered with the historical preservation society to return it to its old glory and turn it into a privately owned museum.

"Everybody gave up on it after Dawkins died. Funny how something so big can be so quickly forgotten."

Ben responded with a humorless laugh, more to fill the silence than because he felt like laughing. But there was something in Carl's pale gaze that didn't quite fit with the rest of their conversation. "You mean the Chateau?"

Carl patted his knee. "That too."

July 1, 1929

George invited me on a picnic today. I was supposed to go to the beach with Jane and Angelique, as Claude is still out of town on his secret mission, but George slipped me a note this morning as we left the house for a walk.

I should not have agreed. It is highly improper. But how could I not when he said he would like to take me to his favorite spot on St. Simons?

I told Jane I wanted to stay near the house. She was concerned about my health, but I assured her I only wanted to stay out of the sun.

God, forgive me these fibs. And my impropriety.

There is just something about George that makes me . . . well, I don't exactly know how to explain it. Sometimes when I catch a glimpse of him in the yard, my heart begins to beat faster, and my head spins. And I think it quite likely that I will swoon, even though I have never done such a thing in my life.

I snuck to the gardener's shed a little before noon, making sure that Jane and Angelique were long gone. Lucille and Mr. Dawkins were nowhere to be found, so I tiptoed down the long corridor and past his study. There was no sound coming from behind the closed door, so I hurried along, remaining as silent as I could.

George was right where he said he would be, a wicker basket in his hand and a shy smile on his face. And my heart responded immediately.

He called me Miss Holiday again, despite my insistence that he call me Ruth. He dipped his chin and probably missed the way I rolled my eyes at his insistence on propriety.

Maddening man. But I could not stay angry as he held out his hand. I stared at it for a very long second—all long, lean fingers and calluses across his palm—and I wanted to reach out and grab it and let it swallow mine. But when I glanced up for a moment, I saw a look of horror in his eyes. It was there only for a flash, as though perhaps he could not believe he had just made such a gesture. Before I could grab him and tell him how I was the opposite of repulsed, he shifted his arm, poking his elbow in my direction as he turned.

I blinked and tried not to let my disappointment show. When I tucked my fingers into the crook of his arm, he set off in the opposite direction of the beach.

I asked him where we were going, and he chuckled. (He has such a nice laugh.) But he said only to his favorite spot on all of St. Simons Island. I nodded like I knew where that was or even generally what direction we were headed. I had not an inkling.

We walked for approximately twenty minutes, all beneath the shade of the moss-covered oak trees. They hung over a path, the grass worn thin from frequent trips. Had George made all of those? There was no time to ask, for just as soon as I opened my mouth, we came upon a clearing. Truly, it was much larger than a clearing. But the break in the hanging branches left room for the sun to shine directly on a small white cross atop a steeple adorning a dark gray roof.

Oh my. It took my breath away.

It was a simple church, having the standard four walls and a wooden door. It sat on a patch of lawn nearly as green as George's eyes. But the spot of sun illuminating it all made it look nearly angelic. Somehow holy.

I could only put my hand to my throat, but George seemed to understand. I tried to find the words to describe just how beautiful it was, but I lost them all as he led me into the open, into the warmth of the sunshine and the coolness of the breeze. It tugged at my hair, and before I could push it into place, George reached for it, tucking it behind my ear.

I must have frozen. He certainly did. Only his eyes changed, growing larger and filling with shock. Twice in the span of half an hour I had caused him to do something he found to be dreadfully scandalous. I barely know this man. What was I doing alone with him, letting him touch my hair and my ear and my cheek?

But if I had not agreed to this walk, I would have missed this church. I'd have missed this moment. I'd have missed him.

A bird sang loud and long, and it must have pulled him from his reverie. George jumped into action, telling me all about Christ Church of Frederica. Nearly 200 years old, it was started by the renowned preacher John Wesley and his brother Charles.

There is so much history in this little slice of heaven, and I wanted to focus on what George said. I really did. But I got lost just past the history of the building in the tenor of his voice, the way it rose and fell with excitement and joy. I think he went on to talk about the graveyard and the grounds. I heard none of it.

By the time he had laid a blanket down to cover the grass and pulled paper-wrapped sandwiches from his basket, I realized my eyes were closed and my face turned up to capture all of the sunny warmth as he told his tale. When he asked if I was well, I jumped, startling us both. I reassured him that I was only enjoying the scenery. I could not very well admit to having been enjoying the sound of his voice. He deserves to be on the radio if anyone does.

One of his eyebrows arched, but he did not point out that I had been looking at exactly nothing. So I attempted to change the subject as quickly as I could, and asked him why this was his favorite place. He looked surprised for a moment but then said the church lawn has everything he needs for peace. Sunshine, roses, and the gospel.

He made it all sound so personal. I had never heard anyone but a preacher talk about the gospel like that, but I could not bring myself to ask another intrusive question, so I took the sandwich he offered and nibbled at the corner.

We barely spoke after that, reclining lazily in the sun until it was time to go back. All I could think about was how glad I was that I had not gone to the beach.

I love the gazebo with all my heart. It is so quiet and calm in the early mornings and still my favorite spot at the Chateau. But George's favorite spot on St. Simons might become mine as well.

July 17, 1929

Claude pulled me into an alcove and kissed me today just as I left my room. I do not know how else to describe it. There were no romantic words or gentle kisses to my wrist beforehand. One moment I was hurrying to meet Jane and Betsy for a swim, and then something grabbed my arm and pulled me right off my feet.

Of course it was Claude. But before I could even realize

that, his hands were on my face and he was kissing me. Thoroughly.

This was nothing like the sweet, chaste kiss of the beach. It was not like the playful kisses that Mama and Papa share when they think no one is looking.

Just when I thought I would never have the opportunity to breathe again, he stopped abruptly to tell me that he had missed me. He nearly growled those words. I didn't even know a man could make that sound.

I hoped that his surprise kiss would make my insides take flight yet again, but instead I wanted to flee. I only wanted to find Jane and sit near her or have her put her arm around me.

No, that was not entirely true. I most wanted to be in that patch of sunshine on the lawn of the church. With George.

There was barely space in that tiny little room off the upper hallway for the two of us to stand. There certainly was not room for me to think about George too. Claude tilted my head up, and I tried to smile. All I could focus on was the strange little curve of his mustache. It sent shivers down my spine, but not the kind I so wanted.

When I finally registered his initial greeting and responded that he had just seen me at breakfast, he assured me that two hours was far too long. And then he called me "my dear."

He was so suave, so debonair. The type of man I have always dreamed of. And the man who could make my dreams come true.

I fled anyway. I am sure I must have given him some sort of excuse or apology, but I can only recall running.

The sunlight through the windows was warm, and my skin felt flushed. By the time I burst through a door on the first floor, I had lost track of where I was. I only truly recognized that I had exited the house because the steady slap of my feet against the hard floors disappeared when I reached the grass.

Free of the house and with no further sign of Claude, I tried to orient myself. Useless.

And that is when I heard a familiar chuckle from behind me. I turned to find George leaning on his rake and grinning like he had won a prize. He presumed I had lost my way and insisted on calling me Miss Holiday.

I insisted on Ruth.

He nodded and promptly called me Miss Holiday.

This again. I was already disoriented, uncertain, and . . . frightened? I was not scared of Claude. He would never hurt me. But I was in turmoil. My insides were scrambled like a batch of eggs. And before I could help it, I burst into tears. I put my head into my hands and tried to muffle the sobs, but I am afraid there was no helping them.

Suddenly something clattered to the ground—it must have been the rake—and two strong arms wrapped around me. They were gentle and warm, and I leaned into them, resting my forehead against George's chest. He rubbed a small circle on my back and offered to help me find my way back.

I wanted to scream. I was not lost, and I assured him so.

His hand stopped moving, and his entire body grew stiff. He said, "Are you injured? Has someone hurt you?"

I believe I will remember those words for the rest of my life. They were so simple but seemed to mask a fierceness, a promise of protection. I pulled back but immediately felt the loss of his arms, so I took a tiny step back into his embrace. I told him I had not been injured. Not really. I am not sure why I added that caveat—I just had to. Truly I had not been harmed, simply shaken up. Surprised. Terribly upset by my response to the man I care for.

And I do care for him—Claude, that is. However, I did not mention such a thing to George. He simply looked at me intently, as though he could see right into my heart. It is not the first time he has done that. But I had to look away.

He kept asking if I was certain I was unharmed. Although I spoke my assurances to him, tears still slipped down my cheeks. I tried to wipe them away, but he beat me to it. His thumbs were large and coarse and as gentle as they had been that day he rescued me from the pool.

He did not quite meet my eyes when next he spoke. But again his words were filled with such depth. "I can take you away from here."

I smiled at that. What a sweet gesture.

As I pulled back all the way, I sniffed but kept my eyes lowered. I looked a mess, surely, and probably a fool too. Mama always says that the tip of my nose turns red when I have been crying. But somehow the weight of George's gaze on me made me feel beautiful, cherished.

I could not help but compare the way he held me with the way Claude had only a few moments before. There was no comparison. And I hate myself for feeling those things with George. It is not right. I have kissed Claude. I am certain that he cares for me, and I for him.

So why did I run into George's arms like a ninny?

I ran away from George just as fast. I am sure I gave some sort of excuse to him as well, but honestly my throat closed right up, and I could barely breathe as I raced for the outdoor pool.

I was so distracted that I nearly missed the breeze off the ocean and the way the palm trees dipped under the weight of the wind. The air felt thick, wetter than usual, and I looked up into the sky. The clouds unfurled, dark and foreboding. As I reached Jane on the pool deck, they opened up and poured out everything they had inside.

We spent the rest of the day in the parlor playing card games. I lost them all. Every time someone passed the door, I jumped, afraid that I would be forced to face Claude. I was not ready to see him again. At least not yet.

I was much calmer by the time dinner came around. "Much" may be too great of a word. But I was at least able to greet Claude with a quiet smile. He took my hand and kissed it as he helped me into my seat. Betsy and Willa scowled at me, but Lucille tittered to Angelique.

Later, after dinner, Jane said that Claude could not take his eyes off me all through the meal. He even missed a bite of his food for staring too intently. I did not dare let my focus waver, even when the conversation turned to more missing pieces of jewelry. I caught a peek of Mr. Dawkins looking rather troubled, and I cannot blame him. He sent Jenny away, almost certainly without a reference, and items are still disappearing. He said even some valuable papers, something to do with the stock market, have disappeared from his study.

If it was Jenny, she had an accomplice. Someone is still at the Chateau.

And yet I am sitting at my vanity scribbling in this journal while Jane sleeps, and thinking only of George.

I cannot help but think he was offering me more than a drive down the lane or a diverting trip to Christ Church of Frederica again. There was something in his eyes. They are so terribly green and expressive, and I almost thought that he might . . . well, it is too embarrassing to even write down. But could he have meant more? Could he have been offering to take me away? Far away? For good?

But how? How could he ever manage that on a grounds-keeper's salary? And he would have no salary at all if he left the Chateau. It makes no sense.

Yet I am rather sad that the prospect is mere fancy. I am a silly girl.

I would never go with him even if he had the means, which he never could. Unless . . .

Oh my. I have the most painful knot in my stomach.

Is it possible? Could George be Jenny's accomplice? Or could he be working on his own to steal from the guests?

What a ridiculous idea.

I'll never sleep now.

EIGHT

Millie slammed the journal closed and glared at the giant red numbers of her alarm clock. Stupid alarm clock. Stupid job. Stupid story. Stupid Great-Grandma Ruth. She was a ninny. Through and through. She'd had one of the wealthiest men in America at her beck and call, and she'd been playing around with the gardener.

Who was rather dashing.

He was not. He was a landscaper with absolutely nothing to offer Ruth. And he could be the thief. Even Ruth had suggested it. Yet she seemed to have some sort of *feelings* for him.

You would have too.

She set the journal—much gentler with it than she'd been before—on the folding tray that served as her nightstand before flopping to her side and smashing a pillow over her ear. Punching it into place, she tried to ignore the little voice still whispering to her.

Admit it. He was a good man. He understood Ruth in a way that Claude never could.

She would admit no such thing. Okay, maybe he was a good man—not the dashing heroes on the covers of the other books by her bed, but still kind. He'd rescued Ruth from the pool, after all. He'd taken her to the church and spoken of the gospel. But that didn't mean Claude didn't care for Ruth in the same way. It wasn't that Claude didn't understand her. It was that Ruth didn't understand her own emotions.

That had to be it.

Yes, she could rest in that knowledge. And she needed to rest.

She flopped to her back, arms and legs splayed, and stared at the ceiling, muttering under her breath at the tick-tick-tick of the fan. It just kept going, ticking along at its uneven pace. Ugh.

Rolling over to her stomach, she burrowed her head beneath her pillow, but her sleeping shorts had twisted around her legs. She kicked to straighten them out. No luck. Another try. Same result.

Flopping to her back, she caught a glimpse of the alarm clock yet again. That was ten minutes of sleep she wasn't going to get.

He's not a thief and you know it.

She didn't care. She really didn't. He could have stolen the London Bridge for all it would matter to her. Just as long as George wasn't her great-grandfather.

He couldn't be. He wouldn't be. Ruth had bigger plans than a laborer. She'd wanted to be a voice actress in the radio dramas of the day. She'd dreamed of the big city far from the Georgia farm where she'd grown up. She wouldn't have gotten in trouble with George.

Millie nodded her head firmly.

With that settled, she could go to sleep. Because she had to be up in . . . She flicked off the hours on her fingers. Six hours. Well, five hours and forty-eight minutes.

"Go to sleep, Millie."

Closing her eyes, she held herself as motionless as possible. But her shorts were still twisted, and the fan still clicked along its merry way.

Stupid fan.

Sweat trickled down her back and across her upper lip. There was no way she could turn it off. Not when the window AC unit had been struggling to keep up with the humidity. Especially when the apartment below her was the center of the sun.

Rolling onto a cool spot of the sheet, she kicked at the covers until they tumbled off the end of the bed.

There. Now she could sleep.

Maybe not. Another fifteen minutes of the ticking fan and coughing AC, and she was no closer to falling asleep. She was only closer to throwing the nearest book across the room. But it was a loaner from the library, and she had no idea where she'd come up with the money to replace a hardcover with a broken spine.

Not an option. She just had to go to sleep.

If she fell asleep right that minute, she'd still have five hours and twenty-nine minutes before her alarm went off. Six hours and twenty-nine minutes before she had to serve coffee to a roomful of grumpy diners in desperate need of the sweet elixir. They were all irritated before their first cup. But she couldn't be grumpy back.

Fall asleep. Fall asleep. Fall—

You know he was good to her.

So what if he was? It didn't matter.

You know he didn't steal anything.

Again, it didn't matter.

Maybe it does.

It did not. It only mattered that she was functional enough to work in the morning. If she wasn't, she'd have to move into her car, and then what would become of Grandma Joy? As it was, Millie only had fifty-three days to find a miracle source of income and a new home for Grandma Joy. Right now it only mattered that she was functional enough to find Ruth's other journal. It only mattered that there was a map in it.

That's what mattered.

No, it's not. And you know it.

She flopped over again, pressing her mouth into her pillow and screaming for all she was worth. She could still hear the clicking of the fan.

When her breath ended and her head thumped in time with the rotating blades, she rolled onto her back and sighed. The moon's light filled the gaps in the blinds, covering her room with shadows as clouds rolled across the sky.

It had rained when Ruth was on St. Simons too.

But that and a bit of DNA were all they shared. Ruth had had two loving parents, a chance for success, and the eye of the richest man in Georgia at the time. Millie had two exhausting jobs, a chance that her electricity would be turned off, and a partner she'd never expected.

Ben's face flashed through her mind, and she tried to forget the way he'd looked the last time she'd seen him, when they searched the maids' rooms. He'd swiped his dirt-covered hands across his face at some point, and there was a swath of black from his forehead around his eye to his chin. It hadn't dampened his grin at all or the twinkle in his eyes. Or maybe that had been her imagination. It had been relatively dark, after all. And she hadn't been staring all that hard.

Liar.

Sticking her tongue out, she blew a raspberry. That's what she thought of that voice in her head. It insisted on keeping her up and calling her names.

She did not need that kind of negativity in her life. Not now. Not when she had a mission to complete. Not when Ben seemed intent on distracting her at every curve.

He wasn't. At least not on purpose.

It wasn't his fault that she still felt his firm grip on her hand as he led her down the stairs. It wasn't his fault that his hair fell across his forehead and he just *had* to brush it out of the way. And that made her insides wiggle like unset Jell-O.

She didn't have time to think about him—or any man, for that matter. She never had. Not since Grandma Joy had needed her help and her care, anyway.

That didn't stop his too-blue eyes from flashing before her. Or that little voice in her head from wondering what it might be like to be the heroine of one of the novels stacked on her floor. Somehow those women found a way to make it work. All of them. They found a way to balance the responsibilities they carried with the men they fell in love with.

But that was fiction. This was real life.

Of course nothing could keep the girl from falling in love with the guy. She didn't have *actual* bills to pay. She didn't have an actual grandma who needed to be cared for. She didn't have to actually find a safe place where her grandma could be cared for.

Of course it was all going to work out in the books. At

least the ones that she chose to read. She made sure of it. A quick peek at the last page was all she needed in order to know if the story would have a happy ending.

Real life didn't come with the same guarantees. And neither did Ruth's story.

Millie flopped over one more time, hunting for a cooler spot free of the stickiness that caked her limbs. There wasn't one. Her bed had turned into a radiator.

Finally she dripped out of bed, crawling across the floor of the semi-enclosed bedroom toward the bathroom. Turning on the cold water, she splashed some on her face. Then a little more. Then she held a washcloth below the cool water—*cold* was far too generous a description. It felt good pressed against the back of her neck. And down her arms, right where Ben had touched her.

Flinging herself back into bed, she tried to wipe that memory away. But it would take a full scrubbing, maybe more.

Maybe Ruth had felt the same. About George, that is.

Maybe she wouldn't think about this right now.

Sure. That was a logical plan. But logical and actionable were very different things. Despite the alarm clock reminding her that she had to be awake in a little more than four hours, she couldn't stop thinking about it all. About Ruth and George. And Ruth and Claude. About why she herself had hesitated to enter the maids' quarters a few nights ago. About whatever Ruth's second journal would reveal.

Millie knew what was keeping her awake. She just didn't want to put it into words. It was easy to look for a treasure. It was so much harder to look for family.

Whether George was a thief wasn't the question. If he was, her great-grandfather was.

And she desperately needed it to be the other man in Ruth's life.

"Are you all right?"

Millie nearly jumped out of her skin at the breath in her ear, and her hands flew to her throat as she stumbled backward. Right into the arms that seemed to be ever-present lately.

"Whoa there." His voice sounded like it had been raked over gravel. "It's just me."

No *just* about it.

"Yes. I'm fine." Her words were barely more than a breath, and she had no doubt that gravel could take her down in a heartbeat. Especially after the night before.

Isabelle Calhoun, the aptly named actress who played the Southern belle of the house party, glanced their way. She seemed quick to dismiss the way Ben held Millie upright and how close his lips were to her ear. Until she zeroed in on Ben.

Who wouldn't? Millie hadn't at first, true, even when Ben's student had pointed it out. But after a sleepless night that involved way too much thinking about Ben on the cover of one of her library books, she understood why women might take another look.

Millie immediately recognized his absence as he stepped away. Probably because he'd noticed that they'd been spotted. Thus far they'd managed to keep from arousing Juliet's suspicions of an inappropriate relationship any more than they had on that first night.

Isabelle, however, wasn't known for her discretion. And if she thought she'd spotted something between tours, it wouldn't take long for the entire cast—and management—to hear about it.

Millie did a quick sidestep, tugging on her gloves and straightening her necklace. Forcing her face into a mild look of surprise, she took a quick breath before diving in. "Ben. How are you? It's been ages."

Oh dear. She sounded like an idiot. Probably because she was one.

The angle of Ben's lips seemed to ask what game she was playing. She didn't know what it was called. She just needed him to play along.

Please. *Please.*

She tried to convey everything flying through her mind in a single glance.

"Hi?" His response was definitely a question rather than a statement. He might not have gotten everything she was trying to send him. So she tried again with a harder look filled with all the things at stake.

"You look great. How is everything?"

Isabelle was still staring at them, leaning toward them, ignoring her partner for the night, Duncan. He was probably rambling on about his new car. It was always about his car or his clothes or some exorbitantly priced steak he'd eaten. Sort of the opposite of Ben, who seemed to always be working and never spending his money.

"Good?" The tilt of Ben's head and furrowed eyebrows said he still wasn't sure what she was up to.

"Great." Now what? She searched for anything that would sound normal. Natural. But she'd forgotten how to have a conversation. "Um . . . You seem . . . How's work?"

Ben's voice dropped a full octave and more than a few decibels. "Did you hit your head?"

Spinning so her back was fully to Isabelle and—she hoped—blocking their conversation, she whispered, "We have to be careful. She's watching us." She hoped her nod toward the redhead across the room was imperceptible from the back. And that Ben would understand.

"You don't look very well."

Wrinkling up her face as much as she could, she scowled at him. "Well, you're too tall."

He laughed right into her face, and for a minute she forgot that she was supposed to be playing this cool and giggled back at him.

"Your gloves keep falling down."

"I know." She jerked them back up again and let her gaze sweep over him, hunting for anything to criticize. It wasn't easy. He *was* tall. Probably three inches over six feet. And a little on the lanky side. But there was nothing wrong with his dark hair, pale eyes, regal nose, and steeply angled jaw. Or the five o'clock shadow growing on it.

"Well . . . well . . ." Argh. Why couldn't she be quicker on her feet? Maybe if she'd gotten more than three hours of sleep the night before, she could be. "Your . . . your . . . eyes . . ."

Their gazes locked, and the bottom dropped out of her stomach.

Those eyes. Looked. Right. Through. Her. And the teasing light that had filled them just a moment before disappeared.

"Seriously, are you all right?" He waved toward her face, and she leaned away on reflex. "You're looking a little tired."

"Is that a subtle way of saying that I have dark circles under my eyes?"

He didn't really have to point it out. She already knew they were there. They had been since she'd dragged herself out of bed, brushed her teeth, looked in the mirror, and groaned.

Ben shrugged.

"I didn't get much sleep last night." She glanced over her shoulder at Isabelle, who had turned her attention back to Duncan and followed him across the room. At least for the moment they had a bit of privacy, and she could be honest. "I was thinking about Ruth."

He squinted. "Something new?"

"The thefts didn't stop after the maid was fired."

He scratched at his chin, his whiskers rustling beneath his fingernails. "It wasn't her." There was a certainty in his voice that made her lean in closer.

"You seem pretty sure for someone who hasn't even read the diary."

"I have my sources."

"You do?" Her voice rose in volume and pitch, and she quickly pinched her lips together.

"Don't look so surprised." A smug smile crossed his lips as the antique clock on the mantel rang the half hour. They both looked toward it and recognized it as their warning bell. Five minutes until the next tour arrived at the parlor.

He turned to find his spot in the hallway, but she grabbed his arm. "Ruth said her room was near a small alcove on the second floor."

His gaze turned distant, like he could see the blueprints rolled out before him. "She said the second floor? There isn't an alcove on the second floor."

Millie mentally ran back through the words she'd read. "Upper hallway maybe? Could there be something on the upper hallway?"

A slow smile made its way across his face until the corners of his eyes crinkled. "I'll meet you outside the women's locker room after your shift." With that, he disappeared between two ficus trees, removing his modern self from the old-time elegance of the parlor. She glanced down at her dress—silk and satin except for the beaded chain at the low waistline—and then at the knit cotton covering Ben's retreating form. He certainly didn't fit into the world created for the guests.

But he was beginning to fit into her life.

He also knew more about this old house than anyone she'd ever met. He could be the difference between finding the truth about her past or losing her future entirely.

NINE

Ben stayed in the shadow of a large sycamore tree for several long seconds after Millie made her exit from the locker room. She looked around quickly, then down at the phone in her hand. He almost texted her his location, but he waited another second.

Right on time, Felicity, the tour guide, walked out behind Millie. She said something that sounded like "good night" and then stalked toward the employee parking lot.

Then the redhead who had stared at them earlier that night joined Millie, her costume traded for jeans and a tank top. Spinning her keys around her finger, she stopped to say something.

He couldn't hear the words, but he could see Millie's profile. First she plastered a fake smile on her face. Then it dipped. She fought to get it back into place, but it was a losing battle. Millie looked like she couldn't be any more uncomfortable if she'd come face-to-face with a rattlesnake.

Maybe she had. And from the flip of the redhead's hand through her hair, she knew what she was doing.

Before he even knew his plan, he stepped forward. The Chateau's lights had been turned low and clouds covered the moon, so he had about a second and a half before he was visible.

Millie's voice rang out clear. "I don't know what you think you saw, Isabelle."

The redhead only leaned in closer, but if she spoke, Millie cut her off. Ben shuffled back into the safety of the shadows.

"Ben and I are acquaintances. That's all. And he noticed that I wasn't looking my best tonight and wanted to make sure I wasn't sick. End of story."

"Hmm." Isabelle seemed to take her time digesting the information. "Then, you know him?"

"I guess." Millie's eyes darted in his direction, but he was still hidden. He hoped.

"Because I've seen him around. Some of the other girls were asking about him, you know. Is he single?"

He crossed his arms and flexed his muscles. Because what else could a guy do when he knew women were talking about him?

Not that he was interested. He certainly didn't have time for anything like that—love and marriage and the whole thing. He'd thought about it, sure. But always down the road.

Still, it was a boon to hear that someone found him attractive. Too bad it wasn't Millie.

He gasped at the thought, hunting for its root and determined to rip it free. He had no business thinking things like that, given their current arrangement. He did not need her to think he was handsome. Even if he thought she was just as stunning in cutoff jean shorts as she was in her costumes.

Millie looked like she'd swallowed her tongue for a split second before answering Isabelle's question. "I have no idea."

He couldn't tell if Millie was still performing or if she really had no idea about his relationship status.

Isabelle shrugged. "Either way." There was a looseness in her words—so cavalier—that made his stomach churn. She either had no respect for him or had no respect for herself. In any case, he wasn't interested in that.

"He doesn't date co-workers," Millie said through clenched teeth.

Had he said that to Juliet? Or was Millie taking license with their friendship? Or did she already know that about him with certainty?

With a "we'll see," Isabelle spun and sashayed across the paving stones, leaving a scowling Millie to stare after her.

When she was gone and the echo of her footsteps had long since vanished, Ben whistled low. Immediately Millie's head snapped in his direction. He could tell the exact moment she saw him. Her eyes went wide, then narrowed, and she marched toward him like a soldier on a warpath.

"How long have you been there?"

Stuffing his hands into the pockets of his navy pants, he shrugged. "Long enough."

Despite the shadows hanging low over them, the pink on her cheeks was undeniable, and she dipped her chin quickly. "You were right."

Closing one eye and glaring at him through the other, she said, "You're not all that handsome?"

He shook his head. "I don't date co-workers."

With a playful slug to his arm, she walked toward the Chateau's main entrance. "So where are we going?"

He led the way to the front stairwell, opposite the one they'd taken to the kitchen a few nights before. She stayed close, but he could tell when she paused to look behind them. "Don't worry, I shut off the cameras."

She didn't budge for a long second, so he reached for her hand, only to find hers halfway there. "Come on." Pulling her up the stairs, he rushed for the alcove she'd mentioned, the only one on the upper hallway. It was a few dozen winding yards from the master suite, Dawkins's private rooms.

"How'd you remember this was here?" She spun around in the little offshoot just large enough for two people to stand in.

Tapping a finger to his temple, he smirked. "Same way I knew where the real maids' quarters are."

"You're a big geek and spend all your time studying ancient blueprints."

Shrugging, he nodded. "Basically."

She smiled at that, flashing her white teeth and crinkling her nose. "Ruth said in her journal that she was leaving her room, heading for the swimming pool—the outdoor one— when she got pulled into the alcove."

Ben turned and played out Ruth's movements in his mind, then stopped short. "Got pulled in?"

"Oh, um . . ." The moonlight through the windows made the flames of her cheeks gentler, but there was no mistaking that she'd revealed something she hadn't wanted him to know. "She was kind of seeing one of the other guests. He pulled her in for a . . . private moment."

"To kiss her."

She nodded.

"Was their relationship a secret?"

She stared at the ornate brass designs on the ceiling for a moment before shaking her head. "No. I think it was common knowledge among all the guests."

That wasn't the full truth—he'd bet every penny his mother had stolen on it. And if she was telling him partial truths about this, what else in that book wasn't she telling him?

He wanted to push, but this wasn't the time or the place. They were already pushing their chances that they'd be caught. A burst of acid reflux reminded him how much he wished he could change the circumstances. Two wrongs did not make a right. But he prayed that what they found might begin to make right some of his mother's many, many wrongs.

Dawdling because he had questions wouldn't help. Later he'd push Millie to explain what she was hiding. Right now he'd find Ruth's old room and pray that she'd hidden her second journal there.

"Well, if she was going to the pool and had to pass in front of this alcove . . ." He pointed to the right, to the only door there.

"Makes sense, I guess." Millie strode in that direction. "After her accident, Ruth said that Lucille had moved her and Jane from one of the bungalows to be closer to her and Dawkins."

Close was a relative word, but in this case, they couldn't get much closer to the banker and his particular friend.

As they stepped into the room, he tried to see it through Millie's eyes. The furniture most likely wasn't original to the room, which sported two twin beds, each with four posters and a blue bedspread. Still, her great-grandmother had fallen asleep in this room to the rhythmic crashing on the beach below. She had stood at that window, overlooking the sand and water, and watched the people strolling along the shore.

Even he—no relation whatsoever to Ruth—felt the physical weight of stepping back in time. It was hard to breathe and hard to think about anything but what Ruth might have felt in this room.

Millie immediately went to the window and rested her hand on the white sill. The glass was foggy, but she stared through the panels like she could see forever.

"She loved being here."

"What's not to love?"

Looking up and focusing her eyes on the present, she smiled. The makeup she'd worn earlier that night was gone, and in its place was the natural glow of her cheeks. "Good point."

Maybe it was the smooth line of her cheek or the way she wrinkled her nose or the way she was lost in the past, but he took a step forward. Then another. Until the space between them vanished.

Something had knotted in his chest, and it refused to let go. Especially when she tilted her head and stared back at him with narrowed eyes. Could she see right through him?

He didn't have even a second to answer that question before she slid around him, strolling across the room. "Let's find out if she stashed that other journal in here."

If it was possible, he was both relieved and disappointed that whatever might have happened didn't. But he refused to focus on it, instead pulling out his knife and setting to work on the grate in the corner.

Unlike the maids' rooms, this one had a closet, and Millie stepped into it. "Ouch!"

"You okay in there?"

She poked her head out, holding up a finger in front of her face. "Splinter. I'll survive."

"Glad to hear it."

The screws in the grate came out without much effort. They twisted with ease, and he almost didn't even need to use his knife.

Because maybe they had been replaced by someone using her fingers?

The thought made his heart stop, then slam back into his breastbone. It could be in here. It *was* in here.

He almost called Millie over to see, but something made him stop. He should find it first. Definitive proof and all that.

Pulling the grate out, he shined the light on his phone into the darkness, giving it a few quick swipes. All was black. Empty.

His stomach sank and he leaned his head into the corner. *Lord, are we even supposed to find this journal? This treasure?*

Still hovering somewhere near his toes, his stomach gave a lurch, and he pressed his hand over his eyes as regret washed over him. This was the first time since he'd met Millie that he'd stopped to talk to God about this. Any of it. Of course, it shouldn't have been. But knowing what he should do and actually doing it were two very different things.

Why hadn't he spent every day since he'd met Millie asking God for direction and clarity and wisdom? Maybe then he wouldn't have ended up with a partner who traded in half-truths and was far too pretty for him to ignore.

"Well, the closet's empty. You find anything?"

He shook his head as he lifted the grate back into place. "Empty. Is your finger okay?"

"Yes. Just a loose baseboard." Her voice stopped suddenly, and he launched himself across the room before he even knew what he was hoping for. Millie had fallen to her knees, her fingers pinching the pale wooden baseboard. It was only about three inches tall, but there was a definite movement to it. Even more, there were notches in the top of the board, as though someone had wedged a screwdriver or other tool between it and the wall.

"Here. Let me help." He dropped to her side and used the blade on his Swiss Army knife to lever the board away from the wall.

Suddenly Millie's fingers vanished and were replaced by the bright flashlight of her phone. "Is that better?"

He nodded just as the board popped loose. They both gasped, and Millie angled her light into the darkness beyond.

Ben stretched out across the floor of the closet, his legs reaching into the bedroom. Pressing his head against the floor, he tried to see into the hole they'd discovered. But it was mostly cobwebs.

He shivered. "I think the spiders beat us to it."

She gasped and jumped back, the light flickering. "Are they still in there?"

"I'm doing my best not to think about it." He closed his eyes and reached into the opening. It wasn't much wider than his hand. Not much deeper either. But suddenly his finger brushed something.

He couldn't help the yelp that escaped as he jerked back,

his hand caked with spiderwebs. Pressing the baseboard back into place, he hoped the spiders would stay behind it.

"What? What is it?" Millie shined her light on his outstretched arm and the gossamer threads clinging to his skin.

He pinched a yellow piece of paper between his fingers.

Millie sucked in an audible rush of air, and his jaw hung slack. "Read it," she whispered.

He wanted to take the moment to point out that she wasn't reaching for the spiderweb-covered clue. But this wasn't the time. This was the time to find the next step.

With his clean hand, he plucked the scrap of paper from its sticky prison and turned it over. Before he could even make out the faded script, Millie leaned over his shoulder and read it herself.

"'I've found a better hiding place. R.'"

"What's that supposed to mean?"

"Um . . ." Her eyes shifted back and forth, reading and rereading. "It's probably . . ."

Ignoring the long thread hanging from the end of his shirt sleeve, she hovered over his arm.

The note had been written in pencil and the charcoal had faded, now barely distinguishable from the yellowed paper. But the words were all there. Just as Millie had spoken them.

"Well, there was definitely something hidden here."

She nodded. Then she swallowed so loudly that he could hear it. "You don't think . . . Was she hiding the . . ."

"The treasure? No way."

Her eyes glimmered with something resembling hope, but doubt seeped in like a shroud.

"Why would she leave a note telling someone that she'd moved a stolen treasure? If you think someone knows where it is, then you move it. If someone had suspected her and searched the room, this note would have been evidence against her. No way would she have risked that."

Millie let out a low sigh. "You're right. But then what—" She bit her lip. "The journal. Someone was reading her journal."

Millie expressed no question about it, and he had a hunch she was right.

"But who?" she asked.

"If she hasn't said anything in her journal . . ." He dragged out the words, wishing she'd say there had been some clue, but with a quick shake of her head, she dashed his hopes. "Then we have to get more details—from someone who was there. Or at least the next best thing."

"But no one who was there is still—"

He knew the moment she realized what he was suggesting. Her eyes flashed and she opened her mouth, but no sound came out. A quick jerk of her head in a decidedly negative direction was all she needed to communicate.

He narrowed his gaze directly to hers. Her sapphire eyes turned to ice, and she crossed her arms over her chest.

"No."

He hadn't even asked a question yet. But she was as smart as she was pretty, and she could probably read his mind.

"We need to know what she does. You know we do."

Her lips puckered, but her gaze never wavered. "We can't. It's not . . . it's not as easy as all that."

"Right." What had Millie called her grandma before? Forgetful? "She might not remember?"

Millie's lashes dropped to her cheeks as her gaze dropped. Her hands shifted from fists under her arms to embrace herself.

A sudden urge to pull her into his own arms washed over him. He wasn't a hugger. His mom hadn't been. Neither had the parade of men who came and went. He didn't really know *how* to be. But when Millie released a pained hiccup that sounded far too much like a sob, Ben couldn't remain still. Grabbing her shoulder with his free hand, he did what his instincts said he should. He pulled her to his chest.

She was stiff as a board for a long moment as he clumsily crossed his untainted arm over her back. Suddenly she let out a breath with a loud whoosh, and her arms went around his waist. Tight.

Tucking her head under his chin, she pressed her face into his shirt. Her breath was warm through the cotton, and his skin erupted in goose bumps under the contrasting air-conditioning. Yes, it was definitely the AC that made his whole body feel like he was on high alert.

The cedar smell that had clung to the inside of the closet faded, and she was all sweet citrus and warmth in his arms. She melted like chocolate in the sun, and he could do nothing but hold on and pray she didn't slip through his fingers.

"Millie?"

She sniffled, and he had never been so grateful that he couldn't see her face and the tears he could feel through his shirt.

Say something. Say something. Say something.

But the mantra did nothing to bring comforting words to mind as the truth seeped through him. Its icy fingers wrapped around his spine until he shivered. Only one word repeated through his mind. *Alzheimer's.*

"Is she . . . worse than forgetful?"

She didn't say anything. Her body trembled like she was

trying to regain her solid state, which came in fits and starts. With her backbone back in place, she shook her head fiercely. Then she stopped. And nodded.

He waited a brief moment to make sure that was her final answer, and it wasn't until she wheezed against him that he realized how hard he'd been squeezing. Quickly relaxing his hold, he thought about dropping his arm. But she wasn't ready for that. He could feel it in her arms still around his waist.

When it became clear that she wasn't going to add any more to her response, he asked another question. "How much worse?"

"Much." Millie sounded like a bullfrog, but no amount of clearing her throat was enough. "It's been diagnosed as dementia."

"Alzheimer's?"

Her head wiggled against his chest in a decidedly negative motion. "The doctors say it's only dementia. She doesn't have the other symptoms associated with Alzheimer's." Her breath was audible, and she cleared her throat again. "But she can't take care of herself anymore. She forgets things she's known her whole life."

Millie held her breath for a quick second before letting it out in a quick rush. "But she was lucid when she told me about the treasure. I promise. Otherwise she wouldn't have known about—"

"The journal," he finished for her.

She nodded but didn't pull back just yet. She probably didn't want to watch him process this particular kick in the pants. He didn't blame her. But he was surprised at how little it actually affected him. They were right where they had been ten minutes before. Nothing had changed, and at least some of Grandma Joy's story had been true.

He wouldn't back out now.

Maybe he should pat Millie's back and promise that it would all be okay. But that was a lie. It was probably going to get worse. A whole lot worse.

At least now he knew what secrets she'd been keeping and why she was after the money. Caring for Grandma Joy would cost a pirate's treasure. Whatever gold the Chateau held might only make a dent. But at least it was a dent.

"Does she live with you?"

"No. I had to . . . I just couldn't watch out for her like she needed. I had to move her into a care facility." She looked away, finally dropping her arms and trying to pull away.

But he kept her close for another moment, rubbing a gentle circle on her back. It was awkward but the only thing he could think to do in the face of her regrets.

When she pulled fully free, her hands folded in front of her and her chin hanging low, she looked about fifteen years old, buckled by the weight of decisions she wasn't ready to make and responsibility that shouldn't have been hers. He wanted to ask about her parents. He wanted to know why she'd had to be the one to decide to put Grandma Joy into a home.

There were so many questions, but only one thing he knew to say. "Let's go see her."

She looked up, a furrow already worming its way between her eyebrows.

"Together."

TEN

Millie cringed as Ben pulled his rattling coupe into the long drive. A faded blue sign at the beginning of the lane claimed this was the Golden Isles Assisted Living Home, but there wasn't anything golden about it as far as she could see. At first glance the row of oaks adorned in Spanish moss seemed a regal welcome, an invitation to visit one of the South's most luxurious plantation homes. And maybe once upon a time it had been. Before the war. Before Reconstruction.

Now it just looked like no one had bothered to bring a hammer to it since. White paint flaked off the two-story columns before twin oak doors that hung at wrong angles, and the red bricks of the front wall had been bleached by years in the hot summer sun.

But Ben didn't seem to notice. He continued to drive in silence, taking the rutted gravel road with its due reverence. That gave her plenty of time to second-guess this plan. It was a terrible one.

Grandma Joy didn't do well with new people. When a new nurse was assigned to her wing, Grandma Joy had screamed through half the night, calling for Grandpa Zeke. But he had been gone for nearly ten years.

Millie shuddered now with the same trepidation she'd had when her phone had rung at two that morning, insistent and nearly as loud as her thundering heart as she raced for the home. It had taken an hour of sitting with Grandma Joy, squeezing her hand and whispering in her ear, to calm the frightened woman down. Nothing worked until she sang Grandma Joy's favorite hymn. No instruments and barely a tune. But the words seeped through a consciousness clouded by time and disease.

> *When peace, like a river, attendeth my way,*
> *When sorrows like sea billows roll,*
> *Whatever my lot, Thou hast taught me to say,*
> *It is well, it is well with my soul.*

Millie had spent the night with her, sleeping in the recliner by her bed, always an arm's reach away. But while the words two generations older than Grandma Joy had held a comfort for her, Millie couldn't muster much hope in them.

Whatever my lot . . .

She didn't know what kind of lot the guy who wrote that song had had. Maybe he did have sorrows. Shoot, maybe he was on a ship in the middle of a storm and praying he didn't fall out. Maybe he was in full-on Job mode.

But one thing was for sure. He hadn't had to send his grandmother to a care facility. He hadn't counted every nickel of every tip, simultaneously hoping it would be enough to pay for another month and feeling shame over having to send her there at all. He hadn't driven down this road, his insides a knot because seeing Grandma Joy was both the best thing in his life and a reminder of his worst failing. He'd never lain awake at night wondering where his grandma would go when Virginia Baker kicked her out. He'd never felt the days ticking by like the clock on a bomb and known that whatever he did probably wouldn't be enough to care for the person he loved most in the world.

Maybe he'd learned to be happy with whatever his lot was. But he hadn't been the granddaughter of the most wonderful grandmother in the world.

Ben kept his gaze straight ahead as he pulled into one of seven empty spots in the ten-car parking area. When he spoke, it was clear he'd noticed something was going on.

"Have you changed your mind?"

Yes.

No.

"I'm not sure." She pinched her lips together, crossed her arms over her stomach, and then uncrossed them just as fast.

"What's worrying you?"

Her laugh was more of a huff of disbelief. "What's not?"

He cracked a smile, turning toward her. His knees banged against the steering wheel, his legs too long for the little car. Readjusting his position, he pressed his hand to her forearm. "We're on the same team, right? We agreed from the beginning. We'd do this together."

She nodded slowly, knowing where he was going with this and at the same time needing him to spell it out.

"We're looking for something that could change both of our lives, and maybe your grandma can help us find it. But we would never do anything to hurt her. Right?"

She nodded, the rope around her chest loosening its hold.

"If today's not a good day, then we'll wait until there is one."

That rope slipped a little lower. If Grandma Joy wasn't up for meeting someone new today, they could wait until tomorrow or the next day, but time was running out. She had to move in six weeks.

She gazed at him for several long seconds, staring into his eyes, reading his face, searching for the truth. And it was in there. The crinkles at the corners of his eyes told her what she needed to know. She could trust him. Even with this.

Then why can't you trust him with the truth?

The question barreled through her, and she had to look down for fear that he'd see it scribbled across her features.

With a quick nod, she opened the car door. "We can only try."

As they walked up the front stone steps, Ben put his hand on the rail and it wobbled wildly. "Guess this old home could use a few new nails."

He'd clearly tried to make a joke, but Millie cringed. "I mean, it wasn't the best, but it was the one . . ."

She could afford.

She didn't have to say it aloud. She knew he knew.

"She doesn't like to be alone." Millie didn't direct her statement toward him exactly, and he didn't seem to think he needed to respond, so she kept going. "She gets scared when she doesn't see a familiar face or the doorbell rings. I tried to keep her with me, but I couldn't be there all the time."

Even she thought she sounded like she was trying to rationalize her decision, although Ben had said exactly nothing accusatory. It didn't matter.

"Sure. I mean, you have to work." As he stepped back to

hold the door open for her, the side of his foot caught on a crack that stretched the width of the cement porch, and he nearly took a tumble.

Millie scrambled for his arm. "I'm sorry!"

Before she could even reach him, he'd righted himself and laughed. "I never was light on my feet. My ballet teacher yelled at me about it all the time."

Her chuckle came out as half surprise and half humor. "You took ballet?"

Shrugging one shoulder, he followed her. "I could have."

"But you didn't."

"No. We moved around a lot when I was a kid. I didn't really get to participate in extracurriculars."

This was maybe the first time he'd ever spoken about his childhood. Or at least opened more than a window. She wanted to dig in. He'd learned more about her life in the last two weeks than she'd ever wanted to share with anyone.

But there wasn't time. Not as they approached the front desk under the watchful eye of a new attendant. Her brown eyes followed their every move, and Millie tried to ease into their visit with a gentle smile.

"We're here to see Joy Sullivan."

Without a word, the woman slapped a clipboard against the Formica countertop, her gaze never leaving Ben.

"Is that Millie?" The disembodied voice from the back room flew out to them, clear and confident.

"Yes," Millie said, but it sounded more like a question than she'd like.

The front desk attendant checked the clipboard, then called out her agreement like Millie needed to be verified.

"Hold on a sec!" It could only be Virginia Baker. What

more bad news could she have? When she appeared at the door to her office, her short brown hair was sleek and flowy, like she didn't even know the definition of humidity. Millie ran a hand over her own curls, which had taken on a life of their own in the misty morning air.

"Millie, I need to speak with you."

She looked at Ben, who nodded quickly and said, "I'll wait right here with my new friend."

The attendant looked like she'd never had a friend in her life and she wasn't currently shopping for one. Ben was un-deterred, his smile nearly blinding.

Millie slipped behind the counter and followed Virginia into her cramped office. Stacks of files filled every corner of her desk, and a computer screen was barely visible behind the central pile. The only chair for guests was also covered in red folders, so she stood at the doorway and smoothed her hands down the front of her cotton Bermuda shorts.

"Have you had any luck finding a new place for your grand-mother to stay?"

Millie pressed a hand to her stomach as it gave a sharp twist, and she squeezed her eyes shut. She'd considered every other possibility within driving distance when choosing this facility. But without an influx of money, she was still without options. "Have you found a pot of gold at the end of a rainbow?"

Virginia clucked her tongue. "I know this is difficult, but we have another resident waiting for the space."

Her eyes flew open, and she stared at Virginia. The woman looked unassuming, but her words had the power to blow up Millie's entire life.

"What are you saying?" Millie tried to keep her voice down, but it rose with each word.

Virginia made a motion with her hands to indicate they should stay calm, but Millie didn't feel calm. Her insides were a hurricane of uncertainty, every piece of her tossed about at the whim of the administrator.

"We're going to need your grandmother's room in thirty days." With a sad smile, Virginia held out a single sheet of paper, but the black print on it blurred as Millie stared.

Her spine tingled, and she fisted her hands at her sides, unable to accept whatever document Virginia had prepared—probably a notice of eviction. "You said we had ninety days. It's only been forty."

"Well, technically, it's been forty-four. But we need her to move out by the end of the month." She turned and picked up a few fliers from her desk, the colorful brochures featuring enormous estates and pictures of smiling seniors. "Maybe one of these will help."

Virginia thrust them at her, and Millie had no choice but to take them and stuff them in her purse. She'd seen these before. And seen the hefty price tags placed on the rooms. Still not an option. And now the clock on the bomb had sped up. She'd lost more than two weeks. And she was no closer to finding a connection to the Devereaux family.

She'd never wanted to crawl into the pages of her books more than she did in that instant. Deep in those stories the heroines never faced more than they could handle. This was so much more than Millie could handle.

Unless . . . Unless Grandma Joy had been telling the truth. Unless she was from the wealthiest family in the South. Unless she was heir to something so grand she couldn't even imagine.

Unless that was all a pipe dream, a wish too good to be true.

Heroes swooped in to save the day in the fairy tales. But her life was all cinders and none of the belle of the ball. Not that she was going to complain about it. It was her lot. Just don't expect her to say it was well with her soul in the midst of it.

"I really am sorry," Virginia said.

Not sorry enough. Millie trudged out of the office, her eyes burning and her hands still shaking. This had to work. It just had to, because *sorry* didn't give Grandma Joy a safe place to stay with staff who actually cared about her.

She didn't even motion to Ben as she slipped out from behind the counter and shuffled down the hall. Natural light seemed to have been banned, but she didn't mind. Not when she'd much rather cover her face and hide the red tip of her nose that she knew was already there.

"Hey." Running footfalls behind her drew closer. "What was that all about?"

"Nothing. Just . . . nothing." She shook her head and stared at the wallpaper that might have been white at some point in the distant past. But the curling edges had lost their brilliance a few decades before.

This was all she could provide for her grandmother. And not for much longer.

A fist squeezed around her heart, and she slowed her walk just to catch her breath. It was broken by a silent sob, and she pinched her eyes closed, turning away from Ben's inquisitive gaze. Hunching her shoulders, she tried to create a wall between them. But he was so much taller than her that it was useless.

He said nothing, but he didn't walk away. There was a strength radiating from him. It was subtle but stable, low-key and constant.

She hated how much she wanted to turn into his embrace and enjoy the warmth she knew was there. She couldn't. Not here. Not now. She scrubbed her hands over her face and tried to find that steel backbone that Grandma Joy had always modeled. It was in her, somewhere deep. She needed only to find the courage to use it.

Letting out a slow breath, she lowered her shoulders from where they nearly reached her ears and forced her hands to her sides. She shot him a glance out of the corner of her eye. "I need to find that treasure."

His dark brows lowered over his eyes, but he nodded slowly, following her down the hall to room 22. The nondescript wooden door was like every other one in the building, but she knew it as if it had a giant X marking the spot. The door was open a crack, but all was silent inside.

Until it wasn't.

Suddenly a loud bang sounded against the door, shaking it hard. "Blasted shoes!"

"Grandma Joy!" There was no time to even consider Ben as she flung open the door, scooped up the sneaker that had clearly been thrown across the width of the room, and raced toward the purple recliner.

The petite woman sitting in the seat had a face redder than a beet, and she glared at the other shoe on her foot. Bending lower, she gripped the white laces between trembling fingers, her hoarse mutters filling the room and certainly spilling out the open door into the hallway.

"Over, then under. No. No." She shook her head hard, her fluff of white curls bouncing with agitation. "Under, then over, then loop and loop and . . ." Her voice petered out, and she looked up, confusion filling the wrinkles of her face. "You changed it on me again. I could tie them this morning. I could."

Millie's mouth went dry, her fingers forgetting how to function. She could only hold the shoe by its laces as understanding dawned. And with it an ache so deep that it threatened to tear her in half.

"It goes over first, right?"

Dropping to her knees, Millie gave her grandmother a soft smile. "Yes. It goes over first. Then loops."

Grandma Joy gave a firm nod and followed the motions with her knobby hands, stiff and uncertain. "I could do it this morning."

"I know." Millie tried to find some other words of comfort but knew they'd be quickly forgotten too, so she let herself off the hook and simply reached for her grandmother's hand. She pressed the paper-thin skin firmly but gently until Grandma Joy looked at her, really looked at her. "Let me help you."

"Camilla?"

Dear Lord.

It was the only prayer she could muster as the hope she so desperately needed was washed away.

How did she not remember? How could she have forgotten the thirteen years they'd spent together with Grandpa Zeke? How had she forgotten the little kitchen table where they'd eaten their meals and put together puzzles? How had she forgotten teaching Millie to drive in the back pasture and the little tree Millie had run over? It never did recover. But they'd been a family, the only one Millie had.

And now Grandma Joy didn't even know her.

"Yes. It's me."

The gold in her grandma's eyes became less fire and more relief as a gentle smile tugged at the corners of her mouth, her pink lipstick seeping into the deep crevices of her skin. "Camilla." This time it wasn't a question as much as the simple enjoyment of saying a familiar name, and Millie tried to let that be enough. "Why—why are you here? How long have you been here?"

"I just got here. I'm going to help you tie your shoes."

"Oh." Grandma Joy patted her bent head. "You're such a good girl. You always take such good care of me."

She had to close her eyes as tears once again threatened to break loose.

Ben clutched at his chest, trying to reel in the top that spun somewhere deep inside. It didn't help.

Watching Millie slide her grandmother's foot into the shoe that she'd thrown across the room and tie it snugly made him want to laugh and cry. It was so sweet and utterly painful at the same time.

But he mostly wanted to run.

This little woman could hold the answers to everything they were hunting for. Yet getting to those answers wouldn't be easy.

"See?" Millie patted the top of the shoes. "All set now."

Despite her perky tone, there was a hesitancy in Joy's responding smile. It seemed to be searching for the true emotion inside, like she was sure the smile was required but not sure why.

Oh, Lord, why do some people have to suffer through this? It wasn't fair.

Then again, life wasn't fair.

It wasn't fair for people who lost their memories. It wasn't fair for people who lost their loved ones. It wasn't fair for people who lost their money. And it sure wasn't fair that someone he loved had caused at least two of those three.

The reminder was enough to turn the pulsing in his sinuses into a full-blown throbbing, and he pinched the bridge of his nose in an attempt to stem the headache where it started. Useless.

So he pushed through, trying to focus on the exchange between grandmother and granddaughter and whatever that might reveal. Despite Millie's assurance to Joy, she wasn't there to help her tie her shoes. This visit was about a book with a map that was still missing. No one was going to hand it to them. They'd have to find it themselves with whatever help was available.

"Camilla?" Joy patted Millie's shoulder, seeming to need a third confirmation.

Millie nodded, and Joy looked across the room. "Do I know you?"

She was obviously speaking to him, but he still pressed a finger to his chest in an unspoken question before barreling on. "No, ma'am. I'm Ben Thornton."

Joy's gaze meandered from him to Millie and back again before settling on her granddaughter. "You know him?" Her Southern drawl became more pronounced, and the blank stare in her eyes was replaced by something that resembled humor. "Or did he follow you in?"

Millie laughed. It was almost sweet enough to overpower the weighty smell of cleaning products and confinement.

"He's a friend of mine."

"Friend?" There was a lingering undertone in the word that danced with romantic suggestion. It was only missing waggling eyebrows to be the stereotypical setup. Meanwhile Ben was still wondering if what they shared could really be called *friendship*.

Acquaintances. Co-workers. Treasure sharers. Yes to all. But *friends*?

Maybe.

He had hugged her. No, that wasn't right. He'd *held* her. He'd let her cry all over his shirt as he'd tried to comfort her. He'd done an extra load of laundry for her. He didn't do that for just anyone. And he hadn't minded a bit.

She'd become a staple in his life. Someone he looked forward to seeing. Someone he wanted to . . .

Well, he'd stick with *friend*. She was definitely a friend.

"My, but you are a handsome man." She motioned for him to step farther into the room. "Like my Zeke. He's tall too."

"My grandpa," Millie said.

He nodded as he took another couple steps into the studio apartment. He'd figured as much. He also had a feeling that Zeke was long gone. If he was still around, the responsibility for Joy wouldn't have been solely on her granddaughter's shoulders. Or Millie would have been taking care of him too.

"Zeke. He's a handsome man."

"You said that already, Grandma."

Those blue eyes laser-focused on Millie. "Some things are worth repeating."

Millie chuckled. "Fair enough."

"Are you from these parts?"

Ben almost missed that Joy's focus was back on him, and he scrambled for the right answer. The one that was true but not too true. "Um . . . no, ma'am. I'm . . . I moved here for graduate school." And to get away from a town where everyone knew his name and what his mother had done. Technically they had lived in Brunswick—just on the other side of the bridge—for a short time years before. But St. Simons had felt like a safe place to mostly disappear. A safe place to forget.

"An academic, then?"

"Ben is a history professor."

"Adjunct professor," he quickly amended. It might not mean much to Millie, but it was the difference between working one job and three.

"At the college?" Joy didn't wait for anyone to confirm. "You know, we all said that Millie could have gone to college. She was smart enough. She just never liked going to class."

Out of the corner of his eye, he saw Millie's cheeks go bright red. He tried to catch her eye with an encouraging grin, but her gaze had fallen to the floor, intently focused anywhere but on him.

"She's smart as a whip, really. Loves those books. She was always up until the wee hours of the morning. I couldn't get her to go to bed, bless her heart."

"That's okay, Grandma. Ben doesn't—"

He held up a hand. "Of course I want to know."

When Millie did finally look in his direction, it was accompanied by pursed lips and a cute little wrinkled nose. He could barely keep in a burst of laughter. Grandma Joy's memories of Millie's childhood seemed more than adequate to annoy her granddaughter. But would she remember the things they really needed to know?

"She insisted on being called Millie." Joy harrumphed,

folding her arms, which were only just long enough to cross her body. As she leaned back in the chair, Ben suddenly realized just how petite she was. Her feet dangled above the floor, and he decided she might not even be five feet tall. But spitfire didn't require a size.

"She wanted everyone to call her Millie, even though her mama named her Camilla."

"Yes, yes. I've always preferred Millie. Not that you ever called me that."

"And she back talked like no child I'd ever seen." But there was a lilt in Joy's tone that revealed even she didn't believe what she was saying.

Millie swatted at Joy's arm with a laugh. "I did not. I was perfect."

"If you call staying up until all hours of the morning *perfect*." Turning back to him, Joy whispered, "She wouldn't close those books. Stayed up all night reading them. I couldn't get her to stop. And if I couldn't find her, I knew where she was."

She didn't have to say it. Somehow he just knew. "The library."

"Yep."

"Well, I'm reading something else interesting right now," Millie said.

Joy pushed herself to the edge of her seat and rested her arms on her knees. "The journal? You found it?" With a tilt of her head, she motioned to him. "He knows about it?"

"I had to tell him. He caught me snooping around."

"So, what's it say? Does it have the map?"

Millie dug into her bag—the substitute suitcase always hanging over her shoulder—and retrieved the carefully wrapped book. Unwinding it from the cloth protector, she slowly shook her head. "There's nothing in here about a treasure. There's no map."

Joy had been reaching for the journal but dropped her hand as soon as Millie confirmed the worst. "No map? But there has to be. She said. She always said." The clouds in her eyes that had blown away flew back in on the winds of a hurricane.

Ben stepped forward, wanting to help her understand but powerless to do anything more than shake his head. It was Millie's comforting hand that settled onto Joy's knee. "But it says there's a second journal. Do you know where it might be?"

Joy's gaze turned distant even as she clasped Millie's fingers in her own gnarled ones. "Another book?"

"Yes. Grandma, it was right where you said it would be. The journal was there. But there's another one."

"The journal? I never wrote a journal."

Millie clutched the diary in her free hand and held it out. "Your mama's. Ruth Holiday's. You told me she left it at the Chateau. In the library. It was there." There was an urgency to Millie's words. They didn't rush but rather came out in waves, imploring Joy to understand, to remember, trying to sweep her back into the land of the present.

Joy's eyes reflected only confusion. Patting her white curls, she frowned. "I don't—that's not right. My mama is—she lives on the farm. Not the Chateau. She loved the farm. Said all the best things were there." She rocked in her chair, her breathing picking up speed.

Millie looked up at him, her eyes wide and fear stamped across her face.

This wasn't something he could fix. There wasn't something he could do to make it better. This felt like when Millie had broken down, and he'd gone on instinct, knowing nothing except that he could hold her.

Dropping to his knees beside the rocking chair, he put his hand on the armrest right next to Joy's elbow. "Tell us about the farm."

"The Chateau?" A childlike smile fell across Joy's face. "It's so pretty at night. All lit up with the electric lights. Mama takes me to see it sometimes."

Just as quickly as it had arrived, hope seeped out of him on a long breath. And something inside his chest split like the *Titanic*.

"What about the farm? Did you live there?"

"Mama said all the best things are at the farm."

Millie looked up at him through long lashes, jaw clenched and lips tight. Silence dragged between them as Joy mumbled on about the farm, her words making only minimal sense.

Finally Millie mouthed two simple words that made perfect sense. "I'm sorry."

He could only nod. There were no words for moments like this, so he simply waited with the two women as one fought for every memory and the other grieved the ones forever gone.

The minutes ticked by. A quarter hour. Then half. The steady squeak of the rocker counted down every second. Until it stopped.

He looked up to see that Joy's eyes had drooped, her chest rising and falling in a smooth rhythm beneath her folded hands.

Millie seemed to have noticed as well. Leaning forward,

she kissed Joy's forehead. "Love you, Grandma." With a pat of her hand, she turned toward the hall and led the way. Outside she closed the door with an almost imperceptible snick.

She didn't move, her head still hanging low and her gaze somewhere near her blue sneakers. "I'm sorry."

He wanted to tell her not to be. He wanted to promise that it was all right. But mostly he wanted to fix this, to do something worth doing. To pursue a lead worth chasing. So he said the first thing that jumped to mind. "All the best things are at the farm."

August 1, 1929

I feel certain that I have ruined any friendship I might have had with George. It should not feel so terrible, but it does. I am sure he will be fine. What is less certain is if I will fully recover.

But I had no other choice. Not after the evening that Claude and I spent together. He has been so concerned about me since he startled me in the little alcove. He is forever checking on me to make sure I am well and that he is not pushing me beyond where I feel comfortable. And the truth is that I feel much more than comfortable in his arms. I like it more than I probably should.

It began two evenings ago. After dinner, Claude invited me for a walk on the beach, and when I suggested that Jane join us, he was insistent that it be just the two of us. I could hardly refuse him. Of course, I did not want to.

He led me by the hand through the parlor and through a side door. Lucille gave me a highly knowing look as we walked by, but I have no idea why. I suppose she assumed that I might be free with my attentions, but she does not know Claude as I do. He is a gentleman through and through. Or, I thought he was.

No, I am sure of it. That evening was simply an anomaly.

We walked along the beach for what felt like hours. The moon was twice as large as normal, and as it cast its great shadow across the rippling waters, it also cast a spell of some sort. I am not entirely sure how to describe it, except to say that I was drawn to Claude in a way that I did not expect. Walking by his side, hearing him speak of traveling across Europe, made me long for a life I have only ever dreamed might be possible. What would it be like to see the great wonders of the world? Paris adorned in her beautiful lights? England's ancient castles? Rome's Colosseum? I have only ever seen pictures in books at the library at Miss Truway's School. Claude describes them with such tenderness that I cannot only picture them, but I can imagine myself there.

He asked me if I would like to travel. I almost responded that I would like to go someday. But Mama says that someday is today. So I simply told him that I would.

He squeezed my hand and said he would take me. I wished I had thought to remove my gloves. Without the silk barrier, I am sure that I could have felt his pulse at his wrist. I wished too that I had worn other shoes. The heels of my shoes sank into the beach, and grains of sand slipped inside, rubbing at my toes through my stockings.

The sand gave way under each of our steps, and he suddenly stopped. Pulling off his shoes, he said we should go barefoot. His shoes and socks were discarded before I could even blink, and he bent over to roll up the hem of his pants.

I have seen a man's ankle before, but this felt oddly personal, strangely intimate outside the context of the swimming pool. His feet are wide and strong, and the dark hair on the lower part of his leg made me realize he is very much a man. I knew that before, of course. But it was a strange realization that I was alone with a man on a beach.

When he looked up, he laughed at me and asked if I had never seen a man's toes before. I assured him I had, and he insisted that he should have the same pleasure. He winked as his fingers cradled the back of my foot and slipped off my shoe.

He wanted to see my feet, and then he said he wanted to see so much more than that.

I should have walked away. Willa or Jane might have slapped him. But I stood frozen. How could I move when my whole body felt afire?

The moon and the lights from the Chateau were plenty bright to see his face, and in his eyes I saw a longing that I'd never witnessed before.

I melted in that instant. My better angels did not try to make their case. There was only Claude and me and the Chateau.

We walked back to the house much later, our feet bare and our hearts full. He stopped me near one of the large trees, cupping my face with his hand and whispering to me of his feelings, calling me "sweet Ruthie."

I thought I should perhaps tell him that I love him, but before I could fully respond, he kissed me well and good. The crashing of a clay pot broke us from our reverie.

Claude stepped back as a knot formed in my stomach. I knew without looking who was there.

Oh, George. His words spouted apologies, but his eyes were luminous and unrepentant. I wanted to run. I wish he had never seen us. He, of all people, must think me a terrible person. But as Mama would say, there's no use crying over spilled milk.

Still, the next morning I woke with a peach pit in my stomach. Why do I feel as though I have treated George poorly when there is nothing between us? Certainly there has been no agreement or even mention of an interest beyond friendship from him. And I have not led him on. Not when Claude's attentions have been so clear.

George did offer to take me away from this place, but I cannot believe he truly meant it. At least, he could not have meant it in the way I thought. He had not offered me a life and a future. He had no means to do so. Even if he did have money, he had no desire to marry me.

Oh my. My mind has conjured far too many unfounded things. I refuse to even wonder about George in such terms.

However, I knew that I must speak to him. But I am a coward, so I wrote him a letter. I thought to have a maid deliver it, but Jenny is long gone, and I realized there was no one I trusted with something so precious. While the rest of the house enjoyed a lounging afternoon around gaming tables, I ducked outside. I even managed to find the same exit I have taken twice, where I have run into George. He was not there.

I walked all the way around the house, past the main entrance and between the rows of sycamores. The air is spicier out there, sweeter somehow. It's as though a few more yards from the ocean, the air is free to highlight the fragrance of all of George's beautiful flowers. Roses. Gardenias. Honeysuckles.

My nose was still pressed into the delights of one of the flower beds when George spoke, addressing me as always as Miss Holiday. I snapped to attention, the silly letter falling right to the muddy earth. I picked it up quickly and shoved it toward him.

He turned it over, looking at the front and back of the blank envelope, and then asked what it said. I almost blurted it out, but how could I say such things face-to-face? So I told him to read it himself.

He stared at the paper again and said only that he would

rather hear it from me. He was so unassuming, rather un-demanding, and he acted as though nothing had changed. As though he had not seen me just the night before in a rather compromising situation. I so wanted to punch him, as my brothers have done to each other a hundred times. I wanted to sock him right in the eye for being so . . . so . . . George.

Instead I yelled at him, waving my arms about like a madwoman, insisting that he knew very well what was in the letter. He assured me that he did not, but I still don't believe him.

I waved my finger between us, my voice rising with each word, and told him that what was between us was terribly inappropriate and must end.

He looked at me through one narrowed eye. "Is it now?" he asked.

Oh, I was so bothered. I screamed at him not to play coy with me. I tried to punctuate my words by calling him by his surname, but I could not remember it. And when I called him George, I lost a bit of my steam. Not all of it, mind you. I was still worked up, but not angry exactly. Unsettled.

He insisted that he was not playing coy and that we had indeed done nothing improper. Walks. A picnic. Always in full view of anyone who might like to watch. He said we had nothing to hide.

Oh, that infuriating man, making so much sense. He thought I had exhausted my arguments, but I still had the truth on my side.

I reminded him that he knew very well that Mr. Dawkins would not like it if he was mingling with guests. George said he would have liked it less if I had drowned on his property. I could not help but touch the spot on my head that had ached for weeks after my accident.

He nodded and held up the envelope. He had been planning to invite me to join him for church on Sunday, but we agreed it would be best for me not to go.

I did think that. I really did. Until his chin dropped, his shoulders slumped, and he walked away.

And I felt as though I had kicked a puppy.

I did the right thing. I know I did. But I am heartsick over George. How can I be so near to pure bliss with Claude and still regret sending George away with every fiber of my being?

August 5, 1929

Things have become quite serious. I do not mean to imply that stolen jewelry is not a serious matter. Obviously Mr. Dawkins believes it to be so or he would not have sent Jenny away.

However, the absolute worst thing has happened. It all began this morning when I slipped out of the house to see George.

That is not quite right. It started before that, and I was not intentionally going to see George. I happened to see him as I walked past the gardener's shed. Actually, it might have been on my second or third time past the open window that he called out to me.

He always sounds so formal, calling me Miss Holiday, and I wonder what his education must have been like. But in that moment, I could only peer through the cloudy glass. He stood beside the big table in the center of the room. A very large pot sat in the middle, and from its rich black earth grew the most beautiful rosebush I have ever seen.

I asked him where it was going to go, and he turned back to his work, snipping at the wayward branches before telling me he thought this might be an improper conversation . . . "Miss Holiday."

Oh, I felt awful. How could I explain that Claude had all but stated his intentions? I am certain that we are close to an understanding. He has kissed me many times now. And I have allowed him to do more. I know that Mama would certainly disapprove, but he can provide for me in a way that I could never have dreamed before. And I do care for him. He is a good man, wise and worldly.

I never meant for George to have feelings for me. But when I told him that I should not, could not, see him anymore and that our letters must stop, I felt as though I might have truly hurt him. His eyes, usually so green, turned to brown, deep and soulful. While he said he understood, how could he, when I can hardly believe what I said to him?

I needed another opportunity to explain myself. I had to.

That is why I went to the gardening shed. Except I could barely find any words. It is not an easy thing to do, breaking a man's heart.

"George. Please," I said. I sounded like I was begging. I probably was, even though I had no idea what I was begging for.

He looked at me then, through the glass that still carried the splatters from the last rain. He did not smile. Neither did he frown. He only stared, and I could feel it like a caress across my skin, deeper than anything that Claude had ever made me feel.

Feelings are foolishness. Mama has told me that a hundred times. I must be practical. I must think about my future. I must think about the opportunities that Claude can provide for me.

I tried to brush George's gaze off, but he didn't waver. So I looked to the side, and that is when I saw it. A piece of pink fabric poked out from behind one of the tall sycamores. The tree's base was so wide that I could not see what was on the other side, but that cloth was familiar. A rock too big to move sat in my stomach.

I looked back at George, who must have immediately read my face. He asked what it was but was already running from his shed.

He told me to wait where I was while he went to investigate, but I did not listen. I followed right behind him, clutching the back of his shirt. Suddenly his hand was over mine, sliding his fingers through mine. I did not mind a bit, as my heart was beating in my throat. It was so loud I imagine the whole beach could have heard it.

As we approached the tree, I could see that it was more than a scrap of fabric. It was a full skirt. And a woman was still wearing it.

I cried out, and George pulled me into his arms. He held me tight as I covered my eyes and tried desperately to erase the image that had been seared into my mind. Willa—talkative, vibrant Willa—lay at the foot of the tree, blood running from her hairline to the corner of her mouth.

George did not hold me nearly long enough. He let me go and dropped to his knees. Pressing his hands to Willa's face, he called her name. She did not respond. Then he touched her arm and shook his head.

I turned and vomited on the spot. I had never seen a dead body before. At least not a person. And dead animals cannot compare.

George hurried me back to the house, leaving me in the parlor, where I sank into the nearest sofa. Before I knew it, Jane was by my side with a glass of water. I drank it empty in one try and then just stared at the crystal bottom as the rest of the house came to life.

It was early and Mr. Dawkins was still pulling on his jacket as he raced down the hallway, hollering for Lucille to telephone the police chief.

The rest of the morning is a bit of a blur for me. I spoke to at least six police officers and told them my story over and over. At some point Claude slipped to the couch beside me, put one arm around me, and held my hand in his.

The day turned rainy just as they drove Willa away. It seemed fitting.

We have all been stuck inside for hours, mostly silent. Except for Angelique. She is beside herself, swearing that she and Willa were to take a walk along the beach this morning. Angelique was running late and blames herself for not being there. Claude and I tried to assure her that certainly if she had been there, they both would have been injured. Or worse.

The worst part of it all is that no one knows why she might have been attacked. Was it an accident? A fluke? Or is it somehow tied to the thefts that have happened here?

This summer is so different than I anticipated. There is more to share. It is a good thing Mama thought to pack a second journal, for I shall have no difficulty filling it.

ELEVEN

How much more?

The question had haunted Millie all night and the one before that, ever since she finished reading the diary.

Ruth had allowed Claude Devereaux certain liberties beyond a chaste kiss, but there was no telling just how far they'd gone on the beach. Or anywhere else, for that matter. It was clear that Ruth had assumed a proposal was imminent. So had she given herself fully to Claude?

If Ruth's story had been a modern one, there'd have been little room for doubt. But ninety years ago? Howard Dawkins had had no shame in bringing his "particular friend" to the Chateau while his wife and child remained in Chicago, but Ruth wasn't afforded the same social freedoms. Her station wasn't even on the same map as Dawkins. How could a farm girl expect to be treated as well as a wealthy banker? Grandma Joy had once said that Ruth's aunt had paid for her niece's education at a girls' academy. But it wasn't enough to set her among the elite.

Millie needed to know where she'd landed. Had Ruth

succumbed to Devereaux's charms? Or had she held fast in the face of temptation? Given their escapades on the beach, Millie wasn't so sure she knew the answer.

And what of George? He was a fine man. She'd conceded that point. Sometimes Ruth's descriptions of him made him sound like he belonged on the pages of her latest library read. Ruth had let him hold her. But Millie had let Ben hold *her*. No big deal.

Except sometimes it felt like a big deal. No, not a *big* deal. But a deal. A situation. A thing.

If that was the best she could do in describing it, then it really wasn't any of those. But that didn't—

"Millie? *Millie!*"

She jerked around, almost toppling the tray in her friend's hand. "Ella!"

"Where were you? Cook's been calling your order for ten minutes."

Millie blinked quickly, trying to erase a vision of grass-green eyes and a warm smile beneath a sunny summer sky. "I'm here. Sorry. I'm here." At least, she was here for another twenty minutes before Ben picked her up for what would probably turn out to be another wild goose chase.

Scooping up the plates at the window, she dodged Cook's salty glare and headed for the end of the counter. All but two of the red padded stools were filled, and the four teenagers on the end scowled as she approached. The only girl in the group said something, but the clanging of Cook's spatula against his griddle mixed with Elvis on the jukebox drowned her out.

"Sorry about that wait. Here you go." She slid each plate into place across the narrow Formica counter and pulled a bottle of syrup from her apron pocket. "Can I get you anything else right now?"

The girl huffed and rolled her eyes as she squeezed out enough ketchup to drown her hash browns. "I'm out of water."

"Of course. Anything else?"

The three boys were already neck-deep in their breakfasts, rich maple syrup drenching their pancakes. They shook their heads, so she reached for the pitcher of ice water.

Just as Millie began to refill the glass around a dancing straw, the girl shrieked. "Ugh! This is cold." And then she shoved her plate.

In an instant Millie dropped the water, the pitcher cracking against the black and white tiles of the floor, and grabbed for the plate, which flew over the counter's edge. She kept it from hitting the floor only by scooping it into her arms. Right against her middle.

The ketchup was cool and wet through her uniform dress, and she froze as it began leaking toward her waist. It didn't pool like the water from the pitcher did in her white tennis shoes, but it globbed against her skin, leaving sticky trails all down her front.

The whole room seemed to freeze. Even Cook's spatula paused. Only Elvis, begging for his girl to love him tender and true, continued.

And every single gaze zeroed in on her.

She tried to find a smile or a chuckle or something. Anything to detract from the fiasco. But before she could break the tension, the rude girl brayed like a donkey. Her laughter was as coarse as her manners, and every other face in the room seemed unsure how to respond. Even the girl's three companions struggled to follow her lead. Each of the teenage boys, all clean-cut and polished enough for Sunday morning, blinked in slow motion as strained smiles pulled at their faces.

Easy for them—they didn't have a midsection full of ketchup, fried potatoes, and runny eggs that had made it to the bottom of her skirt and oozed past her knee.

"Idiot." The girl glared at her, daring her to speak up against the injustice, knowing somehow that she wouldn't. Couldn't. There were unspoken rules about these things. The customer was always right. Treat others as you'd like to be treated. She needed this job.

It was the last that made her clamp her mouth closed and ease the plate away from her. Looking down, she surveyed the damage. She looked like she'd been in a knife fight. More specifically, she looked like she'd taken a plate to a knife fight, and she'd lost. Badly.

The ketchup was still spreading, but there were three distinct splotches in the region of her belly button.

"Millie? Are you all right?"

His voice was both wonderfully familiar and terribly jarring. And it seemed to pull everyone else from their stupor, the whole place erupting with sound and activity at once.

Buddy, the café's manager, lunged for her, holding out a wet towel that had probably wiped down a thousand greasy tables. She deflected it with her free hand, trying to find the face she hadn't seen but knew was there.

Not at the counter. Not in a booth. There, at the hostess stand. Ben in his wrinkle-free shirt. Ben, his damp hair a testament that he'd recently showered. Ben, his eyes wide with concern.

She could only meet his gaze, hold up the plate, and shrug.

He seemed to understand. At least enough to realize that she wasn't gravely wounded and that the attack had been more emotional than anything else. So he offered her a gentle smile, crinkled eyes and all.

That's when her insides, which had been frozen in shock, suddenly twisted with the force of a tornado. Her head spun and her eyes went blurry, and for a moment she thought she'd lost her ever-lovin' mind. Maybe she had. Maybe Grandma Joy and Ruth and Claude Devereaux—or maybe George— had gotten to be too much.

All she wanted to do was curl up in her bed and disappear into the pages of a book. Not forever, but for a while. A long while. Only that wasn't really an option at the moment. Every single one of her worries wasn't going away. Not anytime soon.

So she stared at Ben and sucked every bit of strength she could from his stable, solid stance as three other waitresses fluttered around her. One pulled the plate away while another wiped her hands with a napkin, and the third glared at the nasty girl.

"Come on, guys," the girl said. "We're leaving. This place smells like rotten fish."

Two of the boys followed her across the diner floor, but the last one dug into the pocket of his jeans. "Man, I'm sorry about your dress." He pulled out two twenties, which would barely cover the four breakfasts, and tossed them on the counter. Then he followed his buddies, and they disappeared to the sound of the jingling bell on the door.

"Are you all right, Millie?"

"That girl's the worst. She sat at my table last week."

178

"I'll ask Buddy to comp their meals so you can use the money to get your uniform cleaned."

All three women spoke at the same time. She just couldn't seem to look at them. Not when Ben was making his way over.

"You want me to go take care of them?" His voice was lower than usual, and it sounded like he hadn't used it in days. But his words made her laugh.

"And how exactly would you take care of them?" Foot sloshing in her shoe, she took a step toward the counter.

His brows furrowed and his lips pursed as he looked over his shoulder at the place where they'd exited the diner. "Um . . . well . . . you know. I'd take care of them." He held up a fist and waved it around.

She laughed again. He was one hundred percent history professor in his dark jeans and green button-up shirt. Even with the sleeves rolled up to his elbows, he looked about as capable of "taking care" of those kids as she was able to snap her fingers and make her uniform spotless.

Shaking her head, she managed a genuine smile. "Thank you, though. I'm glad you offered."

Strangely, she was. She didn't want him to beat them up. She didn't think he'd even meant that in his offer. But even if he'd said it only to make her laugh, it had been exactly what she needed. And the spectacle she'd been had suddenly become a lot less interesting to every other patron in the Hermit Crab Café.

"Who's this guy?"

Suddenly Millie realized that she and Ben weren't alone. At the counter between them still sat a dozen other well-behaved diners. And Courtney, Priscilla, and Ella—the other waitresses on the morning shift—were still by her side.

"Um, this is Ben. He's . . . um . . ." She hadn't even had as much trouble introducing him to Grandma Joy. So why was this so hard? But as she looked into the expectant faces of her co-workers and gossip queens, she cringed. "He's a friend of mine."

Lamer words had never been spoken.

"A friend, huh?" Ella eyed him like a medium-rare steak, just the way she liked it.

Ben nodded slowly and spoke like Ella might need him to spell it out. "Yes. A friend. We work together."

Courtney's nose wrinkled. "You don't work here."

Maybe these girls did need Ben to speak slowly.

"We work together at my other job," Millie said. "At the Chateau."

"Oh." Priscilla eyed him up and down, twirling a platinum-blonde corkscrew curl around her finger. "You a tour guide there too?"

"She's not a—" He was halfway to explaining her job to them when she held up a quick hand. She'd already told them a thousand times what she did there. How three women who could remember every "hold the pickle" and "add mayo" for a buzzing party of ten couldn't remember that she played dress-up six nights a week, she'd never understand.

"You girls going to serve some of this food?" Buddy yelled right in her ear.

The others hopped up and took off to deliver the plates stacking up at the window. Millie just turned around and motioned to her dress. "My shift is over in ten. Mind if I go home?"

Buddy rubbed his hands together in front of his too-short tie. Patting his greasy bald spot, he gave her a once-over and then went back for seconds and thirds. His gaze made her skin crawl, but she tried to keep her smile from slipping away.

"Okay. Ella, cover Millie's tables."

She didn't need a written invitation. Sliding around the counter, she ducked into the back room, grabbed her purse and the bag of clothes she'd been planning to change into, and met up with Ben just inside the front door.

As he held it open for her to exit first, he said, "You want to go home?" His tone took a decidedly disappointed dip.

She took another good look at the front of her uniform and sighed. "I don't have much of a choice."

She'd planned to change her clothes at the diner and leave straight from there with Ben. But that was before ketchup started pooling at the waistband of her underwear. Not that she was going to explain that particular discomfort to him. Still, she gave him a hint as she wiggled against her damp underthings, praying that she wouldn't leave stains all over the seat of her car.

Except she hadn't driven that morning. Her car had refused to start. At least she wouldn't have to worry about making a mess.

"Can we go another day?"

He looked toward the far side of the road, over the passing vehicles, like he could see something more than the threadbare clouds. "Today's my only day off for another couple weeks. I'm working a few extra shifts."

"At the Chateau?"

Squinting, he looked back at her. "At the library."

Just how many jobs did this guy have? By her count that made three. Three and a half if treasure hunting took up any more of their time.

She was busy—but Ben was crazy.

Opening her mouth, she started some sort of casual dismissal. She could go on her own. He didn't need to go with her. She probably wouldn't find anything anyway.

But even as she began to form the words, she shook her head at her own arguments. She didn't want to go alone. And she sure didn't want to dwell on why she felt that way.

Maybe Great-Grandma Ruth was right and feelings were foolishness. But they were still feelings. It was that simple. That complex. Sometimes they required untangling, and sometimes she could ignore whatever knotted mess they held.

She'd go with the latter today.

"I do need to run home."

His eyes dropped.

"But I can be fast. I live close by."

As soon as his lips parted in a grin, her ketchup-covered stomach dropped. Why oh why had she said that? Stupid. Stupid. Stupid.

"Okay. I'll drive." There was no question in his words, only a logical plan he expected them to follow. Except his plan included him seeing where she lived. And worse, maybe coming inside.

Her left eyelid began to twitch, and she rubbed her fist against it. It didn't stop.

He walked to the passenger-side door of his coupe and pulled it open. In his best impression of a fairy-tale prince, he motioned for her to enter. Well, a prince with a twenty-year-old two-door carriage that probably had the actual horsepower of a couple of geldings. But the car was impeccable, inside and out. There were no residual water spots from the last rain marring its faded finish. No fast-food wrappers littering the floorboards. Not even the little mulberries tracked in on the rugs.

His car was pristine. She was not.

Holding out her arms, she did a little shimmy. "I'm a mess." Perhaps an unnecessary reminder since he was looking at her, but he seemed to have temporarily lost his good sense.

"Don't worry about it. I have seat protectors."

She'd barely noticed those in her previous trip in his car. She hadn't needed them. But now they were just one more reason he could take her to her home. She needed a new plan. But knowing she needed one and coming up with one were apparently two different things.

He just kept staring at her and gave her another little wave into the car while ketchup baked onto her skin, which promptly started sweating and sent the ketchup rolling once again.

You could have been home and changed by now. Why are you holding this up?

Because . . . because . . .

Great. Now she couldn't even answer her own questions.

Because you don't want him to know that you live in an apartment the size of a postage stamp above someone else's converted garage.

It was possible. Okay, probable.

Get over yourself.

"Are we going to stand outside and melt, or are we going to do this?" Ben asked.

She slid onto the fabric seat protector and immediately began to cook as he walked around and got in behind the steering wheel. No matter how hard the AC blasted, it couldn't cut through air thicker than water, and she held herself as still as possible to keep whatever was oozing down her skin from spreading.

Somehow she managed to give him directions to the house three blocks away, and he let out a low whistle as she pointed to it. It must have looked impressive to an outsider. The two-story main house had been repainted in dazzling blue in the last year. It nearly glowed with bright white shutters and gingerbread over a quaint veranda. A quintessential wooden porch swing squeaked in the wind as they got out of the car. Even among the other impressive homes in the neighborhood, this one stood out.

Ben moved toward the big house, and Millie cleared her throat, heat already making its way up her neck. "My place is over here."

He mumbled something and followed her around to the back of the house toward the two-story structure that had once been a garage and storage. And that was being generous. Where the house was updated and upgraded, the garage had received only just enough attention to call it habitable. Anything beyond that was up to the tenants. And she had exactly no skills in that vein and no money to put into it even if she did.

But at least the rent wasn't bad. And when her car refused to start, she could walk to the diner.

Again Ben walked toward the door on the first floor, and she nodded around the side of the structure. "I'm up there."

She hadn't noticed just how flimsy the wooden stairs were until there were two people on them. Suddenly she worried that a little pressure on the railing might send them both right over.

When they reached the landing, she quickly let them in

and looked anywhere but at Ben as he surveyed her home for the first time. It took him all of three seconds to spin around the single room—complete with a bed, kitchen, and table—and she hated herself for sneaking a peek at his reaction. At his smile.

"This looks like you."

"What? Small and a little grimy?"

He laughed but immediately pointed to a framed picture on the wall. "That must be Grandma Joy and Grandpa Zeke." She nodded, and he continued, "And the note on the fridge." He pointed to a white sheet of paper held up by a magnet. It said only, *It's all for Grandma.*

He leaned into her kitchen, looking at the stacks of mismatched plates and cups, which were visible on the shelves that were stand-ins for cabinets. "And the dishes are so eclectic." He sounded wowed.

But he likely wouldn't feel the same if he knew she'd gotten them all at the thrift store for fifty cents apiece. If he'd known that was her only option. Even saving and reusing paper plates had become too expensive.

"Well, let me just get cleaned up."

She grabbed some clothes from her closet and hurried to the bathroom. It was a bit of a tight squeeze, but she managed to slip out of her uniform, clean herself up, and put on fresh everything. She emerged from behind the accordion door to find Ben reading one of the books that were piled on the table.

Oh no.

"There's got to be something more interesting for you there." She tried to laugh it off, all the while praying he wouldn't realize just how fluffy and fairy tale-y the book in his hands really was.

She'd never gone for the bodice-ripper books. She much preferred leaving some things unread. There really wasn't anything to be embarrassed about.

Except that he—an academic and a lifelong student—would likely discover that she was a silly romantic through and through. And while she liked being a romantic, the thought of him thinking less of her made her stomach ache.

He looked up from the pages in his open hand and smiled. "I was just skimming. Seems like a fun story. Pirates and buried treasure and all that." Setting it back down on its stack, he motioned to the others. "So, I guess you like to read."

Pulling her hair back and fastening it with a rubber band, she nodded slowly. "Mostly just fiction." Since she didn't want to have to explain about the particular kinds of books she loved, she pointed toward the door. "Ready?"

He nodded and led the way, and they were soon on the road headed inland.

"Have you been to this house before?"

Millie's mind had been somewhere out the window and across the green fields, and she jumped at his question. "The house? To my grandma's house? Yes, I've been there. I grew up there."

The car swerved a little before Ben righted it. He worried his lip with his upper teeth for a long moment, and she could almost see the gears in his mind trying to parse her story.

There was no use hiding it—no reason to. "My parents took off when I was a toddler. They decided they didn't like being parents. It was too hard. Too exhausting. Too much." A lump formed in her throat, and she tried to swallow it away. But it refused to budge, so she cleared her throat and tried to speak around it. "They left me with Grandma Joy one day and never came back for me."

Okay, it was out there now. No taking it back. It just hung like a funeral shroud in his car, like she'd killed any chance of a normal conversation.

She opened her mouth to apologize for dropping a bomb on their road trip, but his question beat her to it. "You haven't seen them since?"

"Once, when I was seven or eight, I thought I saw my mom outside my school." She shrugged and tried to conjure up that memory and the hope it had carried for so many years. If it had really been her mother, then maybe she had wanted Millie. Maybe she had realized what a terrible mistake she'd made. Maybe she'd loved her.

But the memory was faded, like a book read too many times, its pages smeared and unclear. Maybe Millie's young eyes had seen what she so desperately hoped to.

"Wow."

She'd almost forgotten she wasn't alone, that she wasn't drumming up those old memories for her own private torture, as she usually did. "You probably had great parents, huh? Packed up your car and sent you off to college with a box of cookies and a tank of gas."

Ben snorted. "Hardly. My mom was a different sort. She was a bit of a hippie, and she never gave it up. We lived in communes and were always moving. She never seemed to have a job, and there was always a parade of guys staying with us." His knuckles on the steering wheel turned white and then relaxed as he took a deep breath.

Millie didn't want to ask. She didn't have any right to. But she did anyway. "Were you close with her?"

Ben licked his lips, which were working hard to fight a frown. He was silent so long that she thought he might not answer the question. Finally he shrugged. "My mom has a lot of problems. She made a lot of mistakes."

She nodded, giving him a silent nudge to keep going.

"When I was a kid, I thought she was the best. She always cut the crust off my PB&J sandwiches. Our house was mostly clean, and she pretty much let me do whatever I wanted."

"Where is she now?"

He didn't say anything, and his gaze never left the road.

"Do you know where she is?"

He gave a quick nod but didn't expound.

"Do you spend much time with her?"

"She's otherwise engaged. And she will be for another seven to ten." His words carried the tiniest hint of bitterness, and Millie's stomach fell to the floorboard.

There was no doubt what he meant. His mom was in prison. And he seemed to think she belonged there. But why?

She wanted to press. She wanted to ask for any teeny detail. But she had no right to do so, so she took a side path and asked something else she had no right to. "What about your dad?"

He narrowed his eyes at the road, and this time his knuckles didn't relax. "I never knew him. I'm not even sure my mom knew who he was."

He said it so matter-of-factly, but it twisted in her chest, tugged at her insides. That was Grandma Joy's story too. At least, that's what she believed.

"I'm sorry," she whispered. If there were other words to say, she didn't know them.

"It's all right." The words were more growl than she expected, and he coughed before continuing. "I made peace with that a long time ago."

She nodded toward a drive off the two-lane country road not even an hour from St. Simons. "Take that one." He did, and they bounced along the gravel toward a square, two-story white house. Its paint was chipped and unfamiliar trucks were parked next to rusted tractors in the yard, but her childhood home had never looked so wonderful.

As he parked the car, she blurted out a thought before it was fully formed. "Do you think that it would have made a difference—knowing your dad? At least knowing who he was?"

"I don't know. Maybe." He crawled out of the car and looked at her over its top. Shadows from the giant oak tree in the yard danced across his face. "Why?"

And then she said the very last thing she'd planned to. The very last thing she should have. "I wonder what difference it would have made if Grandma Joy had known about Claude Devereaux."

TWELVE

laude Devereaux. Grandma Joy and Claude Devereaux.

Ben stumbled to keep up with Millie, who marched toward the front door of the house. He might have called out to her and demanded to know the connection between her grandmother and the wealthiest family in Louisiana, except for the twitching blinds at the window.

Someone was inside and close. Someone whose help they needed. But all he wanted to do was grab Millie by the arm, spin her around, and insist she tell him the truth. Of course, if the wild look in her eyes right after she had spoken meant anything, she hadn't meant to tell him any of it. Not a single syllable.

He needed to know more than ever. But there wasn't time to uncover the truth when the front door at the top of a short flight of stairs swung open halfway. A young woman with mousy brown hair and a baby on her hip filled the opening. Her glare was enough to send goose bumps down his arms. He wouldn't be surprised if she had a shotgun at the ready.

But Millie wasn't deterred. Gravel crunched under her feet

with precise rhythm, and her shoulders squared, as though this home and all of its precious memories belonged to no one else.

"We already believe in Jesus. We don't got nothin' you want. We ain't buyin' nothing you've got." The woman— too young for that moniker, really—poked her chin toward their car. "You best be gettin' on your way. My Danny will be back soon enough."

"Ma'am, my name is Millie Sullivan." She spoke like the other woman hadn't cordially told them to get off her property. With a wave of her hand toward him, she said, "This is my friend Ben Thornton."

Maybe she leaned a little heavily on the word *friend*. Maybe he was reading too much into it, like everyone else seemed to be doing these days.

"I grew up in this house."

Millie was halfway up the stairs, and the woman had closed the door partway. Now only her eyes and scowl were visible through the crack. "We ain't interested in sellin'. We bought it fair and square."

Millie chuckled, and although he couldn't see her face, he could imagine her smile. She didn't have three quarters in her pocket, and this woman thought she wanted to buy the house out from under them. Not likely.

"Of course. You bought the home from my grandmother. Joy Sullivan?"

The door creaked to a stop, held open with the toe of a house shoe, and the scowl turned from distrust to curiosity. "Mrs. Sullivan? This was her family's home."

Millie nodded quickly, eating up the last couple steps to the top and meeting the other woman eye to eye. She reached out a hand and introduced herself again. "My name is Millie."

The woman's gaze dropped to the outstretched hand, her eyes narrowing. Finally she looked back up and toed the door open another six inches. "Samantha. Sam. Williams."

"I'm so happy to meet you." Millie reached out farther until Sam moved her baby to the other hip and opened the door enough to shake her hand.

"I met your grandma. She was a kind woman."

Millie nodded again. "She still is."

"Terrible what happened to her."

He still couldn't see Millie's face from his place at the bottom of the stairs, but he could see her back grow tense and her knees below her shorts lock. She mumbled something that sounded like agreement.

"What're you folks doing out here?" Sam made it sound like they were on top of a distant hill instead of forty miles outside of town among a sea of other family farms.

"I was hoping to ask for a favor."

Sam began to close the door again. "We ain't got much."

"Oh, no. It's nothing like that." Millie looked over her shoulder at him, and for a split second he forgot that she had been hiding something from him. He saw only the kindness in her smile, the warmth in her eyes. The reminder that they were a team—that he was part of a team. For the first time in his life.

The truth hit like a baseball bat to the gut—not that he'd ever swung one. He'd been on his own for so long that he'd forgotten what it meant not to have to do life alone—if he'd ever actually known. And it was nice. No, it was so much better than nice. As he tried to find the word to describe his life after meeting Millie, she offered Sam the barest minimum of their story.

"You see, my great-grandmother built this house with her husband, Henry, and my grandma thinks she may have left something here. Maybe paperwork of some sort. Have you ever found anything like that?"

Sam patted her gurgling baby on the back as he chewed on his own fist. She looked closely at Millie, then at Ben. Her gaze burrowed into them, searching out every half-truth and concealed lie. "What's her name?"

"My great-grandma? Ruth Holiday. Well, Ruth Jefferson after she married."

Sam's mouth dropped open like Millie had given the secret password, and she pushed the door all the way open. "We found a box of letters and such up in the attic. They was all addressed to Ruth. All of 'em."

Millie shot him another look, this one filled with hope. He bounded up the steps to her side as they followed Sam's sweeping arm into the house.

"Can we look at them?" Millie asked.

Sam nodded and closed the door behind them. It wasn't much cooler inside than it had been in the direct sun, and Ben hooked a finger into the collar of his shirt. It was already damp, and air thick enough to cut wasn't helping the situation. He added another roll to his sleeves. It didn't help either.

"You can have 'em if you can find 'em. They're up in the attic, far as I know. But there's some other stuff too."

"Some other stuff" turned out to be a euphemism for a lifetime of junk crammed into a space smaller than Millie's apartment and hotter than an oven. One small vent on the floor didn't do anything to keep air circulating except mock them for every deep breath they tried to secure. After climbing the pull-down ladder and traipsing into the gray unknown, Ben wasn't confident they'd find anything at all, except possibly a stubbed toe.

Millie walked right into an old chest and clapped her hand over her mouth. It didn't do much to muffle the subsequent scream. "Ow!"

"You all right?"

"I'll live. But they might have to take the whole foot." She dug into her pocket and pulled out her phone to turn on its flashlight while mumbling, "That's what I get for wearing flip-flops on a treasure hunt."

He followed her example and held up his light against the darkness. "I thought the treasure was at the Chateau. Aren't we just looking for clues?"

"Who knows at this point?" Her beam illuminated a pile of boxes, and she snaked her way toward it. "Over here."

They opened every lid and peered in every box. They found baby books and baby clothes and little pink baby shoes. They found photo albums and high school yearbooks from the 1950s. They found crayon drawings and pieces of art.

But there were no letters to Ruth.

Kneeling before the bottom box on the stack, Millie leaned back and crossed her arms. Her shoulders slumped, and her chin rested against her chest.

He couldn't blame her. She'd had a long day, and it was only midafternoon. They were both covered in dust and sweat, and he'd give his car for a glass of sweet tea right about then.

Pushing himself off the floor, he followed the beam of his

flashlight through the maze of wicker and wooden furniture. For people who claimed not to have much, the Williams family sure did have a lot of junk. But he kept going, searching for anything cardboard. Preferably it would have the name Ruth scrawled along the side. But he'd settle for anything that looked out of place.

Deeper in, he had to duck his head to keep from smashing it against a beam. And that's when he saw it. Covered in dust and buried beneath a mound of old painting tarps was a white box—or at least it had been white at some point in its life.

It scraped along the wooden floor as he pulled it out from its hiding place and flipped the lid open. It was filled with papers yellowed with time. Newspapers and stationery. Envelopes and postcards. And a bundle of them were tied up with blue ribbon.

"Millie. I found it."

Scraping and scratching to move things out of her path, she clawed her way across the narrow room. She didn't have to duck, and she didn't slow down until she reached him, her hands landing on his back. "What is it?"

"Look at all these letters."

She knelt down, the sagging of her shoulders all but gone. Gently she lifted one of the envelopes from the mess below and pulled out the letter. "George." She said his name in hushed reverence, and Ben racked his brain for any memory of the man from what Millie had told him of the diary. Certainly she hadn't told him every little detail, but he knew that George had been important to Ruth.

"The gardener?"

She nodded. "She . . . she broke things off with him—"

Looking up, she shook her head. "No. That's not quite right. They were never seeing each other."

He was listening to her. Mostly. Except when he undid the ribbon bow around the packet of letters and pulled the first note free. His eyes skimmed the contents, and his stomach twisted into a loop tighter than the script on the page.

Millie rambled on. "She told him she couldn't spend time with him anymore because of—"

"Claude Devereaux."

Her eyes went wide, and she nearly dropped the letter in her hand.

The truth seared through him, and he wanted to yell at her that he had a right to know, that he deserved to know. Instead, he took a deep breath in through his nose and let it out through his mouth.

"What exactly is it with Devereaux and your family? What did you mean earlier about if your grandmother had known about him?"

"Nothing." She looked away as though holding his gaze was far too much weight for her to carry. It seemed the pressure of knowing too much and telling him too little covered all of her as she sagged against the box and put her head in her hands. "I don't know what to say." Her fingers muffled her words as the paper crinkled in her fist.

A twinge of heartburn caught him off guard, and he smashed his fist into the spot right below his sternum. It didn't do much to stem the fire, which could have been a product of betrayal.

But that would require him to care about Millie and whatever they had shared. He didn't. He wouldn't. He'd felt sorry for her. He'd been intrigued by her offer. He'd wondered how she was making ends meet caring for Grandma Joy all by herself.

He did not care about her. Not even a little bit.

Yeah, that wasn't true either.

"I'm sorry." When she finally looked his way again, she'd rubbed two sooty black stains around her eyes. "I should have told you before. I meant to. I planned on it. I wanted to. I just thought that . . . that if I did . . ."

"I wouldn't help you." He didn't have to be a great detective or treasure hunter to put those pieces together.

She nodded. "I do need your help. But also"—she took a big breath that filled her shoulders and lifted her chin even higher—"I like your help."

"You have a funny way of showing it." He could have bitten his own tongue off. He had no business being so outright rude to her. She was obviously about to tell him something important, and he'd just given her every reason to leave him behind. Pressing his forefinger and thumb into his eyes, he sighed. "I'm sorry. Go on."

Biting her lips until they nearly disappeared, she lifted one shoulder. "No. You're right. And if you want to walk away, I won't blame you."

"Just—" He ran his fingers through his hair and pressed his other hand to his waist. He could take her up on her offer and walk away forever. The money wasn't going to be enough to make much of a difference in his life anyway. Okay, sure, it was better than nothing. But it wasn't going to change his course. He was still going to have to work three jobs, still going to have to make right what he could. "Just tell me what's actually happening here. Who is Devereaux to you?"

197

"I don't know for sure. That's what I'm trying to figure out. That's what I'm hunting for." She held up the letters in her hands. "Claude was at the Chateau the same summer that Ruth was there."

"You already told me that."

"But . . . but . . ." She seemed to be searching for words, and he wanted to throw the pile of envelopes with Devereaux's seal at the wall.

"Just tell me when this all started. Tell me why you took the job at the Chateau. Tell me whatever you want. Just tell me the truth." His voice had risen with each word, and suddenly a dog outside the house barked loudly. He refused to let it distract him from watching her reaction.

Another deep breath. Another long pause. Her gaze wandered to a different time and place. And then she started, presumably at the beginning.

"I was visiting Grandma Joy at the home a couple months ago. She looked at me so closely, like she could see right into my heart. And then she said the strangest thing: 'You are your father's daughter.' I laughed because she'd often said how much I looked like him. Then she got very serious. It was strange, but I knew that she remembered. She was fully lucid in that moment, and she said, 'But I'm not.'"

He sucked in a sharp breath, but Millie didn't give him time to digest the information. This wasn't a performance with perfectly delivered lines.

"I asked her who her dad was, and she laughed a little. It definitely wasn't Henry, the man Ruth married. But Grandma Joy didn't seem to know. She kept saying that there was more than treasure buried at the Chateau. She said the truth would be there too."

"And that's when she told you about the diary." He didn't actually ask a question, but she nodded anyway.

"Grandma Joy was born in April of 1930, so it doesn't take much math to put it together. Ruth must have been with Joy's father that summer, the summer she was at the Chateau."

He crossed his arms and took a step back. "And you hoped it was Devereaux?"

"No!" She shook her head hard. "I mean, I do. But I didn't even know he was there that summer until after Grandma Joy told me about the diary. I had no idea who it might be. But I knew there were wealthy guests at the estate."

"And now that you have letters to her from Claude Devereaux, filled with bad poetry and offering a role in one of his upcoming radio productions?"

"What?" She jumped to her feet and reached for the letter he'd only skimmed. "He was going to give her a job?"

Letting go of the slip of paper, he watched as her eyes devoured every word, every detail. "What does her diary actually say? How close was their relationship?"

She looked back up, and even in the gray room, he could see the pink flames licking at her neck.

"Close. He . . . he's the one who pulled her into that alcove to kiss her."

Naturally. He knew that had been a romantic rendezvous. He just hadn't guessed that it involved a poor girl from central Georgia and a man whose family could swim in their millions a la Scrooge McDuck.

"That one kiss—that's a pretty thin connection. And a big leap to having a child out of wedlock."

She cringed, but she had to know.

"Devereaux never married a woman named Ruth. He managed to keep his radio empire afloat during the Depression, and then he married a Rockefeller cousin. That's historical fact."

He should punch himself. Not for telling the truth but for enjoying it quite so much. He hated that he took even an ounce of pleasure in watching the light in her eyes dim.

"I know they weren't married." A muscle in her jaw jumped, and she wrapped her arms around her middle, beginning to collapse on herself. "I know I'm not a legitimate heir. Ruth would have clung to that name for her whole life. There's no way Joy would have become a Jefferson if she didn't have to be."

"Then why put everything on the line looking for that connection?"

"Because even being an illegitimate heir might be enough to provide for my grandma."

And there it was. The whole truth. Everything she'd done had been for Joy—just like the note on her fridge said. For Joy, who had put her life on hold to care for a little girl. It was Millie's turn to repay the sacrifice.

And God help him, he wanted to help her. He had plenty of other wrongs to right and no time to waste on a ridiculous chase—first a treasure they had no claim to, and now a heritage that she couldn't rightfully call her own. Apparently it didn't matter.

"Let's get the letters." He snatched them out of her hand and shoved them back in the box. He slammed the lid back on it, not really sure if he was angrier with her for keeping all of this from him for so long, or with himself for so quickly deciding he'd let it go. He wanted to hold on to at least a glimmer of annoyance. After all, he'd managed to despise his mother for years.

So why was Millie so different? She hadn't exactly lied to him. Neither had his mother.

Still, Millie should have told him what she was really after. She should have let him decide if he wanted to be caught up in all of that.

Millie looked from the box in his arms to his face and back again as he stood. "What? What are you doing?"

"Sam said we could take them. They might have information about Ruth and Claude, right?" He nearly spit the words over his shoulder as he marched a winding path through the attic.

"Y'all doing okay up there?"

Speaking of Sam, there she was. Within earshot, and probably curious to boot why two strangers had spent more than an hour in her attic.

"We're on our way down," he called, moving to the top of the ladder. Turning back to Millie, he lowered his voice. "This time we're going to split up the reading responsibilities, and you're going to tell me everything."

"So you're still with me?"

Narrowing his gaze on her, he adjusted the box in his arms before letting out a soft sigh. "I've done some stupid things in my life, and this may be one of them, but I'm with you until we find that treasure."

August 12, 1929

My dearest Ruth,

I have been distraught without you this past week. Atlanta holds no comparison to your beauty, and I long to return to the Chateau, to your side. I yearn to hold you in my arms once again, to press my lips to yours.

I know you would tell me not to say such things, but I must. For I feel them so fully that I fear they will consume me mind, body, and soul. I hope that they do.

As I walked from the studio to my hotel room tonight, I saw a star in the heavens that could only offer a fraction of your beauty. I sat on a park bench to stare at it but managed only to think of you. These lines came to my mind.

> *How I miss her skin so fair*
> *And silken hair.*
> *She is brighter than the moon,*
> *Her song lovelier than the loon.*
> *I am hers,*
> *Like the cat that purrs.*
> *She has the sweetest kiss,*
> *It is she that I miss.*

I am very busy at the studio here. There is much to be done to launch the new production. My friend Orson warned me of such things, but I foolishly thought that I could spend most of my summer at the Chateau and trust my staff to have everything in place. They are working hard, but they do not have my vision. I suppose that is why I am in charge. Also, it is because I have put up the money to get the production begun.

We are nearly ready, and I wish I had a woman of your talents on set. But the others are under contract, and there is nothing to be done until the next production, or until the writers write a new character. She will be lovely and have the sweetest smile in the world. Would you like that, my dear?

I will be back to the Chateau soon, and you will be the first person I seek out. When I do, I hope to have good news and an important question to ask you.

Yours completely,
Claude D.

August 12, 1929

Miss Holiday,

Perhaps my letter is no less improper than taking you on a picnic or walking with you around the house, but I must check on you. Since we discovered Miss Abernathy under that tree, you have not been yourself. Your smile is a mere ghost of what it can be. You seem quite unwell.

It would be an honor to offer my services to you. I know of a distraction that might take your mind off the shock of what you saw. You need only call on me.

George

August 14, 1929

Miss Holiday,

   Your thanks is not required. I only wish to see your joy restored, and I knew that a trip to the southern creek and the opportunity to put your feet in the water there might help you find a moment of peace, as it has for me. There is such a restorative quality in the sound of the water bubbling back out to the sea.

   I am ever your friend. And as your friend, I must tell you the truth. You asked me on our walk down to the beach what I think of Mr. Devereaux. You must know that we see very different sides of him.

   Quite honestly, I neither like nor trust the man. He is too polished among your people and quite the opposite among the staff. The maids talk of him wandering below stairs after having far too much to drink. I have no proof of it, but I believe that Jenny might have been accused and dismissed for reasons completely unrelated to the things stolen in the big house.

   This is no indictment on you or anyone else in the house. But I cannot in good conscience encourage you to continue a relationship with him.

   I remain ever yours.

9

THIRTEEN

*J*umper! Jumper! He's coming over the south fence. This is not a drill. All hands to the south lawn."

Ben clenched his jaw until he thought his teeth might crack, but he still managed to run. Pressing his walkie-talkie to his cheek, he responded to the call from the security office. "I'm on my way." He was panting already, his chest heaving just to snatch a breath from the evening air. Or maybe it was the sudden thundering in his chest that kept his lungs from doing their job.

He wasn't supposed to do this. He was a historian, a reader of books, a studier of the past. He was not a chaser of kids who thought it would be a good idea to trespass on private museum property ten minutes before closing time.

The house was ablaze in all of its nighttime glory, golden lights lending their glow to the monstrous silhouette. The arches of the front portico were filled with potted palm trees, and he fell off the cement path in an attempt to dodge one.

The final tour of the night was just wrapping up, and the

entrance had long since been abandoned. If the jumper was headed his way, he hadn't made it very far.

As he rounded the last corner of the building and turned into the south lawn with its palms blowing in the wind, he spotted the lone figure. While he was little more than a shadow, one thing was clear. This wasn't a kid. This was a fully grown man—all five and a half feet of his height and nearly that much around his middle.

The man swung a long metal rod from his hand, and for a moment Ben thought it was a cane. But that would have been some feat to climb the wall—even with the aid of a ladder—and need help to walk. Then the man swooped the rod along the grass in rotating circles, and Ben's stomach clenched.

It was a metal detector. This man was looking for something buried on the grounds.

The man looked up, straight at Ben, and he swore a single word that fully expressed the situation. He looked as surprised to see Ben as he was to be seen.

"Well, I figured you'd all be gone by now." There was a note of disappointment in the man's words, and Ben knew how he felt. He'd taken this job in part because the pay was relatively good and in part because they'd promised him that no one had tried to break into the Chateau in twenty years. It was revered and respected by the locals, and no one was interested in defacing the property or barging into the grounds.

It didn't hurt that most of the locals were senior citizens, their hooligan years long since gone. And the visiting youngsters looking to carouse on their spring breaks could find better bars and more trouble in Brunswick on the mainland. Even this time of year, the island was filled with tourist families who didn't trouble the locals much. Which made what he was seeing at the moment a little hard to believe.

The man had to be at least sixty, and his hair was more silver than black. It reflected the moon as he hung his head and jammed the toe of his black sandal into the ground.

"I thought your last tour was at eight." His tone suggested that Ben had personally lied to him.

Ben nodded slowly, shining his flashlight toward the man's metal detector, which was still moving in smooth circles. "It is. It begins at eight and lasts an hour."

The man looked at his watch and swore again. The realization of his poor timing visibly dawned on him.

"Can I ask what you're doing here, Mr. . . . ."

"Fazetti. Milo Fazetti." He shrugged. "I heard there might be something worth finding here. Thought since I was close by, I might beat the rush."

Ben froze, everything inside him screaming that he had to be mistaken. He had to have misunderstood. There was no way that Milo Fazetti—of the loud Hawaiian print and socks with sandals—knew about the treasure. He couldn't possibly have heard about Ruth's prize. The one that no one had looked for in almost ninety years. Ben had searched the treasure-hunting websites just weeks before. There hadn't even been rumors of sparkling silver at the Chateau.

But what other treasure could it be? Carl knew everything about the history of this island. And even he knew of only one rumored treasure—Ruth's. The truth was that the Chateau had only hosted guests for two summers. It had closed quickly after the stock market crash. And after that there had been no one wealthy enough to leave any treasure of substance behind.

They had to be looking for the same treasure. But how did Milo know about it?

"Well, I'm afraid you beat the rush by a few hours too many. Would you mind coming with me? You're trespassing on private property."

Milo shrugged. "If I buy a ticket, can I walk around the grounds?"

"I'm afraid not. Our last tour of the day is coming to a close, and you're about to be banned from this property for at least a year."

"A *year*?" Milo sounded like he'd been sentenced to life in prison. "Do you know how many yahoos will get here in the next year? I can't wait a year."

Ben's stomach sank, and his shoes suddenly felt heavier than cement. How many treasure-hunting yahoos *could* get there in a year? More than he and the Chateau's crack security team of two retirees and a college kid could keep at bay, that was for sure. And there was no telling how fast the wave would approach. They might not have Ruth's diary, but they would sure have the numbers to unearth something. And do it before he and Millie could.

That would leave him and Millie right where they had been at the start. Broke and in need of at least one small miracle.

God, if you're waiting for me to ask, this is me asking. We could really use a miracle right about now.

Millie paced the length of the corridor, her tennis shoes nearly silent on the concrete. She checked her watch again. Nine twenty-seven. They'd agreed on nine fifteen, and she'd arrived two minutes early.

Ben still wasn't here.

He'd said there had been something interesting in a letter he'd read, one of them from Claude. He thought it pointed to a spot in the house. He thought it was worth checking for the other diary, and she had to agree.

The trouble was, she didn't know what the location was. And Ben was nowhere to be found. She texted him again and was greeted only by the call of an owl from its perch in a nearby tree.

"Not helpful," she mumbled as she traipsed the hall yet again, her insides winding tighter and tighter. The stucco arches gave her a view of the waves, their crests glowing white in the moonlight and orange in the reflection of the house. If only she could be as patient and serene as those waves.

Not likely.

Putting her hands to her hips, she blew her bangs out of her face and tucked a stray curl behind her ear. It was crispy from hair spray, and suddenly her scalp and shoulders itched from the three-inch coating they'd received at the start of the night. Her hair had stayed in place, the knot at her neck both graceful and rigid, and apparently so had her skin.

Twitching for a shower, she looked at her watch again. Nine twenty-nine.

Still no sign of him. Either he'd forgotten or he'd run into trouble or he'd set her up.

But why would he set her up? To send her to a deserted hallway in order to keep her out of his hair? While he did what? Searched the spot where the diary might be?

Her brain was filling in the answers to questions faster than she could ask them, and every single one was the worst possible scenario. Every single one sent her pulse racing and her head throbbing and her heart plummeting.

Stupid treasure. Stupid Ben. Stupid her for trusting him.

But he forgave you when you told him the truth about Devereaux.

Stupid conscience for making sense.

The nonsensical arguments worked much better for her. They kept her safe. Safe from relying on anyone else. Safe from trusting too much. Safe from being let down. Again.

"Millie."

At first she thought the sound of her name had been only a mixture of birdcalls and waves against the beach. And then she heard the slapping of feet against the floor. Hurried and urgent, they raced toward her from behind.

"I'm sorry I'm late."

She spun on him, her fists at her sides and her tongue ready to slice. But something about the wildness of his hair—as though he'd been running his hands through it over and over again—and the wideness of his eyes spoke a different truth. He hadn't stood her up. At least not on purpose.

"We have a problem."

Her heart stopped, her breath vanishing with it. "What happened?" was all she could muster on the tail of her gasp.

"There was a trespasser. Someone jumped the fence."

She shook her head. Why should that matter to them?

"He had a metal detector. He's after a treasure. And he's not alone."

Seconds passed as his words sank in. Her knees gave out, and she slumped to the ground, her back pressed to the wall. Wrapping her arms around her bare legs, she tucked them under her chin and tried to process what he was saying. This wasn't fiction. This was real life.

Someone else knew about the Chateau's secrets.

He sagged down beside her, stretching out his legs and gasping for breath. It looked like he'd run a marathon.

"What did he say—the kid who jumped the fence? How did he know?"

Ben shook his head. "He's no kid. He's old enough to be my dad. And he's not alone. There's an article about the Chateau on a website for amateur treasure hunters. They don't have a clue what they're looking for, but they're looking."

"They?"

Ben shook his head and drummed his fingers against his knees. "He said he was the first."

The first of how many? How had word gotten on that site?

The truth zapped her. She hadn't told a soul. Which meant . . . She straightened up, forcing herself not to wave her finger in his face. "Who did you tell?"

"Me? I didn't tell anyone. Who did you tell?"

"Why would I tell someone?"

"You told me."

She gasped. He had *not* just thrown that at her. "I had to tell you. You were going to get me kicked off the property. Besides, if I hadn't, you wouldn't know about any of this."

"So it stands to reason that if anyone else was threatening your chance to search the property, you'd tell them too."

Squaring her shoulders, she turned to face him full on. "Well, *you're* the only one who's threatened to have me fired."

"And I wouldn't have if you hadn't been in the library on the other side of the velvet ropes."

"So you're saying this is all my fault." Something bubbled in her chest, something she couldn't name and didn't really care to. It was unsettling and a bit annoying. Because they were fighting—and she couldn't remember the last time she'd had such a good time.

Maybe this wasn't really fighting. Maybe it was just a squabble. There was something serious at its root, but all she could focus on was the crinkle at the corner of his eye. It always did that when he was smiling. Or about to smile. Or thinking about smiling. That was something she knew about him.

And also that he'd stayed with her. When he had every right to walk away, he'd stayed.

And she knew he was a good man, a kind man, a hero. Villains didn't hold your grandma's hand while she had a complete break from reality. Villains didn't hold *you* and tell you they would stay by your side until it all worked out.

If her life were written in the pages of a book, one thing would be abundantly clear. Ben was the hero. Whether she was the heroine was still up for debate.

"What about your friend from the library?" she asked.

"My boss, Carl?"

She nodded and crossed her arms so they landed with a resounding thump.

"Yes, I told him. I'd also trust him with my life. But he already knew about the rumors of hidden treasure anyway. He's known for years. Why would he wait until now to tell someone else? Besides, he wouldn't know how to post in a forum if you paid him."

She hadn't met Carl, and she had absolutely no picture of him in her mind, so it was easy to fabricate him to fit her story. "Maybe he's been waiting for the diary, and now that he knows we have it, he'll be after us both. First he'll cut the brake lines on your car so you go careening off a cliff and die in a fiery crash. But that's okay with him because you didn't have the diary anyway. Then he'll be after me, stalking me at my house, only he'll miss the C on the street address and think that I live in the big house too."

Ben's eyes grew bigger with each word, each wildly concocted scenario. He opened his mouth as if planning to refute her story, but instead he laughed. Booming and full, the sound echoed around them, bouncing off palm trees and stone archways alike. "Just what kind of books have you been reading?"

"What?" She pinched her lips together, bracing every ounce of her being against the smile that wanted to escape. True, that brake-line plot had appeared in one of the books she'd borrowed from the library. It had involved embezzled money and an angry lawyer. It hit too close to home to really enjoy, but she'd gotten a giggle out of the ridiculous villain nonetheless. Just as she'd hoped, Ben had too.

"There's one flaw with that plan."

"Oh?"

"If Carl killed me, he'd have to do all the grunt work at the library. No way would he willingly get rid of me before lining up a replacement."

"Oh." No matter how hard she pursed her lips to the side, she could feel the smile breaking loose. "Then maybe not Carl."

"Decidedly not Carl." His grin matched her own.

Resting her head against the wall at her back, she watched the hanging moss play in the wind. Even the leaves got in a good rustle or two between the night birds calling. "But then who? If neither of us have said anything . . ." Suddenly her stomach clenched, and she pressed both hands over her middle.

"Grandma Joy." She could only whisper the words, and Ben leaned closer, his brows knitted together and his features tight.

"Huh?"

"Grandma Joy. What if she told someone? She might not even remember that she did. But it would have been so easy to just . . ." She waved her hand, and his eyes followed it, understanding lighting them.

"It could be anyone. It could be that administrator at the home."

"Virginia Baker."

He nodded quickly. "Or one of the nurses. Or a cleaning person. Or even a guest."

"You think the guy that broke in here tonight has been to the assisted living home?"

With a sharp shake of his head, he rejected her premise. "No. But someone who has been there told the world. Milo— the guy who climbed the fence—"

"How'd he get over the wall?"

"Ladders. A metal one on the outside and a rope one on the inside."

She motioned for him to keep going.

"Milo said he was trying to beat the rush. He thinks there's going to be a rush. In fact, he offered me a fifty-fifty cut if I'd give him unfettered access to the grounds."

She tried to chuckle, but it came out arid and tired. "I might have liked this guy."

He raised his eyebrows. "You certainly have something in common."

"When will the others get here?"

"Soon."

Despite the humidity that made her skin sticky with sweat, she shivered at the very thought. They were about to be inundated by people looking for the same thing they were. And not just anyone. These people might be amateurs. They might be pros. Either way, they knew more about finding treasure than she and Ben combined. And without Ruth's other diary, they were fishermen without lines.

"Speaking of the grounds—"

"Were we?"

"Yes. Before. Whatever." She flapped her hands in front of her to clear away the conversation in her mind. "The security manager knows now."

He nodded.

"Things here are going to get a lot tighter, aren't they?"

He nodded again.

"Like tonight."

One more nod.

"What are you supposed to be doing right now?" she asked.

"Officially I'm searching the grounds for any signs of other intruders." He pushed himself off the floor and rose to his feet. "Speaking of which, I guess I should get to that."

"So we're not going to check out Ruth's favorite spot?"

He reached out his hand, and she slipped hers into it. The muscles in his forearm bunched, and suddenly she was standing in front of him. *Right* in front of him. She had to put her free hand up to keep from bumping into his chest, and all of a sudden she could feel the lean muscles there, the ones she'd only glimpsed before.

Glancing up into his face, she could feel his breath in her hair. Slowly—so slowly, as though he was asking permission—he wound a finger into a curl that had escaped that night.

She wanted to lean into his hand, to press her cheek to his fingers and feel his touch. But the only thing she could see was his mouth, his perfect lips, firm and sure and entirely kissable.

She'd gone over the edge. She'd turned into one of those heroines in her books who swooned over a man. But she didn't care one bit.

Or maybe . . . maybe she was more like her great-grandma than she wanted to admit. Ruth had swooned over Claude, without question. Maybe in this very hallway they'd stopped for a short embrace. Maybe they'd kissed and sighed and whispered sweet nothings.

In this moment, that's all she wanted to do with Ben. All she could see were his lips and all she could think about were those lips on hers.

"Millie."

The lips in question said her name. It wasn't so much an inquiry as an urging. She just didn't know what he was urging her to do. She didn't actually care. As long as it meant they could be closer, as long as it closed the distance between them.

Beneath her hand, his heart beat steady, while her pulse pounded a wild tattoo at her throat. He leaned an inch closer to her. Or maybe she'd pressed into him. It didn't matter. It only mattered that they were there—well, almost there.

"Millie?" This time it was definitely a question, and she

managed to raise her gaze to the same emotion reflected in his eyes. He wanted to know that this was okay. That this was all right. That she wanted this as much as he did. That—

"Ben? You still out there?" The walkie-talkie on his belt crackled with the call, and Ben froze. Then he leaned back, his smile filled with regret.

"This is Ben."

"You see anything out there?"

"No, sir. The beachfront is clear. I'm on my way to the north wall now."

His supervisor gave him the go-ahead, and he squeezed her hand before dropping it. "Next time we're working together, we'll check Ruth's favorite spot."

"But where is it?"

"Where would Devereaux think it was?"

FOURTEEN

"He's not here today," Millie said.

"Well, I can see that. But he should be. He's such a handsome young man."

Millie rolled her eyes at her grandma's clear matchmaking attempt and leaned back a few inches. Grandma Joy's eyes were bright, her cheeks pink, and her gaze focused today. Too bad Ben wasn't here to see it.

Yeah, that's why you want Ben here.

Oh, be quiet.

Her mind had been telling her all sorts of things, poking and prodding about what might have been, what almost had been.

But that's all it was. An *almost*. Anyway, maybe it would have been terrible. What if there were no sparks?

Oh, there were sparks when you were five feet away from him.

Pipe down.

What if he was a slobbery kisser? What if *she* was a slobbery kisser?

You're never going to know if you're a good kisser or not if you don't actually do it.

Seriously. Be quiet.

What if they kissed and it was so bad that they couldn't even look at each other?

Really? You think that kissing him could be bad?

Well, maybe not for her, but what about for him? What if he thought it was so bad that he never wanted to kiss her again, and then they were stuck working together, but it was completely awkward and he felt obligated to keep helping her?

How come the heroines in her books never wondered if they were good kissers? How come they just kissed and it was always perfect and wonderful and magical? How come there were always fireworks in the books? What if there were never fireworks in real life?

Her hands clenched into fists at her stomach, and she fell back against her grandma's pillows, wrinkling the previously made bed.

"What are you thinking about, sweetheart?" Grandma Joy rocked back and forth, her eyes closed but somehow fully seeing.

"Nothing."

Creak. Creak. The chair announced each movement. "I thought you came here to make me my favorite soup. Sounds like you're just telling me stories instead."

Millie pushed herself up and took a deep breath, hoping it would wipe Ben and whatever had almost happened—good or bad—from her mind. It did not. She tried to fake it anyway.

"Of course I'm here to make you soup." She was there for

information too, but Grandma Joy didn't need to know that was the heart of the reason.

Walking over to the kitchenette—the standard two burners and four cupboards in each resident's room—Millie took a long look at her grandma. She still looked lucid and thoughtful.

As she pulled a small cutting board from a cupboard and carrots from her own grocery bag, she took a quick breath. "Grandma, we can't find Ruth's other diary."

"Mama's diary?"

Oh no. Already? Grandma Joy sounded distant, fading into the past—or a murky version of it.

Millie swiped the peeler over the length of the carrots harder than was necessary, already seeing where this conversation was going. Nowhere.

"You found my mama's diary."

"Yes, but there is another one." She wanted to ask if her grandma remembered. She wanted to beg her to recall what they'd already talked about. But it would do no good. With each whack of the knife against the carrot, she imagined dementia could be cut and destroyed just as easily. She wished it was so.

"You told me that already."

Millie jumped and turned around. Grandma Joy's eyes were wide open. "Yes. I did tell you that."

"Where do you think it is?" Her features turned thoughtful.

"I don't know. We found a note that makes it sound like Ruth thought someone was reading her diary, so she moved it. But I don't know if it was the first or the second. And I have no clue where she would have moved it to."

With a nod, Grandma Joy asked, "What does your handsome young man think?"

Millie tried not to focus on the reminder of handsome Ben or the implication that he was hers. Instead she thought about what he'd said the night before. "He thinks it might be in her favorite place on the grounds."

"And he knows where that is?"

"Well, we found some letters from—" She slammed on the brakes nearly too late. She couldn't very well drop the name Claude Devereaux to her grandmother. Especially not when it was entirely possible that Joy had been the one to leak word about the treasure to the rest of the world. Accidentally, of course. But remembering to keep secrets required remembering. Not Grandma Joy's strong suit.

Her stomach twisted at the thought of not telling the whole truth—or even what she guessed was the truth. But this was too important to do wrong. And letting word slip out to the rest of the world that there might be another heir to Claude Devereaux's fortune was doing it wrong. She needed proof. No court would call for a DNA test if she didn't have probable cause. That family likely received a hundred fake claims on their money every day. She didn't want to be just another huckster begging for a handout.

She wasn't prepared to fight the court of public opinion. Not until she was ready to fight in a court of law. Of course, she hoped it never got to that level. She prayed that the family would see her plight, understand that Claude's own daughter was in need, and offer a lump sum that would care for Grandma Joy until her dying day.

But first Millie needed more than a scrap of evidence that

he had been her great-grandfather, that Ruth hadn't married him but had still given birth to his child.

Millie looked at her grandma and tried to see in her the dark hair and olive complexion of the Devereaux family. But all she could make out were stooped shoulders from a lifetime of hard labor and eyes that, when focused, told of losing the love of her life.

Pouring chicken broth and water into a saucepan, she tried to pick up where she'd left off with fewer details, grateful that her grandma was prone to long silences and hadn't bothered asking a follow-up question. "We found some letters that Ruth had saved. One of them, from another guest at the Chateau that summer, identified her favorite spot on the grounds. We thought we'd check there."

"Oh, I know her favorite spot. She talked of it often. The very southeast corner of the estate, where the ocean meets the creek. She loved to put her feet in the water. It was cold. She said that when she was pregnant with me, she would put her feet in to keep her ankles from swelling and to listen to the sound of the wind through the moss of the trees."

Millie opened her mouth to argue. The estate didn't have a piece of land like that. The southernmost point along the beach was just a typical beach. No inlet. No copse of trees. Maybe the estate had covered more ground back then.

Or maybe Grandma Joy was remembering wrong. That wouldn't be the first—or last—time.

Her soup base boiled, and she dumped her chopped vegetables into it, stirring slowly, watching the bubbles pop and the steam rise.

There was no point in telling Grandma Joy that she was wrong, so instead Millie diced rotisserie chicken and measured rice and tried to think of something encouraging to say. But before she could come up with a full phrase, Grandma Joy dropped a bomb.

"So they're going to make me move."

Millie spun around, the wooden spoon in her hand at the ready. "Who told you that?"

"My nurse. She's a silly little girl, always giggling when she gives me my medication." She sounded completely detached, like she didn't fully comprehend what she was saying, but it didn't stop her from going on. "She said I'm too much of a handful, but I've been behaving myself. I didn't even point out when that Mrs. Baker had her skirt tucked into her tights."

With a snort and giggle, Millie covered her face. Her shoulders shook until her laughter couldn't be contained and pealed through the room.

"Well, I didn't." Grandma Joy looked nearly offended. "They don't rightly like it when I correct them, so I let her go on out the door with her fanny flapping in the breeze, bless her heart."

Gasping for breath, Millie said, "Please tell me you didn't."

"I most certainly did." Hands on her hips and rocker still going back and forth, she nodded. "It was either that or get a full tongue lashin' for speaking my piece. Why would I want that?"

When Millie finally got her laughter under control, Grandma Joy looked at her, arms folded across her stomach. "Are they really going to make me move?"

Sometimes the questions were easy to answer. Lately they were hard. All of them.

Lying would be easier than telling the truth. And Grandma

Joy might not remember. They might have to have this conversation a hundred times. Did it really matter if she told one little white lie?

Yes. It did.

If she was willing to lie to the woman who had raised her as her own, who wouldn't she lie to? She wouldn't start with Grandma Joy.

"It looks like it. They . . . they say that you deserve more specialized care. And they can't give you that attention here."

"So where am I going to go?"

"I'm not sure." Millie turned back to the simmering soup, anything to keep from admitting that she had exactly zero plans and twenty days to make one happen.

"We have the money for a nicer place. Why not let me move in there?"

Giving her soup another stir, Millie shook her head. "We don't have the money."

"Sure we do. What about the money from the sale of the house? It sold for better than we asked." Grandma sounded so certain that it stabbed Millie through the chest. She leaned against the counter just to keep herself upright.

Taking a deep breath, she reiterated her personal decision. If she was willing to lie to Grandma Joy, she'd lie to anyone. So she wasn't going to start here. It wasn't an option even to stretch the truth. So she took a deep breath and said the most honest thing she could. "That money's gone."

"Well, what happened to it? We just had it."

Millie nearly choked on the lump in her throat. It had all happened before the diagnosis. Before they knew why her memory failed so often. Before Millie had been the responsible one.

She should have stepped in sooner. She should have stopped her. She should have stopped it all. But she hadn't.

"You invested it."

Grandma Joy rubbed her head, as though trying to conjure the memory gave her a raging migraine. "Invested it? Of course not. I would never put my money in the stock market. My mama taught me better than that."

Tears pricked at the corners of Millie's eyes, and she had to keep her back to Grandma Joy. She made a couple listless motions with the wooden spoon in the pan, but even the bright orange carrots bobbing in the broth faded from view. "I'm sorry, Grandma, but you did. You gave it all to Aspire Investments."

As her grandmother muttered that it couldn't be true, Millie could still see the computer screen in her mind, her grandma's savings account showing a giant zero. She could imagine the face of the person willing to target the older generations. He looked a whole lot like Captain Hook from *Peter Pan*, all sinister, twirly mustache. Or that really terrible child catcher from *Chitty Chitty Bang Bang*. Or Honest John from *Pinocchio*.

Probably the latter. Grandma Joy would have taken note of twirling mustaches. She never would have trusted someone like that. But someone came to her, promising to be her friend. Promising to help her double the money from the sale of her house. Promising that Millie would be taken care of for a very long time.

And Grandma Joy had written a check and handed it over.

This wasn't the first time they'd had this conversation, rehashed the past. It probably wouldn't be the last. But somehow this hurt more than it should. For Grandma Joy the truth was new information. For Millie it was a frequent and searing reminder that she'd failed to protect the person she owed everything to. It was a push that she needed to find that treasure. It was a confirmation that she needed to find evidence of exactly who her great-grandfather really was.

Please, Lord, let it be Claude Devereaux. The prayer popped to mind before she could even form it.

Truthfully, those were the only prayers happening these days. Between two jobs, Grandma Joy, a treasure, and a man who kept coming to mind even when he shouldn't, it wasn't easy to think about praying. It was even harder to go to church.

If Grandma Joy knew that, she'd threaten to take a switch to her. Of course, such words had only ever been threats. Millie knew the heart behind them had always been love. Even now—especially now—Grandma Joy wanted her to be safe and loved and to know God loved her. And Millie did.

She did.

Mostly.

But when that piercing pain through her middle reminded her that God had allowed all of it—the dementia, the huckster, the barely making it from paycheck to paycheck—it wasn't always easy to *feel* that she was loved. Feeling and knowing were two different things.

Great-Grandma Ruth's mama had said that feelings were foolishness. But sometimes they felt like more. Sometimes they felt like a stone sitting on her chest, crushing the air from her lungs and making her wish . . . well, she wasn't sure exactly. What did one wish for when she longed for a different life but the same family? She didn't want her parents back or to be someone else's kid. She didn't want to grow up with a silver spoon in her mouth. She didn't want an *easy* life.

She just wanted to be able to say that all was well with her soul. She just wanted to have her grandma—the wise, witty, wonderful woman who raised her—back.

But that was never going to happen.

FIFTEEN

*M*illie read the last four pages of the hard-back in her hands one more time. She'd long since had to crack the door of her car open or suffocate in the direct line of the sun. But she needed this. Just a moment with her book. Just a moment with Genevieve and Sir Robert, who had overcome everything to be together. There had been a war and an evil stepfather, and Sir Robert, who was terrified of the water, even swam across a moat to rescue his beloved Gennie.

Sappy? Terribly.

Did she care? Not even a little bit.

This escape was what she had. And she'd cling to it for as long as it made butterflies swoop in her stomach and love feel like it was within arm's reach. Maybe she'd have to stretch, but all was not lost.

As Sir Robert pulled Gennie into his arms for one final kiss, the image of him in her mind morphed. She had never pictured him as a Fabio knockoff—more like that NFL quarterback who was way too good-looking for his own good, the one in all of those commercials. That was the face of Sir Robert when she'd read this book the first and second time.

But this time he looked different. His hair was shorter, cropped close over his ears but longer in front, a few curls just evident. His eyes were so blue that they rivaled Georgia's summer sky. His chin wasn't square but pointed. And his grin—it was both wry and crooked.

She knew that face. And Ben had absolutely no business showing up in her mind when she was reading about a medieval knight. The two had nothing in common.

Except for brilliant smiles, expressive eyes, and a forgiving heart. There was that.

She tried to keep reading, but suddenly Gennie didn't look a bit like the fierce maiden on the cover. She looked a whole lot like the image Millie saw when she looked in the mirror. And when Sir Robert swept Gennie into his arms . . . well, suddenly Millie was the one being swept away. By Ben. *Her* Ben.

Nope. Not hers. Not at all. Not even a little bit.

Be quiet.

She much preferred to be the one telling the voice in her head to pipe down. And she wasn't comfortable with this shift at all. Not when she was being practical, logical even.

Except there had been that moment, the night of the jumper at the Chateau. It had felt like maybe there was a little something between them. It didn't have a name. It wasn't defined. But it was definitely something.

Told you.

She slammed the book in her lap closed and swiped the back of her hand across her forehead. She needed to drop these books off inside, and with them any reminder that Ben might have played the role of the hero.

Sliding out from behind the steering wheel, she gathered her books to her chest. There were eleven of them in all, and she was halfway across the library parking lot before she began to question the wisdom of this idea.

A gust of wind picked up the front flap of a paperback. It teetered precariously, so she tried to balance her chin on it but only managed to wrinkle the title page.

The hardbacks on the bottom began to slip in her damp palms, and every step bumped them further and further from a secure grasp. She was still at least twenty yards from the library's sliding glass doors, and a quick glance over her shoulder showed that she'd come just as far. There was nothing to do but press on, even as the wind picked up.

Stumbling up a curb, she nearly lost all the books and wondered if she should have just let them go. Then she took another step, and pain shot through her ankle, stabbing like a fire poker fresh from the coals. Her leg buckled and she began to go down. Trying to aim for the grass, she braced herself for the fall.

Suddenly two arms scooped her up from behind. Wrapping big hands under her elbows and around the books clutched to her, he pulled her back against his chest.

"Well, well, well. If it isn't Millie Sullivan, falling all over herself to see me outside of work."

That voice. It was Sir Robert's. Or rather Ben's. How quickly they'd become interchangeable.

"I was not." She tried to straighten away from him to hold herself erect, but the second she put an ounce of weight on her foot, her ankle screamed at her, and she sank back against him. So solid. So firm.

His arms squeezed tight with no indication he was going to let her go again. "You okay?"

"I guess I twisted my ankle. I'll be fine." She rotated it to show that she was all right, but he gave her a doubtful look when she grimaced halfway through.

"Let me give you a hand."

Like Sir Robert gave Gennie, which led to her falling into his arms and being thoroughly kissed?

Yes, please.

Oh, shut up.

"I'm good. Really."

He didn't say a thing. Instead he scooped her books from her hands and stuck out his elbow. Giving her a pointed look and a nod toward his extended arm, he waited.

Grandma Joy would say it was rude not to take a gentleman's arm when it was offered. Sliding her hand into the crook, she leaned on him with every step, each one like fire in her shoe.

"I think Carl has an ice pack in the freezer in the office."

"I'll be fine. Really." She cringed again, and he shook his head.

"You going to run around the Chateau in high heels tomorrow?"

She opened her mouth to argue with him, but the thought of having to walk in even her costume's kitten heels made her consider lobbing off her whole leg. "All right. Some ice might be good."

"Good. Now, how did you know I was working here today?"

"I didn't. I came to return those." As soon as she pointed out the stack of books in his arms, her insides gave a wild lurch. Which was entirely ridiculous. It wasn't like he'd have any clue that she'd been picturing him in the pages of one of those sweet romance novels. Or worse, that she'd been picturing herself with him.

He nodded. "Anything good here?"

"No." Maybe she'd said it too quickly. The rise of his eyebrows suggested that might be the case. She hurried on. "Just filling time until we find Ruth's other diary."

He didn't say much as they entered the library. He simply deposited her books into the return slot and then led her through the library toward a back room. Brightly colored books filled every shelf, and the main room smelled of paper and ink and glue, the sweetest scents in the world.

The back wall contained a row of glass doors, which led to individual study rooms. Millie had never been this far inside. The fiction titles were housed up front, and she'd never needed to dig deeper. But Ben knew where he was going, and he didn't seem to mind that she leaned heavily on him across the patchwork carpet.

Past three rows of tables—all packed with kids at their laptops, earbuds firmly embedded—a single door said *Archivist*. Ben pushed it open, then helped her through. "Carl, this is my friend Millie."

"Friend?" He waggled his bushy eyebrows and patted the top of his balding head, smoothing what little hair remained.

What was with people of a certain age trying to set them up? First Grandma Joy and now Carl.

Ben was quick to the correction. "Just a friend. She's the one I told you about. We found her great-grandmother's diary."

"Oh, that Millie." Carl rushed forward, reaching out both

of his hands to shake hers. "It's quite nice to meet you. Sit. Sit."

Ben quickly explained about her twisted ankle, and Carl shuffled off to a back room with promises of comfort to come.

"So, you've been talking about me?" She raised her eyebrows as she lowered herself into the rolling chair Ben pulled from a desk. It wasn't until she fell onto the cushion that she realized there were actually two desks in the room—smallish metal ones. When she'd entered she'd focused mostly on the two large wooden worktables. Carl had been standing at one, yellowish papers scattered before him.

"Absolutely not. I mean, except for that time I asked if he knew anything about a treasure at the Chateau."

Maybe it was the speed with which he'd offered his rebuttal, but something in his response suggested he might not be telling the whole truth. And butterflies doing a little dance in her stomach suggested that she quite liked the idea that he'd been speaking of her to his . . . well, Carl was sort of a friend.

Just as she was trying to formulate something to say in return, Carl bustled back into the room, his button-up shirt and gray sweater vest as rumpled as ever. As promised, he carried something wrapped in a towel. Rolling over another chair, he patted the seat. "Put your foot on up here, young lady."

She nearly snorted. "Young lady?"

He tsked as she stretched her leg out, and then he set the cool compress on her ankle, which made her suddenly shiver all over. "Well now, you're certainly younger than me, and I'm going to give you the benefit of the doubt for that other descriptor."

Laughter rolled out of her, clear and full and filled with

pure joy. A deeper laugh joined hers, and she glanced at Ben just in time to catch him wiping his eyes as he bent low to catch his breath.

Between giggles, she managed to shoot back, "Do you always come to such rash conclusions, Carl?"

"'Course I do. When y'all get to be my age, you'll see you don't have time to waste on second-guessing."

Ben crossed his arms as he perched on the edge of the nearby desk. "Carl's a smart guy. He rarely gets it wrong."

"Rarely?" she asked.

"Well, I wasn't so sure about this guy when he first started." Carl flippantly waved his hand in Ben's general direction. "Had my doubts he'd be much use, what with his nose in a book nonstop."

"I was working on my thesis." Ben cleared his throat and shifted positions. "And I had a few things on my mind."

There was a strange timbre to Ben's voice. It wasn't entirely different than usual, but there was a gravel to it, a coarseness. It made her sit up and take notice.

He'd said he'd been working at the library a couple of years. What had been going on in his life then? Something with his mother? She used her propped-up ankle to push herself higher, which of course sent fireworks up her leg and forced her to bite her lip in order to keep from squeaking in pain.

"Careful there," Carl said, readjusting the ice pack on her leg.

She nodded, but her gaze held firm on Ben. She thought she'd been the one with all the secrets, but he hadn't told her everything yet either. What exactly was he not telling her?

Carl kept her from asking. Her questions felt too personal

to ask in front of someone she'd met exactly six minutes before. So she tucked them into her mind for later. Later she'd ask why he'd held back, even after she'd told him about Devereaux and the connection she hoped to find.

And after that—much later—she'd be honest with herself about why it mattered at all. Because one thing was certain. It did matter—maybe too much.

"So you're the one with the diary." Carl didn't really ask it as a question, but Millie took the opportunity to confirm.

"It was my great-grandmother's. She was a guest at the Chateau."

"Mm-hmm." Carl nodded and folded his hands in front of him. He took a couple sideways steps and then back again, but always he kept his eyes on her. "How'd she wrangle an invitation? It was supposed to be the best party in Georgia in those days. Wine and liquor, even though it was the height of Prohibition. Fancy dinners and fancy people. She ran in that set?"

"Not at all." Millie glanced toward the ceiling, trying to remember the details she'd read from Ruth's own pen. "She worked in a bank in Atlanta. She'd grown up on a farm, a small one. But her aunt was rich, and she paid for Ruth to go to school. She's a beautiful writer. She must have learned that at the finishing school. Anyway, she met Ms. Lucille Globe at the bank."

Carl whistled long and low, and she knew she didn't need to explain who Lucille was.

"She invited Ruth and her friend Jane to spend the summer at the Chateau. So of course they went. I don't think many people said no to Howard Dawkins. Or Lucille, for that matter."

Carl chuckled and scratched his chin. "Could you imagine? That big white house lit up at night, filled with music and dancing. It must have been somethin' else."

"It still is."

Carl jerked his head toward her, his eyes wide with surprise.

She shrugged. "I play the part six nights a week."

"Of course you do." He patted her shoulder and ambled back to his table, his gaze lost somewhere between the past and the present. "I almost forgot." After pulling on white cotton gloves, he picked up the pages before him, alone in his world yet again.

Millie shot Ben a look, and he shrugged. Maybe this was normal behavior. But she couldn't help but hope that a man who knew the Chateau and the area's history better than anyone else might be able to help them find Ruth's other journal. Although, why would he know more than Grandma Joy or even Millie? After all, she'd read the diary. She knew Ruth's experiences. Well, she knew a couple months of them.

"Did you . . ." Millie wasn't quite sure what she was asking and lost track of it when he didn't look up. Stumbling to find the right words, she tried again. "Did you ever read about a Ruth Holiday at the Chateau?"

Carl didn't look up. "No. Just the usuals."

Ben grunted. "Usuals? The Chateau was only open for two summers."

"Yes, but there was a crowd. A conglomerate of wealthy families—young men and women who ran around together. Dawkins was a bit of an outsider. He was a little older and never quite as well-known as the Rockefellers and the Vanderbilts. His was new money and therefore frowned upon by some of the old-money families. And his Lucille wasn't like the other women in that circle. She was a stage actress who caught his eye, his heart, and apparently his wallet."

Carl had spoken while inspecting and sorting what looked like century-old letters on his table. Finally he looked up. "But there was one family who didn't seem to care too much about Dawkins's past."

"Claude Devereaux."

Carl dipped his head in agreement. "And his sister Angelique. She was as scandalous as Lucille or any of the actresses that ever graced a vaudeville stage."

"Really?" Millie tried to match his description with the one Ruth had given, but the pieces didn't quite fit into place.

"Definitely. She was engaged to at least three men in the two years before the crash. There were rumors that she'd fallen in love with a man who'd lost his fortune to gambling and she was fixin' to marry him, even though her father forbade it. They snuck off to Europe together after the stock market fell."

"What happened to her?" Ben asked.

"Tuberculosis. She died in 1930. Alone and single."

Ben's eyebrows dipped, and he uncrossed his arms, leaning into the story. "What about her husband?"

"Ah, he divorced her when he found out she'd been disinherited."

Carl's words were stoic. Not cold exactly, just factual. But they pricked at something deep inside. Millie bit her lips. Should she feel more emotion than she did at Angelique's sad life and death—especially if she was her great-great aunt?

But there was no proof of that. Not yet anyway.

She risked a quick glance at Ben, who stared at her with a

knowing gaze. He knew exactly what she was going to ask. But Carl didn't, so she tried to play casual. "What about Claude?"

"Oh, he had a good life. There were rumors that he'd planned to wed a poor girl."

Millie's stomach twisted until she thought it might explode. She tried to sit up, but it wasn't easy with her ankle still throbbing. She rolled a little bit in Carl's direction, leaning closer. "Do you know who?"

"That's a family secret that's likely gone to the grave."

Carl hadn't meant to—he probably hadn't even noticed—but he'd just let the air out of her balloon, and she sagged against the chair.

Ben, on the other hand, had noticed. "Why don't you let me drive you home while you rest your foot?"

She glanced over at him as her eyes began to tingle. She had no reason to be upset. Maybe there was still proof out there. Who knew what was in Ruth's second journal? Certainly Carl didn't.

She didn't need much. She just needed enough to compel the Devereaux family—Claude's three remaining heirs—to give her an audience. Then she could ask for the help she needed. It wasn't much, and it wasn't even for herself.

But it might as well be the world.

Ben reached for her, and she let him help her up. Hopping on her good foot, she leaned against his side, his hands at each of her elbows.

"Thank you for your time and your ice pack, Carl."

He nodded but didn't look in her direction. "Some treasure hunters you two are." His low mumble caught her off guard, and Ben's grip on her arms tightened.

After a long moment, waiting for him to continue, she gave Carl a nudge. "What's that supposed to mean?"

He kept right on reading his papers, sorting them into clear plastic covers with the tenderness of a new mother caring for her child. "Only that every other treasure hunter who's called here in the last two days asked about the actual Chateau."

"Wait—"

"What?"

She and Ben spoke over each other, and she could feel his heart beginning to race against her shoulder. She had no illusions that it had anything to do with her proximity.

The others—the ones Milo Fazetti had promised—were already calling. And they couldn't be far away.

"Oh yes. They want to know about the layout and the best hiding places. And they want to know how to sneak in. Some yahoo asked me if his boat would be noticed parked at the dock behind the house." Carl chuckled. "Bunch of hooligans chasing down some lead on the internets."

Ben nodded. "We know about it. I checked it out after I caught the guy on Chateau grounds, but it's mostly wild speculation. All it says is that there's money—lots of money—to be found on the estate."

"I looked too," Millie said. "There's nothing even remotely backed up with evidence. These treasure hunters are just talking about what might be lost there. Some even think it's an old pirate treasure."

Finally Carl looked up from his work. "I know they're just speculatin'. If they knew what they were looking for, bet they'd stop callin' and askin' for help."

"And what have you been telling them?" Ben said.

"Nothin'. Why would I help them? You two, on the other hand—I like you two."

Millie laughed out loud, and Carl gave her a brilliant smile. "How are you going to help us?" she asked.

"I'll tell you about the secret passage."

SIXTEEN

Ben took off after another tour guest. His legs shouldn't have been tight—not after three other chases that night—but they were. And his boots felt like they had been made out of cement. Every step crashed into the stone pavers along the back of the house, jarring his knees, sending sparks up his back.

He wasn't really old. Thirty was still young. So why did he feel like he'd doubled in age and thrown out his back for good measure?

He let out a groan as his mark tossed away an oddly shaped object—surely something intended to help him find a treasure underground—and zigzagged at the bottom of the twin stairways. The Chateau's spires rose before them, the second-story deck stretching a welcome to guests. The curved staircases on each side were as sleek as the rest of the house in the yellow glow of the night lights.

The guest on the lam couldn't have been much younger than Ben, and he couldn't seem to decide which staircase to take. He bobbed to one side and then darted in the other direction.

Ben didn't know why the other guy was having such a hard time deciding, but he didn't complain, as it gave him a split second to catch up. "You. Stop!"

The guy looked over his shoulder, and Ben realized he was more of a kid than a man. His ruffled blond hair looked like straw, like he'd spent every single one of his few years swimming in the Atlantic. His skin was as light as his fair hair, and his eyes were wide, haunted. He was in over his head, and there was no escape. But he kept running.

"Not up the stairs," Ben grumbled to himself, as he tried in vain to fill his lungs. There wasn't anything to be done about it. He had to push through the stabbing pain in his side. It was far too late to start that gym regimen he'd considered six months ago. There was only time to lament his own stupidity and keep going.

God, please let me catch up to him.

The stairs were tough. Wider than usual stairs, they forced him to adjust his stride.

But the kid didn't know to do that. Halfway up the stairs—while Ben was only on the third step—the kid missed his footing and slammed into the steps. He squealed in pain, and Ben picked up speed. He didn't know where the extra burst of energy came from, only that he was suddenly at the kid's side, reaching out to check on him.

The kid groaned and rolled himself over, his back against the steps and his eyes closed. "Guess I'm busted, huh?"

"Pretty much." Ben squatted next to him, taking a quick visual survey. There wasn't any blood, which was a good sign. But that didn't mean there weren't any broken bones.

Cradling his left arm against his chest, the kid sighed. "I just wanted some of the treasure."

"You and everyone else here tonight." Ben wasn't exaggerating. They were coming out of the intricately carved woodwork. An older woman and a middle-aged man had broken free from their tours and set off to explore the grounds, and a man older than Grandma Joy had tried to enter the grounds from the beach side. And those were just the ones Ben had been sent after. There had also been a family trying to hide a metal detector in the dad's pants and two frat boys carrying shovels who had been turned away by security at the front gate.

"Yeah, well, treasureseekers.com knows its stuff, man. If they say there's something here, it's big. Huge." The kid groaned as he tried to sit up, but he moved like his head weighed more than the rest of him.

"Treasureseekers.com, huh?" Ben shifted to sit on the step below the kid's head. His chest still burned, but at least he could gulp in deep breaths. And the thundering pace of his pulse was beginning to slow down.

"Sure. You know, it's like where people post about tips and stuff they've heard about. Some lady found half a million dollars in Arizona last year just from one post on the forum. Like, she just went to her backyard and dug it up."

Ben nodded. He did know about it. He'd checked it out after Milo first arrived on the scene. But it didn't mean that any of the information on the site was more than speculation. No one had any of the details that he and Millie did.

Besides, all these jokers seemed to think treasure hunting looked like it did in the movies. It didn't. It wasn't quite so frantic or fast-paced. At least not like the action movies he'd seen. Treasure hunting was more like searching for clues and then waiting to see how they fit into place—*if* they fit into place. It was a slow grind. Not that he minded that part of it.

But now . . . now there wasn't time to waste. Not when the Chateau was pretty much under siege and he needed that treasure more than ever.

He was apparently a treasure hunter too. He'd never wanted to be one. Never considered it, not once in his life. Not until he'd met Millie. And now it was pretty much all he thought about. Well, the treasure and that list of names on his desk at home. The list of names of people who were owed as much as he could repay them.

The treasure and the list.

And Millie.

He had to be honest with himself. She was taking up a fair bit of space in his brain of late. He didn't really mind. Not when he thought about that wry smile she sometimes had. Or the way she'd kept her cool with a plate of ketchup-covered potatoes all over her. Or the way she wore her hair all pulled back in a knot at her neck. The costumes were pretty, the jewelry flashy. But they couldn't hold a candle to the line of her neck, so elegant, so graceful. And that was all her. He'd wondered more than once what it would be like to press his lips to that hollow where her neck met her shoulder.

And then he'd promptly given himself a swift kick in the pants.

Millie was beautiful. She was smart. She was funny. And she fit in his arms like she'd been handcrafted to be right there. He rather liked it when she slipped into his brain a third—or half—of the time.

But he didn't have anything to offer her. Not now. Not for a long time. Not until every name on that list had been checked off, every person represented on that sheet of paper given back what had been stolen.

It was too late to save those people from his mother's crimes. But maybe—just maybe—it wasn't too late to give them back some of what had been taken from them. More than money. More than security. This was about dignity.

Ben was so lost in memories and scribbled lists and the smell of sunshine in Millie's hair that he almost missed the kid beside him pushing himself up. Jerking back to the present, Ben stood and held out his hand. The kid took it and pulled himself to his feet.

"Guess you're going to turn me in?" There was a slight question in the statement, a hope for leniency.

Ben nodded. "I have to if I want to keep my job."

The kid shrugged. "Figured something like this might happen."

Ben wanted to tell him that if he was going to give up so easily, he might have saved them both a heart-pounding chase and a stumble up the stairs. But he was just thankful the kid didn't fight him on the way back to the security office.

After the paperwork was completed and Billy Cruze was escorted off the property, his name added to the list of *personae non gratae*, Ben sank into a chair in the security office. Maybe he and Millie had brought this on themselves. No one had talked about this lost treasure for ninety years—until they started snooping. And now it was everyone's favorite target.

Putting his face in his hands and his elbows on his knees, he let out a deep breath. *God, what kind of Pandora's box have we opened? And what if Millie really is a Devereaux?*

There was no audible response. Not that he'd expected one.

"Benji!" The least favorite of all of his nicknames—probably because his mother had called him that—was accompanied by a smack on the shoulder and a low laugh.

He didn't need to look up to know who had joined him. "Hi, Theo."

The twenty-one-year-old kid bounced in his chair. "Man, some night, huh? I mean, I knew things were going down and all that when they called me in to work overtime, but . . ." He swore proudly, like he'd just learned the word and wanted to show off that he knew how to use it.

Ben cringed. He'd give his overtime paycheck to have ended up on a shift with Jerome or Richard, two men who'd served in the military, earned the right to say whatever they liked, and respected others enough not to take advantage of that.

"You hear about the new monitors?"

Ben sat up a little straighter and looked Theo right in the eye. "What new monitors?"

"They added some cameras. They're going to keep them on 24-7—like all the time."

Yes, he knew what *24-7* meant. And the growing ache in his gut told him exactly what it could mean for Millie and him.

"They're installing them now, and they'll be up and running by tomorrow. Gotta get the new monitors installed in the morning. This place is gonna be the business." Theo waved his hand to the desk that currently held three computer monitors.

Ben hunched against the riot in his middle. If cameras were rolling, he and Millie wouldn't be free to explore the grounds. They could kiss the second diary farewell and bid adieu to the treasure. Wherever it was.

His stomach rolled, and for a second he thought he'd be sick.

Theo swore again. "You don't look good, man."

Not surprising. His leg bounced, and he pounded his fist against his knee. He needed to let Millie know. They needed to make good use of this night. Their last night. They needed a plan and a map and . . . and more than a couple secret passages hidden in the old home.

They needed to check out Ruth's favorite place. They needed to find the diary right there, in plain sight, because a million restorers and visitors had failed to see it before. They needed the map to be on the first page and so clear that they couldn't mistake the directions. They needed the treasure to be an inch below the ground.

And if—by some wild miracle—all of that happened, they still needed to prove that Millie was a Devereaux and had some claim to the money they'd discovered.

His head began to pound, and a shooting pain behind his left eye was followed immediately by his ever-present acid reflux.

Perfect.

In that list of all the things he needed, a dysfunctional esophagus wasn't one of them. But it was what he had.

Doubling over, curling against the pain, he pressed his face into his hands and closed his eyes. Taking as deep a breath as he could muster, he tried to still his spirit and quiet his soul.

Lord, we need your help.

Such a simple prayer, yet it seemed to lift something from his shoulders. Some of the weight that had been stacking higher, heavier, with each of their needs.

Could it really be that simple? Not that God was going

to automatically give them whatever they asked for. But Ben was reminded that it wasn't all on his shoulders.

It felt like it was. Most of the time anyway. He'd been on his own so long that it was hard to remember he wasn't in this life alone.

Except sometimes—when he was with Millie—it didn't feel like he was doing it all on his own. He had a partner.

He smiled and stood up. If they only had one more night at this thing, then he was going to go find her. They'd make the most of every minute beneath the shadow of darkness.

Millie was hungry and tired and so ready to go home. If her apartment had a bathtub, this would have been the night to fill it with bubbles, sink into it, and wash off the spit-up from the baby during the last tour. The mom had been terribly apologetic. But it didn't change the fact that she was on the hook to get her costume dry-cleaned. Or that she smelled of sour milk.

She gagged as the wind floated the odor past her nose again. Trudging toward the women's locker room, she trailed behind the others, each step like dragging a ball and chain.

"Millie."

The whisper was urgent and so unexpected that she nearly jumped. She really might have if the ball and chain hadn't been so heavy.

Spinning, she saw Ben's face between two of the palmetto trees. He looked around quickly before motioning her toward him.

"What's going on?"

His eyes darted back and forth again, and it made her skin

tingle. She looked over her shoulder as well, but the path between the main house and the offices was empty.

"Ben?"

His eyes were intense, and he pressed a finger to his lips. "They're adding twenty-four-hour cameras. Because of the treasure hunters."

"But you're still security, right?"

"Yeah, but I can't protect us from this—new cameras that are recording at night. After tonight, there's no way for us not to be caught."

"So we have tonight?"

He nodded. "Barely."

"So . . ." She began to wring her hands as her insides churned. There wasn't enough time. This wasn't going to work. They weren't going to find what they needed. She wasn't going to be able to prove anything.

He put one of his big hands over both of hers, and she gulped for air. "I know. Let's give it our best shot."

Apparently he'd learned to read her mind in the four weeks they'd known each other. Since she didn't have anything to hide anymore, she didn't mind. She wouldn't have minded being able to read his mind too. But that was a distraction they couldn't afford tonight.

Suddenly his face twisted, and he blinked hard. "What is that?"

She caught a whiff of it again. "Oh, sorry. That's me. Projectile vomit."

He looked like he had to wrestle his smile down to the mat, and even then the corner of his mouth tilted up.

"Let me go change. I'll be right back. Meet you here?"

"Sure. Then we'll go find Ruth's favorite spot."

She took off for the locker room, which was beginning to clear out, and as she stripped out of the foul dress, she thought of everything she knew about Ruth and everything she knew about Devereaux.

Ben had said that in one of the letters, Claude had identified Ruth's favorite spot on the estate. She didn't know where that was, but something about it didn't sit well in her stomach.

She needed Claude to be her great-grandfather. But she was starting to wonder if she *wanted* him to be.

George had made some valid points in his letters to Ruth. And he had no reason to lie—except that he was clearly in love with Ruth. But even she had questioned Claude's motives and been struck by his forwardness with her.

Millie sighed as she slipped on clean clothes and deposited her costume into the bin to be picked up by the cleaners.

It wasn't that Claude was a bad man. Ruth wouldn't have fallen for someone like that. But maybe he didn't know her. Maybe he didn't really know her at all.

And if he didn't know Ruth, Millie wasn't sure she wanted to risk their last chance on him.

Like a woodpecker trying to get her attention, a memory kept pushing at her. Grandma Joy had said that her mom's favorite spot was on the south end of the property. But there wasn't a creek there or the copse of trees she'd mentioned. That couldn't be it.

As she bent to tie her shoes, careful of her ankle that was still a little swollen, her brain kept going through everything she knew about Ruth's summer at the Chateau. There was that night with Claude on the beach, but that was too broad of a location. And there was the picnic with George at Christ Church of Frederica. George had said it was his favorite place in all of St. Simons. And Ruth had said . . . what? That she loved it too? That it might be her favorite spot too?

But it wasn't on the Chateau's property. And she wouldn't have stashed her diary so far away. Would she? No. No way would she have moved it from the hidden hole in her guest room to a church more than two miles away.

Then another memory struck Millie so hard that she nearly fell off the bench.

The gazebo. Ruth had said she loved the gazebo.

If Millie was going to stake their last chance on anything, she'd rather it be Ruth's own words.

Grabbing her bag, she slung it over her shoulder and slammed her locker shut. She took two quick steps toward the door before her ankle yelled at her, and she had to slow to an easier amble.

When she made it back to Ben, he'd all but blended into the surrounding coverage. The lights had been turned down—standard after-hours protocol—and his dark uniform disappeared into the green leaves. It took her two visual passes of the spot where she'd left him to recognize his shape.

"You ready?" she asked.

He reached for her hand, and she slid her fingers between his without thinking. It wasn't a big deal. They'd touched a hundred times before. But she couldn't ignore the bolt of lightning that zipped up her arm.

Tugging her toward a side entrance, he led the way, but she pulled back and said, "Where are we going?"

"The billiard room."

Millie cringed. "I'm not sure I trust Claude Devereaux's

assumption about Ruth's favorite spot. Besides, that seems like such a strange place to be her favorite."

His eyebrows dipped low. "You think he's wrong?"

"What do you think? You read the letters from Claude. Do you think he knew her well enough to know where she'd hide something so precious to her?"

Ben chuckled, running his free hand down his face. "I think Claude Devereaux was generally a good guy."

"And?"

"And I think he was arrogant and self-centered. And a terrible poet."

Millie let out a short burst of laughter. "And?"

"And I think he knew her about as well as he knew any woman."

She gasped. He didn't really think that Claude was Ruth's soul mate, did he?

He held up his hand as though he could ward off her panic. "I don't think he knew any woman very well. It's hard to when you're so focused on yourself."

Millie couldn't contain her smile. "Way to give me a heart attack."

Between snickers, a question began to ease its way across his face. "I thought you wanted him to be your great-grandfather."

That tug-of-war she'd felt earlier was back. Last time it had felt like a tug on her heart. This time it felt more like a war. "I . . . I do." She paused. "But I . . . want to know that Ruth was happy. You know what I mean. That she was with someone who loved her, not just someone who could give her a fancy life. You know?"

"I get it." He glanced in the direction they'd been headed. "But if Claude was clueless, where would it be?"

"Early on in Ruth's journal, she said something about the gazebo."

"The one on the north lawn?"

She shrugged. "It's the only one I know of. And I think it has benches."

"And you think the journal could be stored in there?"

Millie didn't have much more than another shrug and a whole lot of speculation to offer. "I think that if she was looking for a private place to write her thoughts, the north lawn first thing in the morning might have been just about perfect."

Ben didn't say anything, but the line of his jaw worked back and forth several times. She couldn't read his expression in the light, and her brain tried to backpedal as fast as she could. "You think this is a ridiculous idea."

He squeezed her hand. "Not at all. Let's go to the gazebo."

He took off at a quick pace, and she tried to keep up, but her legs were decidedly shorter than his, and her ankle gave out on the third step. Squeaking like a chipmunk, she jerked her hand free and hopped on her good leg as she tried to massage the pain away.

"Millie," he said on a breath, kneeling on the ground by her feet. "I'm sorry. I forgot. Are you all right?" All puppy-dog eyes and regret, he reached for her waist to steady her.

Not that touching her was exactly the way to keep her on her feet. His fingers were warm and firm, but they set off an earthquake in her middle that threatened her bare knees, tight chest, and everything in between.

"Fine." Grabbing his hands, she wasn't sure if she wanted to hold them in place or push them away. But when her fingers brushed his, she knew. Definitely the first option.

"Can you walk? I could give you a piggyback ride or something." There was a note of humor in his voice, but it was laced with something else that she couldn't quite identify.

Suddenly this Ben disappeared, Sir Robert-Ben taking his place. Decked out in armor and wielding a sword with a silly name, he looked ready to face whatever battle was to come.

And she had absolutely nothing to say to him. Not a single syllable.

"Millie?" He still knelt, still knightly, his voice dropping with concern. "Do you need me to carry you?"

Yes. Definitely yes.

But she closed her eyes and shook her head, praying the motion would dislodge whatever daydream she'd conjured. She blinked slowly and sighed when Ben was back to only Ben. Her Ben.

"All right." He stood. "Want to try this again?"

She could only manage a nod, traipsing after him at a much slower pace.

The lawn was nearly black as they shuffled across it. The deep red wood of the gazebo didn't differentiate itself from the rest of the night until they were nearly upon it.

Ben helped her up the steps, and she dipped her head in a quick thank-you, her breath suddenly too shallow to get the words out. The lawn wasn't that expansive, but taking extra care with her ankle had drained her. She wanted nothing more than to sink onto the closest bench, its wooden seat worn smooth by decades of wind and rain. But they didn't have time for that.

Falling to her knees, she pressed at the lip of one of the benches. It didn't budge. It didn't even pretend to.

She strained harder, pressing her palms beneath the lip and putting all of her weight into it. Still nothing.

She shot Ben a look as he pulled out his flashlight. The beam illuminated first the top of the seats and then the underside. He said nothing as he ran his fingers along the bottom of the lip of the bench beside hers. And then he stopped. With a wink he reached to the back of the seat and pulled it straight up.

She jumped up and did the same to the bench before her. "How'd you know to do that?"

"Hinges." His smirk said so much more than that one word, a subtle reminder that she should be glad he was there. And she was. Not just because he'd figured out how to open the bench seats.

There were so many things she wanted to say to him. Like how glad she was that he hadn't run when he'd discovered the truth. Like how glad she was that for the first time in a long time, she wasn't alone. Like how his touch made her want to melt.

Okay, maybe that last one could wait a little while. But still, it was true.

Ben shined his light into the box in front of her. It was empty except for a few beetles that had found a safe spot inside. Then he moved onto his. Also empty.

They worked their way around the eight seats one at a time. She held her breath and prayed this would be the one as he opened each lid. And let it out on a sigh with each reveal. Her heart beat harder, her hands clenched into fists at her stomach.

Seven empty benches, save for a few spiders unhappy to be disturbed.

That left one. Millie's fists shook and she tried to swallow, but her mouth was far too dry. "I don't know if I should be hopeful or just admit defeat."

Ben looked up from where his beam rested on top of the last bench. "Always hope."

"Easy for you to say."

He grinned. "Sure. But don't forget, my financial future is riding on the treasure map in that diary too."

"Oh. Right." She'd nearly forgotten that he was in this for the money. She'd promised him half of whatever she found. Even if it was just a finder's fee. Amid everything with Grandma Joy, she'd nearly forgotten that he needed money almost as much as she did. But he'd never exactly told her why.

Maybe that was the secret he'd been keeping.

"You ready?"

She pressed a hand to her thundering heart, took a gulp of air, leaned in closer to his shoulder, and nodded. "Do it."

He pulled the bench open, the hinges squealing their unhappiness at being disturbed after nearly a century. But open they did.

When his flashlight beam swung into the open box, it was as empty as all the rest. Her stomach fell, and the back of her eyes burned. She'd wasted their last shot. "I'm sorry." It was all she could muster, but not nearly enough.

Ben didn't appear to be listening. His swung the flashlight beam back and forth over the bottom of the box, his head cocked to the side. "You see that?"

No. But she leaned over his shoulder anyway, seeking out whatever had caught his eye.

"They don't line up."

She frowned and shook her head, still not seeing what he

had focused on, until he reached out and ran his finger along a seam between two boards at the bottom of the box. She gasped. The boards didn't line up. They didn't match. One rested on top of the other. With a small grunt, Ben pulled the top one away.

Suddenly his light swung over something brown. Her heart nearly stopped. And then she lunged for it. It was some sort of thick leather cloth that had been fashioned into a drawstring bag. She flicked away an angry beetle and stared at the package in her hands, which were suddenly trembling.

"Aren't you going to open it?"

She nodded. But she didn't really need to. "This is it." She could feel the sharp corners of a book beneath the case, its covers unbending, and ran her fingers along the book's spine. She didn't need to open it to know that she finally held what they'd been looking for. But whether it contained the map they needed wasn't as clear.

Tugging at the drawstring, she pulled it open, and he lent his light to the process.

"Hey! Is someone out there?"

Millie jumped, her gaze crashing into Ben's and her heart pounding in her throat. Immediately he turned off his light, and beneath the roof of the gazebo it was pitch-black. No moon. No stars. Just darkness.

Another light, bright and long, played across the grass a hundred yards away, but the sweeping motion of the beam was growing closer.

"Theo." Ben whispered it so low that it was more a rumble than a word. But she knew what it meant. If they were found, they'd both lose their jobs, probably be fined, and absolutely lose the journal.

"What are we go-oing to do?" She hated how her voice quaked, but there was no getting around it.

He grabbed her hand and pressed it against his chest, which rose and fell in rapid succession. "We have to run."

She began to nod, then stopped before she remembered that not only could he not see her but she also couldn't run. "My ankle."

He paused. The beam of light grew closer to them. Theo called again, and Ben's heart pounded beneath her hand.

She had to do something. But there was only one thing to do.

She shoved the journal against his chest. "Take it. Run. Hide."

"I'm not leaving you, Millie."

"Do it. You have to. It's the only hope we have of keeping the journal."

He shook his head, but she felt it more than saw it.

"Quit being so stubborn. If you wait, he'll see you. Go." She pushed the package against him again. "Just go. Take it."

His head turned this way and that, but it wasn't the emphatic shake of before. It was like he was looking for something. And not quickly.

"What are you doing?" She managed to hold back the last two words, but her tone definitely implied *you idiot*. "Run."

"All right. But you're coming with me."

"I can—"

Before she could finish the statement, he'd grabbed her arm and swung her around to his back. "Hold on."

She didn't have much choice, so she wrapped her arms over his shoulders and squeezed her knees around his sides as he took off, racing across the grass, racing for the house.

But there was nowhere to hide, nowhere that Theo wouldn't find them.

"Hey, hey, you! Stop!" Theo's voice was high and whining, and his light was still yards away from them. But not for long. Not when they reached the lit aurora of the house. He'd know. He'd see them.

Her heart slammed into her breastbone. There was no way this would end well.

SEVENTEEN

*B*en gasped, straining for air as the darkness surrounded them. He'd thought chasing Billy earlier that night had been difficult, but running from Theo while carrying Millie was liable to put him in the ground. Quite literally. If he stumbled, they'd both be up to their necks in mud.

Stay on your feet. Stay on your feet. Stay on your feet.

He chanted that to himself over and over in his mind. He didn't have enough oxygen to utter a word.

Besides, his ears were focused on listening for the other set of footfalls. Theo didn't look like he worked out a bunch, and Ben was pretty sure his longer legs could win a fair footrace. But this wasn't fair. So Ben had to use any advantage he could think of. And the only thing he could think of was a secret. A secret passage, to be exact.

Carl had said there was an entrance on the north side. Past the main entrance. Down three steps and behind a shrub.

Theo shouted again, but his light didn't reach them. Not yet anyway. But it was close. And getting closer.

Ben's foot slammed against a stone paver, and Millie

bounced hard against his back. She grunted but said nothing else, then she readjusted her clasped hands in front of his throat. No wonder he couldn't breathe. But there was no air to tell her she was strangling him.

Almost there. Almost there. Go. Go. Go.

He wanted to jump down the steps in one leap but couldn't risk it with Millie in tow, his center of balance way off. Slowing just enough to take them carefully, he gasped for whatever breath he could find.

"What are you doing?" Millie whispered in his ear, sending a full-body shiver through him. "The door is right—" Her body stiffened, and he smiled—even though she couldn't see it—when he knew she'd picked up on his plan.

"Come back . . . here!" Theo shouted, but he was clearly winded too. And too far behind.

Ben looped around the palm tree, reached for the wall, and ran his hand along it in the darkness. The handle was supposed to be at waist height, a sun in all its radiant glory.

And it was right where Carl had said it would be. Ben pushed his palm against the sun's face, and a tiny portion of the wall sank in with a groan. It wasn't a wide gap, and he had to set Millie down to squeeze through. But he kept her hand in his, pulling her into the darkness.

Spinning her into his arms, he moved her against the cool stone wall, his arms around her, shielding her. Her face was pressed into his chest. He could feel her gasps.

"Why are you out of breath?" He kept his voice low but couldn't keep the humor from it. "You didn't have to run."

She pressed a hand flat against the front of his shirt and pushed. It wasn't hard enough to say that she wanted him to back off. Which was good, because he didn't want to.

His heart should have been slowing, but its wild tattoo only increased as he leaned his nose into her hair. In a room that smelled of wet rocks and stale air, she smelled of soap and woman. Clean and fresh.

He jerked back only when Theo's cry echoed around them. "Where are you? I'm going to call the cops!"

"Will he see the opening?" Her question was more breath than words, and there was a quiver in it that made his chest ache. Where her breath hit him was warm and sweet and unlike anything he could ever remember.

When he laid his hands on her shoulders, he discovered that her voice wasn't the only thing shaking. Her whole body trembled, and he wanted to make it stop. Not because she couldn't handle it but because she shouldn't have to.

There wasn't room at her back to slide his arm around her. And he couldn't possibly pull her any closer than they already were, chest to chest, nose to nose, breath to breath. But doing nothing wasn't an option.

He couldn't see her in the darkness. He couldn't read her expression or guess at her thoughts. But he could hear her. Beneath Theo's continued calls and ongoing threats, he could hear Millie's tiny gulp, and it tied his insides into a knot.

He didn't know what to do with that knowledge, but his hands seemed to have a mind of their own. Dragging so slowly over her silky skin, he walked his fingers down her arms. At her elbows, she gasped. At her forearms, she gave a full-body quiver. At her fingers, she sighed.

It was hard to tell who made the move, but suddenly their hands were linked, palms flush and pulses throbbing against one another.

He should have stepped away. He should have given her breathing room. As it was, they were sharing oxygen. There was no way to cool down this close.

But he didn't want to. He wanted his heart to pound this hard for as long as it could. He wanted to feel this alive every second of every day. And deep in his gut, he knew it wasn't because Theo had been chasing them—his threats had disappeared into the night. Ben knew his best chance at this feeling was with Millie. Perhaps his only chance was with Millie.

And that nearly knocked him over.

He stumbled forward, which was rather awkward given that there was no more space to move forward. He was already as close as he could be, but there was no denying the urge deep inside. He could be closer.

He could kiss her.

Releasing her hands, he skimmed her arms once again, this time up to her shoulders and then to her neck. Her pulse skittered beneath his fingers, and her skin was like satin, beyond smooth. Beyond perfection.

He let his thumb fall into the curve where her neck met her shoulder, and she leaned into it, leaned into him.

And that was his undoing.

He took a shot in the dark and captured the corner of her mouth with his. It wasn't perfect, but it was like lightning. Millie froze, and he pulled back, staring hard into the darkness and wishing he could see any of her. But it was all black and the color of regret. He had no doubt he'd read the whole situation wrong.

"I . . ." He should apologize, but he wasn't really sorry. At least not about the kiss. "I shouldn't have presumed . . ."

And then from the darkness, the sweetest words he'd ever heard. "Would you mind trying that again?"

"Excuse me?"

"I wasn't ready." There was a smile in her voice. "And I can't see you."

"All right." There was a frog in his throat, and he couldn't pinpoint why. Maybe it was the unsteady motion in his stomach or the hope that flickered with her invitation. Either way, he cleared his throat, cupped her cheeks, and tried again, this time framing her smile with a thumb on each side.

Her lips were firm, still, hesitant.

At first.

And then she fell into him, melting against him, her arms wrapping around his waist, and she clung to his shirt with both fists. She was soft and pliant and fierce all at the same time, giving as much as he gave.

The whole Chateau could have crumbled around them and he wouldn't have noticed. The bottom of his stomach dropped out, and he couldn't be bothered to care. In this tiny passage there was only Millie and him.

And that was all he needed.

He was a really good kisser. Millie didn't need to have anyone else to compare it to. She could have kissed a million other guys and she'd still know the truth, plain and simple. Ben was better than great at kissing.

She felt it clear down in her toes. The tingling that had started in her chest had spread everywhere else, and she had to hang on to him for fear her knees would buckle and her heart would explode. She'd thought it had pounded when

Theo chased them, but this was entirely new. It was a rhythm so wild she was sure her heart had stopped beating altogether before it slammed against her breastbone to jump-start itself. She lurched and he pulled back, and she was empty.

Please. No. That couldn't be it.

It was wonderful. But she needed more. Just a little bit more. And then she'd be satisfied.

Liar.

Put a sock in it.

There wasn't time to argue with herself. There was only time to kiss him again.

But he hadn't leaned back in. At least, she didn't think so. She could hear his breathing, ragged and loud, but he was too far away.

Was it bad form to ask a man to kiss you twice in a row? If he'd started it, could she pick it up right where they'd left off?

Her hands fluttered at her sides, so empty without him to hold on to. She wasn't sure when she'd let go of his shirt, but now she was adrift in an ocean of ink and didn't even know if she could call out for rescue. She only knew he was right in front of her. And if he was right there, then she was a fool if she didn't reach out.

Like a drowning woman grabbing for a float, she pulled him to her.

Their lips crashed together. It was lightning and thunder in one, the shock echoing in all of her senses, leaving her so stunned that she was nearly paralyzed.

Maybe this was normal. Maybe it was always like this.

Unlikely.

If every kiss was like this, nothing else would get done.

Oh, shut up.

Her generally annoying inner voice had a point. Why was she assessing the electricity that shot through her with his every touch? He was still kissing her, and she didn't want to miss a second more.

Turning off her inner dialogue, she leaned in. Their hearts pounded against each other until she couldn't tell which one was hers. They both sounded in her ears, steady and in concert.

She quit thinking long enough to cherish the moment. Long enough to wind her fingers into the silky strands of his hair. Long enough to let him fall into her too.

It might have been a minute. It might have been an hour. She didn't know or care. Until he pulled back. Not all the way—just his lips, really. His hands still rested at her sides, their foreheads still pressed together.

On a haggard breath he said, "Wow."

"Pretty good?" She wanted to take those words right back, but it was too late.

He jerked away, still keeping his hold on her waist but putting decidedly more distance between them. Without his warmth the chill of the stone wall at her back made her shiver.

"Only 'pretty good'?"

"No! I mean, it was great. Really great." She swallowed the lump in her throat and tried again, this time with more conviction. "I liked it. It was wonderful. You! You're great too, and . . ."

Oh, be quiet.

Gladly.

This is not how it went in the books. The characters were always cool about a kiss, and they knew exactly what to say after a romantic interlude. They didn't stumble over their words or fight a storm in their stomach. But this was real life, and only a complete romantic novice called them *romantic interludes*.

Millie dropped her head into her hands, fire flickering up her cheeks, even if he couldn't see it.

And then he chuckled. From somewhere deep in his chest, the laughter rumbled, and she could only shake her head. In all the times she'd pictured her first kiss, it had never ended with the guy laughing at her. With Ben laughing at her.

Sir Robert never laughed at Gennie.

But before her heart could take a good stomping, Ben took her face in his hands, pushing her own fingers out of the way. "Millie, you don't have to describe it. I was here for it."

"But . . . I liked it. A lot. I've just never . . ."

"It's never been like that for me either."

That was good. She guessed so, anyway. But that hadn't been what she was going to say, and if she was going to fulfill her promise to be honest with him, she'd have to tell him the whole truth.

Squaring her shaking shoulders, she gave a quick nod that didn't come close to dislodging his hold on her. "It's not that it's never been like that for me. It's just that . . . um . . . I'm twenty-four years old, and I've never been kissed."

His breathing stopped, and the space was too silent save for the pounding in her ears as she waited for him to say something. Anything.

He didn't.

So she reverted to filling the space with anything else. "My grandpa died when I was younger, and I started working young. I had a boyfriend in high school, but it was really more of a group-of-friends thing. And then my grandma got sick and I didn't have time to think about that. And I've never really—"

He ran his thumbs across her cheeks, and she gasped when he caught a tear. She could just break away, make a run for it, and be done with this whole mortifying moment. Maybe Theo would catch her and throw her off the property, and she'd never have to see Ben again.

Sure. That sounded like a reasonable response.

And then suddenly his lips pressed to hers again. This wasn't a storm over the ocean. It was like butterfly wings, gone in a moment.

When his chuckle returned, it wrapped around her, warmer than a hug. "I'm surprised you didn't have guys knocking down the door to be with you. But I'm glad you didn't have time for them. I'd have hated to fight them all off, but I would have."

Heat washed over her, and she bit her bottom lip. "Really? You don't seem like a fighter."

"I'd have gone to the gym or something." He laughed again before tucking a strand of her hair behind her ear. "Whatever it took. You're worth it."

That wiped every thought from her mind, and she full-on sighed against him. "I don't know what to say. Thank you?"

"Ha!" It was a burst of humor that seemed to escape untamed. "How about we just have a look at that diary?" His hand dropped from around her waist, and suddenly a light filled the space. He pointed his flashlight at the floor, but she still blinked furiously against it after so long in the dark.

She quickly scanned the space. It was much smaller than she'd suspected, and fully enclosed. It was less passageway and more earthy closet. The coolness made it feel like an underground cave, but the other stone wall was nearly at Ben's back.

An image of her pressing Ben against the wall instead of the other way around suddenly flashed across her mind's eye. And with it came another rush of blood to her face.

Ben's grin dipped a smidge, and she wasn't at all sure she liked being able to see him. Except for his beautiful smile. And the firm line of his jaw. And the perfect slope of his nose. But those eyes—they saw too much. It had been so much easier in the dark.

Funny. Her books never talked about that.

"Are you all right? I didn't mean to . . . I didn't know it was your . . ."

She nodded and ducked her head to avoid his hand, which reached for her cheek. Because she wanted him to hold her again. Maybe too much.

But he was right. They had a diary to look at.

"I'm really fine," she said as she pulled the leather bag from the waistband of her shorts. When she reached inside, he shined his light onto it, and they both held their breath.

The book was thin, barely half the pages of the first volume, and the casing had taken a few hits, especially at the corners. But the words scratched onto the yellow paper were as clear as ever. It began on August 14. And there was no map in it.

She flipped gently through each page, and Ben's light bobbed quickly, a silent acknowledgment that they still didn't know the location of the treasure.

"What's that?" He pointed at the last page, shining his light directly into the fold where the pages met, and she saw that the final page had been ripped almost halfway down.

"It's a letter to George. But it was never sent." She pinched the covers between her fingers, longing to scan it, to read the last line at least. She ought to know how this ended. She should know if this was Ruth's final dismissal. It was what she wanted.

Is it really?

Of course. What would she be looking for, if not proof of her Devereaux heritage? Without that name she was worth exactly the $5.89 in her checking account.

Her hold on the back cover felt off, and she had to readjust it, but she couldn't tear her gaze away from the top of the page.

My dearest George . . .

No date. No tears that indicated a terrible breakup. No red-lipstick kisses.

Only the certainty that this was the last thing of Ruth's that Millie would ever read. And it was going to either change her life forever or crush every hope she'd ever had.

"I guess we better read this."

"Together?" His question didn't suggest that he wanted to, but as soon as he said it, she knew she needed him by her side to face whatever was in there.

"Meet me at my place?"

"I'll follow you home."

August 14, 1929

I screamed at him. How could I not after that letter he wrote to me?

George doesn't even know Claude, and he had no right to say such things. I told him that as I waved that scrap of paper under his nose, nearly pressing mine to his.

He gently tugged the paper out of my fist and glanced at it, as cool as if he hadn't written such incendiary words about Claude with his own hand.

"I am sorry if I have offended you, Miss Holiday." His words were deferential, but his eyes sparked with something that promised he still believed what he had written to be true. And always with the "Miss Holiday."

He was not really sorry, and I told him I did not believe him. I told him he was probably glad to have the words off his chest. And I shoved at just that spot.

I have never pushed a man before in my life, except for my little brothers. And this was quite unlike that. He did not budge. His chest was like a wall, hard from years of manual labor. But even though I knew it to be useless, I pushed again.

He did nothing to stop me. He only stood there, looking at me like he felt sorry for me. As though I was the one being attacked. That made me even angrier. Everything inside me felt too tight, like my insides had outgrown my skin, like a foot wedged in a shoe two sizes too small.

I yelled at him that he had called himself my friend, yet he spouted such drivel and spread such terrible rumors. A friend would not do that. I yelled it at him until I was nearly out of breath.

He just waited until I had to pause before coming to

his own defense. He said that I had asked for his honest opinion. I had. But it did not mean that I wanted it.

I stumbled to find an appropriate retort. We were all alone by his shed, and I could have sworn and gotten away with it. I nearly did. I wanted to. I had heard men on the farm say such things my whole life, and this seemed just the right time to unleash a string of words that would make my mother blush. But before I could, he kept going, asking me if I was unhappy that he had told me the truth about my love.

"He's not my love!" I yelled those exact words, but they popped out before I even realized what I was saying. I had not meant to say any such thing. It was just that George made me spitting mad.

Of course I love Claude. I mean, I think I do. I have never actually been in love before, but this must be what it's like. And I was not about to have George speaking ill of him.

I demanded he take back his words. But he said the most shocking thing. He said that I deserve someone who will care for me more than he cares about his money.

The bottom of my stomach dropped out. I don't know why exactly. Except that there was an implied promise in every one of his words. A suggestion that he is the one who could care for me so.

I went to push him again, but this time he grabbed my wrist and held it there. I tried to yank it back, but the harder I pulled, the tighter his grip became. And the more I wanted to kick him in the shin.

In a low voice I demanded that he let go of me. I wasn't afraid of him. George would never hurt me. But I was terrified of what he was making me feel. All of these emotions. They were so new and strong, and I just wanted to get away.

He dropped my hand and made a snide remark about getting my head out of the clouds.

Ooooooh. I stamped my foot in the grass, and it gave a very unsatisfying thump.

He snorted, and I wanted to scream at the top of my lungs. I had thought about this. I had. I knew what I felt for Claude. And I did not need George's condescending snorts trying to sour my feelings.

I swung my arm back, ready to give him another hard push. But before I could touch him, he grabbed my arms, both of them, and pulled me straight up against him. He did not say a word, but I could feel his chest rising and falling in rapid succession beneath my hands. And his eyes were brighter than the lighthouse, so intense and staring right through me.

I thought he was going to shove me away and storm off. There was thunder in his expression, and I deserved all of it.

And then suddenly his lips were pressed to mine. I froze up, sure that I should push away from him. Only I did not. I melted right there on the spot. I melted into him, letting his lips move against mine in gentle strokes.

When he pulled his hands away from my arms, I thought he might be done, and I did not want to be done. I wanted to be . . . well, I did not want it to end, and I clutched his shirt with both of my fists.

I needn't have worried. He slipped his arms around my waist, holding me even closer. I could not imagine that was even possible, but it must have been. Suddenly our hearts were beating at the same tempo, racing faster than mine ever had before. I could hear them like the thunder of horse hooves at the end of a race.

My entire body tingled as his hands squeezed against my back. He was like granite, and I knew I was safe inside the wall of his embrace. I forgot everything in that moment. Claude. Jane. My mama's warnings. I had nothing to fear from George, so I kissed him back. He made a little noise of surprise, and it was followed by a groan from the back of his throat.

If I could cause him to make that noise every day for the rest of my life . . . Well, that is far beyond any discussion we have had. But I could be happy to the tips of my toes to hear that.

Just when I thought my heart would burst, he pulled back, gasping for breath and pressing his forehead to mine. And then he called me Ruthie, the sweetest name I have ever heard. He told me he was certain he had crossed a line, but he could find not an ounce of regret.

My insides had taken a ride up and down the washboard and been wrung out to dry, and I could offer only a mumbled agreement.

And then he said the words I had been waiting for all summer, words I had expected to hear from another. He said that he could not promise me the world, but he could give me a good life. And he would gladly spend every minute of it making me smile.

How could I not smile at such an offer?

But my head swirled, and I could not let go of him or I would surely stumble to the ground. These were the words

I'd been waiting to hear from Claude. These were the words I'd expected after every late-night beach stroll and secret rendezvous. Yet they were coming from George.

So I fled.

I fear that I left him without an answer. How could I give him one when I clearly do not know my own feelings? George is perhaps the best man I know, and I fear that I must break his heart.

But oh, when he speaks my name, it is better than hearing angels sing.

August 15, 1929

I think I might have seen something I was not supposed to. Oh, I am certain I have seen more than I should have here at the Chateau. And I can never forget the breathless shock of finding Willa's body, something I never want to experience again.

But this time it was dark. I had gotten lost and ended up in the wrong corridor again. It is so easy to do, and only that much more so when I have been able to think of nothing but George and his kiss.

When the rest of the party had retired to the parlor after dinner, I claimed a headache and left for my room. However, I had missed a turn and ended up in a hallway near the kitchens. I could hear the cook and maids singing, but all I could think of was the first time I had gotten lost in this house and George had so kindly walked me back to the front entrance.

I took a handful of other turns and a flight of stairs up before finally reaching a hallway that I had been to only once before. Lucille had taken Jane and me down this hall once and pointed out Mr. Dawkins's private study. She said he did not allow anyone else inside.

But tonight I saw someone exiting the room. The shadows were so thick that I could only see an outline, but I know it was not Mr. Dawkins. It was not any man.

Perhaps I should have shouted or drawn attention. But I was frozen in place and could only think of poor Jenny, who lost her job when she was accused of theft. What if this woman was only a maid cleaning up while Mr. Dawkins was out of his office?

But something in my stomach is so unsettled that I cannot fathom that it could be so innocent.

August 16, 1929

I should have said something last night. Instead I went to bed and tossed and turned all night while someone took off with Mr. Dawkins's stock certificates, ones he had recently acquired for a company right here in Georgia. He was nearly purple this morning at breakfast, his fists shaking and his voice loud enough to take the roof off. I have never seen him so riled, and I think maybe Claude has not either. He sat by my side at our morning meal and held my hand. He looked strained. Almost nervous.

But it was hard to focus on Claude when Mr. Dawkins was yelling. Lucille tried to calm him down, but he brushed her off—I think rather too roughly. She stumbled to her knees, but as Jane and I got up to check on her, she waved us off.

Claude pulled me back to my seat, but I did not particularly want to stay. I really just wanted to be in George's shed. Safe. Peaceful. Quiet. And in his arms.

The realization hit me so hard that I dropped Claude's hand and did not allow him to pick mine back up.

What was I supposed to do? What does one do when she's been determined to marry one man and realizes she's in love with another? What does she do when she realizes she's done things for which the man she loves may never be able to forgive her?

I felt like the piano was sitting on my chest, and I could not swallow a bite.

No one ate during Mr. Dawkins's tirade. He demanded that every room be searched for the certificates. He offered a reward for anyone with information.

Yet I sat there mute. I had some information, but it is still only an inkling. And I daren't begin spreading rumors when I know that doing so could only cause more pain if I am mistaken.

I thought about it through every sleepless hour last night. I do not think the woman I saw was a maid. I am almost certain I recognized her as one of the guests. So I am going to follow her. But I dare not reveal anything until I am certain. It should only drive a wedge in the relationships I have forged here.

In the dim light of this lamp, I do find myself longing for simpler times. There was not so much intrigue or scandal on the farm or even at school. Certainly there were no stolen kisses in a stairwell or a secret rendezvous with a millionaire. And when I came here, that is what I longed for. It was what I had spent my life wishing for—excitement and passion.

And now I long for a simple life, secure in the arms of the man I love. I do not need to see the lights of Paris or to dine in the best restaurants. I do not need to sit at concerts with wealthy men and dance with millionaires.

I do not believe Mr. Dawkins to be a bad man, although I must question some of his choices. Most of all I question whether he cares for his money and his stolen certificates more than those he claims to love.

And I have no doubt that Claude would be the same.

Never once in all my time with Claude has he made me feel more than I did the first time I met George. Mama always says that feelings are just feelings. Perhaps it is true, but perhaps it is not. Perhaps feelings are an indication, not of love or commitment, but of that still small voice the pastor talked about on Sunday last. George had taken me again to his favorite spot, to Christ Church of Frederica. The pastor preached with such conviction of God speaking to us. Not audibly, but silently in the quiet of our hearts. And I wondered if I had ever heard God speak to me even once.

Now I wonder if sometimes that voice is the tug on my heart, a feeling I cannot deny.

Of course, this was before George kissed me. And certainly before I was sure that Claude is not the man for me.

But before I find my way back to that simpler life, I must do what I can to restore what has been taken. And I am almost certain that she will act tonight.

August 17, 1929

I write tonight with a trembling hand as someone who almost did not survive. I would not have, save for the intercession of one man. But I find I must chronicle tonight's events while they are fresh. Jane continues to ask me for details, and I can speak none of them. It is far too difficult to explain all that happened. Perhaps if I write it down, I will show Jane my book, even though I have found her looking for and reading it on two occasions and had to move it.

But this time I may share it with her so that I do not have to relive the moments again. Each time I close my eyes I see that shovel bearing down on me, and I know that I am so close to the end. All I could think about was how much I would miss having a future with George.

It was foolish, really, to follow Angelique last night. I should have told Jane where I was going. Perhaps I should have told Claude or Lucille. Even Mr. Dawkins had calmed down by the evening enough for me to tell him that I had seen someone leaving his study, and I had a pretty good idea of who it could be. But they are all crazy about Angelique, and I was nearly certain that they would try to convince me that I had not seen her head of wild curls exiting the study, or that it had all been entirely innocent.

But the feeling that seemed like so much more than a feeling compelled me to follow her. So I did. I waited in the shadows at the south exit closest to her guest room. I hid behind the trunk of a palm tree and tried to keep my breathing shallow, silent. It was much harder than I thought it should be as my heart pounded in my ears.

Then she appeared. Her hair was tied back and she was wearing trousers, but I could not mistake her porcelain skin or the almond shape of her eyes, so exotic and so secretive.

I stayed back, hoping I wouldn't lose sight of her in the night. Even the moon seemed to be on her side, hidden behind a cloud, blanketing the night in ink. I nearly did miss her turn toward George's small shed, and when she disappeared I had nowhere to hide. So I squatted behind a rosebush and prayed that she could not see my pale shirt. How silly of me to wear such light colors. In my defense, this was the first time I had ever gone sneaking around in the night—except with Claude. And that had been less about sneaking and more about scandal.

When Angelique reappeared, she was carrying a rather large shovel. I thought perhaps it would be awkward in her hands, but she carried it as though she had dug a thousand garden beds, and she set off for the beach. When she was far enough ahead of me, I followed her yet again. The crashing of the waves and the wind covered the sound of my footsteps and, I hoped, the thunder of my heart.

Near the beach, before the grass fully turned to sand, she made her way south. We'd long since abandoned any foliage I might hide behind, and my stomach was in a knot the size of the Chateau itself. But I continued on. It was far too late to abandon my plan now. And if I went for help, I could not possibly find her again.

When she picked up her speed, I did too. Especially when I saw what was ahead. A copse of trees reached right up to the beach, their long arms black against the deep blue sky. I knew immediately that if she reached the trees, I would lose sight of her and lose any proof I might have.

I began to run, but the grass was slippery, and I was losing ground with each step. She seemed to be flying by now, her hair a trail of wild abandon in her wake. I must have been gasping for breath by the time I reached the tree line. But it was no use. She was gone.

I fell to my knees, sucking in the thick air and praying that I might see a glimpse of her among the trees. I did not. I only felt fire in my shoulder.

The pain came first. And then I heard the clang of metal against something solid. It happened so quickly and yet seemed to drag on for hours. Twisting to cradle my injured arm with my other hand, I caught a glimpse of the edge of the shovel blade, and I knew. I had not found Angelique. She had found me.

"You silly little girl," she cried as the tip of the shovel sliced across my arm. And then she said I was just like Willa, always in the way.

Willa? I could hardly believe what she said, but I knew immediately that she had killed her friend. Why? Because she was going to steal some stock certificates?

Then I suddenly realized the terrible truth. Angelique hadn't only stolen some stock certificates. She was behind all of the disappearances—the brooches and necklaces, silver and diamonds. She'd taken all of it, but why? I could not make sense of it. She is a wealthy woman, and her father and brothers have more money than I could even conceive of. Could they not care for her? Surely they would make certain that she did not go without.

But there was no time for me to parse the facts and come to any sort of conclusion.

I ducked as the shovel scraped my ear, and I lifted my arm only to find that it was nearly useless. Blood dripped from my shoulder, and immediately my head began to spin. But I refused to give in. Pushing to my feet, I tried to look her in the eye and make her see me. Her eyes were cold, like there was no soul behind them, only hatred. Why did she hate me? I have not even refused Claude yet.

I begged her to tell me as I lifted my other arm to deflect another pass of her shovel. But my question went ignored. I tried again, reminding her that we were friends.

The head of her shovel dropped to the ground, and her eyes narrowed. She laughed as though it was quite the joke before spitting out that I had no idea what her life has been like.

I knew that I could not possibly best her in a fight, so I tried to reason with her. I tried to keep her talking, asking her to tell me, to explain it to me.

She did pause then, leaning against the shovel handle. Her eyes stared over my shoulder, maybe seeing the whitecaps of the open ocean. But she looked as though she was seeing something much farther away. And then her voice broke as she explained that her father is forcing her to marry a man she does not love because the one she cares for is not acceptable. He is not wealthy. He does not come from means. Her father believes him to be after her money.

She was silent for a long moment before her gaze returned to me, and she said I knew about that. I tried to assure her that I was not after her brother's wealth, yet my insistence fell on deaf ears.

But for me, speaking the truth was like being released from prison. It was true, and I was suddenly free to love the man I did for the rest of my life, no matter how short it was.

I closed my eyes and prayed that George would have a life filled with joy and love, even though I could not be there to see it. I opened them just in time to see Angelique swing the shovel, and it was almost to my head. I was nearly to heaven when the shovel stopped quite suddenly, and she cried out.

Then George was there, stripping the tool from her hands, and she screamed as loud as the seagulls that he had ruined everything. She went on and on about his roses and how they were too close. Too close. Too close.

She made no sense at all, but her words rang inside of me over and over again as though I should understand them.

I still do not, hours later. But her words are not what haunts me. Nor the vision I see behind my closed eyes.

What haunts me is that I may have missed my final opportunity to tell George how I feel.

Mr. Dawkins has declared that he is closing the Chateau for the rest of the year, and we must all go home tomorrow. Angelique refuses to reveal where she has hidden the stock certificates, even after the deputies questioned her.

They have taken her away, but Jane is certain she will be released. The Devereaux name holds sway anywhere in the South, and a small-town judge will not be able to hold her, even for Willa's death. She never truly confessed it to me, and they have found no other evidence.

But I'm not afraid of her. She tried to kill me to keep her secret from being revealed. Now the whole world knows.

Claude was beyond apologetic. It was clear that he was appalled by his sister's behavior, all of it. He tried to comfort me, but I had to be honest with him. Despite the exhaustion that had settled over me as soon as George escorted us back to the Chateau, I pulled Claude to the side. His hands were on my face and around my waist, and my skin crawled. Not because he reminded me of Angelique but because for the rest of my life I only want one man to touch me. And I told him as much.

Well, I did not tell him there was another man but rather that I was certain we would not be the right match and we should not spend time together any longer. He did not seem particularly disturbed by it, but for me it was like the last chain had been broken.

Jane insisted I be seen by a doctor, and Mr. Dawkins called for one. The doctor bandaged my arm and assured me it will heal with a minimal scar. Lucille was quite kind to bring me a warm cup of chocolate. They sat with me for hours no matter how many times I assured them I was fine. But I could not tell them what I really wanted, which was to see George.

Jane and I are on the first train to Atlanta tomorrow. I fear I may never see his green eyes and kind smile again.

I am not sure I am ready to live the rest of my life without air.

August 18, 1929

My dearest George,

Do you think it possible that you could still love a fool? For that is certainly what I have been. I should have seen you from the beginning and recognized your kind heart. You have been saving my life from that moment by the pool and through the rest of this summer.

You have made me see a love I could not have imagined possible. I thought that love was about committing to a man no matter how he treated me. But you have shown me tenderness that makes my heart soar. I could not have imagined how this love I feel for you makes me want to care for you in the same way. Could I possibly make you as happy as you have made me?

I leave for Atlanta this morning—Jane and I are off in only a few minutes—but I long for the opportunity to try. I want to try to make you happy. I want to cook for you and care for you and wash your clothes after you jump into a swimming pool to rescue a silly girl.

And I have been silly. I thought that money and wealth and traveling the world would make me happy. I thought that I could belong at fancy house parties and dress in the finest gowns. I thought that my education should afford me a position in a brick house in the best neighborhoods of New York and Chicago.

Now I know none of that matters. None of it makes anyone else happy. Why should I be any different?

I want only the opportunity to be with you. That would make me happy.

You said that day that you loved me. You said you wanted

to take me away from here. You said you would like to marry me.

Please, tell me I am not too late to accept.

Yours forever,
Ruthie

EIGHTEEN

Millie looked up from the last page of the diary, her eyes glassy and filled with a sadness Ben hadn't seen there before.

"The letter is still here." She pressed her finger to the final page, her other hand flat against her chest. "Why didn't she give it to him?" There was a strange tremor in her voice, and she blinked hard and fast as a single tear made its way down her cheek.

Ben leaned across her table, the one that looked like it belonged on a front porch between two Adirondack chairs, the one she'd cleared of books and set with coffee mugs when he arrived at her apartment the night before. They'd read until the sun's morning light broke over the horizon, taking only a short nap to see them through.

Swiping his thumb across her cheek, he gave her a gentle smile. "You okay?"

She shook her head, covering her face with both of her hands, her elbows leaning on the edge of the table. "I don't know. I'm just . . . I know that she married Henry and they were happy. But what about George? What if she never got to tell him that she loved him?"

She was a hopeless romantic, his Millie, and it made him chuckle. It also made his heart beat just a little faster.

"I thought you wanted to be a Devereaux."

She dropped her hands and glared at him, her lips pursed to the side, showing off the dimple he hadn't bothered to notice before because he'd been too busy trying not to notice her at all. Until the night before, that is. Somehow a kiss in the dark had suddenly freed him to see what he'd been missing out on.

"I did." She huffed, clearly not satisfied with her answer. "I do. I mean, I need to be. But . . ." Jabbing her fingers through the long hair of her ponytail, she sighed again. "But I want Ruth to get what she wanted."

She shoved back her metal folding chair and picked up her coffee mug. It took all of two strides to get to the other side of the kitchen, where she clunked her mug on the counter with a bit of extra force. It rang in the silence, and she flexed her neck and shoulders several times before picking up the coffeepot and pouring its contents, which were certainly room temperature by now.

"Why did she run off and marry Henry when she was clearly in love with George? You don't just love someone and then run off with someone else." She spun around, a drop of coffee sloshing over the lip of her mug.

"And you have a lot of experience with that kind of thing?"

She shot him a hostile glare, her nostrils flaring and her eyebrows turning into thunderclouds. That just made him laugh harder. Perhaps it was a low blow given that she'd only had her first kiss several hours before. Then her second, third, and fourth. And her fifth when he arrived. And if he didn't mess this up in the next hour, he was hoping she had her sixth before he left.

"You can't read fifty romance novels a year without learning a thing or two."

He eyed the stack of books she'd set on the floor by her chair. White tags on each spine identified them as library loaners, and he raised his eyebrows in question. "All right then. What have you learned?"

"Well." She swung her hand toward the pile and dipped her chin. "I've learned that you don't give up on love. Ruth wouldn't have given up on George. Unless . . ."

He didn't know where she was going exactly, but she seemed to need a nudge. "Uh-huh. Unless what?"

"Unless she was expecting another man's child?" She fell into her chair, setting her cup on the table so hard that coffee splashed across onto the metal top. She mopped it up before it could mar the diary, but the glare she gave the book indicated she wouldn't have cared if it had been tarred and feathered.

"We don't know that she was."

"We don't know that she wasn't. There was the night on the beach. She alluded to a scandal, and that perhaps George would have to forgive her."

"There's not enough here to convict her."

She took a sip of her coffee, cringed, and put it back down. "Says you."

"Yes, says me. And I think you should give her the benefit of the doubt."

"But there are too many unanswered questions. If Henry isn't my great-grandfather, then who is? Ruth didn't tell us.

And why would she tell Grandma Joy there was a treasure map in these old diaries? There obviously isn't. I've read every page, and it's useless." She threw up her hands and let out a short breath. "Grandma Joy is going to be homeless in seventeen days, and I've spent the last month on a wild goose chase for nothing."

Ben reached for her hand and gave it a gentle squeeze. He wasn't certain he could take away her frustration. But he could try. "Maybe it's not for nothing. Ruth did tell us where Angelique buried her treasure."

She let out a little puff of air that sent her bangs flying. "I think I'd have noticed if she did."

"Or maybe you were too focused on Ruth falling in love with George."

She opened her mouth, sure to argue her case, and he held up a finger to hold her off.

"Hear me out." She nodded, and he caught and held her gaze for a long second. "Angelique did not have the stock certificates on her when she was arrested, right? I mean, if she had them on her person, they would have been found by the police when she was booked at the jail. And word would definitely have gotten back to Dawkins before Ruth left that last morning. So if she didn't have the certificates, then she had to have hidden them before she was found out."

Millie's pale eyebrows drew so tight that they almost appeared to be one line, but she nodded a slow concession.

"So then why did she take a shovel with her that night?"

"Because . . ." She bit her lips until they nearly disappeared. "I have no idea."

"I think she took it with her to dig up the treasure and move it."

Her eyes got round, and he could almost see the moment she reached the same conclusion he had.

"When she said that George's roses were too close."

He nodded.

"He was planting new roses too close to where she'd buried it."

He sat back and crossed his arms. "If I were a betting man, I'd put good odds on that."

She flashed him a broad smile, all straight white teeth and sass. But when she lifted her cup to her lips and swallowed, the smile was gone, replaced by a frown that didn't go away. "But that was ninety years ago. It must be long gone by now."

"Why would it?"

"Well, Angelique . . ."

"Went to Europe and died there."

She drummed her fingers against the table, her eyes shifting back and forth. "Her dad's lawyers must have gotten her off the charges or at least free on bail. Just like Jane said he would. And then she fled."

"Probably with that gold digger that her dad didn't want her to marry." His mind raced for the next steps, organizing them like a term paper. Somehow it helped to say things aloud, and Millie's agreement kept him going. "So she never had a chance to go back for it. At least as far as we know. And Ruth never went back for it, or she wouldn't have told Joy that there was a treasure and a map."

"But why not? Why didn't she go back? That doesn't make sense."

Why, indeed. He flipped it over and over in his mind, trying to put together everything he knew to be true about Ruth Holiday. "Well, she didn't forget about it."

Millie shook her head in agreement.

"She might not have known exactly where it was."

"But as far as we know, Ruth never even looked for it," Millie said. She chewed on her thumbnail, her eyes a window to the same mental acrobatics he was performing.

"So what did she do? She got married to Henry, had a baby, and weathered the Great Depression."

They both slammed their hands down on the table at the same time, making the open diary jump.

"Of course." Millie got back on her feet and marched the length of the kitchen. "Just two months later the stock market crashed, and those certificates would have been next to worthless."

"Dawkins never came back to look for them because he was hit so hard. He knew they couldn't save him. Whatever Georgia company he had bought stock in would have tanked too." Ben tapped his foot in time with Millie's stride. Bouncing his fist against his leg, he tried to make the next logical step. But there wasn't much to go on.

"So why didn't Ruth come back for it after the Depression?" His question was meant to be rhetorical.

Millie didn't settle for that. "She told us why in her diary."

He stared at the open pages, gently flipping back a day or two. He let the words roll across his mind. They'd spent an hour reading and talking, and he was certain—never once had Ruth said she didn't want the money. "No she didn't."

Millie leaned against his back, her arm stretched out over his shoulder, and for a moment he forgot to care about the diary and the treasure. He couldn't follow the line of her finger, not when he looked up at the underside of her chin and all the smooth skin of her neck. He remembered how sweet she tasted, like sunshine and strawberries. And he didn't want to argue with her. He didn't care about being right. But she didn't know that.

"Yes, she did. Remember?" She looked down, and their eyes locked.

Sparks shot through him, lighting a fire that burned somewhere deep in his chest. Would it always be like this with her? Could it always be like this?

Always. That wasn't something he'd ever thought about before. Not when his childhood had been nomadic at best. But with Millie, it didn't seem far-fetched. It seemed right. It was right.

Because he had gone and fallen in love with her.

Forget the spark. That fire inside him turned into a raging inferno. And only one thing could quench his thirst.

Stretching his neck up, he kissed her chin. Just a peck. Plenty to get her attention.

"Nice try, bucko. You're trying to distract me because you know you're wrong." But her giggle betrayed that his kiss wasn't unwelcome.

He knew no such thing. He couldn't even remember what they were disagreeing about.

"It's not going to work." She ran a finger along his jaw, her eyes tracing the movement as she bit her lip.

Oh, those lips. He could practically feel them against his own even now.

"Ruth said it clear as day. She said that Dawkins loved his money more than he cared about people. And Claude would do the same. Why should George or Henry or anyone else be different?"

He tore his gaze away from the pink bow of her mouth

just long enough to look into her eyes and hear the truth of her words.

"Maybe Ruth didn't want the money," Millie said. "And maybe she never told another soul about it."

"Which means it's right where Angelique left it."

"Too close to George's rosebushes, where the trees reach the beach."

He couldn't not kiss her again after such a brilliant announcement. "You're smart. You know that, Millie Sullivan?"

She shook her head, her cheeks turning pink, that blush all too familiar and beyond pretty.

"It's true." He pressed his lips to hers again, and she let out a low giggle.

"You really think so?"

"I know so. After all, you chose me to be your partner."

She rolled her eyes and pushed away from him. "I don't recall having much choice in the matter."

"Well, you were smart enough to trust me."

She considered it for a long moment, her hands on her hips and her head tilted. "I suppose that's true. Now let's go find Ruth's treasure."

Millie could hardly breathe. Not because of the long walk from the car to the beach, or because she was carrying a shovel that weighed more than a beluga whale. Not even because the July air was thicker than water.

She couldn't breathe because her heart was in her throat, beating a million times a minute.

And that was because Ben had stopped and pointed. He'd

said nothing, but a muscle in his jaw twitched. His knuckles turned white on the handle of his own shovel, and his eyebrows had risen almost to his hairline.

Now she couldn't look away from the row of bushes in front of them. Roses. Pink and white and blooming.

"I'm not sure I really thought those would be here." She choked out the words around her heart.

Ben stabbed his blade into the soil and leaned over the flowers. Pressing his nose against the petals, he took a deep breath and sighed. "George sure knew what he was doing."

"Uh-huh." But Millie didn't stop to literally smell the roses. Her gaze landed on the rock wall to their north, the Chateau's southern property line. "How did they get down here, off the grounds?"

"The wall is relatively new, within the last thirty years or so. Maybe this land was sold off by Dawkins's nephew at some point. We know for sure that the land the museum occupies ends at the wall."

Millie dug the toe of her tennis shoe into the soft soil. It was rich and black, protected from the sun by the canopy of trees above. A small creek trickled along ten yards away, its bubbling a soundtrack of tranquility. "So who owns it now?"

"I don't know. I didn't see any 'No Trespassing' signs on our way. Did you?"

She shook her head.

"But one thing's for sure. If we find a treasure on this land, whoever owns it won't stay silent for long."

With a chuckle, she stepped toward the end of the row of roses. "I'm pretty sure you're right about that. So, where do you want to start?"

Ben surveyed the ground around them, a clearing not more

than five feet. The place where Ruth had been nearly killed and George had rescued her. And Angelique had cried out that he was getting too close.

"I mean, it's pretty clear that the treasure isn't under the roses, right?" She didn't really need his agreement. She knew her argument was solid. "Otherwise George would have found it when he was planting them."

"Makes sense." He picked up his shovel again and dragged the point along the ground, seeming to test how hard the dirt had been packed. "And she would have wanted to make sure there was a marker, something that would help her identify the spot."

Millie's eyes roamed the clearing. What would Angelique do? Nothing too brazen or obvious. After all, she'd kept the entire house party in the dark about her thefts for months. She knew how to be low-key, to fly under the radar. So what would that look like here?

She turned a slow circle, surveying every tree and root and fallen twig. But the ground cover wouldn't have been there—at least not as it was now—ninety years ago. She turned again, trying to see what would have been there then. The trees would have grown wider, taller. The branches were thicker now, and they let in only patches of light through the leaves.

And then she saw it. It wasn't remarkable at all—not really. But it made her stomach flip and her heart leap at its spot in the base of her throat.

It was a simple mark on the birch tree. Its white trunk had been marred with a single line longer than an axe head. It was almost at shoulder height now, but ninety years ago it would have been at her shin perhaps. Just right for slamming a shovel through the bark.

"That's it."

Ben stopped his own survey and followed the line of her finger. And when he gasped, she knew he realized it too.

Without any more conversation they began to dig. Their shovels took turns sliding into the earth and tossing it aside. The damp dirt thumped as it landed in the ever-growing piles behind them. The air filled with the scents of dirt and leaves and the outdoors. And sweat.

In a matter of minutes Millie had to stop to wipe the drops from her forehead. When she missed one, it rolled into her eye, the salt stinging. She winced and blinked and wiped her face with her sleeve.

That's when she saw Ben watching her.

Perfect. The man who was used to seeing her in all of her Gilded Age glory now saw her for what she really was. Her silks were gone, her pearls forgotten. Her hair, always so carefully arranged and sprayed permanently into place, ran stringy and wild down her back. And she undoubtedly had sweat marks around her neck and down her back.

Nothing said "kiss me again" like sweat dripping off her nose.

But Ben didn't look away. And he didn't look disgusted. Instead he gave her a smile. It wasn't mocking or filled with pity. It was gentle and sweet, and it promised that they would do the tough things together.

And somehow that hit her harder than the roses or the tree trunk or Ruth's unmailed letter to George. Because this was real life. It was her life. For the first time in almost eight years, she wasn't alone. And more than that, she didn't want to be alone.

Her heart slammed into the back of her throat, and she

tried to smile back at him. But she knew it came out shaky and uncertain at best. He didn't seem to care. He just kept right on shoveling and smiling at her. Shoveling and smiling.

And then he struck something.

It echoed through the clearing and across the grounds, and Millie didn't know if she should fall to her knees or make sure that no one else had heard their discovery. Her stomach dropped, and she followed it, hitting the dirt with a quiet thud. Ben knelt on the far side of the shallow hole, his shovel abandoned and his hands clawing through the mud.

They brushed and scraped at the black earth until it revealed a pale blue metal box. Its corners had rusted over the years, and the silver buckle closure had certainly seen better days—probably right around 1929.

Ben dug his hand down the sides and pulled the box free of its burial place. And there, engraved in the metal below the buckle, were two little letters.

AD.

NINETEEN

Ben tried to pry the metal open with his bare hands, but the rust wasn't going along with his plan. It squealed and groaned and didn't budge at all. "Come on," he mumbled.

"Come on," Millie joined in.

It didn't help.

He was breathing hard by the time he set the box back down. It wasn't particularly heavy, but it was sturdy and built to last. That boded well for whatever was inside it. Not so much for the people trying to crack it open.

He looked at Millie, and she put her hands on her hips, her eyebrows forming an angry V. "We need some sort of leverage. You know, fulcrums and force and all that."

He quickly agreed. Setting the box on its back and wedging it securely between two tree roots, the buckle facing the sky, she shoved the tip of her shovel beneath the lip of the lid. Then she leaned on the handle.

Nothing happened.

She scowled and leaned harder, up on her tiptoes, hips wiggling and body shaking. Still nothing.

He wanted to laugh at her antics, but more than that, he wanted to know what was in that box. So he joined her, adding his weight to the pressure of the handle. The wood in their hands groaned, and he cringed, expecting it to splinter.

And then with no warning, the buckle popped and pieces flew at them. He ducked as his heart skipped a beat and the box clattered end over end.

They raced to it, kneeling on either side. He prayed this was what they'd been looking for, what they needed. He prayed that what they found would let him finally lay his mother's sins to rest.

Millie reached for the lid, but her hand stilled just before opening it. She looked up through thick lashes, and he could read the question in her eyes. Was it going to be enough?

And maybe that was the real question. Could it ever be enough? There was only one way to know.

"Open it," he said.

Squaring her shoulders and sucking in a quick breath, she gave a dip of her chin and popped the lid open.

His mind couldn't make sense of what was inside. Sunlight sparkled off of a chain of silver like nothing he'd ever seen. And beside it sat a ring with a glowing red ruby the size of the moon. Gold necklaces had tangled together, and strings of pearls pooled in a corner. The missing brooch lay over it all, pink and green gemstones outlining the wings of a butterfly. It was everything Ruth had written about and so much more.

Millie gasped, but Ben didn't have any air to do so. This was beyond what he could have imagined. And it was theirs. All theirs.

Or at least theirs to turn in to the authorities. And then, if unclaimed, unlooked for, unwanted, it could be theirs. Even a fraction. A finder's fee, as Millie had put it, would change their lives. His mom's debts could be paid. Every person he knew she'd swindled would be restored. Grandma Joy would receive the best care money could buy.

Because—for the first time in his life—money wasn't the issue.

Millie squealed as she pressed her hands to her face, then threw her arms around his neck. "We found it! This is really it!" She pressed a wild kiss to his lips and then leaned back on her heels, hands covering her face. Her shoulders shook. He couldn't tell if she was crying or laughing or both. It didn't matter.

His cheeks ached from smiling so hard, and there was a lump in his chest that he couldn't name. It was all so much.

Forcing himself to find out what filled the rest of the box, he pushed the glittering pieces to the side. Paper crinkled beneath his fingers, and his stomach did a full barrel roll, the pressure on his chest suddenly making it hard to breathe.

The stocks. Angelique's final theft was right here with the other things she'd stolen.

He pulled the papers free and read the heading. Across the top in bold letters was a word he knew well. *Coca-Cola.*

A chuckle broke free. Then a full-on laugh. And then his shoulders hunched and his whole body shook with mirth.

"What's so funny?" Millie asked.

It took him two tries to get the words out. "You know—that Georgia company—the one that Dawkins bought shares in?"

She nodded.

"It was Coca-Cola."

"Are you serious?"

He showed her the documents, ten pages of them, all with the same company name emblazoned across the top.

"What are these worth?"

"I don't know exactly. But if they're real, millions."

Her eyes welled with tears as laughter spilled out of her. And he could do nothing but hold her close.

"Can you even imagine? What would you do with this kind of money?" Millie couldn't hold back another giggle as Ben pulled his car into a parking spot in front of the sheriff's office. She hugged Angelique's box to her chest, her head still spinning with the possibilities.

It wasn't theirs yet. But maybe some of it would be.

He chuckled and seemed to think about it for a moment.

She didn't have to. "Of course, I'd find the very best home for Grandma Joy, somewhere I could visit her all the time, and when I couldn't be there, I'd be sure that they were taking the best care of her. I'd know she was happy and not scared when she forgot. I'd know it was clean and her sheets would get washed every week. And they'd never make her move again."

"That's a good dream. But nothing for you?"

"Oh, for me? I'd buy a car that always runs. I'd buy a house with real air-conditioning. No more of that useless window unit for me. And I'd buy myself a steak. A real steak—that someone else cooked. And I'd buy bookcases and fill them with books. Books that *I* owned!" She straightened in the passenger seat. "Definitely the books before the steak."

Ben laughed, his gaze off somewhere beyond the brick building before them.

"What about you? What will you do with your half?"

His gaze dropped, and his eyes drooped at the corners. "I'd try to make things right."

His words were vague, but they struck a memory in her, something that reminded her of all the times she'd thought he was holding back.

"Seriously, Ben. What would you do?"

"That's what I'd do. I'd make things right." He stared straight ahead, and his fingers gripped the steering wheel so hard that his knuckles turned pale.

"What things?"

Silence hung between them for so long that she thought he hadn't heard her, until his chin fell to his chest. He took a deep breath and kept his gaze somewhere near his feet. "All of them. As many as I could."

She pressed her hand against his arm. "What's the first one?"

He looked at her out of the corner of his eye. "Who?"

"Who, what?" She squinted at him, but while his face was in focus, his words were as obtuse as ever.

"Cora Aguilar."

She racked her brain for any memory of the name, but it didn't fit in Ruth's journals or their talk of treasure or anything that Ben had said to her. "Who's Cora?"

"My mom's first mark." When he was silent for too long, she squeezed his shoulder to keep him going. "I wasn't quite ten. I didn't understand how life worked. I didn't know where money came from. I just knew that the kids in my class sometimes made fun of me because my clothes had holes or my lunch was a can of sardines. And then one day there would be new shoes, the two-hundred-dollar ones that everyone wanted. I hadn't had three meals a day in two weeks, and suddenly I was wearing brand-new clothes. There were packed lunches and cookies when I got home from school. And then a few days later we had to move, sometimes sleeping in our car until my mom could find us an apartment."

Millie rubbed her eyes, which burned as he recounted his childhood. She hadn't always had much, but she'd had Grandma Joy and Grandpa Zeke. She'd had a home she didn't have to leave. "I'm sorry."

But he didn't seem to hear her. "I should have asked where the money was coming from."

A fist tightened around her stomach.

"But I didn't. If I wondered, I never asked. I couldn't. Not when whatever money was coming in was the difference between sleeping in our car and having a roof over our heads and a real shower. And you know the worst thing about being a homeless twelve-year-old boy?"

She shook her head. There was no way she could get a word around the lump in her throat, the weight on her chest.

"The other kids always make fun of the smelly one."

"Oh, Ben. I didn't know." She couldn't fuse the image of the clean-cut man before her with the picture in her mind of a little boy in need of a simple shower.

"So I didn't ask. I didn't question. I only wanted to survive. It wasn't until I was a sophomore in high school and I had this history teacher. I was only at that school in Jacksonville for a semester, but this teacher, Mr. Cunningham, made me fall in love with history. He made it so interesting, and I wanted to be just like him—to make students care about the past because it informs our future."

Whatever she'd felt for Ben before grew new blooms. She'd

cared about him, really liked him. And now . . . well, she wasn't sure what this was. But it was special. Different. And it swirled inside her, wiping out every doubt that might have stood between them.

"That was the first year I heard Cora's name."

Oh, right. There was more to Ben's story, and she leaned into it, into him.

"One day my mom said that the money had run out. We had to move. She needed another mark, and she had a tip from a friend at a retirement home near Nashville."

The twister inside picked up and took her stomach with it. "A tip?"

"I didn't ask her. I couldn't. I finally had a dream, and I wasn't about to lose out on it because my mom might have been doing something underhanded. But I knew she was."

Bile rose in the back of her throat, and she had to swallow convulsively to keep it down. She knew the type of person his mother was. She knew the damage that person could bring to a family. Damage it had brought to her family.

Ben let go of the wheel long enough to stab his fingers through his hair, rearranging the already wild style. "We were only there for a few months. But within weeks, money was rolling in. We had a new car, then two cars, one for each of us. It was luxury I had never known. I was in town long enough to get decent grades. I had a guidance counselor who convinced me I could go to college, so I weaseled away every dime I could. When Mom would leave me twenty bucks for pizza while she went out on the town with her boyfriend of the week, I would eat tuna sandwiches and tuck that twenty into a box under my bed."

"And that's how you paid for college? With other people's

money?" Her voice rose with each word, anger bubbling low inside her like a geyser searching for release.

He nodded. "And I regret it every day. Which is why I—"

"Which is why you want the money."

Again he gave her a nod, but he still didn't look in her direction. His shoulders slumped a little more with each word.

Everything inside her longed to fling open the car door and march into the sheriff's office, turn in the treasure, and hear that they could keep even a fraction of what it was worth. But something inside her had to dig deeper. It demanded to know the rest of his story. He'd given her clues along the way—just like Ruth had—and now she knew she was missing a key piece of the puzzle.

"And now your mom is in prison?"

"Yeah."

"How was she caught?"

His swallow filled the whole coupe. "About eight years ago she started a fake investment firm. She promised big returns on midsize investments, and she targeted retirees, mostly between here and the Florida state line."

"And she took their money and ran?"

She didn't really need to ask the question. The truth was right in front of her, and she could see it like it had been printed on the cover of a book.

And she was going to be sick.

He scrubbed his face with his palms. "When she was convicted, she was ordered to pay restitution, but her lawyers found a loophole. She filed for bankruptcy, and now she'll never pay a dime."

"So that's what you're doing? That's why you're working three jobs? To pay back those people?"

He looked at her then, his head still bent forward but a question in his eyes. Maybe her words should have been—if not pleased—at least accepting. But she couldn't keep the venom from filling every syllable.

"I am. At least the ones who were named in the court case. As many names as I can find, I'll make it right for them."

"And what about the years that they've lost? What about the ones that were homeless because of her? What about the ones who lost everything, who lost all hope? What about the ones who wouldn't have had to suffer at all if you'd just spoken up when you were a kid?"

He leaned his head back against his seat. "You think I don't think about that? I wish I'd made another choice. But at the time, it didn't feel like I had one. It was my mom or foster care. It was my mom or sleeping on the street. What kind of choice is that?"

Her fists shook in her lap so hard that the metal box rattled, and he looked from it to her face and back, his eyebrows raised with more questions.

But how could she explain? How could she tell him about the war inside her when it stole her breath? Every single thought was replaced with one word. When she closed her eyes, she saw it in the letterhead on her grandma's table like it had been emblazoned across the sky.

Aspire.

Her throat constricted, and she doubled over as tears filled her eyes.

"Millie? I'm sorry." He touched her back, but she couldn't bear it. Flinching away, she hugged the door and the box to her chest.

"I should have told you," he said. "I know it's a lot to ask you—to ask any woman—to deal with."

Yes. He should have told her. He should have told her when she offered him half of the treasure. He should have told her before she took him to see Grandma Joy. He should have told her before he kissed her.

He should have told her before he made her go and fall in love with him.

Stupid Ben.

Stupid Millie.

"Millie? Millie? What is it? I'm going to make it right. I'm doing everything I can to make up for it."

"It's not enough. It'll never be enough."

He blinked hard, jerking back in the tight confines. "What's that supposed to mean?"

But she answered him with a question of her own. "What's the name of the investment company that your mom set up?"

"What? Why?"

"*What* was it?"

Please, please, please. Let him say any other word. Let this all be a hoax, some sick joke. Let the ache in her stomach that threatened to tear her in half be from a misunderstanding.

Please, God. Let me be wrong. Let every coincidence be just that.

But she wasn't wrong. And she knew it from the tips of her toes to the top of her head. She'd followed that case from the jump, and there was no way his mom wasn't the woman she thought she was.

He frowned. "Aspire."

She flung her door open and vomited on the ground. Her

stomach rolled and rolled, and she hugged what had been her hope while her insides emptied.

"Millie?" Suddenly Ben was by her side, helping her up, but his touch burned, and she ripped herself out of his grasp.

"Stay. Away. From. Me."

"What is going on?" He tossed up his hands and took a couple steps back. "I don't understand why you're so upset."

"Because." She walked away and then back to him and poked him in the chest. "Your mom. Your mom—who you could have stopped—she stole everything! She took every penny that Grandma Joy ever earned!"

His jaw dropped open, his eyes wider than she'd ever seen them. "Grandma Joy. But she's not on my list. She's not—she wasn't named in the case."

"She didn't want to press charges. She said that justice was going to be done, and she didn't need to have her name on that list. She said . . . she said she could forgive that woman."

She spun and marched away, but she wasn't done. Flinging herself back around, she wagged her finger at him again. "But I can't. I won't!"

"I don't know what to say. I'm so sorry."

She snorted at him, derision dripping from her every cell. "Like that could begin to help." She pivoted and marched away, blind and uncertain where she was going.

"What about the money?"

"The money? Is that what you care about? Then keep it!" She flung the box in his general direction, her vision blurred and her lips trembling. "Keep your stupid money. I don't want it! I don't want you!"

And then she ran.

TWENTY

You look like someone ran over your dog."

Ben looked up from the keyboard at his desk with no idea how long he'd been staring at his motionless fingers. He was supposed to be responding to an online request for information. Instead he was stuck in a parking lot in front of the sheriff's office, the weight of the box landing in his arms as Millie took off like an Olympic sprinter.

She hadn't returned a single one of his phone calls. And there had been more than several.

He tried to smile at Carl's remark, but it took far too much effort. He managed only to lift one corner of his mouth, and it dropped immediately back to the frown.

Carl pulled on a pair of white cotton gloves and began to open a journal twice as old as Ruth's. "What's wrong? Treasure hunt not going well?"

"No. I mean, it's fine." He shook his head, trying to focus on Carl and not on the image of Millie's sweet lips as he saw them every time he closed his eyes.

One of Carl's bushy eyebrows raised, clearly doubtful.

Ben blurted out the first thing he thought of. "I mean, we found it. We found the treasure."

"Sure. That's why you look like a kid that got left at Mount Rushmore."

"Really." Ben turned back to his computer screen, his back to Carl. But he could still feel the other man's eyes on him. "We found it. It was south of the security wall—off the property."

"You don't say." Carl abandoned his project and sidled up to Ben's desk. "What'd you find?"

Ben shrugged, unable to muster any enthusiasm for their discovery. It didn't matter that he'd invested a month in trying to locate the treasure. It didn't matter what it contained.

None of it mattered without Millie.

"Well, it has to be better than sweet potato pie," Carl prodded. "If not, no one would bother looking for it. And those treasure hunters are still calling. Fewer than before the Chateau beefed up its security, but still, they're looking. So what was it? Worth the hubbub?"

"If any one of those hunters had found it, they wouldn't have been disappointed."

Carl gave a low grunt. "Uh-huh."

"More jewels than I've ever seen in one place. A handful of silver and gold necklaces, diamond pins, ruby rings."

Shaking his head, Carl let out a long whistle.

"And that's not the most valuable stuff." Carl raised his eyebrows, and Ben gave in. "Stock certificates from Coke."

Carl's jaw dropped. "From 1929? For *the* Coca-Cola Company?"

Ben nodded.

"Those are worth a fortune. Millions maybe."

"I know."

Clapping him on the back, Carl laughed. "So what'd you do with it? Put it in the bank? Does your girlfriend have it?"

"She's not my girlfriend." He snapped the words so quickly that even he wondered why he'd been so sharp. Carl assumed they were a couple. Ben only wished it were true.

He took a deep breath and tried to wipe Millie from his thoughts. Carl hadn't really been asking about his relationship status. Rubbing his hands over his knees, Ben shook his head. "I turned it in to the sheriff."

"I suppose you would have to. And they're going to track down the rightful owners?"

Ben shrugged. "I guess so. They're going to try anyway."

Carl tapped his toe on the ground, uncrossing and then recrossing his arms. "So do you know whose property it was found on? If it's not the museum's, it must belong to someone other than the Dawkins family. Maybe they have a claim to it."

"I don't know. And I don't really care at the moment."

He couldn't believe those words had just come out of his mouth. Even if they were true.

The money didn't matter without Millie. He'd work a dozen jobs to take care of her and Grandma Joy and to repay what his mother had stolen.

But Millie had been right. He couldn't give back the years. He couldn't erase the heartache or stress or give them back that time free of worry and fear. He could never make it right. So why should she forgive him?

Carl gave another long, low whistle. "Tell me what's going on in that head of yours, boy. No man alive would give up a treasure like that. Not without a fight. Or not unless he knew he was beaten."

It didn't take him even a split second to know the truth. "I'm beaten."

"What'd she do to you?"

"Nothing." Oh man. He sounded like a petulant teenager now. He rolled his eyes at himself and leaned back in his chair—the same one Millie had sat in when she'd sprained her ankle. The ankle that had hurt too badly for her to run, so he'd carried her to make sure they were both safe. Which was why he'd arrived at the secret passage out of breath and feeling far too warm. And probably why he'd kissed her like a lunatic.

But being out of breath and overly warm did not explain why he'd enjoyed the kiss so much. Or why he'd thought about a repeat performance every day since. Which was why knowing she didn't want to be any part of his life ever again made his heart feel like it had gone twelve rounds with a meat tenderizer and lost.

Yep. He'd been beaten.

"I'm going to need more than that," Carl said.

"More than what? More than 'nothing'?"

Carl nodded, kindly ignoring what a jerk Ben was being to his own boss.

Ben leaned forward, resting his elbows on his knees and his face in his palms. "What do you need to know? That Millie and her grandmother are broke because of me?"

All pretense of good humor vanished in an instant. "You best start talking. Right now. That girl was sweet as sugar and put a light in your eyes like I've never seen. And if you treated her badly, then we're going to have words."

"I didn't mean to. I didn't even know I had." And then it all spilled out. About his childhood and his mother and how he was trying to pay them all back. And how he had discovered that Grandma Joy had been swindled but wasn't listed in the court files.

"She's never going to forgive me. And I can't blame her. I've made her life miserable."

Carl sniffed, folding his gloved hands in front of him. "Seems like you weren't really to blame. You were just a kid."

"Well, it might sound that way to you. Millie doesn't agree." Ben sighed into his palms. "And she's not wrong. I messed up. Badly. I thought I could make up for not doing anything. I didn't even realize—until I talked with her—just what my actions had cost my mom's victims."

"The sin of inaction," Carl mused.

Ben sat up enough to see Carl's face. His eyes had taken on a distant look, and there was a pain in the set of his jaw.

"I think maybe we all have regrets. I've read enough letters and journals and newspapers from the last two centuries to know. It isn't a new affliction. People have been struggling with it for years. Good intentions but bad results."

"Yes. But she can't see past the results."

Carl strolled across the room, back to his worktable, his hands moving around the papers in front of him. "Here's what I know for sure. People have been messing up for centuries, millennia. We've been ruining relationships, hurting others, seeking only what's best for ourselves. It's human nature. It's what we do. We're imperfect people."

"Is that supposed to be a pep talk?"

Shooting him a scowl, Carl kept going. "But it's the imperfect—the broken—who need mercy. The perfect don't need anything. But you and me and the rest of the world, we need mercy. We need forgiveness. Even someone like your mom."

Oh man. That was a knife to the heart.

He clutched at his chest and tried to take a deep breath. But there was no air.

"You're more than that, you know."

Ben tried to look up at Carl, but he couldn't lift his chin.

"You know that, right? You're not what your mom did. You're not the bad choices you may have made. You're who you are right now, and you're the next decision you make."

"How can I be who I want to be if Millie can't ever forgive me?" Ben asked.

Carl huffed like he was getting frustrated. "Millie's forgiveness doesn't define you. God's forgiveness takes care of that."

Had he been defined by God's mercy or his mother's scandal? Had he been characterized by grace or by making it right on his own?

Well, now he knew. He could never make it right. There was nothing he could do that would be good enough to wipe it away. There were consequences for his actions.

But there could be forgiveness too.

"Why's it so important to you what Millie thinks of you?"

Ben threw his hands up and groaned. "Because I'm in love with her. I think I am anyway. I never have been before, but when I'm with Millie, I see a different future. It's not about my past. It's about what we could be—together."

Carl nodded like he found the response satisfactory. "And what is it that she wants?"

"To never see me again?" He managed to quirk the corner of his mouth and let out a half chuckle, half groan.

"Or . . . to know who she is?"

"How'd you know about that?"

Carl shrugged. "She doesn't seem the kind to be consumed by money, so when you said her great-grandmother had been at the Chateau, I figured there was more to her story than all that treasure hunting. So I did a little digging."

Ben pushed himself out of his chair, marching to the work-table and forcing Carl to look at him. "What did you find?"

"Oh, this and that."

Pressing his hand to the tabletop, Ben leaned in closer.

Carl chuckled. "Only that Ruth Holiday was married."

"Right. To Henry Jefferson."

Carl's lips twisted with a Cheshire grin. "To someone else. Before Henry."

"And I kissed him. A lot!" Millie flung her arm across her face. Somehow admitting to the last was so much worse than everything else that she'd just told her grandma. Worse than not knowing where her grandma was going to move. Worse than discovering Ben was the son of the woman who had made their lives miserable. Worse than throwing away the treasure in a fit of anger.

The only thing worse was that she really wanted to kiss him again.

Not that she'd admitted that to Grandma Joy. She had no intention of ever doing such a thing. She'd never tell another soul for the rest of her life.

And maybe by then she'd have stopped thinking about Ben altogether.

Dreamer.

Oh, knock it off. That's what readers did. They dreamed. She dreamed. And if she wanted to dream that she'd some-day forget Ben, then she was going to do it.

From her favorite chair, Grandma Joy rocked forward to reach for her hand, and Millie rolled to her side. Lying on her grandma's bed, she was nearly eye to eye with the woman who had raised her.

Gnarled fingers moved to her hair and combed through the strands over and over again. For a second Millie was once again a child. Comforted and cared for. She wasn't the one in charge, and she certainly wasn't responsible for someone she couldn't support.

"I'm sorry," Millie said.

"Whatever for?"

Her stomach swooped, and tears burned at the back of her eyes. Millie had lost her again.

But then her grandma continued. "You have nothing to be sorry for. You couldn't have known Ben's role in his mother's scheme. And you couldn't have known who his mother is."

"But now I've given away any chance—"

Suddenly her purse vibrated on the tile floor. It rattled and shook her keys. But she didn't get up to answer her phone.

Grandma Joy gave her a hard look that traveled to the bag and back. "Going to get that?"

"No, ma'am."

"You know that every single one of us is more than the worst thing we've done. All of us. We bear the image of our Maker. Even Ben."

Millie stiffened, and perhaps her grandma could feel her trying to pull away. Her hand grew heavier, keeping her in place.

"And we're surely more than the worst thing someone in our family has done."

"But . . . but his mother is the reason we're in this situation. Because of her, I can't afford to take care of you. And Ben was complicit in all of it."

"My dear, he was a child. And there is so much more to life than money."

"But she stole those years from us."

"She stole no such thing. That's life. The struggle and scraping. The figuring out how to find joy in the midst of pain. That's the good stuff." Grandma Joy took a deep breath and closed her eyes, rocking back and forth for a long second. "For as long as the good Lord has us here on earth, that's what we'll keep doing. Can you find happiness, my sweet girl?"

Millie shook her head, not sure she could give the Sunday school answer.

"Losing the money means so much to you. And not being a Devereaux?"

She sat up then, pulling her hand out of her grandmother's grasp, leaning against the wall, and looking her in the eye. "Do you really think I only care about money? I'm doing all of this to care for you. I just want you to be safe and taken care of." Suddenly her grandmother's form swam before her eyes, her dear face wrinkling with concern.

"Honey, you know that money is never going to be enough."

She looked toward the ceiling in an attempt to keep the burning in her eyes from turning into a full-on flood. It was easy for Grandma Joy to say that money wasn't important. She didn't have any idea how much it would cost to put her in a new home. Or how hard Millie had worked to make sure they had all they needed.

"I wish it was that easy, Grandma."

A gentle pat on her hand followed a low hum. "Oh, I never said anything about it being easy. There were times when your grandfather and I thought we'd have to sell the house and every acre we had. But it was never about how many nickels were in our savings account."

"Then what?" Millie threw up her hands. "How can we survive without enough money?" She hated how petulant she sounded, but her grandma was off on another fantasy. Maybe her memories were lucid, but her problem-solving skills left something to be desired.

Grandma Joy patted her hand. "You're looking for money to be your provider."

Millie began to nod, and her grandma cut her off quickly. "Money isn't what provides for you. Money is a tool. God—" She paused and looked hard at her granddaughter. "God is the one who provides. Let him take care of you."

The tears began to leak in earnest then, rolling to her chin and dropping to the front of her shirt. "It's not that easy. How can I trust him when he's taken everything from you? What that woman didn't steal, God has. What's to say he won't take everything from me?"

"And what if he does? Will you fault him for that?"

Honestly? Probably, yes.

"Who am I to question God's ways?" Grandma Joy's smile was filled with concern but as radiant as ever.

Millie wanted to punch a wall. "But he took your memories." As sure as Ben's mother had stolen Grandma Joy's retirement, God had left her a mere shell of the woman she had been.

"Oh, he didn't take my memories."

Millie let out a low snort. Easy to say but contrary to every piece of evidence.

"Sometimes they may not be easy for me to retrieve, but that doesn't make them any less mine. The experiences—those years raising your dad with my Zeke, then a chance to raise a little girl like I'd always wanted, all those years farming and serving my community and my church—those are my story. And even if I can't remember them, God hasn't stolen them. Every little face I taught in Sunday school. Every woman I brought a care package to after she gave birth. And every time I look at your face, I'm reminded that my story lives on in all of you. God used me then, and maybe he'll use me now. No check or dollar amount can take that from me. No matter if I forget, I know there are those who remember that I was there during a hard time or brought a measure of comfort in a difficult season or helped to raise a young woman who can change the world."

Millie's chest ached, and she'd entirely given up on trying to stem the flow of tears.

Could it be true? Could all that her grandmother said be true? Maybe a person's story wasn't like a book that became useless after the pages were too worn to read. It wasn't about how much that person could remember. It was about how many lives they had touched. It was about making a difference in the little ways.

"Sometimes I can't remember his face—your grandfather's. And sometimes it is so clear that I think he might be sitting on the bed next to me."

"Oh, Grandma."

"No, no, dear." Her grandma patted her arm. "It's not sad. I love thinking that he's right by my side. Even if I'm mistaken, I know that we were together. I know we shared a life that mattered. Even when I can't remember the details, I'm sure of that. Because even the hard times are manageable when you have someone to share the pain with."

"You have me. I'm right here."

With a laugh and a sigh, Grandma Joy shook her head. "I do love you, my sweet girl. But you need more than me. You need someone to lean on, someone to lean on you. Life is so much sweeter when you're not in it alone. Why do you think God gave Eve to Adam?"

"But she betrayed him." She spit the words out much more vehemently than she'd planned, the story far too close to the one she was currently living.

"Oh, Adam didn't need any help finding sin. He needed someone to be with him after the garden. He needed someone who understood everything he'd lost and could walk by his side anyway."

Someone who could understand loss. Ben had lost his parents. Not exactly like she had, but the result was the same—a life of trying to pick up the pieces all alone. A life of failing to make good out of the pain of the past.

She hiccupped on a restrained sob as another rush of tears covered her cheeks, and she pressed her forehead to her grandma's hand. Had she missed out on her chance to be with someone who could truly understand? Someone who not only cared about her but also cared *for* her?

"But even if he cares for me, how can I forgive him?" She couldn't. It wasn't that simple.

Grandma Joy's eyes turned sad. "All of us are more than the worst thing we've ever done. All of us. Your dad is more than running off and leaving you behind. Because in his selfishness he gave me a gift—you. And that handsome young man of yours is more than failing to turn in his mother."

"You sure about that?"

"What is he?"

"What do you mean?" Millie rubbed her head, trying to push away the pain behind her eyes. "He's a history professor and a security guard and an archivist."

"So, a hard worker?" Grandma Joy looked rather smug, and Millie wanted to contradict her, but she couldn't. He *was* a hard worker. "And what did he do when you told him you'd been hiding your real reasons for looking for the treasure?"

Millie scowled. She hadn't told Grandma Joy that so she would use it as ammunition. "I suppose he forgave me."

"Not only did he forgive you, he did it quickly. On the spot."

"Yes. And he's loyal. And he works at a library."

Grandma Joy's smile turned even more smug. "He likes books, does he?"

"Well, not novels so much. But yes."

This was not good. Grandma Joy was making far too much sense, and Millie didn't want sense. She wanted to be angry. She wanted to hang on to a grudge. She didn't want to put herself out there and risk being hurt again. Because she knew how badly it could hurt. Because she was just protecting herself. Because . . .

Because you're an idiot.

Yeah, she deserved that.

"I don't know what to do. It's too late." Her heart had been shattered, and it was too late to put the pieces back together again.

"Oh my, no. It's never too late for love. It's never too late for forgiveness. Tell him how you feel."

A line from Ruth's diary jumped to her mind, and she shook her head. "Ruth's mama used to tell her that feelings were just feelings. Maybe it doesn't matter what I feel. Especially if he doesn't feel the same."

Grandma Joy clucked like an old hen. "You've piled those excuses higher than cow patties. And that's all they're worth— a load of manure."

"But—"

"You're sure quick to give up on love for someone who reads so many romance novels. Don't you believe in what you're reading? Don't you think that true love is patient and kind and it doesn't hold a grudge? What kind of drivel is in those books you read if they're not showing that kind of love? Real love isn't love because it's easy or always feels good. It's love because you choose not to be self-serving."

"But . . ." Her mouth flapped like a fish out of water.

"But what? You know I'm right, and you'll never know what he's thinking if you don't return his phone calls."

She glanced at her purse, which had vibrated at least three times since she arrived. "How do you know he's been calling?"

"Because he's followed you on a hunt with no promise of riches, except your time. Because I saw the way he looked at you on that first visit. Because he's a good man who won't let you run off without trying to win you back." She pushed her rocker, setting off the squeaks. "He cares for you the way that George cared for Ruth. And I'd wager a week's worth of pudding that you care for him too. And that you'd like to kiss him again."

Millie dropped her gaze and pressed a hand to her neck, trying to cover the flames that were already rising toward her ears. How did her grandma know her so well?

"I'll take that as a confirmation. Was it nice?"

Nice? A glass of milk was *nice.* A warm shower was *nice.* Finding a new pair of shoes at the thrift store was *nice.*

Ben's kiss had been like fire and ice in one. It had been a choir of angels singing. It had been forget-everything-but-his-lips-on-hers fantastic.

And if she didn't do something about it, she would never have another kiss from him. Ever.

There were things she could live without. Financial security. A two-bedroom home. A purse that had never been owned by someone else.

Ben was not one of those things.

Grandma Joy leaned over and cupped Millie's face with her hands, her skin as smooth as butter. "He's so much more than the mistakes he's made. He knows he was wrong, and he's a history professor."

Millie's eyebrows bunched together.

"Studying history is all about learning from our past so we don't repeat mistakes in the future." Grandma Joy leaned in until their foreheads nearly touched. "Ruth may have missed out on the love of her life because she didn't tell him how she felt. Don't make her mistake."

Millie let out a dry chuckle devoid of any humor. It was true. If she didn't learn from Ruth's mistakes, she was bound to repeat them. And Ruth may have chosen love over money, but if she never told George, what good was it?

Millie might never know how it all ended.

Grandma Joy leaned back in her chair, picking up the old

diary once again. She flipped through the pages, landing on the final letter to George. "Imagine missing out on true love by half a page. That's all that connects this letter to the journal."

Millie cringed. Imagine missing out on love because she held on to a grudge.

The thought made her stomach ache, and she doubled over as Grandma Joy studied the back cover of the diary.

"Well, I'll be."

Millie didn't have the wherewithal to ask what had caught her grandma's attention.

Suddenly Grandma Joy howled with delight. "Will you look at that?"

TWENTY-ONE

*M*illie clutched the folded pieces of paper in her hands, trying not to wrinkle them, but shaking so much she thought she might drop them if she wasn't careful. She wasn't sure if it was what she was holding that had her shaking or the man she hoped to find.

Well, actually, there was a good chunk of her hoping not to find him, even though she really needed to. If anyone could help her make sense of the diary's biggest secret, it was Ben Thornton.

She was fully capable of asking for his help without throwing herself into his arms and begging him to kiss her again. Although that had worked well for Gennie and Sir Robert. Just when it had seemed that all hope was lost and her father would never allow them to find happiness together after Sir Robert swam across the moat, Gennie had climbed out of her bedroom window on a rope of bedsheets and run to the stables, where he was preparing his horse for a midnight ride. She'd flung her arms around him, buried her face in his chest, and whispered the words she'd been holding back for so long. "I love you, Robert. I always have."

Not that Millie would say that to Ben. She wouldn't. Not even anything remotely related to that. She would remain professional and poised. She'd ignore every moment that they'd shared and forget the gentle rasping of his whiskers against her skin or how he'd refused to leave her behind at the gazebo. Or the way he'd forgiven her when she'd been a little less than honest with him about her interest in the Devereaux family. Or the way he'd been so incredible with Grandma Joy.

Or the way his face had melted with heartbreak when he realized that Grandma Joy had suffered at his mother's hand.

Tears began to pool at the corners of her eyes as she marched across the crisp green grass, and she rolled her eyes to keep them at bay. As she walked through the library's sliding glass door, she took a deep breath. It didn't help. Everything inside her was wound as tight as a spool of thread.

The librarian behind the front desk greeted her by name, but Millie could only wave in response. A lump was growing in the base of her throat, and it took everything inside her not to turn around and run. Because she didn't know what she'd say to him. Because she wasn't sure she could be in the same room with him. Because she was a big old chicken.

Only one thing kept her weaving through the stacks of books and refraining from disappearing between the rows of fiction titles. The name on the paper in her hand.

George Whitman.

She paused in front of the closed door at the back corner. Maybe Ben wouldn't be here. Maybe he'd be teaching a class.

But that wasn't probable unless he'd changed his schedule in the last three days.

Or unless he was avoiding anywhere she might be looking for him.

It was possible but not likely, given the myriad of messages he'd left on her voicemail. Not that she'd listened to them. But the calls had come more frequently in the last day and a half, and she couldn't help but wonder if she'd left a void in his chest half the size of the one he'd left in hers.

Raising a trembling hand, she formed a fist and knocked twice. The door swung open before she could strike it a third time.

Suddenly face-to-face with Ben, she took an unsteady step back. His eyes lit with something she couldn't name, and a tentative smile spread across his lips. Oh, those lips. Full and pink and as firm as she remembered.

"Hi." His voice sounded like it had gone through a meat grinder. "Did you get my message?"

"You mean, all seventeen of them?"

If he'd had any proclivity toward it, she was certain he would have blushed in that moment. But her cheeks burned instead.

"I got them."

His entire face transformed from uncertainty to pure joy. "So you know!"

"Know what? I got them . . . but I didn't listen to them."

His eyebrows dipped low again, his voice holding her at bay as much as his arm that kept the door from fully opening. "Then why are you here?"

She shouldn't have come. This was a terrible idea.

Oh, shut up.

No. She would not shut up. She'd let Grandma Joy talk her into coming to see him after her shift at the diner, still smelling of grease and syrup. She'd told herself some story about how they could go back to how it was before she'd known the truth.

But she wasn't sure she could. Because when she saw him, she saw his mom. She saw the face of the woman with no heart and less conscience.

But that's not Ben. You know it's not.

As if he could hear her internal dialogue, his features softened again. "I'm glad you're here. I'm so glad." He swung the door open into the archivist room. "Carl's at lunch. But we found something."

She shouldn't do it. This couldn't end well.

You can trust him.

She took a step in, then leaned away. Finally she held up the paper in her hand, waving it at him. "I really only came to ask if you could help with this."

Ben held out his hand. "I'll try. What do you have?"

She lowered it onto his palm, keeping her hold on it for a long second.

Let go!

She released it with a sudden jerk, and he opened it up, his eyes scanning the page. With no choice but to follow him inside, she slipped in before the door could close her out.

"This is a property deed. And it belongs to George Whitman."

"I know." She stopped at that, but the silent *I'm not an idiot* was more than implied.

He looked up with a smile. "Of course. Where did you find it?"

"It was hidden in the back cover of Ruth's diary. The second one."

Ben snorted. "Why am I not surprised?"

"What's that supposed to mean?" Millie wrapped her arms around her stomach. It was more of a settling hug than a barrier between them.

"I'll tell you in a minute." Ben plopped down in the chair in front of his computer. "Do you know where this plot is located?"

"That's what I was hoping you could help me with. Do you have access to the county records that far back?"

He nodded, already clacking away at the keys. Suddenly a map appeared on his screen, the land divider a clean white line across a sea of green trees. It was a relatively small plot of land, especially compared to its northern neighbor. But Millie gasped all the same.

"Is that . . ." She pointed at a pale blue line that wiggled its way toward the clearly defined beach. "Is that the creek? The one by where we found the treasure? And that's the . . ." Well, there was no use pointing it out, really. The giant white structure in the adjoining piece of land could only be the Chateau.

"Yep."

"So George owned the land. That land. Where we found the treasure." Her words weren't making a whole lot of sense even to herself, and she leaned over his shoulder to get closer to the truth.

"He owned the property, all right. And if this is still accurate"—he waved his hand toward the screen—"it still belongs to his family. The treasure, even though it was on his land, probably still belongs to the family of the original owner. The sheriff's office will track down Dawkins's heirs and return the certificates and probably the jewelry too."

Millie sagged against his desk, her heart thundering. She'd known that would be the case for the treasure, but it still didn't explain one thing. "Then why did Ruth have it? She never told him how she felt, so why would he have given her the deed to a plot of land worth thousands?"

"Well, that's not exactly right."

Millie's gaze snapped toward him, but she couldn't find the words to formulate a complete question.

Ben pushed back his chair, and with a quick tilt of his head he invited her to follow him to the adjacent table. "I found something. I mean, really Carl did. But he thought it might help."

"Help what?" As soon as they were out there, she wished she could reel her words back in. She knew what. But for a split second she'd forgotten. She'd forgotten that she had to remember that he was more than the worst thing he'd done.

He just was. He was more than the boy who hadn't known how to turn in his mother. He was more than the son of the woman who had conned Grandma Joy. He was more than she'd given him credit for.

He was a child of God, created in his image. Infinitely lovable. And she did love him.

"I'm sorry. I'm so sorry." The words flew out of her mouth of their own accord, but she meant them from the very depths of her soul. "I shouldn't have yelled at you. I shouldn't have thrown the box at you and run away. I was shocked. I was hurt. It just all hit me at once, and I couldn't see past my own past."

Her breaths came in short gasps, and her cheeks were suddenly wet with tears. "I was heartbroken and I was scared—I am scared. I don't know how I'm going to take care of my grandma, and I've blamed your mom for so long. Suddenly I had someone else to blame, and I hated it. Because—because—" She tossed her hands up in the air, fighting for the words she wanted to say and the ones she knew she couldn't.

Just say it, you chicken.

Yes, she was a big chicken. So what?

So, are you going to make the same mistake Ruth made?

"Because I think I'm falling in love with you, and I don't know how to do that and blame you too. I just want—"

She didn't have time to tell him what she wanted because suddenly his hands cupped her cheeks and he pressed his lips to hers. Her stomach tanked, swooping low and fast, and she grabbed at his forearms to stay on her feet.

An electrical current raced down her spine, sweeter than syrup.

And then she was too far away from him. Grabbing his sides, she pulled him against her and wrapped her arms around his waist. He was trembling. Or maybe that was her. It was hard to tell this close, but somehow it didn't matter.

His thumb brushed a tear off her cheek, its path warm and tender. "Sweet Millie. I'd do anything to make it right." His words were little more than warm breath against her skin, his thumb dragging across the bottom of her lip. It built something inside her that she couldn't name, something that burned and churned and begged for more. His gaze followed the same path, and it was more tangible than even his touch, setting her entire being on fire.

"I didn't know how much I needed someone in my life until I met you." He cleared his throat. "I was so used to doing it on my own, and then you showed up in my life, a means to an end. I thought the money might . . . I thought it would help me make up for my regrets. But then, all of a sudden, I couldn't imagine my life without you. I didn't realize just how empty it had been until I lost you. And now I have nothing to offer. Nothing to give. I can only beg for your mercy."

Her lips trembled until she thought she'd never be able to respond, and even as she began, the words were uneven and stuttered. "Grandma Joy always said that those who have been shown mercy give mercy."

His breath hitched, and suddenly his whole face swam before her.

"I forgive you, Ben Thornton. Will you forgive me?"

He tugged on her hand, pulling her into his side and wrapping one arm around her waist. "I'll do you one better."

"Always trying to one-up me, huh?"

He chuckled. "You're going to like this one."

"Better than that last kiss? Doubtful."

He gave her a full belly laugh at that. "Okay, maybe it's not that good. But it's close."

"I might need another example just to make sure."

Leaning over, he obliged her. This one wasn't quite as urgent, not quite as fierce. It was gentle and sweet and as tender as any touch she'd ever known. She could stay in his embrace for the rest of her life.

And she might have if Carl hadn't barged in on them.

Millie jumped back, but Ben didn't let her go completely, even though he couldn't miss the flames licking up her neck.

"Ah, I see you told her then."

Ben shook his head. "I was just about to get to it."

"Get to what?"

Ben's grin made her knees tremble. "We found a picture of your grandma."

"Grandma Joy?" She squinted at him, then at the newspaper clippings printed out and scattered across the worktable. "What do you mean?" She felt like an idiot but she couldn't put any of these pieces together.

"Well, actually, we found a picture of Ruth—clearly pregnant—in *The Herald*." Ben looked at Carl as though waiting for approval to continue, but Millie could only push at his chest.

"Was there an article? What did it say?"

"Her loving parents were enjoying a church picnic and eagerly awaiting the arrival of their baby."

She gasped, searching for a full breath and knowing it wouldn't come until he confirmed what she already knew somewhere deep within.

Ben rubbed his hand up and down the full length of her bare arm. "Her loving parents, George and Ruth Whitman."

The tears didn't bother with an introduction. They just poured out of her eyes, down her cheeks, and rolled off her chin. "They—" She hiccupped loudly, slapping a hand over her mouth. "They were married?"

"Carl was the one who found their wedding announcement. It was a small one in their local paper, but as soon as he had George's last name, he was like a hound on a scent."

She turned to the grizzled archivist and reached out to him with both hands. "Thank you. Thank you for finding my heritage."

Carl tried to pull away, but she wouldn't be denied a full hug.

"And he found a building permit request in the county

archives," Ben said. "George was going to build her a home on their property, a gift from Howard Dawkins."

"The property." She squeezed Carl again.

Ben swallowed audibly. "There was an obituary only a few weeks after the picnic. George died in a farming accident before he could build her that house, and Ruth remarried."

"They were hard times," Carl said. "It wasn't unusual for a man and woman to marry because they simply needed a partner."

"Henry." She whispered the name, sending up a quick prayer of gratitude that he'd loved Ruth well and Joy as his own all those years. He might not have been the love of Ruth's life, but at least she'd had a short time with George and a constant reminder of him in Joy's smile.

"So, you're definitely not a Devereaux." There was an implied question in Ben's words, and Millie mulled it over, letting the truth fully form before she responded.

"No. I'm not. And I'm good with that. I'm . . . I'm actually really happy about it." Which was true but made no sense considering that she was crying again. Not loud sobs or uncontrollable tears. But her eyes kept filling and leaking with every rapid blink.

Ben reached over and brushed her cheeks dry. Then he leaned in and kissed away one tear that he'd missed. She nearly melted into a puddle at his feet.

Who did that kind of thing? Who was so tender and kind even when she was falling apart for no identifiable reason?

Sir Robert? Probably.

Ben Thornton? Apparently so.

And she'd rather have Ben any day of the week.

But that didn't change the truth. She wasn't a Devereaux,

so there would be no money from them. She and Ben had no claim on the treasure—even if it had been found on Ruth and George's property. And Grandma Joy was still about to be kicked out of her room at the home.

All this time. All this effort. All this energy she'd put into finding the diaries and the treasure. It was all a waste. She was no closer to being able to care for Grandma Joy.

But at least you don't have to do it alone.

For once she didn't want to argue with the voice in her head. Instead she leaned against Ben's side, thankful. Maybe everything they'd been through over the summer was for that only—for the certainty that she had a partner. In treasure hunting. And in real life.

"I don't know what I'm going to do with Grandma Joy." Taking a deep breath, she stepped out in faith. "Maybe we can figure it out together?"

He squeezed her, and it was better than all the century-old stock certificates in the world. "As it turns out, Joy happens to be a very wealthy landowner."

"No. She sold her house, and the money . . ."

Ben picked up the deed to the property. "She's the sole heir to George Whitman's estate, which happens to include almost half an acre of beachfront property on St. Simons Island. Do you know what that's worth?"

Millie shook her head and tried to ignore the bells ringing in her head.

"Only about a million and a half or so."

"Dollars?" What a stupid question. Yes, of course, dollars. American dollars. More than a million of them.

Something inside her chest filled to bursting and then exploded with joy and hope and pure relief. She flung her arms around Ben's neck and let all those pesky tears make a pool right on the front of his shirt.

"Unless you want to keep the land. You know, for sentimental purposes."

She chewed on her bottom lip for a long moment. "I guess property is nice. I've never owned any before. But how could a patch of land compare to knowing that Grandma Joy is safe and cared for? With that kind of money, I could get her a spot in a home right on the beach. Can you imagine?"

He chuckled. "She could have any room she wanted. She's a millionaire now."

Millie shook her head, her face still pressed against his chest. "Not quite. Half of it is yours."

He stiffened, his lean body turning immobile. She couldn't manage to look into his face.

"I can't take that money," he said.

"Can't take the treasure?" Carl's voice boomed. "What kind of idiocy is that?" He shook his head and strolled toward the door, mumbling something about being as silly as some woman.

It seemed to shock Ben from his stupor. "Oh, I almost forgot. Sam, Sam Williams. The woman that bought your grandma's house. She's the one who was looking for the treasure and told that crazy website. She's the reason all those treasure hunters visited the Chateau."

Millie nearly had whiplash from the change in topic, and she scrambled to catch up. "How do you know?"

"She showed up here at the library. She was looking for information on the Chateau's history, and when I asked her one question, she folded. Confessed the whole thing. She overheard us talking about it when we went to the farmhouse, and then when she contacted that treasure-hunting website for help, they published the rumors."

Her laugh was little more than a dry cough. "Some people will do anything for a treasure. But you don't seem to want the half I promised you."

His heartbeat picked up speed beneath her ear. "I turned in the treasure to the authorities. All of it. Your land isn't part of that. It's not what we agreed on. Besides, if it hadn't been for me and my mother, you never would have needed it in the first place."

"Um . . . technically that's true. But here's the thing." She risked a quick peek at his lips, which were pursed to the side, his jaw tight. "I think Grandma Joy likes having you around. She's asked about you—at least, I think 'that handsome fellow' is referring to you."

His laughter reverberated in his chest, and it echoed inside her too.

"I think she'd like to have you around some more. I think I'd like that too. And maybe if I could get a good home for her and you could repay the money your mom stole—well, we might only have to work one job apiece. Maybe then we would get to spend some time together."

"And maybe we could see where this thing leads?"

Those bubbles were back in her chest, better than sweet tea on a sunny day. She felt strange and new all over. And she was pretty sure it was almost entirely Ben's fault.

She didn't really need the money. Maybe she never had. She just needed him.

He hooked his finger under her chin and lifted it up, forcing her to meet his gaze. "Is that something you'd be open to?"

"Seeing where this thing"—she thumped his chest and then her own—"goes?" She pretended to think about it, but there was no thinking required.

He squeezed her until she squealed with laughter.

"Yes. I think I'd rather enjoy that."

"Good. Because otherwise I was going to have to study every one of your books to figure out how the guy woos the girl so I could win your heart."

"You'd be willing to read a romance novel to do that?"

He shrugged, whispering against the corner of her mouth. "Whatever it takes."

"You don't have to try too hard. You already did."

Then he kissed her again, full and strong, a road of possibilities they had yet to explore.

This was so much better than the happily ever afters in her books. Because it was real. And it was only the beginning.

EPILOGUE

Six Months Later

"Ben! Are you here?" Millie burst into his home without an invitation. They'd pretty much given up on those after about a month. Millie wasn't great with waiting to be let in, and Ben didn't much care, as long as she kept coming back. Which she did with appealing regularity.

After all, they both had a lot more time on their hands since Juliet had fired them when the truth came out that they'd taken two antique books from the Chateau. That the diaries belonged to Millie's great-grandmother didn't sway the historical preservation society. When local reporters caught wind that a ninety-year-old treasure had been unearthed, it didn't take long for the *hows* to quickly follow.

The head of the historical preservation society had made a few threats. The sheriff, on the other hand, was so impressed that Ben and Millie had turned over such a lucrative treasure that he persuaded the society to let the missing diaries pass with nothing more than a pink slip for each of them.

In all honesty, Ben was relieved that the truth had been laid bare. Insurance companies with long memories had quickly claimed the jewelry from the box, and the stocks had been returned to Howard Dawkins's family. With half the earnings from the sale of Joy's property—which Millie insisted he keep—he'd paid back all twenty-three people on the list. And he'd begun searching for the others who hadn't been named.

Ben finally had nothing to hide and plenty of time to spend with Millie. He couldn't ask for anything more.

"Ben! Get down here." She raised her voice to make sure it reached to every corner of his two-story craftsman home, a gift for himself when every debt had been repaid and Grandma Joy had been secured in a room with an ocean view, safe and cared for.

Ben patted his pocket as he loped down the wooden stairs, an odd knot forming in his stomach. He hadn't expected to be nervous. He was pretty sure they were on the same page. They had been since that day at the library. Every step, every task, they'd tackled together. The only thing they'd argued about was that hideous rug she'd wanted to put in his living room. And now he kind of liked it there.

But still. She was clearly more than a little excitable today, so maybe he should wait.

This could be good news or terrible news. Either way, they'd figure it out together. Which was absolutely the best thing about being with Millie Sullivan. He'd never thought he minded being alone. Until he wasn't. And he didn't plan on doing that again.

When he reached the turn in the stairs, he caught Millie's gaze and held it. Her cheeks were flushed, and she waved an envelope in her hand.

"What is it?" he asked.

"It's a letter."

Hustling down the last eight steps, he stopped in front of her, only then seeing the shimmer in her eyes. "Who's it from?" He reached for her arm and gave it a gentle squeeze.

With a trembling lower lip, she sucked in a quick breath. "It's a message from the Dawkins family. They . . . they're so thankful we returned the stocks, they decided to give us a finder's fee."

He laughed. "You always did say that's all we could claim. So, what is it?"

Her lip trembled again, and he bent his knees to look directly into her eyes. "Millie? What does the letter say?"

"They want to give us ten percent."

His insides did a swift barrel roll, and he blinked twice. "Ten percent of how much?"

She swallowed. "Seventy-three million."

"They're going to give us seven million dollars?"

"Seven point three." She pulled a slip of paper from the envelope and held it out to him. "And they already gave it to us."

The multicolored background of the certified check danced in the light, but the zeroes could not be denied. He let out a breathless laugh, scooped her up in his arms, and spun around the entryway.

"You can buy a whole library of books with that. You can go back to school. Or just never have to work again. Or you could give it all away."

When he finally stopped spinning her, she wrapped her arms around his neck. "What are you going to do with your half?"

Well, he wasn't going to get a better lead-in than that. Taking a deep breath, he looked her square in the face. "I think I'd like to take a vacation."

She smiled. "That sounds wonderful. You should take a break. You've earned it. You work so hard."

"I was thinking we should go together."

She nodded quickly. "Where would you like to go?"

He swallowed the lump in his throat and steeled everything inside of him. "I was thinking more about when I'd like to go."

"Okay, when do you want to go?"

"After we get married."

"Okay—wait. What? You want to . . ." Her eyes grew big and round and as blue as the ocean, and he wanted to set her down, but he never wanted to let go of her again in his life. "You want to marry me?"

He nodded very slowly, holding her gaze as he set her back on the floor. "I do."

"You know you can have the money. I already promised it to you." Her voice kept dropping, each word softer than the one before, and he couldn't tell if she was trying to talk herself into believing this was happening or talk him out of proposing.

He reached into his pocket and pulled out the velvet box, then dropped to one knee. "I don't need money or treasure or Coca-Cola stocks. I just need you, Millie Sullivan. Forever."

"You and me forever?" Her smile eclipsed her face before she leaned forward and pressed her lips to his. "That's the greatest treasure I could ever imagine."

• • • • •

READ ON FOR A
SNEAK PEEK AT THE NEXT

GEORGIA COAST
ROMANCE!

• • • • •

ONE

$\mathcal{A}$nne Norris knew two things for certain. Some things could be forgiven. Some things most certainly could not.

While she knew a whole lot about the latter, at the moment she prayed her current offense might fall under the former.

"You're late." Lydia. She'd been paying her rent at this coffee counter for more than a year, and more often than not Lydia's scowl made the bright yellow walls seem three shades darker and about as welcoming as a shark at the shore.

"I know." Anne dug into her floppy bag, her fingers searching out the sharp corners of the check she'd written just minutes before. She tried to give Lydia a smile, but even the effort faltered. "I'm sorry."

"Mm-hmm." Forget Southern hospitality. Lydia had skipped the serving of sweet peach pie in favor of a double portion of sour apples. She leaned her forearms on the counter next to the cash register and held out her hand. Slowly she dropped it as her eyes grew wide, roaming the scene before her. "What on earth are you wearing?"

Anne dropped her gaze to the floor and the black boots that reached just to her knees. They nearly met her purple skirt below the silk sash that she'd tied around her waist. Her white blouse was loose enough to let the breeze cool her down, even beneath the summer sun. She reached for her hat, brushing her fingers through her hair before remembering that she'd left the hat in her car.

Good thing too. The sweeping red feather in the black felt probably wouldn't have helped her case.

Anne tried again, her lips straining to provide at least a hint of kindness. "I'm Anne. Anne Norris. I run—it's my job."

"I know who you are, and you're late." Putting her hands on her slender hips, Lydia narrowed her gaze.

Anne sighed. Something deep inside her warred at the correct response to Lydia's attitude. She should apologize again. She should find the check, which was playing a pretty convincing game of hide-and-seek in the depths of her purse while she jabbed her hand into the darkness. And she should bow out of the just-closed coffee shop as quickly as she could.

But she'd spent five years and seven months cowing to bitter women who took advantage of their positions. And she'd moved three thousand miles to try to forget it all.

Taking a deep breath, Anne tossed her bag onto the midlevel counter between them. Something inside cracked against the wooden slab, and Lydia clucked her disapproval. Anne gave her a tart smile before diving into her handbag/ luggage. Her dad always said she'd throw her back out carrying around something this big, but if she'd learned one thing over the last seven years, it was to keep the important stuff close by. At all times.

This bag was pretty much her whole life.

Business license? Check.

ID? Check.

Rental agreement for the apartment above the coffee shop that said her payment was three days past due? Check.

"Rent is due on the first of the month."

Anne didn't have to pull her head clear of her bag to sense Lydia's frown. "I know." She pushed a red scarf and clean white shirt out of the way and caught sight of a pale blue slip of paper. "Got it!"

She yanked it free, waving it like it was a golden ticket and Lydia was Willy Wonka.

In a decidedly un-Willy-Wonka-like move, Lydia snatched the check. With one glance, she handed it back. "I can't accept it without the late fee."

"But I'm . . ." Anne scrambled for the words. "It's only three days."

"And our policy is that each late day incurs an additional one percent fee. You owe an additional three percent."

Anne wanted to pull her hair out. There was no way Lydia would understand that she'd had a more important bill to pay—for a little girl waiting for the check that would pay for her groceries and keep the roof over *her* head.

Why had she signed a lease with this angry landlord? Because she'd had to check a specific box on the application. And everyone else had used that as an excuse to turn her down.

Having her own apartment was supposed to feel like freedom. And it did. To an extent.

She'd started her own business. She gave tours six days a week. And she had a key to the door. Definitely an improvement over her previous living situation.

But in moments like this, she wasn't entirely sure she was free. She owed an extra twenty-one dollars. Once upon a time it would have been the difference between a nice dinner out or ramen noodles in her dorm microwave. Now it was noodles for dinner every night and the difference between eating three meals a day or two so the peanut butter didn't disappear too fast.

Anne sighed, the choice like a rock on her shoulders.

Lydia pursed her too-pink lips, put one hand on her hip, and held the other out expectantly. "It's twenty-one bucks. I can't accept your payment without it."

Which meant that the late fee would just keep growing. And her checking account would keep dwindling.

She forced a smile back into place, putting every effort into making her voice match. "Please. Could you make an exception? I can pay you the fee next week." She had two full tours scheduled for the weekend, and the tourists this time of year were usually good tippers. That is, if they showed up. They'd missed their cancelation window, but it didn't mean they'd risk sticking around for whatever show Hurricane Lorenzo had in store.

"No."

Okay. So basic courtesy was out.

She bit back the scowl that threatened to fall into place. Only God could help her if she ticked off her landlord and landed out on the street. Especially with the hurricane scheduled to make landfall within hours.

Sucking in a staggered breath, she jabbed her hand back into her bag. "All right. Let me get you a new check then."

Lydia didn't even smile at that. She just held out her hand

as Anne scribbled the new amount on the check, ripped it free, and passed it over.

"Remember, it's due by the first."

Anne nodded, hoisting her bag onto her shoulder.

"Every month."

"Uh-huh." Clamping her mouth closed lest she get herself in trouble, she spun and walked outside.

The sun had almost disappeared beneath the unfurling clouds, a red carpet for the coming storm. She could relate. Her whole life, she'd just been making the way for things to go from bad to worse. She hadn't thought it could get much worse, but maybe God had brought her to Savannah to kill her off in a hurricane. That sounded about right.

Except that usually the bad consequences were her own fault. She didn't have a thing to do with the coming storm.

She strolled around the outside of the white-brick building, which was at least a century and a half old. The shutters had been painted green, and wrought-iron lamps at the front door flickered a welcome that Lydia didn't know how to reflect. The top two stories had been converted into apartments, but the rooms were about as big as they had been when the building served as a boardinghouse before the Civil War. That meant rent was low and she didn't have much space to furnish.

Stopping by her car, she snagged her hat and lunch box from the passenger seat, then dragged herself up the metal stairs on the outside of the building.

Her hand was already in her bag, hunting for her keys, when her phone began ringing. Digging through the rest of her keep, she peered into the abyss. A faint blue glow was her only beacon, and she clasped her hand around the vibrating phone.

"Hello," she panted before even looking at who was calling her.

"The hurricane. Lorenzo. It's supposed to be bad."

"Hi, Mom."

"Well, hello to you too. Are you prepared for this thing?"

Anne nodded before remembering that her mom couldn't see almost three thousand miles through the phone line. "Don't worry," she said, opening up her apartment and slipping into its muggy interior. "I'm watching the news. I'll be fine."

"You can come home, you know."

"I know, Mom." It was more something she said because it was what her mom wanted to hear than reality. Because she really couldn't. Going back to California wasn't an option. It hadn't been in exactly two years, three months, and twelve days.

Her mom paused, and there was a long silence on the other end of the line. She leaned harder against the phone tucked between her ear and her shoulder as she threw her bag on the counter, waiting for the sound of the television in the background. It usually served as both a distraction and a conversation piece—especially when Anne had already seen the cheesy made-for-TV movie that her mom couldn't turn off. But tonight there was no spirited dialogue, and the bright strings in the background were missing.

"Is this about money? I know things are tight."

That was an understatement. But it also wasn't the deal breaker. Money was an issue, but California was *the* issue.

"Thanks, but no . . . I'm fine. Really." She sounded like

she was trying to convince herself, and she didn't like it one bit. Or maybe she really was trying to convince herself. That was even worse.

Falling into the lone chair in her living room, she put her face in her free hand and sighed. In all honesty, the weatherman on channel 11 had done a terrific job of scaring her pants off. Lorenzo sounded like a pretty nasty dude, and he was supposed to make landfall right along the Georgia coast sometime before midnight.

She'd done everything the newscasters had recommended. She'd picked up bread and milk—the last half gallon at her grocery store. She'd even splurged on an extra jar of peanut butter—before she'd given her last twenty-one bucks to Lydia downstairs. Just in case. She'd charged her phone in her car. Also in case.

In case her power went out—pretty likely. In case her phone died—almost certain. In case she was cut off from the rest of the world—she already felt like that most days, so this wouldn't be much different.

But no amount of planning could really prepare her for what was ahead. The unknown.

"I'll buy your plane ticket. I'm sitting at my computer and can get it for you right now. It'll just take a minute." Suddenly the once-silent background was filled with the clicks of a mouse and the frenzied typing on an ergonomic keyboard. Anne could picture it. It hadn't changed in ten years. Not since before she'd . . . well, before.

In her life there was only a before and an after. And never the twain shall meet. Her life was defined by one solitary event, and the whole of her history was divided by it.

Her parents' computer had been the same in both. A black

tower and jumbo monitor and that oddly shaped white key-board with the gel wrist pad. She'd used it a lot before, but only once after—right before she'd left for Savannah.

"Please don't. I can't come home."

The silence was so loud on the other end of the phone that she prayed her mom would turn on a movie. Even the news. Anything to break up the deafening silence. She didn't.

"You mean you won't."

Anne meant both. But it didn't really matter. She couldn't explain. There weren't enough words in the world to make her mom understand that when she'd left California, she hadn't been leaving her parents. She hadn't been leaving the sweet memories of her childhood or the joy of her first two years of college.

The library had had a book about words for which there was no precise English translation, and she'd savored every strange and wonderful page. And right about now she wondered if she should be included in that book. There was a pain inside her with no exact translation. Not when her mom had hugged her so tight. Not when a tear had slipped down her dad's cheek. Not even when her kid brother had begged her to stick around for his college graduation.

Her heart was filled with a mixture of regret and sorrow and the deepest certainty that what had been done could never be undone.

"Annie?" Her mom's voice changed to the one she always used when her children were ill. "Please. Come home."

"I . . . I love you, Mom."

"Then trust that we love you too. And we'll take care of you."

If only she could. If only it were that easy. It would be so

354

simple. She had only three weeks' worth of tours booked. And then . . . Then she could pack up everything she owned into her Civic. It would fit easily.

And then what? She'd go back to a place where memories slammed into her at every turn, crushing and relentless.

Her mom sighed. "Honey . . . you've got to let this go. You've paid for it."

"According to who?" She spit the words out, instantly regretting them. "I'm sorry. I'm just . . . you don't know what it's like."

"You're right. I don't. But I know that you're my daughter and I love you. I want you to be happy and safe and cared for. Please."

"I want those things too." But wanting them didn't mean she deserved them. Even in her dreams, she couldn't imagine deserving happiness. She certainly didn't deserve to be cared for. At least no more than the state of California had cared for her for almost six years.

"Mom, I can't explain what it's like facing that city. Every corner of Santa Barbara has a memory. It's a museum, a monument to every stupid, trusting decision I made. Every second I'm there is nothing more than a reminder that I . . ."

"It wasn't your fault."

"The jury disagreed." She pressed her toe into the stained carpet of her living room, remembering the narrowed eyes and tight mouth of the jury foreman. He'd stared at her hard as he read the verdict, and she'd wanted to slide beneath the table. But there was no hiding from the judge and jury in the courtroom. She'd deserved every ounce of his disdain.

"I could have stopped it." Anne sighed. "I should have."

"Your dad and I love you. You always have a home with us. Okay?"

"Okay."

But she'd moved as far from the California coast as she could, and she wasn't going back. Her parents' home wasn't big enough for all her baggage.

And try as she might, she couldn't set it down.

ACKNOWLEDGMENTS

*D*aughter. Sister. Writer. Friend. These are some of the names I'm called, identities I'm known for. And the people who call me by them are the reason you're holding this book in your hands. I owe an enormous debt of gratitude to them.

To my mom and dad, who call me daughter and let me disappear for months at a time to write a book they won't get to read for many more. Your love story might not have come from the pages of a novel, but it is stable and steady and has given me wings to dream.

To Micah and Beth and Hannah and John and their families, who call me sister and Auntie E. You're the best encouragers around. I love being part of this family.

To the team at Revell—Vicki, Karen, Hannah, Michele, Jessica, and so many more—who call me writer and friend. Thank you for cheering me on. Thank you for believing in my stories and helping them become the best versions of themselves. What a privilege and a joy to work with this team.

To Rachel Kent, who calls me writer, client, and friend.

Knowing you has been one of the great joys of my writing journey. I could not ask for a better agent.

To Amy Haddock, who calls me friend and willingly reads my very first drafts, red pen in hand. As always, your feedback is invaluable. Your friendship more so.

To Jessica Patch and Jill Kemerer, who call me friend. Your encouragement is such a boost, especially when I hit a rough writing patch. I look forward to each and every Vox from you both, knowing you'll have wise words and so much laughter to share.

To my heavenly Father, who calls me his own. The name you've given me is the one I cling to. Thank you for inviting me to join you on this creative journey.

Liz Johnson loves stories about true love. When she's not writing her next book, she works in marketing. She is the author of more than a dozen novels—including *The Red Door Inn*, *Where Two Hearts Meet*, and *On Love's Gentle Shore*—a *New York Times* bestselling novella, and a handful of short stories. She makes her home in Arizona, where she dotes on her five nieces and nephews.

"The Red Door Inn took my breath away! Highly recommended!"

—**Colleen Coble,** author of *The Inn at Ocean's Edge* and the Hope Beach series

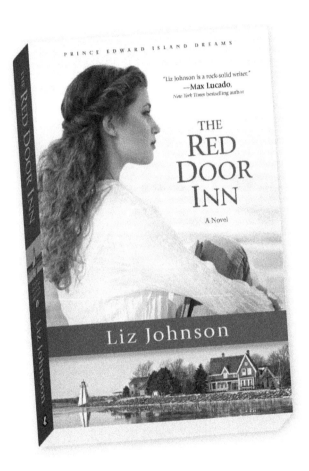

Two brokenhearted strangers are thrown together on Prince Edward Island to restore the Red Door Inn. Will they learn to trust again?

R Revell
a division of Baker Publishing Group
www.RevellBooks.com

Available wherever books and ebooks are sold.

"A delightful, yummy tale of faith and finding truth at the lovely Red Door Inn."

—**Rachel Hauck,** *New York Times* bestselling author

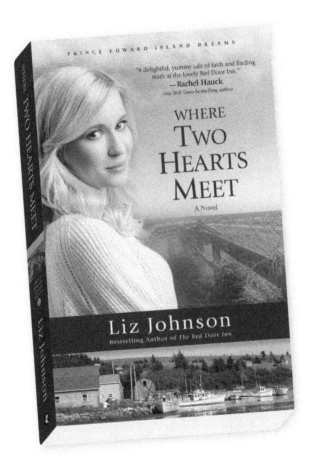

Bed-and-breakfast chef Caden Holt needs to persuade Adam Jacobs to write a glowing article about the Red Door Inn. But he's not the secret travel reviewer she believes him to be.

"This is a story to be savored long after the last page is turned."

—**Catherine West,** author of *The Things We Knew*

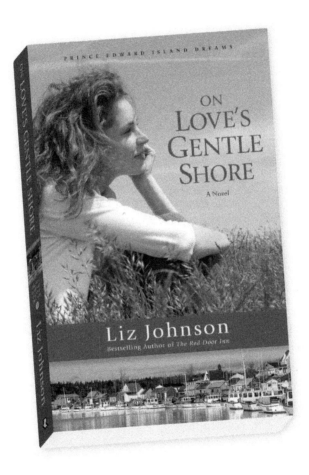

When Natalie O'Ryan returns to Prince Edward Island to plan her wedding, she runs into her childhood best friend—and discovers that the love she's been looking for is right where she left it.

Revell
a division of Baker Publishing Group
www.RevellBooks.com

Available wherever books and ebooks are sold.

Meet
LIZ JOHNSON

LizJohnsonBooks.com

| Read her BLOG | Follow her SPEAKING SCHEDULE | Connect with her on SOCIAL MEDIA |

Be the First to Hear about Other New Books from REVELL!

Sign up for announcements about new and upcoming titles at

RevellBooks.com/SignUp

Don't miss out on our great reads!

CPSIA information can be obtained
at www.ICGtesting.com
Printed in the USA
LVHW02*1620151018
593651LV00007B/89/P